SHRAPNEL

ISSUE #16   **THE OFFICIAL BATTLETECH MAGAZINE**

SHR▲PNEL
THE OFFICIAL BATTLETECH MAGAZINE

Loren L. Coleman, Publisher
John Helfers, Executive Editor
Philip A. Lee, Managing Editor
David A. Kerber, Layout and Graphic Design

Cover art by Germán Varona Galindo, a.k.a. Wallok
Interior art by Jared Blando, Eldon Cowgur, Mark Hayden, Stephen Huda, Alex Iglesias, David A. Kerber, Duane Loose, Natán Meléndez, Marco Pennacchietti, Gerhard Mozsi, Anthony Scroggins, Florian Stitz

Published by Pulse Publishing, under licensing by Catalyst Game Labs
5003 Main St. #110 ▪ Tacoma, WA 98407

Shrapnel: The Official BattleTech Magazine is published four times a year, in Spring, Summer, Fall, and Winter.

Available through your favorite online store (Amazon.com, BN.com, Kobo, iBooks, GooglePlay, etc.).

ISBN: 978-1-63861-159-2

(CONTINUED)

GAME FEATURES

COMMANDER'S CALL
FROM THE EDITOR'S DESK

It's said no battle plan survives enemy contact, so it's worth noting that I originally had quite a different issue lined up for all of you MechWarriors, but a monkey wrench thrown into those gears meant I had to shelve it for a later date and call in some reinforcements. That said, this issue is the result of a truly Herculean effort by the whole *Shrapnel* team to make sure we deliver another terrific batch of stories and game content on time. They're the real heroes of this battle, and I can't thank all of them enough. If you see any of them at a convention or in various places online, take a moment and let them know how much you enjoyed their story, article, or art; I'm sure they'd love to hear from you!

So, on to business: In case you've been living under a rock since 1984, 2024 marks the 40th anniversary of *BattleTech* and the stompy war machines we all love! Four whole decades of combat between massive metal avatars of war. Four decades of BattleMechs and MechWarriors, tanks and aerospace fighters, DropShips and JumpShips. Forty years of betrayal and backstabbing, politics and alliances, massive wars and small-scale raids capable of changing the entire face of the Inner Sphere and beyond. It's hard to believe it's been that long: seems like my first game was only a few years ago... That said, there's plenty of great anniversary stuff coming down the pipeline, so keep an eye out for all the upcoming surprises, and let's celebrate forty years of armored combat!

One last thing I'd like to mention before I go further: earlier this year, the BattleTech community lost Kelly Bonilla, who was instrumental in developing WizKids' *MechWarrior: Dark Age* game. I know many of our readers first encountered *BattleTech* via *MW:DA*, and if you played any of the other Clix games, you owe her a debt of gratitude. For this issue, Jennifer Bixby wrote a touching tribute in Kelly's memory, which features the 'Mech piloted by Kelly's in-universe character straight from *MW:DA*. Let's all raise a glass in Kelly's memory and honor her enduring legacy.

For fiction, this issue kicks off with "Flushing the Competition," by returning author Steve P. Vincent, whose previous story "All Those Left Behind" was featured in issue #10. In this story, you'll follow a Periphery pirate's quest for some unusual Star League-era *lostech*. Among our other returning authors is Craig A. Reed, Jr., who brings us "Riding the Tiger," a tale of Capellan Thuggee cultists and the lengths they'll go to achieve their goals. David Razi, who brought us "Sackcloth and Sand" all the way back in issue #4, travels to the Clan Homeworlds on the cusp of the Wars of Reaving in "Of the Dust of Dreams," and Russell Zimmerman's "Range War" offers another entry in the continuing saga of Mountain Wolf BattleMechs and their quest to return to their former glory. And finally, we have the long-awaited conclusion of Bryan Young's *Lone Wolf and Fox*, which is immortalized in the cover art of this issue, by Wallok. You know you don't want to miss this!

We also have two new authors debuting in this issue. Devin Ramsey's "Sacrifice of Angels" puts us aboard the mighty battleship SLS *Chieftain* during a pivotal battle in the fight to wrest Terra back from the Usurper, Stefan Amaris. Closing out the issue, Benjamin Joseph's "Locust Alone" demonstrates the desperation that gripped many worlds in the wake of the communications loss on Gray Monday.

For game content, we have an in-depth look at various aspects of space travel: "Voices of the Sphere: Terror on the Spacelanes" discusses the potential dangers spacefarers might face; "Captains and Loadmasters Symposium" offers some helpful advice on how to make the best use of your DropShip's limited cargo space; "WarShips Quarterly: SLS *California*" features a historical overview of the titular *Texas*-class battleship, from its inception to its ultimate fate during the Amaris Crisis; and "The Pony Express Rides Again" explores the courier JumpShip system and its vital role during the Blackout. Also, in "Infamous Arms Dealers," you'll find some gunrunners you might not want to cross, and "Mystical 'Mechs and Giant Monsters" demonstrates House Kurita's attitudes toward its enemies, as seen through the lens of the Draconis Combine's pop culture. "Technical Readout: COM-7T *Commando*" covers the "Blazing Inferno II" variants, and "Chains: Alternate Pilots for the Clan Direct Fire Star" offers a story-based set of pilots, perfect for use with that forthcoming Force Pack. "Unit Digest: Tarantulas Battalion" covers one of Wolf's Dragoon's striker-battalion experiments, and "Planet Digest: Zathras" details the history of a Canopian world that once declared itself its own miniature empire. And finally, "Chaos Campaign Scenario: Rocking Gibraltar" allows you to play out the pivotal battle in which the Free Worlds League strives to eject occupying Marian Hegemony forces from the capital of the Gibraltar Military District.

No matter how you enjoy the *BattleTech* universe, be it primarily through the fiction, tabletop game, or video games, we're all glad you've been here for the first forty years of this incredible ride, no matter whether you played the first edition in 1984 or if you've only recently discovered the Inner Sphere in the last year or so. Here's to another forty years, and then some!

And perhaps, when we hit the 800th anniversary in 2784, our descendants will remark about how Commanding General Aleksandr Kerensky is slated to depart on the Exodus that year...

Happy 40th, everyone!

—Philip A. Lee, Managing Editor

FLUSHING THE COMPETITION

STEVE P. VINCENT

LEOPARD-CLASS DROPSHIP LUCKY BUCK
CALIBAN'S ROCK
ANTI-SPINWARD DEEP PERIPHERY
11 MARCH 3022

"Toilets that clean you up with a squirt of water, without even needing to press a button!" Kevin "One Eye" Broderick grinned in the cockpit of his *Vindicator* as he regaled his lancemates with the promise of treasure to come. "Imagine!"

"It'd be convenient and all..." Kalissa—*just* Kalissa, or else—chimed in over the network. "But then what would your mother do with her time?"

As their other lancemates roared with laughter, Broderick grinned. Stuffy Inner Sphere types would get uptight about Kalissa's backtalk and the crew's laughter, but he considered it a vital part of his unit's success. Because if they liked each other, they were less likely to stab *him* in the back.

He let the chatter continue, but tuned it out, focusing instead on their landing. Their venerable *Leopard*-class DropShip—the *Lucky Buck*—was coming in for landing on Caliban's Rock, so close the 'Mech bay doors on the port and starboard sides of the ancient aerodyne DropShip had already started to open.

Few people in the Inner Sphere had heard of Caliban's Rock, but that still left plenty of people in the Periphery—clinging to the edges of human civilization like moss on a rock—who had. And when they spoke of it, they spoke the same language as dreamers the galaxy over, of life-changing fortunes and technological treasures.

They spoke of *lostech*.

The moment the *Lucky Buck* touched down, Broderick disengaged the gantry lock on his 'Mech and throttled it up out the 'Mech bay door and onto Caliban's Rock—a cratered, volcanic hellhole with few redeeming features except the long-rumored but never-found *lostech*.

"Welcome to paradise." Broderick laughed as he led his crew off the ship. "Let's do a quick sweep to make sure there's no nasties waiting to steal *Lucky* while we're gone, then we'll move on to the objective."

"You sure about this, One Eye?" Bishop scoffed, griping as usual. "We *could* just land the ship right on top of the target, given the guy who told us about the cache said it was undefended..."

"I don't trust guys who spill secrets over a beer, Bishop. And I *especially* don't trust the volcano right next to our objective to stay quiet. If it blows on *us*, we're in trouble. If it blows on the *Lucky*, we're stranded here."

"If you don't trust the guy, why are we here at all?" Bishop wouldn't give up on it, and hadn't since Broderick had first told his lance about the job. "We could *also* just get the hell out of here."

"Without the squirty toilets?" Broderick said. "Cut the shit, Bishop. We're here, like it or not, so try and be more like Wilkins over there."

Wilkins, for his part, said nothing.

Like usual.

After a quick—quiet—perimeter search, they moved out in a loose diamond formation, which was about as coordinated as the lance got. Kalissa led the way in her *Jenner*, while Bishop's *Clint* and Wilkins' *Phoenix Hawk* took the left and right points of the diamond, with Broderick in the rear—right where he liked to be.

If he could see *their* backs, he could stab *them* in the back first if he had to.

Some would call him paranoid—fingers already on his triggers, his targeting reticule shifting between the three 'Mechs in front of him— but Broderick considered himself pragmatic. He'd won leadership of the lance after taking it from his predecessor in a poker game, and he wasn't about to let *his* guard down and lose it all.

Such was life among a small group of bandits in a part of the Periphery where banditry was the only way to get ahead. Sure, he could have tried farming, but he preferred shaking down the locals clinging to life on a dozen different rocks, kicking over their mud huts and incinerating their livestock with his 'Mech if they refused to pay up over trying to grow soybeans.

As his crew continued to talk shit among themselves, Broderick focused on his surroundings. There was little to see except volcanic soil of different shades of gray, occasionally punctuated by a rocky outcrop or the bulbous cacti that seemed the extent of local flora. He saw no bodies of water, no other plant life, no animals, no human settlements...

But then his 'Mech's sensors blared a warning about new targets being detected.

"Contacts!" Broderick cried out over the network, silencing the chatter of his lance. "Two 'Mechs and some armor, sitting right on top of our objective."

"I see them! Engaging!" Kalissa responded first, her *Jenner* already throttling up to get into the action. "Looks like a pair of *Centurions*."

"Careful..." Broderick trailed off, mainly because he already knew his words were wasted. "Stay inside the umbrella of our long-range fire."

Broderick cursed as Kalissa didn't respond, apparently determined *not* to heed his warning. She was already pushing past the extreme range of his LRMs, let alone the weaponry of the rest of the lance, to tangle with two 'Mechs totaling three times her tonnage to once again prove she was the baddest MechWarrior within a thousand light years.

If she wanted to throw her life away, that was her business—but not today.

Today, he needed her.

Broderick had asked Kalissa out, and they'd started dating a month ago, after he'd heard scuttlebutt about Bishop looking to replace him. It was sound planning, which had put Kalissa—the most fearsome woman he'd ever met—in his corner. But her death would complicate matters, so he throttled up and got into the fray.

The others had already started to fire on the two *Centurions* and half-dozen armored vehicles when Broderick loosed his first volley of LRMs, peppering one of the enemy machines. As the first missiles landed, the next lot fired, his finger squeezed tight on the firing trigger.

He thought about getting in closer, to add his 'Mech's medium laser into the mix, but hesitated, given that previous battle damage and a lack of spare parts had his *Vindicator* missing its PPC. And that was *before* mentioning the 'Mech's pockmarked armor, its wireframe damage indicator already orange all over.

Such was life on the fringe of civilization.

As his missiles pounded one of the *Centurions*, Kalissa worked her usual violent magic. She jumped high into the air, firing her brace of medium lasers at the enemy 'Mechs, then landed right on top of the turret of one of the enemy armored vehicles. As it exploded in an impressive fireball, she waded ever deeper into the battle.

Bishop and Wilkins were also doing their best to cover Kalissa. A second vehicle, then a third, then a fourth were all destroyed in short order, the firepower of Broderick's lance proving telling, although the *Centurions* were getting their licks in on Kalissa and the others.

As if to prove the point, Bishop's panicked voice came over the comms. "I need support! I've got this *Centurion* on me like spots on a zebra!"

Broderick grinned, aware that Bishop's *Clint* was not up to squaring off against the heavier 'Mech, even before considering the damage his would-be Brutus had entered the fight with. And while it would've been the easiest thing in the world for Broderick to switch his fire to bail Bishop out, treason had a price.

As he unleashed another volley of LRMs at the *Centurion* Kalissa was engaged with, Broderick opened a direct channel with Wilkins' *Phoenix Hawk.* "Bishop will have to fend for himself."

"Copy." The single word reply came back a second later, which was one more word than anyone usually got out of Wilkins. "He's about to blow..."

Broderick glanced out his cockpit at Bishop's *Clint*, which was already close to destruction. The battered 'Mech was missing its left arm; acrid, greasy brown smoke spewed from several holes in its torso, and the *Centurion* was continually probing it with autocannon and medium laser fire.

"Disloyalty has a price," Broderick whispered. "Time to get it done, One Eye..."

He fired another volley of LRMs at the other *Centurion.* Finally, instead of stripping more armor from across the torso of the enemy 'Mech like sandpaper working a piece of lumber, his missiles hit pay dirt. The right side of the heavier 'Mech exploded outward, its ammo cooking off.

"Enemy down," Broderick said to the rest of his lance. "Focus fire on the vehicles."

"The *vehicles*?" Bishop's shrill cry hurt Broderick's ear. "I need help with this *Centurion*!"

Broderick didn't respond. He simply smiled and kept supporting Kalissa with long-range-missile fire, glad he'd soon be done with Bishop's treachery. As Bishop's overmatched *Clint* continued its death dance with the second *Centurion*, the man himself started to unload expletives. "Pack of scum, the lot of you!" Bishop's aggression didn't hide the panic in his voice. "Bastar—"

His *Clint* exploded in a fireball as its ammo cooked off, unable to resist the continuous assault of the *Centurion*'s autocannon, even as the rest of Broderick's lance finished off the final enemy vehicles, cut open by withering missile and laser fire by three medium 'Mechs.

That just left the *Centurion.*

Broderick, always the pragmatist, was keen to seal the deal and reduce the risk that his already battered crew would be further harassed by the heavier 'Mech. He broadcast wide. "Disengage and you won't be harmed."

"Disengage?" The *Centurion* pilot laughed as he backed his 'Mech up. "We're just getting started with you assholes..."

Broderick's eyes narrowed as he turned his 'Mech on the spot to face the *Centurion*, now almost a thousand meters away and increasing the distance between them with every passing second. He used his external camera to zoom in on the enemy 'Mech.

Then, among all the battle damage on the retreating *Centurion*, he spotted it: the logo of the thing he hated the most in the galaxy.

Van Dyk's Reavers.

If Bishop had been a looming problem now dealt with, the Reavers were a dormant one now active.

Rudi Van Dyk was a drunk and a sadist, hated by his own people and feared by his enemies. In command of a couple combined-arms companies in this region of the Periphery, his penchant for atrocities was well known, making a regular bandit like Broderick seem like a ComStar acolyte in comparison.

Van Dyk was also the man Broderick had beaten at poker for his lance of 'Mechs.

Given his reputation, several of Van Dyk's pilots had been all too happy to jump ship when their 'Mechs had been won by Broderick. Kalissa was the only person left of that group, with Wilkins and Bishop picked up along the way since then, but Van Dyk hadn't taken the loss of four irreplaceable 'Mechs lightly.

The rest of Van Dyk's force had besieged the city Broderick's newly won lance had holed up in, but he'd managed to negotiate passage off-world with an enterprising young DropShip captain. The man had landed his *Leopard*—the *Lucky Buck*—inside the city, Broderick and his people had rushed aboard, and they'd blasted off to safety.

Free of the Reavers, Broderick had quickly manipulated his way into control of that DropShip, as the young captain's debt collectors finally found him at the edges of human existence. It had been worth it, giving Broderick and his people their own transport. From there, his crew had spent years in the bandit business.

And always staying one step ahead of the Reavers.

Nowadays, the Reavers were in the pocket of Gregor Abramovich, a two-bit warlord who ruled over four poor planets in this region of space. When he wasn't using them to crush dissent, Abramovich sent the Reavers further afield to loot, a mission that had had them breathing down the neck of Broderick and his lance more than once.

"Should we pursue that *Centurion*, One Eye?" Kalissa's voice came over the radio, shaking him out of his thoughts. "We can catch it if we move quickly..."

"Let it go." Broderick sighed. "We're gonna have to get the loot and back to the DropShip quickly, 'cause the Reavers always travel in packs."

Broderick sighed and ran his hand through his hair, which was slicked with sweat thanks to the face-melting humidity of Caliban's Rock, then shouted into his portable radio. "Do it again!"

Standing next to the few outbuildings they'd driven the Reavers from, Broderick was getting frustrated as he watched Wilkins try to pull open the door to the bunker in the middle of the compound. A high-tension cable was now taut between the door and an O-ring they'd welded onto the *Phoenix Hawk*'s torso, but the door was proving stubborn.

As Wilkins continued to work at it, the 'Mech's feet started to slip in the dirt, requiring some skill to handle. Broderick could hear the actuators in the *Phoenix Hawk* working overtime as Wilkins fought to keep the machine upright, but again the door didn't budge.

"Cut it." Broderick sighed again as he radioed the order, finally convinced the door wasn't going to open. "We'll need to find another way in."

Kalissa scoffed next to him. "The door's thick, so we can't blast through it. Its hinges are concealed, so we can't work on those. And you've seen the result of trying to force it..."

"We'll figure it out. I'm not leaving without those toilets." Broderick crossed his arms over his chest, glaring at her despite the fact they'd been dating recently. "They'll be worth a fortune on the black market."

"We'll see." She laughed, turned and started to walk back to her *Jenner*, parked fifty meters away. After a few steps, she turned and gave an impish grin. "I'll tell you what, if you get us inside and we find the gear, I'll make it worth it."

Broderick grinned, his poor mood improving a little. "Don't make bets your ass can't cash, Kalissa, because I'll come to collect..."

As she smirked, shrugged and walked away, Broderick couldn't help but focus on her for a second or two. Then his mind returned to the job, driven by equal parts profit and fear. He wanted a score—*needed* a score, after so long without one, his debts mounting and his people growing impatient—and now he had the Reavers on him.

Those two facts focused Broderick's mind.

And, when combined with an offer from Kalissa that intrigued him, the feeling was electric.

He returned to his *Vindicator* and spoke into the radio, a new idea having formed in his head. "Hey, Spicer, I need you to land the *Lucky* near the door we're trying to crack."

There was a long pause, before the voice of Spicer—the young, hotshot captain of the *Lucky Buck* who now worked for Broderick—

came over the radio. "I know what you're thinking, but I'm not sure that's the best idea—"

"You're not paid to think—"

"Uh, now might not be the time to point it out, but none of us have been paid at all in the last few months. But, aside from that, I'd like to remind you of the *giant dormant volcano* near to the LZ..."

Broderick sighed yet again. It was the same story every time he tried to give Spicer an order, constant backtalk with plenty of attitude. It was like the pilot resented his circumstances in life, his spacefaring career limited to hauling a lance of bandits around the Periphery in a beat-up *Leopard*, tethered to whatever JumpShip they could convince to take them. It was hardly the stuff of legends, unless they *did* manage to find some *lostech*.

But, despite the griping, a few minutes later the *Lucky Buck* touched down a safe distance away, kicking a cloud of dirt into the air. The distance was necessary, lest Broderick and the others be cooked by the fusion plasma thrusters, so the DropShip took a few minutes to taxi at low power over to near the bunker door.

"You sure about this?" Spicer tried his luck one more time over the radio when the ship was stationary. "If that door's too strong, there's a chance you'll damage the ship."

"That's your problem, Spicer." Broderick's tone was a bit harsher now, exasperated as he was with the continual resistance. "If you'd rather have this argument with Kalissa, I'd be happy to send her your way..."

Immediately, Spicer responded by having one of the DropShip's crew rig up a long, thick, high-tension cable to an O-ring on the ship's exterior, his fear of Kalissa legendary after he'd tried to hit on her and ended up with a broken arm. When the task was done, several crew members walked the cable over to the bunker door and secured it there as well, then returned to the ship.

"Let it rip," Broderick ordered. "The rest of you keep an eye on your sensors, because once we crack this egg open I don't want the Reavers to get the jump on us."

Broderick crossed his fingers as he watched the *Leopard* slowly start to taxi away from the door at low power. This time, unlike when the 'Mech had been trying to force the door, the sheer power of the DropShip got the job done.

Broderick saw the door warp, buckle and then finally pop open.

"*Lostech...*" he whispered, trying to stay calm. "All your work has got you this far, so stay focused."

He checked to make sure Kalissa and Wilkins were still on overwatch in their 'Mechs. It'd be just his luck to finally score a life-changing haul, only to have the Reavers steal it out from under him. Besides, keeping

Kalissa and Wilkins *outside* reduced the risk of *them* stealing his find and made sure *they'd* be the ones to deal with the Reavers first if they showed up.

After all, all great generals had to deal with loss sometimes.

After ordering Spicer to get the *Lucky Buck* back in the air, he dismounted from his ride, ran to the breached door and took the stairs two at a time, descending so deep the temperature quickly became far cooler than the inferno he'd left outside. Except for the staircase, there was nothing of note, the design of the place clearly from one point to another.

He took the stairs down, farther and farther, until he emerged in a large, cavernous storage area—a huge underground warehouse, the size of which baffled him. He'd never seen a facility of this size anywhere in the Periphery. It was filled with hundreds—thousands—of crates.

"That's a *lot* of toilets," Broderick muttered. "Or I've been fed some bullshit..."

He moved inside, quickly inspecting the closest crates, conscious the clock was ticking before the Reavers arrived in force. He found lots of stuff inside—weapons, gold, jewels, household appliances—but nothing that gave him any confidence of finding the *lostech* he sought. It seemed there were no wonder toilets to be found here.

It was just a bandit stash, like so many others hidden across the galaxy.

Broderick had a sinking feeling that, instead of the location of a great treasure that would change the fortunes of humanity *and* himself, the drunk guy had led him into a trap. And, a second later, the crackle of his radio all but confirmed it.

"Bro... I... Att..."

The message was gibberish, static interspersed with half a word every few seconds, but it told him something outside the bunker was wrong. He waited for a clearer broadcast to come through, but this far below ground he didn't like his chances.

Until he could get back to the surface, he was all alone.

Broderick stood rooted on the spot, frozen with indecision.

Part of him wanted to ignore the chaos aboveground, continuing his search for the elusive, high-tech toilets. Or, failing that, he could settle for picking over the best of the loot in the stash, then try to load it aboard the *Lucky* and get the hell out of Dodge before the Reavers arrived in force.

But the other part of him—the more rational part—suspected they were already here.

With a sigh, Broderick looked longingly at the crates full of valuables he'd be forced to leave behind, even if there wasn't a toilet to be seen. Stopping long enough to pocket enough gold and jewels to pay his crew for the next few months—and pay the arrears he owed them—he drew his sidearm and headed for the door.

He didn't make it more than a few steps before he heard footsteps and chatter from the stairs, at least two people coming *down* when he was hoping to go *up*. His mind racing, he ducked down behind cover, waiting to confirm the voices were a threat and not his own people coming to check on him after the radio had failed.

He confirmed it a moment later, because as the voices and the footsteps got louder, he guessed at least six people were coming for him. Staying low, Broderick moved away from the mystery arrivals, deeper into the underground warehouse and the maze of crates inside.

As he scooted from crate to crate, risking brief seconds of exposure, those searching for him didn't relent. The deeper he retreated into the warehouse, the further they followed, a hunting party looking for their prey. And, finally, the voice Broderick least wanted to hear confirmed it.

"I know you're in here, Broderick..." Rudi Van Dyk's gravelly voice was mocking as he and his goons continued to fan out to search for him between the crates. "I bet you thought you'd found *such* a score..."

Broderick froze, as if doing so might end the nightmare he was stuck in.

"You see, my people and I have known about this little trove for years. It belongs to Gregor Abramovich, by the way, which means *my* people couldn't even *consider* breaking in and stealing..."

The penny dropped for Broderick, and he silently cursed himself for not spotting the trap sooner. The Reavers would *never* dare move on the stash that belonged to their employer, the warlord of this particular region in the ass-end of humanity's great expanse, a man known for punishing disloyalty with brutality...

"...but if, in the conduct of our protection of said trove, *you* were to shoot past my people, breach the door and get caught red-handed, then it would be my duty to destroy you. It's just a shame some items couldn't be recovered..."

Broderick was the fall guy for one of the most audacious heists ever attempted in the Periphery, a player who'd been played. From the drunk guy in the bar—almost certainly a plant—to being trapped in the underground warehouse, he'd walked blindly along a path to his own doom, led by the nose by his enemies.

The thought infuriated him.

Still, he'd be damned if he was going to let old man Van Dyk do him in. He'd gained his own small dose of notoriety at the expense of the mercenary leader, rising from Dispossessed MechWarrior to commander of a lance of treasure hunters thanks to one hand of poker...

...and a card or two in his pocket.

The thought of the past gave him an idea in the present. With a grin, Broderick reached into his pocket and pulled out the gold and jewels he'd stashed only a few minutes ago. After looking down at them longingly for a second, he flung them as far as he could, back in the direction of his pursuers.

The valuables pelted the floor, the crates and—in one case—one of his pursuers, who cried out in wounded protest. But his barrage had the desired effect, sowing some confusion and chaos amongst Van Dyk's crew, enough to frustrate them and have them chasing false noises.

Although he'd bought some time, he was now two-thirds of the way to the back of the warehouse and almost out of options. He could try to sneak back past them, but Van Dyk probably had guards on the door, so he kept retreating toward the rear wall of the underground warehouse.

The end of the line.

When he reached it, Broderick frantically looked around for an option, then his eyes settled on a half-dozen heavy-duty braces propping up the wall. They were spaced several meters apart, no doubt key to the structural integrity of the cavernous room.

The nugget of a plan forming in his head, Broderick used the precious few seconds he had to search through some of the nearby crates. All pretense at stealth and secrecy abandoned, he rummaged through one crate after another, rapidly tossing aside any that didn't contain what he wanted. He was gambling, but he had no choice left.

Then, on the fourth crate, as he heard Van Dyk's mocking laughter, he hit pay dirt.

He took two of the small charges from the packing crate, doubting he had time to use more than that anyway. Keeping low, he headed for one of the braces, planted the simple charge at the base, then set it. He repeated the process with the next brace along, the whole process taking only twenty seconds.

As much as he hated the idea, blowing the struts and collapsing the warehouse in on himself—and his foes—seemed like his best bet. He had no desire to die, but he had *far* less desire to let Van Dyk win or be tortured by Abramovich, so he'd go ahead with the plan unless a better option presented itself.

"Freeze!" Van Dyk's voice was filled with menace. "You move a centimeter, you're gonna be sorrier than your 'Mech outside..."

Broderick froze, his hands concealed from Van Dyk by his torso. "Good to see you, Rudi. Feels like just yesterday those sorry 'Mechs were sporting your colors..."

"Good. Keep playing ball and we might leave you to die in here rather than take you to Gregor. Now, turn around, slowly."

Broderick did so, letting his enemy feast his eyes on the remote detonators in each of his hands while he laughed. "Looks like you've been outplayed again."

"You're bluffing," Van Dyk scoffed. "You won't blow yourself up, so why don't you drop the act and accept the inevitable."

"The only inevitable thing here is the destruction of your boss' main stash..." Broderick grinned. "I don't have any friends or family for him to torture, but last I checked you had a son..."

Broderick enjoyed the wave of doubt that crossed Van Dyk's features. The man was old—a few decades past his prime 'Mech-driving and poker-playing days, which explained how Broderick had taken the lance from him—but his already wrinkled brow furrowed further at the thought of what Abramovich would do to his kid.

The one thing Van Dyk seemed to care about more than revenge.

"We can make a deal." Van Dyk's tone was now conciliatory, although he kept his gun leveled at Broderick. "We'll walk you to your DropShip and you can get the hell out of here."

"And in return?"

"You toss those detonators on the ground before we let you board. You live, Gregor's stash has no damage except a door that needs replacing, and my son stays safe."

"And my people?"

"They're already dead and their 'Mechs are scrap..."

Broderick thought for a second. If it was true, he was disappointed his lance had been wiped out, but Van Dyk was offering a better option than any other available to him. He nodded. "Deal."

Van Dyk lowered the gun, although he kept it at his side, and the half-dozen goons he had in tow were also packing enough heat to turn Broderick into Swiss cheese in less than a second. On the other hand, Broderick could blow their paymaster's stash if they crossed him. It was a standoff that could end with them all living...

...or all dying.

It took them a minute to reach the stairs, then another few to ascend back to the surface of Caliban's Rock. They walked in silence the whole way; Broderick kept his mouth shut to make sure he'd keep breathing, Van Dyk because he didn't want to spook his enemy into blowing the stash, and the other goons because they had nothing to say.

And when they reached the surface, Broderick wasn't sure he *could* say anything, because the sight took his breath away.

Broderick could see two companies of assorted metal on station— light and medium 'Mechs, tanks, and infantry transports—forming a perimeter around the bunker entrance and the outbuildings. For their part, Wilkins' *Phoenix Hawk* was a smoking carcass, while Kalissa's *Jenner* was stationary and surrounded.

His own 'Mech was standing with its cockpit canopy still open.

"I want to walk out of here with my 'Mech." Broderick turned to glare at Van Dyk, aware he was changing the deal on the fly. "And Kalissa's."

"*My* 'Mechs, Broderick, *my* 'Mechs." Van Dyk's face clouded over. "You're already lucky to be getting out of here with your life and limbs, but now you want me to give you the 'Mechs you stole *and* the turncoat?"

"Better than your boss finding out his stash has been destroyed." Broderick waved the detonator remotes. "Swallow your pride or your family swallows a few bullets, Van Dyk—it's your choice."

There were a few seconds of silence—a tense standoff by two men who hated each other, neither of whom wanted to back down—until Van Dyk finally nodded. He barked orders at his people, Broderick was escorted to his 'Mech, and soon enough he found himself back in the cockpit.

"Pleasure doing business with you, Rudi," Broderick spoke into the microphone on his neurohelmet once he was safely strapped in. His voice boomed over the 'Mech's external speakers. Then he switched to radio. "Kalissa, on me."

In formation, the two 'Mechs turned their backs on the Reaver forces and headed for the *Lucky Buck*, which he ordered to land several kilometers away. Usually, Broderick would be nervous turning his back on the enemy, but with the detonation remotes resting in his lap he had all the insurance he needed against Van Dyk's possible treachery.

The closer he got to the ship, the more relieved he felt to have survived a close call with his most hated enemy. Although they were about to leave without the high-tech toilets—and two of his lancemates—Broderick considered any mission that ended with him breathing to be a success.

"Uh, boss, just letting you know Van Dyk tried to convince me to turn on you once we lifted off..." The voice of Spicer in his ear over the radio popped Broderick's bubble of self-congratulation. "I told him to shove it."

"I appreciate it, Spicer." Broderick sighed with relief, now only a few hundred meters from the DropShip, the enemy's weapons now out of range. "What did he offer you?"

"The...*freedom* of working for him instead of you..." Spicer laughed. "You always order me around and usually fail to pay on time, but at least you're not a sadist..."

Broderick grinned, despite the situation. "Well, there's no pay coming our way out of this giant waste of time, but I appreciate the loyalty. We'll get a big score soon enough."

"Count on it." There was enough of a pause to suggest Spicer didn't believe it, but he was along for the ride for a while longer anyway. "The 'Mech bay doors are open. Welcome home."

Broderick went first, boarding the *Lucky Buck* on the starboard side, while Kalissa boarded on the port side. Wasting no time, Spicer dusted off, the ship ascending even before the 'Mech bay doors were closed, not wanting to stick around to tangle with the Reavers for a second longer than necessary.

And, in this instance—for the first time ever—because he'd followed Broderick's order.

As soon as he'd reached the cockpit of his 'Mech, Broderick had communicated with Spicer via a tight beam that he needed to be ready to take off the *second* they were aboard. That was because Broderick having the detonation triggers had been a bluff all along—their signal couldn't reach underground any more than the earlier radio broadcast could...

"Holy shit!" Spicer's panicked voice came over the network, right on schedule, sounding like music to Broderick's ears. "The ground that warehouse is under just collapsed! It...caved in...and took a few of the Reavers with it!"

Broderick grinned. "Keep us climbing, Spicer. I don't want old man Van Dyk to have any way of reaching us, not after what we just did to Abramovich's stash..."

When Spicer confirmed the order, Broderick sat back in the seat of his cockpit and closed his eyes, even as the side bay doors closed fully. While they were walking away empty-handed and had lost two 'Mechs to the enemy, the fact they'd survived at all was a triumph of ingenuity and a little bit of luck. They'd hitch a ride out of the system, find somewhere quiet, and take a breather.

Opening his eyes, a smile still on his face, Broderick looked at Kalissa's 'Mech. The *Jenner* was facing him, and he could see right into her cockpit. As he reached up to remove his neurohelmet, smiling at her as he did, a frown replaced his grin when he saw the blank look on her face. Kalissa was many things, but she was always expressive.

So when her mouth moved as if she was having a conversation, he became more concerned.

"Kalissa?" he said over the radio, even as he raised an eyebrow so she got the message. "How about I get you a cold one once we're out of the cockpit?"

Broderick's concern levels went off the dial when her face stayed neutral but her mouth kept moving, talking to someone that wasn't him. He never did remove the neurohelmet, instead slowly moving his hands back to the control sticks of his 'Mech...

...and fired.

As the *Vindicator's* medium laser bored into the *Jenner* from point blank range, Broderick kept his eyes locked on Kalissa. The second the shot landed, her face screwed up into an angry scowl, and she glared at him with as much fury as the laser he'd just shot into her ride.

"Finally saw where the threat was coming from, One Eye?" Kalissa laughed over the network as she fired her *Jenner's* quartet of medium lasers into his machine. "More like *no* eyes…"

Broderick cursed in his cockpit as molten metal started to sluice in great rivers down his 'Mech, the lasers having cut deep into his already damaged ride. The wireframe indicator stayed orange all over, for now, but he knew his ride couldn't take many more full salvos from the *Jenner*.

Fury burned in the pit of his stomach, because now he knew. Not only had the story of *lostech* been a ruse by Rudi Van Dyk to lure him into a trap, but Kalissa had been in on it. She'd worked her way into his confidence, concocted the story about Bishop's potential treachery to cut away one of his allies, then driven the knife—or laser—in herself.

"We were clear, Kalissa!" Broderick shouted at her over the comms network as he fired his medium laser—again and again—taking four hits from her weapon for each one he dished out. "We could have lived to score another day!"

"Always over-promising and under-delivering, Broderick—in business and the bedroom…" She laughed as another salvo of lasers cut deep, one finding his internal structure, at the cost of sending her heat levels sky high. "You promise, but Van Dyk *delivered*."

Broderick didn't respond.

He was done talking.

He'd turned the tables on one foe already, burying the cache and getting one over on Van Dyk; now he just had to do it again. The only problem was being locked in a stationary, point-blank-range BattleMech death match aboard a DropShip that was rapidly climbing, its pilot screaming over the network for the pilots to cut it out.

Wincing as yet another of Kalissa's lasers probed his 'Mech's internals, his armor more memory than fact right now, Broderick decided to take a gamble. The same spirit had won him his lance, but since then he'd been so careful about *losing* his lance he'd played it safe.

No more.

Firing his medium laser one more time, he throttled his 'Mech forward, then used the *Vindicator's* hand to grab the high-tension cable that had been rigged up to rip open the door of the bunker then been disconnected by the crew and discarded in the corner of the bay. As that same crew ran for cover deeper inside the vessel, he braved further salvos from Kalissa's *Jenner* to get in close…

...then wrap one end of the cable around the narrow section of the *Jenner*'s hull in between its torso and the mounting of its left pair of lasers...

...and the other end over a gantry.

It seemed to take Kalissa a moment to realize what Broderick was doing, but when she finally did, she thrashed her 'Mech and fired her lasers like a madwoman to prevent the inevitable conclusion of his plan. Steam rose off her 'Mech as her rate of fire exceeded the ability of her heat sinks, but she didn't let up.

"Shit," Broderick said as the *Jenner*'s fire disabled his medium laser, although he was thankful its fire hadn't found his LRM ammo bin. Then he keyed the radio to speak to the other man he needed to enact his plan. "Spicer?"

"Are you batshit crazy, Broderick?" The pilot's panicked voice was shrill, as it had been for the entire duration of the firefight, ignored by Broderick until now. "Stop firing immediately!"

"Not gonna happen," Broderick said as he maneuvered his hand to push the *Jenner* back a few centimeters. "Here's what I want you to do..."

"You're *crazy*," Spicer replied after Broderick had quickly explained the plan, but he got on with doing what his boss had asked for anyway. "Now!"

Broderick didn't need to be told twice. The cable in place, he lowered the shoulder of his *Vindicator* and rammed the *Jenner*. The impact caused more damage to both 'Mechs, but it also forced Kalissa's ride back a little. Squeezing the control sticks so hard his knuckles were white, he repeated the process, again and again...

...even as Spicer opened the 'Mech bay door behind Kalissa.

As she realized what he was trying to do, Kalissa throttled her 'Mech forward, focused on survival rather than victory. Like Broderick, she clearly knew his only way to win this encounter was to push her out of the DropShip, but while his *Vindicator* was heavier, her *Jenner* had more raw power, so the physics favored her.

Until Spicer banked the ship slightly to give him a helping hand.

As the feet of Kalissa's *Jenner* sparked on the deck of the DropShip, she broadcast over the network. "Broderick! Let's talk about this! Please!"

"I didn't find the toilets I was after, Kalissa," Broderick replied, continuing to push her back. "Doesn't mean I can't flush the competition..."

Her reply was a scream as the left foot of her *Jenner* finally reached the edge of the deck, sending her 'Mech toppling out of the DropShip as the *Lucky Buck* continued its climb. The high-tension cable went taut, keeping the *Jenner*'s 35-ton weight tethered to the ship, despite the squeal of protest from the overloaded gantry, but she had no way to get back aboard.

Broderick's next challenge was to make sure he didn't follow her out the door. He immediately worked his controls, throttling back at the same time as he used his 'Mech's hand to brace against the frame of the 'Mech bay door, arresting even more of his forward momentum. His 'Mech leaned over the edge—too close for comfort—but his footing held.

"Well, that was a first," Broderick whispered, exhaling with relief now that he had Kalissa neutralized and the *Lucky Buck* was burning to safety. He keyed the radio to speak to Spicer. "Now you can say you've had a 'Mech battle aboard..."

"You're a maniac, One Eye, but I'm glad I'm on your side..." Spicer's voice was filled with relief as he piloted the DropShip away from the surface of Caliban's Rock. "Want me to release the cable?"

"No," Broderick said, putting his fingers back on the firing triggers. "We've already lost so much on this job, I can't afford to lose another 'Mech. We'll need some crew with breathing devices up here to figure out how to bring the *Jenner* aboard, right after I take care of *her.*"

He lined up his targeting reticle over the *Jenner*'s cockpit, tracking the target as the 'Mech continued to spin and hang on the high-tension cable. It was a difficult shot, but he pulled on the trigger, his small laser striking true. A few more shots—some hits, and some misses—and the job was done. Kalissa was dead.

Van Dyk and his Reavers had been foiled.

Broderick's position as commander of his—admittedly reduced—lance was ensured.

He'd live to find fancy toilets or some other treasure some other day. In the Deep Periphery bandit business, that counted as a win.

"Now get us out of here," he said.

"Where to, boss?"

At that, Broderick grinned. "Well, do I have a score to tell *you* about..."

VOICES OF THE SPHERE: TERROR ON THE SPACELANES

LANCE SCARINCI

9 NOVEMBER 3151

Our knowledge of the void is dwarfed by the endless volume of our ignorance. We ply a realm of swirling chaos where stars are born and rent asunder, thinking we can tame it. Danger begins before we ever leave atmosphere and abates only once our feet ground on stable rock. Strange things happen in space because space *is* strange. Despite our thousand-year invasion, we have not tamed it. The void is intrinsically hostile and, in many ways, beyond our understanding. Space boils over with natural perils, next to which man's refined brand of cruelty pales.

—INTRO TO *THE PILLARS OF HEAVEN SHAKE*, NEW AVALON PRESS, 3121

Dr. John Whateley, Kathil, Federated Suns: JumpShips work because they do. Except occasionally, they don't. Misjumps are generally benign, resulting in minor distance errors, but in certain places things get odd. There exist navigational anomalies where the math simply fails and ships are sent far off course. We know the wheres through observation, but the whens elude us. It's random, like the whim of some fickle being. Salford, in the Combine's Pesht District, is infamous for minor displacement of almost every vessel passing through. Savonburg, in the Periphery March, is known for similar behavior, as is Fronc. Comparable events at The Rack are often put down to piracy, but in truth, such happenings predate the system's fall into chaos. It was a treacherous place even when the Rim Worlds called it Port Vail. Every jump is a roll of the dice. Sometimes, we roll snake eyes.

Chu-sa **Yasu Hamasaki, Styx, Draconis Combine:** Do not ask me of the Red Hunter, unless you wish to know of shame and treason. His ancestors served the Dragon, but he seeks only its enmity. He has turned coat on his homeland and on two Clans who mistakenly accepted him as their own. He sells his services, but only a fool would buy them. Abdoun Ricol serves only himself. They say he wants his ancestral home of Rodigo back. He will never have it, but mark me, he will have something. Wherever he settles, his neighbors will have no peace. We should destroy him now.

Sergeant Pernella Silva, Loyalty, Free Worlds League: Periphery pirates suck, but internal pirates are worse. They hit worlds thought safe. Lincoln's Rotting Corpse terrorized our area for decades until Clan Wolf cleared them out, but did they? Word came from Molokai just last week about a band of pirates who communicated only through a mummified corpse dubbed over with maniacal laughter. No ID, but who else would that be? Copycats? Why resurrect LRC instead of, say, Anti-Nick and the Elves from Hell? Guess we're heading to Thirty Weight for some house cleaning.

Technician Trest, *Invader*-class CSF *High Tides*, Clan Sea Fox: You Spheroids ply the black, but it is not your home. We are born to it, modified through surgery and breeding to excel in it, and still we puzzle over it. Hyperspace is beyond our ability to comprehend, yet we shove ourselves heedlessly through it. Jumps are quick affairs, but still move smoothly forward in time, *quiaff*? When you arrive late, you shrug it off. When you arrive before you left, I promise your thinking will alter. What of those whom hyperspace will not release? The SLS *Enigma* vanished during the Liberation of Terra, but it is still periodically sighted. Early reports spoke of transmissions from a confused crew before the ship immediately jumped again. Later transmissions became cries for help. I cannot speak to their truth, but last year, I did receive an incoming ping from a *Congress*-class ship over Wasat. It sent only animalistic growls before jumping out.

Scientist Merle, Pollux, Wolf Empire: What? Why ask me that? My field is robotics, not fanciful storytelling. I know nothing of Necromo, and the idea of spacefaring independent drones is preposterous! Even Star League science was not so advanced. *Sibkin* nonsense. Next question.

Zhong-shao **Sergei Zakharov, Shipka, Capellan Confederation:** Privateering is not dead. Being at peace with a neighbor only means the flag is not flown when they come to steal and murder. The Celestial Throne may be above such deviousness, but the Davion barbarians will come with or without their colors, and cowards behind the Republic's failed Fortress struck at us for years with state-sponsored terrorism. When unknown forces strike, think twice before branding them mere pirates.

Leftenant Simon Auclair, Skepptana, Filtvelt Coalition: Malfin' Tortuga. It never ends with that place. They're like a virus you can't shake, lying dormant until conditions are ripe. Like now. There's a raid every other month, all along the border, and too many of our people are off helping Erik fight the Combine. The Brotherhood of Randis is some help, except for that Brother Perseus and his doomsaying. Tortuga's bad enough; we don't need tall tales and ghost stories!

Star Captain Dancey, Ramora, Raven Alliance: The Outworlds Wastes grow more hostile by the day. Perseus Schell speaks true. I will say no more.

Della (surname withheld), Furillo, Lyran Commonwealth: What made me quit spacing? Space! It hides so many secrets. How far out did the Star League go? Five hundred light years, plus the Periphery? We're told only the odd devolved colony exists past that. Really? We reached the current borders of the Inner Sphere within a century of discovering space travel, and that was many centuries ago. You really think we stopped there? You think the Clan Homeworlds are the only advanced colony out there? Maybe what I saw out beyond Circinus will change your mind. Encountering another ship out there is rare, but we didn't stumble on one, oh no. It was a convoy! Dozens of ships, at least one pinging back at over two megatons. No IFF, no answer to hails other than to send some droppers our way. Thank God for lithium-fusion batteries. Before we jumped, one of them ships moved... It wasn't a ship.

RIDING THE TIGER

CRAIG. A. REED, JR.

He who rides the tiger can never dismount.

—Chinese Proverb

LIUBU MOUNTAIN
XI'AN PROVINCE
XIENG KHOUANG
SIAN COMMONALITY
CAPELLAN CONFEDERATION
21 MAY 3066

It took the man three minutes to die.

The attack was swift and sudden, turning the camp from a peaceful dinner scene into a killing ground. The murderers outnumbered the victims nine to three, and they were old hands at the task. None of the three victims had a chance to escape once the *rumāls*—the strangling scarfs favored by the cult for centuries—encircled their necks.

Salmalin Takeri watched the dying, middle-aged man before him with detached interest. The man sprawled face down on the ground; one member of Takeri's gang held the man's legs, while a second pinned his arms. Asad, Takeri's second-in-command, held the *rumāl* firmly in place around the man's neck, a knee planted between the shoulder blades to provide leverage and keep the victim on the ground. A radio playing Rajasthani folk music drowned out any chance of the struggle being heard beyond the camp.

A quick glance at other victims told him they had already succumbed to death. The campfires revealed the bodies on the ground. The *bhuttotes* were in the process of removing the yellow scarfs and looking to Takeri for instructions. With a motion of his head, he indicated the grove of trees behind him. The team that had helped each *bhuttote* perform the rite then picked up the bodies and carried them into the darkness.

Takeri looked back at the man before him. His name was Shen Hung, and he still struggled to escape from his assailant, but his attempts were weakening. After another thirty seconds, Hung went limp. Asad kept the pressure on for another minute, then removed the yellow scarf from the dead man's throat and stood. With a small gesture, Takeri instructed the two assistants to pick up the body and carry it away.

"Very good," he whispered.

Asad nodded. He was slightly above average height, but his arms and shoulders were well muscled. "Next time," he said in a harsh-sounding whisper, "I will be the *sotha,* you can be the *bhuttote*."

"Of course, my friend," Takeri said. He reached into a waistcoat pocket and pulled out a small radio. "Dasya," he said, his voice even, "have you finished digging the holes? The rubbish is on its way."

"Yes, *Jemadar*," a voice replied. "We will be done in about ten minutes."

"Good. Kanaka, have you checked the inventory?"

"Yes, *Jemadar*," said another voice. "They have more than we thought. Chen can pick up the excess on the way back."

"Excellent. Make sure we leave a clean camp in the morning." He pocketed the radio. "The Goddess will be pleased with our work tonight, my friend."

"The omens were right for it," Asad replied. He groaned as he stretched. "I am getting too old for this."

Takeri laughed. "You. Getting old?" He slapped Asad on the shoulder. "We will serve as the Goddess wills. Come, let us observe the rites and get some rest."

SHAANXI CITY
XI'AN PROVINCE
XIENG KHOUANG
SIAN COMMONALITY
CAPELLAN CONFEDERATION
10 MARCH 3067

Tobe's was an Irani café near the south gate of the city. Those pilgrims who could afford it made a point to partake of at least one meal there before making the trek to the Namdroling Nyingmapa Temple. It was a popular destination for both members of the planet's Han majority and the Indian minority. Takeri always spent time here before the start of the pilgrimage, drinking *khari chai*, renewing acquaintances, listening to gossip, and keeping an eye out for the Goddess' next offerings.

In Shaanxi, Takeri went by the name of Achir Sahir, Master Merchant, who traveled nearly anywhere across the planet to make a profit. He was well known as a generous man who had been a regular along the pilgrimage trail for most of the last two decades. And unknown to all but a few trusted men, he was the planetary leader of the House of the Setting Sun, a front for the Thuggee Cult.

Across the marble-topped table sat his oldest son, Pakava. He was eighteen now, taller than his father but slimmer, with tightly curled hair, deep brown eyes, and an easy smile. Like his father, he wore the clothing of a moderately successful merchant, a good disguise in this quarter of the city.

"Tell me, son," Takeri said softly in *Ramasi*, the chant used by those who served Bhawani in this holy mission. "The four men at the table by the window. What do you make of them?"

Instead of looking directly at the men his father had indicated, Pakava turned his head to look at one of the many large mirrors lining the wall. After a few seconds, he replied, "Workmen. Probably from the construction site down the street from here."

Takeri shook his head. "No. All four are wearing military-style boots. One might, or two, but all four?" He shook his head again. "They are all wearing baggy clothes. Their hair is uniformly cut, and they are all clean shaven. Notice how they do not say much to each other, and they spend too much time looking around. They are not workmen."

A flicker of worry crossed Pakava's face, but he quickly removed it and took a sip of his *masala chai*. "Could they be looking for us?"

"Maybe. I will speak to Valnar later today and see if there is anything we should be concerned about."

The front door of the tea shop slid open with a hiss of pneumatics, and a tall, lean figure wearing a police uniform entered. Takeri frowned.

"What is it?" Pakava asked.

"A lion has just entered, my son. Stay silent and watch."

The police officer scanned the room until he spotted Takeri. He moved through the tables until he reached Takeri's table. "Sahir."

Takeri smiled. "Inspector Kaleka, it is good to see you again!"

Inspector Harbir Singh Kaleka scowled. His dark beard matched his dark eyes, and his sun-darkened skin was only offset by his blue turban. "Back again, I see."

Takeri spread his hands. "Of course! I am a merchant, and I have wares to sell."

"If I could believe that is all you did, I would not be here."

"This is my son, Salmalin."

Kaleka switched his gaze to the younger man. "So, the next generation starts its work?" he asked, his tone cold.

"He needs to learn the family business."

The inspector looked back at Takeri. "Fencing and moving stolen goods? Maybe even murder?"

"You wound me, Inspector. I am an honest businessman."

"You are many things, but honest isn't one of them."

"You are obsessed with finding something that is not there. Come, let me buy you a cup of tea."

The inspector shook his head. "No. Don't think this is over, Sahir. You and your band of thieves will make a mistake one day, and I will be there to see it. You can only ride the tiger for so long before he eats you."

"The only animal I ride is my horse, and the only thing he eats is grain."

Kaleka's scowl deepened. "Keep looking over your shoulder, because one day, I will be there."

Takeri waited until the inspector had walked out the door, passing a party of four entering the café. Three were men, while the fourth was a woman, all dressed in worn but well-tended clothes. The two larger men wore backpacks, while the woman and the third man only had a bag slung over one shoulder.

"Father," Pakava said, after sipping his tea, "is he onto us?"

"He suspects," Takeri replied, his gaze watching the newcomers reach a table and sit. "But he does not suspect our real allegiance. If he did, he would have been here with a dozen officers and taken us away for questioning."

"Is he dangerous?"

"Very. He is the senior field investigator for the regional police force. He is tough, smart, honest, and dedicated. But his weakness is he will not violate his own code of honor or the law to bring in criminals. He suspects we are thieves and maybe murderers, but he cannot prove it."

"Maybe we should introduce him to the Goddess."

"No, he is too well-known, and is rarely alone. He also is a formidable fighter. I saw him once defeat three toughs trying to kill him with only his bare hands. No, it is better to let him seek the scent we choose for him." Takeri made a slight motion toward the table where the four newcomers sat. "What do you make of them?"

Pakava used the mirrors again to looked at the party, then looked at his father. "Travelers."

The older man nodded. "What else?"

"They have spent a lot of time outside, even the girl. She's pretty."

"Mind your focus," Takeri reminded him gently.

The younger man took the mild rebuke with a nod. He watched the newcomers place their order with a shop's waitress. "The man with the bag is the leader, the girl his sister or lover. From the cut and material of their clothes, they have money."

"And the other two?"

"Servants or bodyguards. They're deferring to the other two."

"Good. What else?"

"They don't appear to be armed, though there may be weapons in the bags."

Takeri brought his teacup to his lips. "Good. You are learning, my son."

The man Pakava had identified as the leader glanced around, then looked directly at Takeri. He stood, whispered something into the girl's ear, and walked toward Takeri and Pakava. He reached their table and bobbed his head to Takeri. "Forgive my rudeness, sir," he said in a soft, slightly nervous voice, "but are you Master Achir Sahir?"

Takeri, looked up at him. "I am. May I help you?"

The man was maybe in his middle to late twenties, with dark hair and a worried expression. "I need to speak to you," he said. "May I join you?"

Takeri frowned. "I am not in the mood for business," he said slowly. "I do—"

The man's expression looked crestfallen. "Please, Master Sahir. We need your help. Master Merchant Hari Valnar suggested I speak to you about this matter."

Takeri smiled slightly. "Hari is an old and valued friend. If he thinks I can help you, then the least I can do is listen. What is your name, friend?"

"It's Chen. Sying Chen."

"Please, sit." Takeri motioned to the table. "Would you like some tea?" Chen nodded eagerly. "Salmalin, please pour friend Chen a cup of the *khari chai*."

Pakava placed the filled teacup in front of Chen as the man sat in one of the black, wooden chairs. "Thank you, Master Sahir," Chen said.

"Please, call me Achir. Would you like something to eat? The service is excellent, and the food is even more so."

Chen grimaced. "No, thank you. We've just come off the ferry from Fanlu, and I fear my stomach is still somewhat unsettled." He sipped the tea and made a face. "Maybe I shouldn't indulge right now."

"That is understandable. Where are you from?"

"Yunfu, in Guizhou Province."

"You are a long way from home, Friend Chen," Takeri said. "It must be, what, at least fifteen hundred kilometers from here?"

"You are right. Most of the way was by rail, but we had to cross the Dongsha Straits, and the sea was rough."

"It usually is at this time of year. So, how can I help you?"

"We are here to find someone," Chen said. "Sheng Hung, my fiancée's uncle."

Takeri frowned. He faintly remembered the name. "I fail to see how I can help you, my friend. Surely the militia or the police would be the people to contact?"

Chen shook his head. "I have tried them, and they are worse than useless! Ling is worried about her uncle." He glanced at the table where his group sat and flashed a smile at the woman. When he looked back at Takeri, he said in a softer tone, "Shen is her legal guardian. I wish to marry Ling, but we need his permission to do so."

"I still fail to see why you need my help."

Chen nodded. "He came here last year to make the pilgrimage to the Namdroling Nyingmapa Temple. We have not heard from him since he sent a message that he was starting his pilgrimage."

"Ah," Takeri said. "I see. You think he might be at the temple."

"He is a very devout man, and it would not surprise us if he resided there. But it is also possible something happened to him along the way. When we were asking around for someone to help us, I was given Master Valnar's name. From him I got your name. You are well known for your trips to the temple."

Takeri shrugged. "I do good business selling to the pilgrims along the route. And I always give the temple a generous percentage of what I earn. While I am not of their religion, I have always respected the monks who live there."

Chen nodded again. "We were hoping we could travel with you, to retrace the steps Shen took. If something did happen to him, then we must find out."

"I see." Takeri smiled slightly. "I should warn you that this won't be easy or cheap. No motorized traffic is allowed along the route, with the exception of emergency vehicles. Riding animals are expensive, and the local dealers always inflate their prices around this time of the year. And while most pilgrims are decent and honest, many will not speak to anyone without some monetary inducement."

Chen leaned in, his eyes bright. "We have money!" he whispered excitedly. "My family is well off, and Ling and Shen's family are far from poor. Money is no object."

"Indeed?"

Chen nodded. "We'll have enough to reasonably pay for any information. And should the news be bad, we will make an offering of what we have left when we reach the temple."

Out of the corner of his eye, Takeri caught a flash of excitement on Pakava's face. *Youth*, he thought. "I will tell you what, Friend Chen," he said, smiling. "I will make a few inquiries around the city and see if anyone remembers Shen. If they do not bear any fruit, you will be welcome to travel with my party."

Chen bowed his head. "Thank you, Master...Achir. I promise you will not regret this."

Takeri waved his hand in dismissal. "No need for thanks, Friend Chen. It will be my pleasure to help you in this worthy cause." He removed a small notebook and pen from his waistcoat and wrote quickly. He tore the page out and handed it to Chen. "This is my address here in the city," he said. "If I am not there, leave a message. We will leave in four days."

Chen took the paper with a look of hope. "Thank you!" he said eagerly. "We are in your debt!"

Takeri smiled. "A debt that can be repaid by inviting me to the wedding."

Chen nodded. "Of course! Thank you again!" He turned and hurried over to the table, and was soon in whispered conversation with his fiancée and the others.

"The Goddess smiles on us!" Pakava whispered in *Ramasi*.

"Does she?" Takeri whispered back. "I am not one to accept ripe fruit when it just drops out of the sky into my lap. I would not put it past Kaleka to plant some undercover officers in my party. Finish up your tea. I need you to run some errands for me."

"What?"

"Go find Valnar and find out if he talked to Chen. After that, find Asad and ask him to find out all he can about Sying Chen and Ling Hung from Yunfu. Also, have them contact our brothers inside the police force and find out what Kaleka's plans are. Finally, have him put the word out on the street that someone is looking for Shen Hung."

"But what if they find him?"

"They won't. We gave Hung to the Goddess last year." He looked at Chen and the others. "And if the Goddess wills it, he will soon have company."

LIUBU MOUNTAIN
XI'AN PROVINCE
XIENG KHOUANG
SIAN COMMONALITY
CAPELLAN CONFEDERATION
18 MARCH 3067

The mountain trail was ten meters wide, and centuries of travel had made it smooth and level. It climbed at a gentle incline at this point, though the closer they came to the Temple, the steeper and more difficult the trail became. Birds were singing in the trees, the air cool but not cold, and the late afternoon sun was low on the horizon.

There was a total of thirty in Takeri's group, including Chen, Ling and their servants. The rest were his people, every one of them a loyal servant to the Goddess and her Avatar. Most of the group walked along the trail or rode in one of the four donkey-pulled wagons Takeri used to carry his wares. The rest, like Takeri, Pakava, and Chen's entourage, rode horses.

Takeri heard a horse trot up to him. He turned to watch Chen guiding his horse up the trail until he was even with the disguised assassin. "Achir," he asked, smiling, "are we camping soon?"

Takeri smiled back. "Less than half an hour," he called back.

Something still bothered Takeri about Chen and his party. Asad's contacts had come back with confirmation of Chen's story. Both he and Ling were from Yunfu, engaged to marry, and had left Yunfu to find Shen Hung. As for Kaleka, the Thuggee members inside the police force had reported he hadn't requested or received additional personnel and had left Shaanxi to pursue a lead in Hua-lien, a city along the south coast.

Despite the confirmation, Takeri felt uneasy about the entire situation. They had been on the road for four days, leaving Shaanxi four days after the meeting in the tea shop. The locals had been able to supply little information, as was expected. From what he had known of Shen Hung, Takeri knew the man had not been the gregarious type. Still, enough sources had indicated Shen Hung and two servants had left the city on the pilgrimage trail.

Much of the time on the trail was uneventful. Every time they came across another party, Chen and one of his servants would stop and question the party about Shen. When they were done, Chen would give the pilgrims a small gift, then rejoin Takeri's party. Again and again, the ritual repeated.

Several times, the group encountered militia and police patrols. As with the pilgrims, Chen and one of his servants would stop and ask them about Shen. The only difference was there was no gift for either the police or military.

Takeri had one of his men stay close to the conversation, in case it was an attempt for Chen to pass along information. But his men all reported the same: the conversations were always about Shen and if anyone remembered seeing him last year. Always the answer was no, as most pilgrims were not regular travelers, and thousands of people made the journey.

From these conversations, Takeri discovered Shen Hung had been a sculptor of some renown, and had created a series of statuettes for the monastery. Takeri vaguely remembered the cargo Shen and his servants were carrying had been taken off-world to be sold elsewhere.

The other servant stayed near Ling and a donkey carrying a small chest. Twice, members of Takeri's party had seen the chest's contents when it was open, and both reported it was full of money.

Chen's servants were silent and stayed near their wards and the chest. Despite neither one moving like a trained martial artist, both had the look of experienced brawlers. But once the *rumāl* was slipped around their necks, it wouldn't matter what fighting skills they had.

Once in the morning, and once in the afternoon, the party would stop, the wagons opened, and wares displayed for passing groups to browse. Practical items like packs and walking sticks were common, along with small religious merchandise that could be left as offerings at the temple. Business was always brisk, and Takeri consistently made a tidy profit on the sales.

But, under his watch, the traveling bazaar also had another purpose. It allowed other groups of Thuggees along the trail to make contact, trade information, and alert each other about problems and groups to avoid. With over 50,000 people on the 150-kilometer trail at any one time, the sixty or so followers of Kali under Takeri's authority easily blended in with the masses.

Normally, it would take Takeri's caravan seven days to travel the trail, but Chen's continuing questioning had slowed them down, and Asad glumly estimated it would add another two days to the trip. "What are you waiting for?" he had asked his leader and friend late on the third night.

"I need to be sure," Takeri had replied.

As the sun was lowering itself to the horizon on the fourth day, he still wasn't sure. Was the Goddess testing him? If he was going to commit himself to offering those souls to his goddess, it must be soon. He saw his men looking at Chen and his party like wolves eyeing prey. So far, none of the four had made any sign they knew they were in danger. Either they were oblivious, or they were very good actors.

Takeri wasn't sure which one was the reality.

LIUBU MOUNTAIN
XI'AN PROVINCE
XIENG KHOUANG
SIAN COMMONALITY
CAPELLAN CONFEDERATION
19 MARCH 3067

The sound of helicopters woke Takeri from his slumber. Light was just peeking over the mountains through the opening of his tent. He threw off the thick covers and got out of the bedroll.

His son, who shared the tent with him, opened his eyes slowly. "What is it?" he asked sleepily.

"I don't know, but get up. Helicopters along the pilgrimage route are never a good sign."

By the time Takeri was dressed and out of the tent, the helicopters were in view. He recognized the three incoming helicopters as Sky Lions, used exclusively by the regional police.

The area was a widening of the path, enough space for two dozen tents. Even now, people were crawling out of their tents, most sleepily staring up into the clear dawn sky. A few early risers had several fires going, but the air was cold and biting.

"What do you think?" Asad asked in *Ramasi* as he strode up.

Takeri frowned. "I do not know."

"Kaleka?"

"Probably. We shall not take any chances. Alert the men and watch Chen and his people."

"Right." Asad strode away.

"What's going on?" Chen asked as he approached.

"I don't know," Takeri admitted. "Vehicles are forbidden along the trail, unless there is an emergency."

Chen shielded his eyes with his hand as he stared at the helicopters. "I think one of them is going to land!"

Takeri looked up and saw a Sky Lion descending toward them. The pilot maneuvered the helicopter over the trail with some skill, adjusting for the air currents. Five meters above the trail, ropes were kicked out on both sides of the helicopter, twisting and writhing like snakes as they fell. As soon as the ropes hit the ground, armored figures slid down. When the last of eight men landed, the Sky Lion rose into the air, the ropes retracting nearly as fast as they had been thrown out. Once the first helicopter was clear, the second came in, and the process of deploying men repeated.

Takeri saw the blue turban at once. "Kaleka," he muttered.

"Who?"

The Thuggee leader looked at Chen. "Police officer. He has a vendetta against me."

"Why?"

Takeri shrugged. "He is convinced I am an evil man, despite no evidence against me."

"Evil? I find that hard to believe."

"Some people will believe what they want, no matter the evidence."

Kaleka strode toward them, surrounded by heavily armed police officers. "Sahir!" he shouted.

"Inspector Kaleka!" Takeri replied cheerfully. "What can I do for you today?"

"We're here to search for stolen goods."

"Stolen goods?" Takeri frowned. "Why would I have stolen goods?"

"I just returned from Hua-lien. One of your shipments there had several valuable items in it reported stolen."

"Who would accuse me of such things?"

"The relatives of pilgrims who never returned from this trip."

"That still doesn't explain why you accuse me of being a thief."

"Inspector," Chen said, stepping forward. "I must protest your actions against Master Sahir."

Kaleka's gaze went to Chen. "You are?"

"I'm Sying Chen, from Yunfu, in Guizhou Province."

"You are a long way from home, Master Chen."

"We are seeking my fiancée's uncle, Shen Hung. He was last seen making this pilgrimage last year."

"I see. Has he been reported missing?"

"Not yet. We are hoping he is at the monastery."

"I see." Kaleka looked back at Takeri. "I don't suppose you know where Shen is?"

"Me?" Takeri spread his arms wide. "I am a simple merchant, not a detective. How would I know?"

"Inspector," Chen said, "I repeat my protests."

Kaleka gave him a withering stare. "I don't care. Now, unless you want to be searched too, I suggest you get out of my way."

Chen bowed his head and stepped back. "I still think you are wrong."

"Master Chen, I suggest you and your party get away from this man here. He and his men are dangerous. You just might wake up with a cut throat."

"I trust him more than I trust you."

Kaleka shook his head and strode past him. "Then you are either a fool or in league with this criminal."

"I am neither, Inspector."

"We shall see, Master Chen."

The police had searched for an hour, but it had taken Takeri's men three hours to clean up the mess the police left behind. As expected, Kaleka's men hadn't found anything—any wealth the Thuggees took from their victims was buried, to be picked up later by Takeri's men on the way back to Shaanxi. Still, the search had been thorough and, Takeri suspected, deliberately done to make a mess.

It was close to noon before the group got underway again. Takeri rode at the front, while Chen and his group hung farther back. Asad's horse caught up with Takeri's, and for a moment, neither one said anything.

"Well?" Takeri asked in *Ramasi.*

"They made no contact with the police," Asad replied in the same language. "Chen and his servants stood in front of their tents and didn't let any of the officers get within five meters. The girl stayed inside her tent, peeking out on occasion to watch the search. No officer spoke to them, and the inspector never even looked at them. One of the men did hear him radio headquarters, demanding to know who Sying Chen was."

"No chance of messages being passed between Chen and the Inspector?"

Asad snorted. "Not unless they've developed a code with angry facial expressions, shouted curses, and threats. No personal contact, no quiet conversations, and no radio calls. If this was a ploy for Kaleka to make contact with his undercover team, I don't see how they could have done it."

Takeri nodded. "Agreed. Chen was more concerned with protecting his possessions and his girl than talking to the officers. Which makes me wonder if he had something more valuable to protect."

"Your orders?"

"For today, do nothing but watch them. I would not put it past Kaleka to double back on us, and his men have delayed us enough that we will not reach the next camp until after dark, too late for our purposes."

Asad scowled. "We are running out of time."

"Patience, my friend. We have a couple days left before we reach the monastery, and there are a few places along the way where bodies can be lost forever. Let me think about it overnight."

"Right." Asad reined his horse around and trotted back to the caravan, leaving Takeri alone with his thoughts.

LIUBU MOUNTAIN
XI'AN PROVINCE
XIENG KHOUANG
SIAN COMMONALITY
CAPELLAN CONFEDERATION
20 MARCH 3067

Takeri guided his horse to the side of the road, allowing the wagons to pass. Asad rode over as he climbed off his horse, making a display of checking the saddle's clench.

"Well?" Asad asked softly. "The double moons we saw last night are a good omen."

Takeri exhaled slowly. "Tonight. After dinner."

Asad nodded. "The girl too?"

"We cannot leave witnesses. Give Pakava the task of being her *bhuttote*."

Asad looked a little surprised. "Is that wise?"

"He will need to learn sometime. She is light and weak. She shouldn't be a problem. Assign Raplka and Mufta to hold her."

"I will tell the others. The signal?"

Takeri smiled. "I'm feeling nostalgic. The signal will be when I say, 'Bring the tobacco.'"

The campsite was another widening of the trail, already occupied by a dozen tents, but with enough room for Takeri's group to set up camp. By the time the camp was finished, the sun had gone down.

After setting up their tents, Chen and one of his servants started a fire while Ling and the other servant began preparing their dinner. Takeri had offered to share his meals with Chen and his group, but the young man had politely, almost reluctantly, declined. He explained that Ling couldn't eat meat, and to honor her, Chen was doing the same. So, the four prepared and ate their own meatless meals.

Asad found Takeri in his tent, sitting at a folding desk, counting money and making notes on a handheld noteputer. "All is ready."

Takeri nodded and turned off the device. "Come, let us get this done."

The night was clear, and one of the moons was rising in the east. Several cooking fires were scattered around, and the wagons were formed up into a square around the perimeter of the camp. Between the wagons, small groups of Takeri's people sat or stood, swords and vibroknives close at hand but out of sight. A radio playing Rajasthani folk music was loud enough to prevent any noise from inside the camp reaching beyond it. Half a dozen Thuggees were scattered outside the camp on watch.

Good, Takeri thought. Still, he couldn't shake the feeling something was wrong.

He sighed. Maybe Asad was right. Maybe the Goddess and her Avatar had blessed him and his group with an easy mark as a sign of her favor.

He gave Asad a quick look and gesture, and the man began a tour of the camp. Takeri counted to one hundred under his breath, then started walking. As he walked, he thought he heard a helicopter, but when he looked into the night sky, he saw nothing but stars. He continued on, resolving himself for what was about to happen.

Chen's people were sitting around a small fire, and they looked up as Takeri approached. "May I join you?"

Chen waved to a flat rock across the fire from him. "Of course, Achir! Did you have a good day?"

"It went very well," Takeri replied as he sat. "The temple will be pleased with my contribution this year."

"I am glad."

"How have your own efforts been?"

Chen's smile faltered. "Not as promising as I had hoped. A few pilgrims thought they recognized Shen from last year, but they are not sure."

"What happens if you do not find him?" Takeri asked.

Chen sighed, then looked at Ling. "We would be forced to find Ling's cousin. But he is in the military, so he will be hard to track down. Even if we find him and he agrees, it will be at least another six months after that until we can be wed."

"I see," Takeri replied. The small fire had ruined his night vision, but he knew the *bhuttote* and their assistants were moving in. It was up to him, as *sotha*, to keep the four occupied until it was too late. "What would happen if you two were to elope?"

Chen looked horrified. "We couldn't! Neither family would condone such an action!"

"So elope off-world," Takeri said with a shrug. "Surely you have enough money left to make a new start somewhere else."

"No," Ling said firmly. Takeri looked at her and thought what a waste it would be to sacrifice her to the Goddess. "Our families would hunt us down!"

"And there is no chance we could get a permit to go off-world!" Chen added.

"I know a few people," Takeri said. "They could get you a permit, for a suitable fee."

Chen shook his head. "My family has contacts throughout the Commonality. We would run out of money before we could outrun their influence."

The sounds of the fire and crickets were loud enough to mask the sound of the Thuggees' approach. Takeri saw shadows moving behind Chen and the others, but he kept his eyes on the group. "I am sorry for suggesting such a thing," he said, lowering his head. "Please forgive me."

"That's all right," Ling replied. "We are fortunate to have found a friend like you in our time of need."

Asad came out of the darkness. "We've finished making camp."

"Good!" Takeri said. He smiled at Chen and the others then stood. "Enough about such matters. Let us enjoy the evening. Asad, bring the tobacco!"

The night around the four came alive as the *bhuttotes* came out of the darkness to drop the *rumāls* over the newest sacrifices to the Goddess. As they did so, the Thuggees assigned to help dashed forward to tackle and pin the tributes down before they could react. Takeri stepped back slowly, keeping attention on him until the last instant.

Then, things went horribly wrong.

Takeri heard the sound of a helicopter getting louder, and from the night sky, the beam of a searchlight stabbed down on the camp. The Thuggees faltered when the intense light passed over them as the four sheep they were about to kill suddenly became tigers.

Something metallic appeared in Chen's hand. Without standing, he spun and flung the item at one of the Thuggees that was trying to tackle him. The Thuggee grabbed his throat, blood welling around his hands as the thrown blade found a vital point. Even as his would-be murderer collapsed, Chen hurled himself to the side and back, easily avoiding the *bhuttote's* attempt to strangle him. He smoothly rolled to his feet and gutted the second assistant with a vibroknife that had suddenly appeared in his hand. He withdrew the knife, spun, and slashed the *bhuttote* across the throat, nearly decapitating the Thuggee.

As the dying *bhuttote* fell, Chen spun and flung something at Takeri. Takeri bit off a scream as his right leg folded under him. He managed to avoid striking his head on the rock he had just been sitting on, but his shoulder hit it hard enough to numb his arm. He looked down and saw a throwing knife buried deep in his right thigh.

Shouts and screams made Takeri forget his pain and look up. The searchlight showed everything that was happening, and it horrified him. Both of Chen's servants, each wielding a pair of long knives, had exploded into a storm of slashing blades, sending two Thuggee to their deaths in sprays of blood. Their *bhuttotes* died within an eyeblink of each other, cut apart like sides of beef. Ling's paired rattan sticks rapidly broke one Thuggee's arm, then crushed his windpipe with a snapping blow. A second Thuggee tried to stab her with a vibroknife, only to go down under a storm of vicious strikes.

Night suddenly became day, and it took Takeri several seconds to realize the helicopter was landing. As soon as it touched down, men spilled out of it and raced toward the fight. A few stopped long enough to point weapons at any Thuggee in sight and opened fire. Several of Takeri's men fell, while the survivors ran.

"It's a trap!" Asad roared, moving toward Takeri. "Brothers, fl—"

Chen, a vibroknife in one hand and a pistol in the other, covered the distance between him and Asad in two strides. Asad managed to draw a long knife from a sleeve and blocked Chen's first thrust, but it left him open for a pistol across the jaw. The Thuggee stumbled back, but Chen surged forward, his face hard and cold.

Asad slashed at Chen's throat, but the man leaned back just enough to avoid the slice, then fired a kick to the side of Asad's knee. The *crack* of the Thuggee's knee joint breaking was almost lost in the violence around them. Asad fell, his curse cut short as Chen stepped in and rammed his knife into the Thuggee's right eye.

Chen released the knife and spun back to where his allies were moving through their opponents like a scythe through grain. "Leave some alive!" he barked.

Two Thuggees went down under the pommels of the servants' knives. Ling ducked under Pakava's knife and hit him several times with her sticks. The young man fell, his consciousness snatched from him by the well-placed blows.

Chen shifted his pistol on a nearby Thuggee, who was trying to stab Ling in the back, and pulled the trigger. The crack of the shot was loud, despite the sound of fighting. The Thuggee's head exploded. As the now-dead assassin fell, Chen shifted his pistol back to Takeri. "They have three seconds to surrender," he intoned. "Two seconds..."

"Brothers!" Takeri shouted. "Surrender! In the name of the Goddess, surrender!" The sounds of fighting died away and the helicopter's searchlight shut off.

Several men from the helicopter charged at Chen, rifles raised, yelling at him to drop the weapons.

Chen glowered at them. "Who is in charge?" he demanded. "Bring them here now!"

"I am here," Kaleka said, emerging from the darkness. Like the newcomers, he was dressed in all black, including his turban, and carried a submachine gun. "Who are you? You're not Sying Chen. He and his fiancée are under house arrest in Yunfu."

"They are there on my orders," Chen replied.

"And you are?"

"*Sang-wei* Raymond Chow, and I serve Chancellor Sun-Tzu Liao."

Kaleka frowned and looked around the camp. "Unless I am mistaken, you and your comrades are Death Commandos."

"You are correct. Contact *Sang-shao* Grendell in the capital. He will confirm our identities."

The officers lowered their weapons slowly, and a couple of them stepped back.

Kaleka stepped forward. "I will accept your word for the moment. What is going on?"

Takeri stared at Chen—*no, Chow*—who returned the stare with the same coldness a tiger has for its prey. "Achir Sahir," he said, his voice flat. "Or should I use your real name, Salmalin Takeri?"

"You knew," Takeri spat out.

"Of course. Master Valnar was most helpful."

"He would not talk."

Chow shook his head. "Everyone has a weak point. Valnar's was his family. He chose to talk instead of watching his family die slowly." He looked at Kaleka. "This man is a Thuggee cultist, as are his men."

"Thuggee?" Kaleka spat in anger, glaring at Takeri. "I knew he was a criminal, but I did not think he had sunk that low."

Ling walked over to Chow, still carrying the sticks she had used to knock Pakava out. "We left a few alive," she said flatly.

"Good," Chow replied. "Make sure the dead remain so."

Ling nodded and walked away.

"What brought you here?" Kaleka asked.

"Shen Hung."

"Yes, I remember the name. You were looking for him."

"What many people did not know, Shen's full name was Shen Hung Liao."

Kaleka looked surprised. "Related to the Chancellor?"

"Fourth cousin. He did not use the Liao name because he wanted his work as a sculptor to be judged on its own merits, not because he was the Chancellor's cousin."

He looked back at Takeri. "One of the statues you took from Shen Hung was purchased by someone seeking to curry favor with my lord Chancellor. When he presented the statue to the Chancellor, he recognized his cousin's work. The statue was one of a series he was creating for the Namdroling Nyingmapa temple. Hung was quietly loyal to the Confederation and the Chancellor, but he would not have willingly parted with the statue under any circumstances."

"You suspected he was dead," Kaleka said.

Chow nodded. "The Chancellor ordered the Maskirovka to locate his cousin, but they found no trace of him over the last year."

"So, Hung was dead."

Chow nodded. "However, the Chancellor sent us to investigate what happened to Shen Hung, and we found evidence of Thuggee activity on this planet."

"I was not aware of that."

"The cult was protected by several senior members of the planetary government. Sian is sending an investigation team to uncover the traitors. As for our investigation, we traced the statue back to Valnar, and he told us Achir Sahir had given him the statue. We located Sahir and after an intense background check, identified him as Salmalin Takeri, a known Thuggee leader."

"You could have taken it to the local authorities," Kaleka said.

"Out of the question. We still do not know how deep the cult is here, and my orders were to locate and punish Hung's killers."

Ling came back. "We have nineteen bodies and seven prisoners."

"Bring the prisoners here and line them up across the fire from Takeri."

Ling nodded and returned to the prisoners.

"What are you going to do with us?" Takeri demanded.

"As far as I am concerned, you and the rest are already dead. The only thing left to decide is the manner of your death."

Takeri looked at Kaleka. "Inspector! We demand our day in court!"

"You don't deserve one," Chow replied coldly. He looked at Kaleka. "My orders from the Chancellor are clear. Do you wish to dispute them?"

Kaleka didn't look happy, but held up his hands in a gesture of defeat. "I don't like this, but since it's the Chancellor's will, I cannot oppose this, *Sang-wei*."

The last of the prisoners was being dragged into line on the other side of the campfire. They knelt, their hands bound, all looking dazed and showing signs of inflicted brutality. Takeri saw Pakava, the left side of his face bloody and swollen, dragged into place at one end of the line. Four policemen stood behind them, rifles ready.

"Inspector," Chow said. "My team will handle the prisoners."

Kaleka motioned to his men, and the officers stepped back into the darkness, replaced by Chow's team. Each was armed with a pistol held by their side.

"Unlike Shen," Chow said, walking around the fire until he was standing in front of the row of prisoners, "I am not a gentle man. I kill enemies of the state."

"What are you waiting for, then?" Takeri half shouted.

Chow turned to look at him. "I want the rest of the Thuggee cult on Xieng Khouang. You will tell me everything—leaders, meeting places, middlemen, everything."

"Why should I?" Takeri managed to growl out the question. "As you said, we are already dead."

"The method of execution is up to you," Chow said. He looked at the line of prisoners. "If you don't tell me everything, not only will every one of you die slowly, but your immediate families will die first, in front of you." He looked back at Takeri. "Not only your families, but the families of those who died here, no matter how old or young. They will die in every way we can think of, with the exception of strangulation. I will not grant your people that release."

"*Sang-wei,*" Kaleka said quietly. "That seems excessive."

Chow looked at him. "This is not a criminal matter, Inspector. It is a matter of state. My orders are to eradicate the Thuggee presence from this planet by any means necessary. The Chancellor's will supersedes local law."

Kaleka scowled, but said nothing as he turned and walked away.

Chow looked back at Takeri. "You have three minutes to decide. After that, you'll be able to explain to your Goddess in person why you failed."

"Don't tell him anything!" Pakava shouted. "Remember that—"

Chow turned and shot the young man in the head. Pakava's head snapped to the right, sending a spray of gore into the darkness as the bullet exited his skull. Chow turned to Takeri, ignoring the now-lifeless body as it toppled over onto its side. None of the other Death Commandos displayed any emotion at their leader's action.

Shock struck Takeri like a lightning bolt. "You—you killed my son!" he gasped, staring at what had been his offspring a few heartbeats before.

"And you killed innocent people, including the Chancellor's cousin. Not an even exchange, but it will do, for a start."

"You are a monster," Takeri whispered.

Chow shook his head. "I am the Chancellor's will, given form. You now have two minutes, thirty-five seconds to decide." He walked off into the darkness.

Takeri stood there, staring at the body of his son. His service to the Goddess was over. To talk would lead to the deaths of others, but what else could he do? A glance in Kaleka's direction showed the inspector still had his back to everyone, resigned to doing nothing. For a moment, Takeri felt sympathy for him.

He then looked at the faces of those who still lived, and he knew the truth. Most would talk, to save their families. He suddenly realized he would be one of them.

Kaleka was right. I rode the tiger too long, and now I will be consumed by it.

"*Sang-wei!*" Takeri called out. "We will talk! But on two conditions!"

"What are they?" Chow's voice asked out of the darkness.

"First, our families are not to be harmed. They are innocent of our crimes!"

"If you tell us everything, there will be no need to harm them. The second?"

"When it comes time to execute us, we want to be hung."

There was silence for a few seconds. "All right. You have my word. When it comes time, you will be all hung."

Takeri relaxed. At least he could die in service to his goddess. He just hoped that when the time came, he had the strength to place the noose over his head himself.

COM-7T COMMANDO "BLAZING INFERNO II"

Mass: 25 tons
Chassis: Foundation Ultralight Endo Steel
Power Plant: Omni 150
Cruising Speed: 64 kph
Maximum Speed: 97 kph, 118 kph with Triple-Strength Myomer
Jump Jets: None
    Jump Capacity: None
Armor: Lexington Limited
Armament:
    4 Defiance Model XII Extended-Range Medium Lasers
    5 Diverse Optics Extended-Range Small Lasers
    1 Ompec-J Small Laser
Manufacturer: Coventry Metal Works (Refit)
    Primary Factory: Coventry (Various)
Communications System: Cyclops 14
Targeting and Tracking System: Cyclops Multi-Tasker 10

Long the darling of the Lyran Commonwealth's scouting formations, the *Commando* has enjoyed vast success over its seven centuries of service. Once exclusively Lyran, the Succession Wars spread the capable little 'Mech to various mercenary companies, where a score of variants commonly called the -7 series emerged. Thrifty mercenaries often swap missile racks for energy independence, and the *Commando* is a common sight in Mech-it-Lube franchise refit bays.

Capabilities

Debuting during the FedCom Civil War but not gaining traction until recently, the "Blazing Inferno II" carries the spirit of the popular Succession Wars variant into a new age. This refit runs hot even with its double heat sinks, but the installation of Triple-Strength Myomers turns the heat into a benefit. Though still a competent scout, the COM-7T's prodigious volume of fire more often sees it deployed as a striker.

Battle History

Traditionally cordial relations with the Lyrans allowed Hansen's Roughriders to purchase several *Commando*s for their scout lances. A handful of the newer -7T was gifted for testing shortly before the Bromhead Massacre of 3067, and it saw significant service during the Roughriders' subsequent savaging of the Taurian Concordat. Locally produced Taurian *Commando*s, refit to the -4H model, clashed often with the Roughriders' newer variants. Though holding an initial edge, once the Taurian machines exhausted their limited supply of rockets, they became easy prey for Roughriders Blazing Infernos and their fusillades of accurate laser fire.

In 3133, Jasek Kelswa-Steiner's Stormhammers saw some success during the chaotic battle for Irian, thanks to *Commando* pilot Duncan Havelock. In the low-gravity, airless environment of the moon Prospero, Havelock pressed his 'Mech's maneuverability to the limit, stressing its frame to position himself for perfect shots against his Swordsworn opponents. Sadly, Havelock and his *Commando* were lost to the Dragon's Fury shortly after landing on Irian itself. The Fury salvaged Havelock's 'Mech, but lost it in its next battle when stress fractures incurred on Prospero caused its right leg to snap off. Fury technicians learned to carefully scour salvaged 'Mechs for any trace of the Curse of Havelock.

Lyran Commonwealth Armed Forces Leutnant Famke Keller bartered safe passage off Gallery after the Clan Wolf invasion of the early 3140s by challenging the Wolves to a Trial of Possession in her *Commando*. Bid as the defender, MechWarrior Halsey equipped his *Mist Lynx* with several anti-missile systems and vowed to capture this honorable warrior for his Clan. Keller's Blazing Inferno annihilated Halsey's 'Mech in under a minute, securing her passage to Tharkad. Ironically landing with the Wolf invasion force, Keller immediately entered battle alongside the Wolves against Clan Jade Falcon. She has a standing offer to take a Trial of Position and join Clan Wolf as a warrior.

Variants

The COM-7X swapped the -2D's SRM 4 for two more medium lasers and extra ammo for its SRM 6. The similar -7Y layers on another ton of armor instead of expanding the ammo box. The -7Y2, the beloved "Blazing Inferno," sacrifices both missile racks for an array of lasers. The recovery of Cellular Ammunition Storage Equipment technology saw the emergence of the durable -7Z and its sub-variant, the -7Z2. Both trade the SRM 4 for lasers and armor, and a Beagle probe for the -7Z2.

Later variants incorporated recovered endo-steel technology to provide more protection and hitting power. The -7A simplified ammo requirements with paired SRM 4s and maximum armor. Jump jets and a return to the original armor layout differentiate the -7J from the -7A, while the -7W reaches for longevity with extra ammo and a Streak launcher. Task Force Serpent used these variants to great effect on Huntress, prompting Coventry Metal Works to dedicate factory space to producing official re-creations.

Notable 'Mechs and MechWarriors

Lieutenant Rex Pearce: Pearce has served as executive officer for two incarnations of the Crescent Hawks. By his own admission not a leader, Pearce found his niche as a first officer, providing level-headed advice while loyally enforcing the commands of his captain. Converting his *Commando* to the Blazing Inferno was only logical, as the Hawks' missions frequently place them behind enemy lines.

Grady Kiefer: A man of incredible luck, Kiefer was the sole survivor of Team Venom, an ill-fated merc outfit obliterated by the Draconis Combine in 3044. Kiefer inherited the unit's funds along with his COM-7X and struck out on his own. His career includes being stranded behind the lines of the Clan advance, an alliance with pirates of the Oberon Confederation, a stint with Hansen's Roughriders, and an utterly improbable win in the 3049 Solaris Championships.

Battalion Chief Sergeant Declan Rayne: A Free Worlds League expatriate who stumbled into Taurian service after a stint as a freelancer, Rayne fit well with the Taurian Guard and rose rapidly. Given the call sign "Karma Samurai" for his tendency to dole out justice in unexpected ways, Rayne will hunt any enemy he thinks behaves dishonorably on the battlefield. His luxurious, belly-length beard has won several tongue-in-cheek contests throughout the Taurian Defense Force.

Type: **Commando COM-7T "Blazing Inferno II"**
Technology Base: Inner Sphere
Tonnage: 25
Role: Striker
Battle Value: 1,018

Equipment		Mass
Internal Structure:	Endo Steel	1.5
Engine:	150	5.5
Walking MP:	6 (7)	
Running MP:	9 (11)	
Jumping MP:	0	
Heat Sinks:	11 [22]	1
Gyro:		2
Cockpit:		3
Armor Factor:	80	5

	Internal Structure	Armor Value
Head	3	8
Center Torso	8	10
Center Torso (rear)		4
R/L Torso	6	8
R/L Torso (rear)		3
R/L Arm	4	7
R/L Leg	6	11

Weapons and Ammo	Location	Critical	Tonnage
ER Medium Laser	RA	1	1
2 ER Small Lasers	RL	2	1
ER Medium Laser	RT	1	1
ER Medium Laser	H	1	1
ER Small Laser	CT	1	.5
Small Laser	CT	1	.5
2 ER Small Lasers	LL	2	1
ER Medium Laser	LA	1	1
Triple-Strength Myomer	*	*	0

Notes: *Triple-Strength Myomer occupies 4 critical slots in RA and 1 critical slot each in LT and LA. Features the following Design Quirks: Narrow/Low Profile, Exposed Actuators.

Type: **Commando COM-7X**
Technology Base: Inner Sphere (Introductory)
Tonnage: 25
Role: Striker
Battle Value: 623

Equipment		**Mass**
Internal Structure:		2.5
Engine:	150	5.5
Walking MP:	6	
Running MP:	9	
Jumping MP:	0	
Heat Sinks:	10	0
Gyro:		2
Cockpit:		3
Armor Factor:	64	4

	Internal Structure	Armor Value
Head	3	6
Center Torso	8	8
Center Torso (rear)		4
R/L Torso	6	6
R/L Torso (rear)		3
R/L Arm	4	6
R/L Leg	6	8

Weapons and Ammo	**Location**	**Critical**	**Tonnage**
2 Medium Lasers	RA	2	2
Ammo (SRM) 15	RT	1	1
SRM 6	CT	2	3
Ammo (SRM) 15	LT	1	1
Medium Laser	LA	1	1

Notes: Features the following Design Quirk: Narrow/Low Profile, Exposed Actuators.

Type: **Commando COM-7Y**
Technology Base: Inner Sphere (Introductory)
Tonnage: 25
Role: Striker
Battle Value: 684

Equipment		Mass
Internal Structure:		2.5
Engine:	150	5.5
Walking MP:	6	
Running MP:	9	
Jumping MP:	0	
Heat Sinks:	10	0
Gyro:		2
Cockpit:		3
Armor Factor:	80	5

	Internal Structure	Armor Value
Head	3	8
Center Torso	8	10
Center Torso (rear)		4
R/L Torso	6	8
R/L Torso (rear)		3
R/L Arm	4	7
R/L Leg	6	11

Weapons and Ammo	Location	Critical	Tonnage
Medium Laser	RA	1	1
Medium Laser	RT	1	1
SRM 6	CT	2	3
Ammo (SRM) 15	LT	1	1
Medium Laser	LA	1	1

Notes: Features the following Design Quirk: Narrow/Low Profile, Exposed Actuators.

Type: **Commando COM-7Y2 "Blazing Inferno"**
Technology Base: Inner Sphere (Introductory)
Tonnage: 25
Role: Striker
Battle Value: 728

Equipment		**Mass**
Internal Structure:		2.5
Engine:	150	5.5
Walking MP:	6	
Running MP:	9	
Jumping MP:	0	
Heat Sinks:	10	0
Gyro:		2
Cockpit:		3
Armor Factor:	80	5

	Internal Structure	Armor Value
Head	3	8
Center Torso	8	10
Center Torso (rear)		4
R/L Torso	6	8
R/L Torso (rear)		3
R/L Arm	4	7
R/L Leg	6	11

Weapons and Ammo	**Location**	**Critical**	**Tonnage**
Medium Laser	RA	1	1
2 Small Lasers	RL	2	1
Medium Laser	RT	1	1
Medium Laser	H	1	1
2 Small Lasers	CT	2	1
2 Small Lasers	LL	2	1
Medium Laser	LA	1	1

Notes: Features the following Design Quirk: Narrow/Low Profile, Exposed Actuators.

Type: **Commando COM-7Z2**
Technology Base: Inner Sphere
Tonnage: 25
Role: Scout
Battle Value: 543

Equipment		Mass
Internal Structure:		2.5
Engine:	150	5.5
Walking MP:	6	
Running MP:	9	
Jumping MP:	0	
Heat Sinks:	10	0
Gyro:		2
Cockpit:		3
Armor Factor:	88	5.5

	Internal Structure	Armor Value
Head	3	8
Center Torso	8	11
Center Torso (rear)		5
R/L Torso	6	8
R/L Torso (rear)		4
R/L Arm	4	8
R/L Leg	6	12

Weapons and Ammo	Location	Critical	Tonnage
Small Laser	RA	1	.5
Beagle Active Probe	RT	2	1.5
SRM 6	CT	2	3
Ammo (SRM) 15	LT	1	1
Small Laser	LA	1	.5

Notes: Features the following Design Quirk: Narrow/Low Profile, Exposed Actuators.

Type: **Commando COM-7Z**
Technology Base: Inner Sphere
Tonnage: 25
Role: Striker
Battle Value: 661

Equipment		Mass
Internal Structure:		2.5
Engine:	150	5.5
Walking MP:	6	
Running MP:	9	
Jumping MP:	0	
Heat Sinks:	10	0
Gyro:		2
Cockpit:		3
Armor Factor:	88	5.5

	Internal Structure	Armor Value
Head	3	8
Center Torso	8	11
Center Torso (rear)		5
R/L Torso	6	8
R/L Torso (rear)		4
R/L Arm	4	8
R/L Leg	6	12

Weapons and Ammo	Location	Critical	Tonnage
Medium Laser	RA	1	1
SRM 6	CT	2	3
Ammo (SRM) 15	LT	1	1
CASE	LT	1	.5
Medium Laser	LA	1	1

Notes: Features the following Design Quirk: Narrow/Low Profile, Exposed Actuators.

Type: **Commando COM-7A**
Technology Base: Inner Sphere
Tonnage: 25
Role: Striker
Battle Value: 625

Equipment		Mass
Internal Structure:	Endo Steel	1.5
Engine:	150	5.5
Walking MP:	6	
Running MP:	9	
Jumping MP:	0	
Heat Sinks:	10	0
Gyro:		2
Cockpit:		3
Armor Factor:	88	5.5

	Internal Structure	Armor Value
Head	3	8
Center Torso	8	11
Center Torso (rear)		5
R/L Torso	6	8
R/L Torso (rear)		4
R/L Arm	4	8
R/L Leg	6	12

Weapons and Ammo	Location	Critical	Tonnage
SRM 4	RA	1	2
Ammo (SRM) 50	RT	2	2
CASE	RT	1	.5
SRM 4	CT	1	2
Medium Laser	LA	1	1

Notes: Features the following Design Quirk: Narrow/Low Profile, Exposed Actuators.

Type: **Commando COM-7J**
Technology Base: Inner Sphere
Tonnage: 25
Role: Striker
Battle Value: 599

Equipment		Mass
Internal Structure:	Endo Steel	1.5
Engine:	150	5.5
Walking MP:	6	
Running MP:	9	
Jumping MP:	5	
Heat Sinks:	10	0
Gyro:		2
Cockpit:		3
Armor Factor:	64	4

	Internal Structure	Armor Value
Head	3	6
Center Torso	8	8
Center Torso (rear)		4
R/L Torso	6	6
R/L Torso (rear)		3
R/L Arm	4	6
R/L Leg	6	8

Weapons and Ammo	Location	Critical	Tonnage
SRM 4	RA	1	2
Ammo (SRM) 25	RT	1	1
CASE	RT	1	.5
SRM 4	CT	1	2
Medium Laser	LA	1	1
2 Jump Jets	RL	2	1
Jump Jet	CT	1	.5
2 Jump Jets	LT	2	1

Notes: Features the following Design Quirk: Narrow/Low Profile, Exposed Actuators.

Type: **Commando COM-7W**
Technology Base: Inner Sphere
Tonnage: 25
Role: Striker
Battle Value: 608

Equipment		Mass
Internal Structure:	Endo Steel	1.5
Engine:	150	5.5
Walking MP:	6	
Running MP:	9	
Jumping MP:	0	
Heat Sinks:	10	0
Gyro:		2
Cockpit:		3
Armor Factor:	64	4

	Internal Structure	Armor Value
Head	3	6
Center Torso	8	8
Center Torso (rear)		4
R/L Torso	6	6
R/L Torso (rear)		3
R/L Arm	4	6
R/L Leg	6	8

Weapons and Ammo	Location	Critical	Tonnage
Streak SRM 2	RA	1	1.5
Ammo (Streak) 50	RT	1	1
Ammo (SRM) 50	RT	2	2
CASE	RT	1	.5
SRM 4	CT	1	2
2 Medium Lasers	LA	2	2

Notes: Features the following Design Quirk: Narrow/Low Profile, Exposed Actuators.

IN MEMORIAM: KELLY BONILLA

JENNIFER BIXBY

Born August 28th, 1971, Kelly Ann Bonilla-Dillon was the only child of Patrick and Christine Dillon. She spent her childhood in Chicago, Illinois. She married Vic Bonilla in 1999. They welcomed their son, Leo Enrique Bonilla, in 2005. She passed away on January 31st, 2024 after a battle with cancer.

As a game designer in a field full of men, she became known for how she brought teams together. Her passion and creativity drove her to become the Lead Game Designer for *MechWarrior: Dark Age* and *MechWarrior: Age of Destruction*. She also contributed to *HorrorClix*, *HeroClix*, and *Pirates of the Cursed Seas*. She also worked on Unity UI as a screen building support contractor. She was the Lead Developer for *MechWarrior: Age of Destruction* from 2004 until 2008. To date, Kelly is the only woman to have ever been the lead developer for a *BattleTech* product line.

In an interview with *Game Trade Magazine* (Issue 93, November 2007), she said, "Like a 100-ton assault 'Mech resting squarely between my shoulders, working its way up to my cranium, *MechWarrior* is a game with a huge following and a well-established universe, which should be enough to make just about anyone slump their shoulders a bit. Working within that universe, while trying to expand it and move it along into its future, is a huge challenge. Envisioning what sort of technologies might have developed after decades of peace, and what new methods of war the inhabitants of that universe may have been developing anyway during that peace, is a difficult task."

While she was the line developer for *MechWarrior: Age of Destruction*, *HorrorClix*, and *HeroClix* at the same time, Kelly received little credit for her capabilities during her lifetime. She was understated, wonderfully snarky, and phenomenally capable. After the *MechWarrior: Age of Destruction* line ended, she turned her creative talents to *Magic: The Gathering*. She listened to all the players, not just the hard-core ones, and inserted randomness into games to keep them fun for everyone. Regardless of the game system and game world, she took all players' opinions about the games into consideration and kept them in mind as she worked on the game itself.

> *"When you're a game designer, you are working on the nitty gritty. When you're a developer, you're working on the universe. Kelly was able to do all those left-brain, right-brain things well, and was quiet about it. She just did her job, and did it well. She was really compassionate about the people she worked with.*
>
> *"Kelly didn't get nearly enough credit for what she did. I just don't think anyone understands how much she did. I don't understand how she kept it all straight in her head, with hundreds of minis to create.*
>
> *"So many people have enjoyed the games she has created for them. We have gotten so much enjoyment and satisfaction out of what she has created. A lot of people can't say that, and it's not something everyone can understand. I just want the world to know just how capable, talented, and wonderful she was. If she can be an inspiration to any women game designers out there, let's blow this horn as loud as she can."*
>
> —TONI RIVERA

The lesson Kelly Bonilla leaves with us is a very simple one: love deeply, whatever it is—your job, your family, your friends, or online friends. Love what you do deeply. Love the people deeply. It doesn't have to be the big things; in fact, often the small things are what make a big impact in people's lives.

> *"Poor monkeys. For some reason they need constant reassurance that they look 'fabulous.' The bunny has transcended all requirements of such things. The bunny simply IS. I advise all to accept themselves as they are, to simply 'be,' and perhaps then be the bunny."*
>
> —KELLY BONILLA

JLP-KB JACKALOPE

Mass: 30 tons
Chassis: Triumph Dynamic Endo Steel
Power Plant: Victory 240 XL
Cruising Speed: 86 kph
Maximum Speed: 129 kph
Jump Jets: VC Dynamo
    Jump Capacity: 240 meters
Armor: Advantage Ferro-Fibrous
Armament:
    2 Conquest Extended-Range Medium Lasers
    2 Victory Conditions-C SRM 4 Launchers
    1 "Fullback" Advanced Point Defense System
Manufacturer: Eris Enterprises Design Group
    Primary Factory: Capolla
Communications System: Angst Clear Channel 5
Targeting and Tracking System: O/P TA1240

In the two decades since its introduction, the *Jackalope* became the bane of many a force commander. High speed, long-reaching jump capability, and a host of ClanTech weaponry and sensors made this light 'Mech a persistent and troublesome battlefield pest in the years after Fortress Republic was raised.

Capabilities

The JLP-KB was inspired by the personalized *Jackalope* of a Ghost Knight sent to operate outside the Fortress Wall. As the Republic braced for the Clan invasion of Terra, the *Jackalope* was overhauled to accept one of the few successful innovations from the Republic Institute for Strategic Combat—the advanced point defense system. The APDS fit naturally, given the *Jackalope* had originally been built around the Clan Laser Anti-Missile System; however, the bulk of this new system required engineers to use a small cockpit, making this variant a significantly less comfortable ride for its MechWarriors.

Battle History

During the mass recall of Republic forces to Prefecture X, the *Jackalope* proved its value on the planet Milton II. Anastasia Kerensky's Wolf Hunters were assaulting Milton's spaceport to capture valuable supplies from its military warehouses. Despite overcoming the Republic Standing Guard forces, reinforcements from Paladin Otto Mandela stymied the Hunters long enough to permit Republic forces to evacuate lighter equipment and nearly all consumables. It was the low altitude drop of a company of *Jackalopes* that forced Paladin Mandela to retreat and go to ground in the mountains.

Jackalopes used by Katana Tormark's Dieron Regulars proved vital at delay and counterassault roles during Clan Nova Cat's rebellion. On Piedmont, several *Jackalopes* from the Third Regulars were regularly sent out on wide ranging maneuvers to disrupt rear lines of *Kanrei* Toranaga's forces. It was these persistent attacks that turned the projected three-day battle into a protracted five-week siege.

During the Siege of Terra by Clans Wolf and Jade Falcon, *Jackalopes* were intended as raiders, where their APDS could provide an umbrella for each other and other 'Mechs they were escorting. Clan Wolf's ardent refusal to adhere to Clan doctrine and Clan Jade Falcon's use of orbital bombardment made such plans irrelevant. After Clan Wolf took Australia, most of the *Jackalopes* were distributed to various units to function as hypermobile close-in weapon systems. The largest single deployment of APDS *Jackalopes* on Terra was during Operation Four Horsemen. Multiple *Jackalopes* and Angerona "Aegis" Squads were assigned as escorts for the massive superheavy OmniMechs employed by the Republic. The combined missile shields performed admirably against the Wolf *solahma* Clusters that acted as the bridge between Chance Vickers' and Alaric Ward's forces. It was only when met by the Tactical Response Cluster that even the massed *Jackalopes* were overwhelmed. With so many forces firing on their charges from all angles, the Four Horsemen's escorts were quickly overwhelmed and dismantled with the rest of the task force.

Variants

Eris has produced a limited run of JLP-NH *Tepoztēcatl* using stealth armor systems. These *Jackalopes* were widely distributed, with no single force procuring more than one. Examples of the *Jackalope* salvaged by Clan Wolf's Watch particularly impressed the Wolf Touman, which is refitting the 'Mechs with ferro-lamellor armor for the expected expansion of the Star League Defense Force.

Notable 'Mechs and MechWarriors

Ghost Knight Kelly Bonilla: Lady Bonilla was often described as an esoteric personality with a passion for speed in all its available forms. Like many of the Ghost Knights, her mission was to rain havoc among the Republic's former prefectures, making sure no single government could maintain a hold on worlds annexed in the Republic's absence. Her personal *Jackalope*, nicknamed *Harvey*, was stripped of Clan weaponry and equipment to ease repair and maintenance on the other side of the wall. In its place was a new advanced point defense system,

which allowed Bonilla to act as a rapid-response missile shield to the rest of the Fuzzy Bunnies command she raised as part of her mission. After-action reports transmitted to Terra were so impressive that the APDS was being evaluated for wider deployment on *Jackalope* platforms. Lady Bonilla never made it to Terra in time for its defense against Clan Wolf, and presently is considered missing.

Hunter Scott: A freeborn Clan Jade Falcon MechWarrior, Scott's life was one of overcoming the prejudices of the traditionalist Clan. Proving his worth in the Falcon *desant*, he was shot out of his BattleMech in the second Battle of Skye and captured by the Steel Wolves. Following Anastasia Kerensky into the Wolf Hunters, Scott was the designated commander of the air drop that forced Paladin Mandela to stay loyal to the Wolf Hunters. After he left the Wolf Hunters in 3146 over their decision to join Clan Wolf, he drifted from planet to planet. Eventually he made his way back to Alyina, and has thrown his lot in with the Alyina Mercantile League.

MechWarrior Robert Wilson: Nicknamed "Skippy" by his friends, Wilson was one of the many wandering freelancer mercenaries who rose to prominence during the collapse of the Republic. Wilson found his way to Galatea and traded out his scrapped *Hellbringer* for a *Jackalope*. For the next decade, he stayed close to the old Mercenary's Star, where his bright yellow *Jackalope* and tendency towards smaller contracts led to whispers he may be "the next Ace Darwin." The creation of any such legend was cut short by Clan Jade Falcon's invasion of Galatea in 3144, when Wilson was killed defending civilians from Mongol Elementals looking to put homes to the torch to try and draw out the Northwind Highlanders.

Type: **Jackalope JLP-KB**
Technology Base: Mixed Clan (Advanced)
Tonnage: 30
Role: Striker
Battle Value: 1,259

Equipment		Mass
Internal Structure:	Endo Steel	1.5
Engine:	240 XL	6
Walking MP:	8	
Running MP:	12	
Jumping MP:	8	
Heat Sinks:	10 [20]	0
Gyro:		3
Cockpit (Small):		2
Armor Factor (Ferro):	86	4.5

	Internal Structure	Armor Value
Head	3	9
Center Torso	10	13
Center Torso (rear)		4
R/L Torso	7	9
R/L Torso (rear)		2
R/L Arm	5	8
R/L Leg	7	11

Weapons and Ammo	Location	Critical	Tonnage
ER Medium Laser	RA	1	1
SRM 4	RT	1	1
Ammo (SRM) 25	RT	1	1
APDS (IS)	H	2	3
Ammo (APDS) 12 (IS)	LT	1	1
SRM 4	LT	1	1
ER Medium Laser	LA	1	1
4 Jump Jets	RT	4	2
4 Jump Jets	LT	4	2

Notes: Features the following Design Quirks: Compact 'Mech, Narrow/Low Profile.

Type: **Jackalope JLP-BD-L "Harvey"**
Technology Base: Mixed Clan (Advanced)
Tonnage: 30
Role: Striker
Battle Value: 1,028

Equipment		Mass
Internal Structure:	Endo Steel	1.5
Engine:	240 XL	6
Walking MP:	8	
Running MP:	12 (20)	
Jumping MP:	4	
Heat Sinks:	10 [20]	0
Gyro:		3
Cockpit (Small):		2
Armor Factor (Ferro):	86	4.5

	Internal Structure	Armor Value
Head	3	9
Center Torso	10	13
Center Torso (rear)		4
R/L Torso	7	9
R/L Torso (rear)		2
R/L Arm	5	8
R/L Leg	7	11

Weapons and Ammo	Location	Critical	Tonnage
ER Medium Laser (IS)	RA	1	1
M-Pod (IS)	RT	1	1
MASC (IS)	RT	2	2
APDS (IS)	H	2	3
Ammo (APDS) 12 (IS)	LT	1	1
M-Pod (IS)	LT	1	1
Supercharger (IS)	LT	1	1
ER Medium Laser (IS)	LA	1	1
2 Jump Jets	RT	2	1
2 Jump Jets	LT	2	1

Notes: Features the following Design Quirks: Compact 'Mech, Narrow/Low Profile, Unique.

Type: **Jackalope JLP-IC**
Technology Base: Clan (Advanced)
Tonnage: 30
Role: Striker
Battle Value: 1,337

Equipment		Mass
Internal Structure:	Endo Steel	1.5
Engine:	240 XL	6
Walking MP:	8	
Running MP:	12	
Jumping MP:	8	
Heat Sinks:	10 [20]	0
Gyro:		3
Cockpit:		3
Armor Factor (Lamellor):	98	7

	Internal Structure	Armor Value
Head	3	9
Center Torso	10	15
Center Torso (rear)		4
R/L Torso	7	10
R/L Torso (rear)		4
R/L Arm	5	9
R/L Leg	7	12

Weapons and Ammo	Location	Critical	Tonnage
ER Medium Laser	RA	1	1
SRM 6	RT	1	1
Laser Anti-Missile System	H	1	1
Ammo (SRM) 15	LT	1	1
ER Medium Laser	LA	1	1
4 Jump Jets	RT	4	2
4 Jump Jets	LT	4	2

Notes: Features the following Design Quirks: Compact 'Mech, Narrow/ Low Profile.

Type: **Jackalope JLP-NH**
Technology Base: Mixed Clan (Advanced)
Tonnage: 30
Role: Striker
Battle Value: 1,208

Equipment		Mass
Internal Structure:	Endo Steel	1.5
Engine:	240 XL	6
Walking MP:	8	
Running MP:	12	
Jumping MP:	6	
Heat Sinks:	10 [20]	0
Gyro:		3
Cockpit:		3
Armor Factor (Stealth, IS):	88	5.5

	Internal Structure	Armor Value
Head	3	9
Center Torso	10	15
Center Torso (rear)		4
R/L Torso	7	9
R/L Torso (rear)		2
R/L Arm	5	8
R/L Leg	7	11

Weapons and Ammo	Location	Critical	Tonnage
ER Medium Laser	RA	1	1
MML 3 (IS)	RT	2	1.5
Ammo (MML) 40/33 (IS)	RT	1	1
ECM Suite	H	1	1
MML 3 (IS)	LT	2	1.5
Ammo (MML) 40/33 (IS)	LT	1	1
ER Medium Laser	LA	1	1
3 Jump Jets	RT	3	1.5
3 Jump Jets	LT	3	1.5

Notes: Features the following Design Quirks: Compact 'Mech, Narrow/ Low Profile.

CAPTAINS AND LOADMASTERS SYMPOSIUM

CHRIS WHEELER AND MIKE MILLER

SALTY SPACER INN
GALATEA
3145

[Begin Partial Transcript]

Welcome, and thank you all for joining me today at the grandly named "Captains and Loadmasters Symposium," here in the conference rooms of the Salty Spacer, purveyor of the finest beers, wines, and spirits on Galatea. And yes, I am on commission—so drink up! [*Laughter.*] I'm Captain Conrad Grumman, late of the LCAF, and an independent for the last twenty years. I've seen service from The Barrens down to the Calderon Protectorate, and everywhere in-between.

Spacers are an ingenious and hardy breed—they have to be. Something breaks down in the big dark, and you're dead if you don't improvise. We DropShippers are a middle ground. Treated as a taxi service sometimes, we get the worst of both environments—gravity, atmosphere, and vacuum, with reentry to boot. What won't kill you on the ground will do in space and vice versa. [*Chorus of assents.*] And we get regularly shot at, too—some folks are just darned rude! [*Laughter.*]

This talk is about working smarter, not harder. Making those precious H-bills or Fox Credits go further. Cargo space is always at a premium on combat droppers—yeah, you *Mule* pilots can be smug! [*Laughter.*] As the saying goes, "An army marches on its stomach." The supplies you can haul in—and the salvage you can haul out—can be the life and death of a mercenary unit at times. [*Murmurs of agreement.*]

The purpose of this talk is to maximize those cargo numbers in ways that work for you. Starting with the transport bays themselves, or "Back to Bay-sics" as I like to call it! [*Groans.*]

You'd be surprised at what extras can be crammed in when the need arises, or when you need to quickly depart a hostile LZ. Some of this is common sense. [*Faint booing.*] What's that? Ah, I see ya, Mr. Calliope, you old pirate! Pipe down and let an honest merc earn a living. [*Laughter drowns out the heckler.*]

Where was I? Oh, yes. You can use transport bays for far more than the specific cargo they're designed to carry. I'm not just talking about putting multiple vehicles in a vehicle bay either—that's rookie stuff—but vehicle bays are a good place to start. You gotta get creative if you wanna make the most of the space you have. You wanna shove a few standard ten-ton cargo containers into a light-vehicle bay using Savannah Masters as packing peanuts? [*Laughter.*] Sure, go right ahead. Just don't expect to be able to deploy anything quickly.

What's that?

[*A member of the audience asks a question.*]

Oh, can you fit small craft in large vehicle bays? I've seen it done, but it really ain't pretty! Which brings me to my next topic: fighter bays. Given the usual placement of these bays toward a vessel's nose, it takes a lot of crane work to pack extra things in easily. Vehicles can fit without too much drama, but you're better off with bulk cargo. Those *Hamilcar*s have got it sweet with their low-slung fighter bays! Or better yet, what about those collapsible fighter bays on the *Leopard*, eh? Except if you wanna move that cargo internally—yeah, sucks to be you then! [*Various members of the audience laugh heartily.*] Shifting cargo around in orbit can be done, but it's a massive pain. Just make sure you've got plenty of null-G packs handy. No-one wants to vent a deck unnecessarily—that's just asking for trouble. I'll cover the repair and storage areas when I get to the 'Mech bays.

Got fighter bays and want a side-gig? There's always someone wanting to deploy satellites. Telecommunications networks, the local militia, or just nosy nobles. It's a great way to supplement a merc's pay on DropShip-poor worlds. Now, if they're light enough, you can just strap them to a fighter's external pylons and deploy them individually. Or deploy them from the cargo bay of a small craft or your DropShip itself. Wanna do it quickly? Why not use the launch catapults in a fighter bay? Better check the limiters first, though, so you don't crush a light satellite when your catapult was still set for a *Thunderbird*. Your contract won't cover breakages, that's for damn sure! [*Laughter.*]

I won't go into detail on small craft bays, as those are pretty uncommon on DropShips. Just remember, small craft of 100 tons or less will fit in a fighter bay, and fighters will fit in a small-craft bay.

Not got much to say about infantry bays either, they're just too small to pack much in. Plus the meatheads don't take kindly to you trying to store extra ammo in there! [*Laughter.*] Those bays are pretty easy to reconfigure though, so if they don't have any occupants, they can make handy nooks for keeping stuff in.

On a similar topic are passenger quarters. You may have fares, you may not; it all depends on where your contract takes you. But if you're lucky enough to have all your crew looked after, those extra quarters can help you out in a pinch, and you'd be surprised at how much stuff you can cram in them. The same goes for empty bay quarters, too. They're just a royal pain in the ass to load and unload though, so arguably you're better off with stuff like consumables that you'll use up going in, and any "additions" going out. Heard of one crew venting a section of steerage quarters and using them as impromptu freezers for Mizarian venison. Reckon it would have improved the natural smell of the quarters, too! [*Chuckling.*]

Besides passenger quarters and vehicle bays, 'Mech bays are probably the next most common. We'll start with the parts and storage areas first. Most 'Mech bays—and fighter bays, too, for that matter—have an open space set aside for more extensive repairs or refits. Often centralized, with parts and ammo storage and machine shops, the anchor points here are specifically designed for storing extra gear. Obviously this depends on the DropShip, but you can easily get an extra twenty-five tons of equipment into this area, per bay. And best of all, it won't stop you from normal operations, either.

Yeah, you can sometimes strip the bays back a bit further. Some droppers aren't even configured for combat drops, like the *Excalibur*-class, while others have limited repair gear, all of which frees up more space. But if you're doing that, then you may as well strip the 'Mech bays out entirely and have everything as bulk cargo. And just hope you never have to deploy in a hot LZ!

Sure you can park vehicles in empty 'Mech bays too, or even around a 'Mech that's already in one. At least the tankers will be happy with the upgraded quarters! [*Loud laughter.*] We've all stuffed whatever salvage we can in there, too. [*Murmurs of assent.*] You can even have multiple 'Mechs in there. Just don't expect to have them combat ready in most cases.

[*A member of the audience asks a question.*]

Double-dropping—yeah, heard of that. Having two light 'Mechs sharing a customized 'Mech bay, and both being able to combat drop. Kinda risky. Kinda crazy. Kinda genius. You lose flexibility, but necessity is the mother of invention and all that. If you wanna be the next Captain Ravannion with a bug swarm, then so be it.

If combat dropping ain't your thing, then sell off your drop kits. Those drop cocoons and jump packs are pretty bulky, far better to dedicate that storage space to more useful supplies. The kits can raise a pretty penny as well. Unless your first mate beat you to it and already sold 'em off; ain't that right, Mr. Calliope? [*Calliope's denials are drowned out by howls of laughter.*] I ain't even mad, just jealous I didn't think of it first!

And just remember: the tighter you pack it, the harder it is for your pesky customs inspectors to do their jobs too. They ain't gonna want to waste their time with that, if ya know what I mean. Not that an honest merc like me would condone that sort of behavior! [*Raucous laughter.*]

But whatever you do, just make sure it's damn well secured. Use all the cargo tie-downs you can, and then double- and triple-check them. We've all heard of unfortunate captains that lost a bay door due to badly secured cargo. At best this is an expensive inconvenience, but it can easily get you captured, and at worst dead. [*Contemplative silence.*]

And on that sobering note, I suggest we take a short break. I'll remind everyone there is a fully stocked bar behind you. Drink up, I've got bills to pay! [*Laughter.*] When we return, we'll discuss some more in-depth topics such as cargo overloading and how everything is air-droppable at least once! [*Laughter.*]

[End Transcript]

RANGE WAR

RUSSELL ZIMMERMAN

FAMINDAS
ALPHERATZ IV
OUTWORLDS ALLIANCE
19 MARCH 3034

Cameron watched the two men meet and shake hands, a pair of some of the biggest fish in their not-inconsiderable pond. They weren't the sharks and whales that truly ran the Inner Sphere, the leviathans and krakens of the Great Houses, no. But compared to the average galactic citizen—and especially the average citizen here in the Outworlds Alliance—their wealth was almost unimaginable and their influence almost inhuman, while their most seemingly casual decisions were matters of grave importance to a great many other people.

One of them, their host, ran the nation, dozens of worlds, a long-struggling but stubbornly independent state bordered by the looming titans of Houses Davion and Kurita. He was a President, reluctantly and perpetually beleaguered, disrespected within and without his star nation. He had a new wife, though, and with a little luck a child soon on the way. Reasons to press on. Reasons to adapt, to change, to evolve. Reasons to take more direct action, despite what the media called "a bone-deep dislike of directness."

His important guest was, put simply, a businessman. He ran a corporation struggling, still, to regain its footing, but a corporation that was one of the oft-flimsy beams propping up the Outworlds Alliance. Mountain Wolf BattleMechs wasn't a large company, and, in fact, they were one of the galaxy's smallest in their field. They were underdogs, perpetually ice-skating uphill, determined to sleep well at night, and Cameron knew more than most they were risking their profit margins by playing fair and shooting straight in a universe cruel to the generous. But they existed. They created. They contributed. They endured.

The relationship between the nation and the business was a symbiotic one, theoretically good for both, but just letting them both survive, if not thrive. The relationship between the two men themselves was just as mutually beneficial, but just as tenuous. They predicted one another more than they trusted, and they both knew just how desperate the other one always was. They appeared relaxed around each other, but never quite were, and Cam thought both of them wished otherwise. They both were men well accustomed to being the ultimate decision maker in whatever room they were in—which made it awkward any time they disagreed.

Neither the President nor the businessman were young men any longer, but neither was—quite—old yet, either, as between them they looked to be a century old, give or take. They had more gray in their hair than they might like, but they *had* hair, and more importantly they still had straight spines, clear minds, and sharp eyes. Their meeting room was luxuriously furnished and far more empty than full.

Aside from the two men, only two others met with them that day. The President was accompanied by a stunningly handsome woman of a like age who carried herself like nobility, the businessman by a darker-hued copy of himself roughly half his age; a son. Cameron. He knew there was no mistaking the relationship between him and his father, the shape of their brows, their noses, and their jawlines.

"*As-salamu alaykum*, Mr. O'Leary," the President said, wife at his side. He said it carefully enough to make it clear he had practiced his pronunciation. "And *Ramadan Kareem*."

"*Wa 'alaykumu s-salam*, Mr. President," CEO Brandon O'Leary responded, reaching out to shake Neil Avellar's hand with a wry smile. "But I imagine this 'urgent conversation' you mentioned will determine just how 'generous' my Ramadan will be."

Cameron and his father had planned to visit Alpheratz later in the year. Much later. Their trip from Vendrell hadn't been a short one, and Brandon's wife, the duchess of said Vendrell, hadn't been terribly pleased at their changed plans. Their travel plans had been accelerated at Avellar's request, and Cam knew his father wanted to know why. A head of state sending a hasty summons and refusing to elaborate via long-range communications hadn't left Brandon O'Leary feeling very comfortable and relaxed on their journey.

"I hope you don't mind." The President's new wife, Rebecca Avellar née DeSanders, wouldn't be dissuaded from playing hostess. She gestured to a table with platters of local delicacies and decanters of specialty drinks. "We know you're expected to fast until nightfall, but I'm afraid habits of hospitality die hard. Please, help yourself if you're so inclined, gentlemen. But know that we mean no offense, if you'd rather wait."

"Oh, no offense taken at all!" Brandon O'Leary leaned in cheerfully, plucking up a little berry-filled tart. "I don't precisely share my wife's faith. Good manners and the occasional prayer are enough for me. I'll leave acts of devotion to the younger generation. Cameron! Not a word to your mother, hmm?"

Bran tossed the tart into his mouth and chewed it around a smile. Cameron—the spitting image of his father, but cast a bit darker, and with tightly curled black hair—shook his head and smiled at the elder O'Leary's good-natured blasphemy, tempered with a wise fear of his formidable wife.

"None for me, thank you, ma'am." Cam gave their hostess a small head shake. "Even though I'm as far away from my mother as I've ever been in my life, I'm worried she'd find out I cheated. Somehow, she always just *knows*. I'll have to wait until *iftar*, I'm afraid, or the guilt would ruin it."

"Well, you certainly won't be alone in eating after nightfall," the President answered, smiling in return, and for a moment his plain, almost weak features lit up. "We've had a number of *madrassahs* established in recent years, especially on the western side of the city. I'll have my people take you to one tonight, to break your fast with a few dates and, er, I'll be honest, I'm not sure what else. Oh! But perhaps tomorrow we could arrange a proper tour for you? Let you see Famindas proper and all that?"

Cameron nodded politely. "That would be lovely, Mr. President. I look forward to it."

"Perhaps before we make plans for touring the city, though, we should have a discussion about..." Rebecca trailed off, pointedly arching one perfect brow her husband's way. Cameron appreciated that she'd refused to leave guests hungry, but he also appreciated that she'd clearly picked up on his father's eagerness to get down to business.

The change to their travel plans had not left the Duchess of Vendrell a happy woman, as Brandon had reminded his son repeatedly during their long spinward journey.

"Ah! Yes, of course. The matter at hand!" Neil bobbed his head agreeably. "Terribly sorry, of course, of course. You didn't come all this way to drive around the capital, no, no, of course not. Come, please, sit!"

Avellar gestured them toward the plush seating near his desk. While they all relocated and got down to business, his wife gestured for a few waiting servants to clear the unwanted food away. The feast wouldn't languish, ignored until it spoiled. Not while so many were hungry so close to the capitol building. Not every empty belly on Alpheratz was due to Ramadan.

"As I'm sure the media has made clear, things have not been... easy...for the Alliance recently. And, er, by 'recently,' I mean 'ever,' but most especially *more* recently."

He neither beat around the bush nor sugarcoated it, not with the O'Leary clan. The Outworlds Alliance had been struggling to survive since the first President Avellar had founded it, nearly by accident, centuries earlier. Food shortages and pirate raids in equal measure continued to keep life expectancies short, and the citizenry was always eager and willing to blame all their woes on their leader. The Alliance's parliament, built to stop tyranny, instead all too often seemed tailor-made to stop *anything*; any Alliance-spanning legislation required unanimous approval from every member. From his studies of their governmental system and Brandon's lectures, Cameron had picked up the impression that herding cats would be easier, more fun, and generally accomplish a great deal more, than being President of the Outworlds Alliance.

Still and all, a few media outlets grudgingly admitted Neil had been *trying*. The President sat down behind his large desk and sighed. Cameron and his father settled into the plush chairs opposite it.

"Some changes of late bring the promise of future prosperity, but theoretical prosperity tomorrow doesn't fill empty stomachs today. If I might speak frankly? Too many of my people, Mr. O'Leary, are starving."

There was little question which O'Leary he meant.

"I don't see how Mountain Wolf BattleMechs can help you with that, Mr. President, but if you'll explain it to me, I'll be glad to see what we can do." Brandon leaned forward, paying rapt attention.

Cameron's father had trained him to recognize when an opportunity presented itself to curry favor with powerful people, *and* to genuinely help the people that work for you whenever you can. It wasn't often a businessman's wishes aligned so neatly. Here in the Periphery, Brandon constantly reminded his son, their wealth could be put to good use, while still leading to longer-term benefits. It had been a *long* flight from Vendrell, filled with more than a few such lessons.

"You have JumpShips, Mr. O'Leary. And you have DropShips. And, worse come to worst, you have 'Mechs." Neil Avellar rattled off the list plainly, almost abruptly. He reached out and spread open a folder full of papers, laying them out for the O'Learys to read.

"You have all of those things, too, Neil, and more of each of them," Brandon said, raising an eyebrow. He had taught his son that the Outworlds Alliance wasn't an Inner Sphere powerhouse, but their Alliance Military Corps wasn't a pushover either. Especially where flyers were concerned. Especially compared to the paltry fleet of Mountain Wolf BattleMechs.

But they're purely defensive. Cameron frowned, racking his brain. *The President must want something more proactive than usual.*

"I do. But there have been raids aplenty of late, so my troops and ships are needed at their stations. Beyond that, however, I don't *want* them on this job, I need it to be...not *quite* me, not quite the Alliance military, undertaking this task. The final reason I'm asking for your help, however? You have something I *don't* have, and I am willing to help you with in return; you have a burden I could lift. An agreement with my mother, legally bound into the contracts that prop up your facility here. In the end, you offered us almost sixty million C-bills worth of sixty-ton 'Mechs."

"I did." Brandon nodded, watching the President carefully. "A full company was the precise deal. We've given you that, and sold you more than that many again, at cost."

"So you have, and we are grateful." Avellar nodded. "But she also got you to promise her sixty years. Sixty years of Mountain Wolf BattleMechs only producing and manufacturing *Merlin*s, and only right here on Alpheratz. How would you like to *not* have that promise holding you back for quite so long? If you lend me these JumpShips, Brandon, and those DropShips, and enough of those 'Mechs, I will cut what remains of that agreement in half."

The President of the Outworlds Alliance spoke grimly, almost sternly. He gave the reminder a moment to settle in.

"You've served twenty-four years of that...sentence...as it were. I'm willing to halve the remainder. 3052! In 3052, Mr. O'Leary, not 3070, I'll release you. You'll be free to open a new plant anywhere you'd like, doing whatever business you'd like, without violating the agreement you made with my mother."

Brandon stared, deep in thought.

Avellar extended a hand for a shake. "Mountain Wolf BattleMechs and the Outworlds Alliance have always been friendly. Do me this favor, and I will prove that friendship by freeing you well ahead of schedule."

Brandon's eyes lit up, despite any savvy negotiator exterior he otherwise tried to keep. Cameron knew he wanted, *desperately* wanted new Mountain Wolf facilities to open. Especially to reopen one in particular: on Vendrell, the distant planet he now called home, where Mother ruled and Cameron had been born. Brandon O'Leary had plans for the future, the long game, the expansion and diversification of Mountain Wolf BattleMechs. He longed to restore the family name, the family company, to former glory. Brandon wanted to make *Night Hawk*s again.

Cameron had heard the story more times than he could count. Decades earlier, Brandon had had to negotiate, and hard, with the former Alliance President, Ronaine Avellar. Getting a facility on Alpheratz in working condition and *Merlin*-capable had been no small affair, and she had charged no small price. Old and ailing, she had demanded *time* from him. She knew she was dying, and she'd wanted all of Mountain Wolf's prosperity for the Alliance, to see to future Avellars after she was gone. She'd demanded sixty years from Brandon O'Leary, six full decades where Mountain Wolf would bring economic strength and military might to her successors, and *only* to her successors.

Cameron's father, desperate for the plant to open and the first *Merlin*s to be produced, had agreed. He'd needed the win to keep the company afloat, and sixty years of waiting to branch out had beaten the alternative, death. In the decades since that first, desperate deal, though, Brandon had started to resent the old promise. Sixty years of stagnation instead of growth had turned sour.

And now, the very first of Ronaine's successors was offering him some of that time back. Brandon gave the Outworlds President a long look, and Cam could almost see the numbers and possibilities alike dancing in his head.

His father nodded. "That's a big offer, Neil, a big offer." Brandon looked down at Avellar's hand, but just lifted an eyebrow. Cam knew his father would have to *know*, before he could shake on it. A Brandon O'Leary handshake meant something. "Which means it must be a big ask. So let's hear it."

The President and his wife nodded as though it was the answer they expected, and Neil pointed down to a star map. "Gentlemen, what do you know about...the planet Joshua?"

JOSHUA
OUTWORLDS WASTES
4 MAY 3034

The air was thick with flies, heat, and the stink of death.

The insects roiled through the valley in surges and waves, a rippling, droning, black mass clinging to the area like an oil slick atop churning surf. Whole generations of stinging black dipterans would feed on the rotting bodies heaped on the valley floor, then breed, deposit maggots, die of old age, and repeat the cycle. The thousands of corpses they fed and lived and died on was invisible beneath the cloud from up atop the high valley walls, but even that far away, the incessant, buzzing drone of the swarm was inescapable.

As inescapable as the stench.

"Well, shit." Johnny "Dozens" de la Cruz peered over the edge, reaching up to push his broad-brimmed hat higher on his head. He had a thin, new beard and luxurious, long dark hair he kept in a ponytail. He was wrapped in denim and leather, like everyone else, but was a little paler; less years alive meant less years in the sun than his fellow ranch hands.

"Mm-hmm," Brownpants grunted an acknowledgment around a mouthful of bitter green leaves—Joshua tobacco, often called Joshua leaf, a mild stimulant and hardy, drought-resistant plant luxury that was affordable even on a ranch hand's pay because *here*, at least, it was an actual weed—then he spat down into the valley below. His skin was as worn and leathered as the chaps he wore, thanks to Joshua's harsh sunlight, but his splendid mustachios were still more black than silver. He was the oldest and most experienced hand on the Castillo Verde, but still lean and hardy enough to work, day in and day out.

"That's a whole lotta death." Stringer grimaced, lip curling at the smell even up this high. She was older than Johnny's twenty, but younger than Brownpants' forty-some-odd. The Joshua sun had given her the same bronze-dark skin, the wind had given her the same squint, and the work had given her the same calluses. She had more tattoos than Brownpants, but he had more wrinkles. She turned away from the cliff edge, having seen more than enough of the churning black swarm below. Her dark eyes swept the area warily, like those who had done this might be back any moment.

"Mm-hmm," Brownpants nodded sagely.

"How many is it, y'think?" Johnny looked, as he often did, to Brownpants. The man was the oldest hand on the ranch *and* a real-life combat veteran. Johnny had looked to him since he'd been a boy.

"Two thousand, I reckon," the bunkhouse chief said, wrinkles around his eyes as deep as his frown. "Might could be three."

Johnny de la Cruz had spent his whole life here at the Castillo Verde ranch—naturally, as it was going to be his someday—and plenty of those days had ended with plenty of dead sheep. But he'd never seen three *thousand* dead sheep before.

The ground all near the cliff's edge was churned by trotters, thousands and thousands of them, a scar across the increasingly dusty soil of the Castillo Verde. Johnny's bootprints, and those of the gathered hands, were lost in the wide swath of upturned soil. Not so the footprints and burn marks of those who'd herded the sheep off the edge and down into the valley. There was no hiding *those* tracks.

'Mechs had done this, some with flamers, and every hand at the Castillo Verde knew whose.

A sharp whistle drew Johnny and the rest over. His father, Jonathan de la Cruz XI, was a cleaner, more dignified man than his workers, but no less hale or worn by the elements; skin tanned a deep, dark brown by the harsh sun, his slicked-back hair going gray, and wrinkles around his eyes from the perpetual squint Joshua demanded of all those who lived beneath its broken solar shades. He was a rancher, through and through, and he had precious little patience for his hands when they weren't working.

"Quit your staring," de la Cruz said, voice gruff, confident, and disgusted. "You've all seen dead sheep before, and will again. There's work to do, and we're going to do it. Those Saltrock bastards killed a few head, that doesn't mean you lot can neglect the rest of our stock. You want to eat tonight, you earn your stew, same as any other. You know the drill. Run your patrols, stay in pairs. Check the herds, check the fences, check your ammo, but most of all check your goddamned *guts*. Now go on. Saddle up."

He waved them off. As the men—and Stringer—scattered and did just that, sped on by Brownpants' curses, Johnny Dozens lingered to talk to his father. The crown prince of the Castillo Verde, he was used to his father having a few more words just for him, either to teach him, chastise him, or both.

"Don't gawk," was what the elder de la Cruz ordered this time. "Don't overthink it. We've been raided before, and we've raided 'em back. They're just getting bigger, is all. It's nothing new."

"We fixing to do it again? Raid 'em back?" Dozens perked up. "We have to teach those Ortegas a lesson, show those *pendejos* they can't get away wi—"

"They *already* got away with it!" His father's eyes flashed angrily. "They came, they did it, they left. That's getting away. You didn't stop them; the time to try has passed. They killed two thousand or more of our sheep. We don't know how many, because you're staring and dreaming of a fight instead of doing your job and seeing to those that remain."

Johnny licked his lips and nodded.

"You aren't just one of them, son. Stop thinking like they can, like they must, like they are allowed to. You aren't just a hand. You aren't just a *soldado*. You're my son. My *son*. Act like it. We run a business. You tend to the business first. Your ego second, or never."

With that, he put his hat on his head and turned and walked away.

Just in case the rest were watching, Dozens nodded like his father had told him something important, like he'd given him some special instruction instead of...what he'd given him...then he turned and jogged toward his 'Mech and clambered up the ladder.

A dozen of the ranch's hands rode horses, and had already started off to get back to their own daily chores. The rest of the cowboys were ready to go and waiting on him, though, in their own 'Mechs. The bare steel of each machine gleamed in the sun, except the drab brown on the lower half of Brownpants' machine. Inside them, the regulators, ranch hands turned MechWarriors, were already brims off, buckets on.

Now Johnny did the same, removing his open-crown cowboy hat for a bulky, Rastaban Agricultural-branded neurohelmet.

Johnny's *CattleMaster* was a 25-ton machine, and by far the newest 'Mech in the Castillo Verde stable. His was a Hunter variant, bristling with proper, military-grade small lasers and machine guns. Stringer's *Crosscut* ED-X2M, five tons heavier than Johnny's 'Mech, was registered for brush-clearing, but in many a tight situation her oversized chainsaw and flamer had done serious damage to enemy wranglers. Pico, St. Croix, and Rawlins all piloted well-worn *Sidekicks*, lighter, leaner, 20-ton machines armed only with retractable blades and the spit and vinegar of the cowpoke in the cockpit. The lot of them had internal combustion engines, softly spewing smoke as they idled.

Towering over all of them, nearly twice the tonnage of Stringer's *Crosscut* and by most accounts the most lethal machine on Joshua, was Brownpants' signature ride, a lethal *Shadow Hawk*. It was the only Castillo 'Mech to be painted, although the flat brown only covered it from the hips down, and Brownpants had paid for it out of his own salary. Half-clad or not, it was a proper, full-on BattleMech. Taken from the Alliance Grenadiers when Brownie had deserted years earlier, the medium 'Mech had been a fixture around the ranch for as long as Johnny could remember. As the seasons rolled past, the de la Cruz family had gotten more use by far out of the *Shadow Hawk*'s size, strength, working hand actuators, and eternally reliable fusion engine, than the 'Mech's weaponry.

That said, Brownie's reputation was long since secure. The *'Hawk* had seen enough fights to slowly deplete its store of missiles, but that still left the SHD-2K's Donal PPC. The need for it had been greater as things continued to escalate with the Ortegas. Brownpants, who still wore the color to honor the brother and sister Grenadiers he'd lost more than the regiment he'd left behind, was the most dangerous gunhand the de la Cruz family had. He was arguably the most dangerous man on Joshua, in fact, and he was a good part of why the Castillo Verde continued to hold their own in their feud with Saltrock Ranch.

While Johnny and the ranch hands brawled with Saltrock's crew, Brownie *fought*. Brownie *soldiered*. There was a difference, and they all knew it. Johnny was always glad to see Brownie, in or out of his 'Mech. The elder ranch hand had been omnipresent in his life. Since he'd been a boy, Johnny had felt like his father held up the sky. Just as long, he'd felt it was Brownpants who held down the dirt beneath them.

Brownpants rounded out and, alongside Johnny, led the Castillo Verde regulators. The six of them did work around the ranch, of course, and their 'Mechs had the hand actuators to show for it, tools more than weapons. Each of them had worked their way up out of the saddle and into a cockpit after proving loyalty and ability in equal measure, even

Johnny. They were ranch hands, not soldiers. They, in and out of their 'Mechs, still wrangled, herded, branded, roped, fenced, welded, calved, chopped, cleared, rode, and worked, and every one of their 'Mechs, even the *Shadow Hawk*, was laden with cargo netting and tools. But still and all, they were the wall of steel that protected the Castillo Verde from outside threats.

Or, at least, they were supposed to. Last night, they had failed, and two thousand sheep—a not-inconsiderable percentage of Castillo Verde's net worth—had died for it.

Across the Verde, ranch hands got back to work, whether from horseback or cockpit. Fences were mended. Turf was repaired as best it could be. Spooked stock was rounded up, driven farther from the borders of the ranch when possible. Patrols were kept up. Life went on. Life always did. Raids—even monstrous ones like this, the worst in their history—were as much a part of ranching on Joshua, ranching *anywhere*, as storms were, and sickness and drought and simple bad luck. Ranchers worked, ranches suffered. It was the way of things. The de la Cruzes and their loyal ranch hands could, at least, take solace in knowing the Ortegas and their Saltrock hands suffered most of Joshua's calamities alongside them.

Joshua was ranching, writ large.

Never a terribly populous or wealthy planet, Joshua had barely been considered worth the investment of the Star League terraforming work it had received centuries earlier. The Department of Mega-Engineering had manufactured and installed a solar shade, a high-tech, outsized umbrella of sorts, shielding the people of Joshua from the too-intense heat of their nearest star. The flora on Joshua, such as it had been, had evolved mostly to hardy scrub and coarse grasses.

Once the DoME solar shields were in place, the Star League took a longer, harder look at the world and wondered if they'd made the right call. It was light on rare minerals and precious stones, had no oil to speak of, even its oceans were barely workable with standard desalination protocols. What it had was open space, rugged grasses, and livable climates. Perfect for ranching, munitions testing, and little else...and it was too far out of the way, on the very fringe of the very fringe of the Periphery, for munitions testing.

And that had been *before* the solar shade started failing.

Like many failures, it was a slow process. Once upon a time, the shade had absorbed, not merely diverted, the tremendous solar power raining down on Joshua. What little electricity the world needed had been provided by the array. The danger of Joshua's sun had been turned into a resource instead, so long as the sunshield was upkept and its orbit corrections maintained. Even after the Star League fell, local engineers had done what they could do. Unfortunately, it hadn't been enough.

Some people say the trouble started in 2761, back in the Star League days, when pirates had attacked and seized the solar shield controls. The very next day, the Seventy-Fourth Royal Dragoons jumped in-system via pirate point and combat-dropped from orbit, decimating the pirates and reclaiming the ground control center. While Joshuans celebrated Sunshield Day and their liberation, year in and year out, there were some concerns that the piratical manipulation, or the devastating assault that followed, had initially started the solar shield's slow decline.

Whatever the cause, it happened. Two hundred years ago and more, the planet had been...not thriving, no, but getting by. Working as intended. Providing, for itself and its neighbors, ton after ton after ton of meat, wool, leather, gelatin, and more. It had been a meat market, if not a breadbasket, of the Baliggora Province, back when the Baliggora Province had meant something.

Then the temperature began to climb. Higher. Higher still. Too high. Sunshield Day after Sunshield Day came and went, and every year it was a little hotter, the climate a little more extreme, than the year before.

Over decades, then centuries, people simply died or...left. The merchant-piloted DropShips still came and went, trading industrial goods from faraway stars, leaving filled with huge cooler-cars of frozen beef or lamb, bales of wool, Joshua leaf, or sometimes sprawling cargo holds filled with seedstock or whole herds of livestock bought up. The Baliggora Province, never a bustling administrative entity to begin with, became a memory, and the Outworlds Alliance hadn't cared about Joshua since the days of Johnny's grandfather's grandfather.

Things got worse. The equators became inhospitable to life, then the greatest landmasses, and now only the south pole was habitable. And just who inhabited it? A population of thousands, not millions. Joshua was kept alive, technically, by a starport in the heart of the small, new capital city, by the Saltrock and Castillo Verde ranches, and not much else.

The Saltrock Ranch was a cattleman's affair, all bluster and longhorns, big herds of thin-haired, hardy range-bulls. The Ortegas had once dominated the cattle industry on Joshua, buying out, gobbling up, and bullying smaller range-beef affairs until it had first a virtual, then a literal, monopoly. Now they *were* the cattle industry on Joshua.

Opposite them, the de la Cruzes had done the same, twelve generations of them, but with sheep. The two families had inherited the traditional feuds between their industries, and their own sheepshooter war had grown more and more personal and intense across a dozen generations. Three times, they'd tried to marry the problem away. Three times, it had failed. If the ongoing Succession Wars could teach anyone anything, it was that those who consolidated power wanted to *keep* consolidating it. Just as the Davions and Kuritans would never be content near one another, so too, writ small here, would the de la Cruzes and the Ortegas never make for comfortable neighbors.

As the population of Joshua had grown more and more miniscule, as the industry had grown more and more concentrated, as the arable land—even by Joshua's harsh and brutal standards—had grown smaller and smaller and the temperature kept climbing...the feud had grown hotter as well. As hot as the star overhead that had burned through the Star League's best attempt at keeping it in check.

Three marriages hadn't stopped it from turning into a war.

And hell if I'm gonna be a fourth. I already got me a number. Johnny Dozens, the twelfth Jonathan de la Cruz, stomped his 'Mech across the grasses and shrubs of the ranch he'd been born to run, dragging his thoughts away from Joshua's history and into the present. *We're settling this feud the other way.*

His father had finally authorized reprisals with a simple, three-word order to his regulators. Johnny knew the eleventh de la Cruz had been in touch with *Señor* Ortega in the weeks following the raid, and he had overheard enough of the conversations to fill his veins with fire. He'd heard the curses, the insults, the threats, the quiet rage getting louder as calls continued. None of it had worked. The Ortegas were the only family on Joshua that rivaled them for wealth and power, and they seemed determined to press the issue until the de la Cruz family sold them their land and fled, like so many had already left Joshua.

Johnny's father wouldn't have it, though. He'd called Johnny and Brownpants into his office and given them simple instructions: "Call their bluff."

Oh, we'll call their bluff all right, Jefe.

Johnny's *CattleMaster* was the tip of the spear, taking point, the front of their line and the first of them to stomp carelessly over the meters-tall, electrified fence separating Castillo Verde from Saltrock. Sparks flew as the security system shorted out, and Johnny flashed his teeth in a feral smile as his sensors—proper, military-grade TharHes Mars-1 affairs—tracked the rest of the hands following in his wake. Stringer and her *Crosscut*, the trio of *Sidekick*s jockeyed by Rawlins, Pico, and St. Croix, and in the rear, watching out for all of them, came Brownpants' *Shadow Hawk* with its murderous PPC.

Cruising at fifty kilometers an hour, it didn't take them long to come across Ortega range-bulls. Genetically engineered from ancient Terran aurochs and newer, hardier breeds of cattle, even the comparatively lean Joshua stock could mass upward of four tons. A lone range-bull was nothing to be trifled with, much less a herd.

Still and all, the ranch hands of the Castillo Verde had come specifically with the intention of trifling, and so trifle they Goddamned *did*.

"Yee-haw!" Stringer laughed into their "lance" comms channel as her *Crosscut* charged and waved its huge sawblade-arm. "Git along, you bastard beef!"

The *Sidekick*s followed suit, their own smaller industrial blades revving, gouts of flame from their flamethrowers blasting up into the air, their spotlights glaring balefully down at the beefstock. Between the stomping titans, the bursts of fire and light, the revving engines of most of their 'Mechs and the higher-pitched roar of Stringer's monstrously oversized chainsaw, even the hardiest Saltrock range-bull wanted to move the other way.

And when a range-bull wanted to move, it moved.

Johnny's plan wasn't to butcher thousands. He wasn't an Ortega. That sort of cruelty and slaughter wouldn't do, not in the name of the Castillo Verde and the honor of the de la Cruz line. They were simply out to provoke a good, long stampede, to snowball as many Saltrock beef as possible into a big, panicked mass, and to send the wave of beef rushing at the Ortega ranch house proper. Let a few hundred tons of range-bull roll past the Saltrock bunkhouses in the middle of the night, let Saltrock ATVs, fences, and sheds get trampled. Let an avalanche of cattle rush through and past their ranch, and let the Ortegas rouse their gunhands. Let their 'Mechs come deal with the raiders, let 'em duke it out, and then let whatever of them could limp away operational to deal with the chaos and destruction of the stampede.

Johnny'd call their bluff, all right. He'd provoke a fight, smash up some Ortega iron, and then he and the regulators would be on their way, message delivered. With luck, before sunup they'd all be back in the Castillo Verde bunkhouse, and Stringer'd be doodling up tattoos to immortalize the night's raid on whatever ranch hands had earned some glory.

It didn't take long for the plan to come to fruition. The first part, at least. Once panicked, there wasn't much on Joshua—wasn't much *anywhere*, truth be told—that could stop dozens, much less hundreds, of range-bulls on the run. There was no stopping 'em, and no hiding them, either. The Ortegas and their sensors saw the trouble coming from kilometers and kilometers away, and soon enough they moved to intercept.

Johnny's fancy electronics were still outdone by Brownpants and his *Shadow Hawk*, a genuine weapon of war.

"Incoming OpFor," the old hand said matter-of-factly, voice low, calm, as laid back as talking about the weather—which was, in fairness, itself a life-or-death affair all too often. "Eyes right."

The *Sidekick*s slowed their playful chasing of the running-amok beefstock and turned to their right, shoulder-mounted spotlights searching. Stringer's *Crosscut* revved as her slower machine didn't stop to search, just turned and rushed after them. Johnny's *CattleMaster* and its fancy TharHes tracking systems pinged multiple threats inbound.

Then, they got a look at 'em.

"Whoa," St. Croix said over their comm, the nearest *Sidekick* and the first to see.

"What in tarnation?" Rawlins gawked.

"Boss?" Pico sounded like he wanted to call the whole thing off.

"Ah, screw it." Stringer throttled up even faster...just before a flight of missiles exploded across the front of her machine and nearly made her fall over.

Coming at them weren't the pair of light *Sidekicks* and pair of 35-ton *Powerman* IndustrialMechs they'd expected. Or, rather, the problem was that those were coming, but they weren't rounded out by the last few 'Mechs Johnny expected. The Ortegas themselves and their custom 'Mechs were nowhere to be found, and replacing them on the field were a pair of downright giants.

In the lead was a hunchbacked titan Johnny's TharHes systems designated as a *Lumberjack*, but an LM4/P variant; which meant not only was it a looming 70-ton beast, bigger even than Brownpants' *Shadow Hawk*, and sporting a chainsaw to match, but it also bore a proper weapon of war, an LRM-10, and with some military-grade armor and fire control systems to go with it. Even on the battlefields of the Inner Sphere, a long-range missile array was a serious affair. On Joshua, it was a statement of deadly intent.

Just as bad, though, behind it, scuttling on four stomping legs, was a *Scavenger* SC-V-M, a MilitiaMech proper. Somehow the Ortegas had gotten their hands on their own combat machine, and an 80-ton assault 'Mech at that! This was no IndustrialMech or AgroMech with a bolted-on weapons kit or two, but a purpose-built machine sold to protect against pirates and other troublemakers. The quad 'Mech was even heavier than the *Lumberjack*, similarly armored, and sported an even more terrifying weapon. It had a medium-bore autocannon—a weapon type perhaps not fired in anger on Joshua since the days of the Star League—believed by many to be the best all-around, jack-of-all-trades gun in existence, the second-most destructive ballistic weapon Johnny'd ever heard of, and a hell of a nasty surprise.

This wasn't going to be some casual skirmish of wrecked armor and broken hand actuators, some ranch-hand brawl that would lead to

Stringer slapping some fresh ink onto boasting regulators and everyone having a beer later. This wasn't their usual clash, no. It was an ambush, a lethal trap, an all-or-nothing bushwhacking—and Johnny Dozens had led his regulators right into it.

The stakes were made clear to the de la Cruz regulators very simply and brutally, from the outset. The autocannon announced itself by blowing out Pico's cockpit in a long, scathing burst of automatic fire that sent tracers clean through the back of his *Sidekick*'s head and into the night sky. For just a heartbeat, Johnny saw, or imagined he saw, a red mist in the cone of light from Pico's shoulder-mounted spotlight before the 'Mech crumpled.

Silence fell just as Pico's *Sidekick* did. Quiet filled the night for a long moment as the gravity of the situation was made apparent to one and all.

"Well," Brownpants drawled, slurring slightly from a lower lip filled with Joshua leaf, "We got us a scrap."

Both sides charged, one outnumbering and outmassing the other in outrageously unfair fashion. There was only one way the fight could end, and they all knew it. Still and all, they made a go of it, the regulators of the Castillo Verde bunkhouse, they really did.

St. Croix had always been close with Pico, and he proved his loyalty to the Castillo for the hundredth and final time as he led the charge in the most literal sense possible. His *Sidekick* rammed bodily into a *Powerman* HaulerMech nearly twice his weight; and he did so at speed, revving his lighter 'Mech's engine as hard and fast as it could go, no hesitation or preservation to be seen. He slammed into the *Powerman* with such an impact both of them went down in a tangled mess. His *Sidekick*'s fuel tank opened up the night sky in a ball of flame and steel and the larger *Powerman* was sent sprawling, myomer threads exposed and torn, one arm hanging useless as the 'Mech tried to clamber awkwardly to its feet. Johnny searched the darkness with his eyes and his mil-grade sensors alike, but saw no sign of St. Croix having ejected.

Our makeshift ejectors've saved our hides plenty of times in these fights...but this don't feel the same. It'll take more than improvised auto-ejectors to get us home from this one.

Rawlins staggered under a flight of LRMs, but waded in close enough for a soccer kick to knock down a Saltrock *Sidekick* faster than any Ortega pilot could react. Shouting obscenities into their shared comms, he used his flamer and brutal 20-ton stomps to extract terrible screams from his downed enemy, then another kick ended those screams suddenly and awfully.

The rest of Ortega's men responded just as quickly and brutally, though. Rawlins went down beneath the bashing fists of the other Ortega 'Mechs, as *Powerman* and *Sidekick* limbs pummeled his 'Mech mercilessly. Armor plating flew. His searchlight got blasted off his shoulder. Sparks seared the night sky. Then his cockpit, too, went dark, and so did his icon on Johnny's sensors.

Stringer avenged Rawlins almost immediately as her slower *Crosscut* got in close and savagely peeled open a distracted *Powerman*'s back with her screaming, spark-spewing chainsaw. She waded into the fight, but got not only physically assaulted back, but shot at for her trouble. Her armor, already pockmarked by that first wave of LRM fire from the *Lumberjack*, fell off in sheets after another volley—the precise targeting systems of the heavy 'Mech unerringly blasting at her even in the twisting melee, the bar brawl gone 'Mech scale—before the *Lumberjack* dashed in to finish her off.

She sawed up the *Lumberjack* something fierce, but the fight had been too unfair from the start. Eventually a kick from the larger machine sent her *Crosscut*'s left leg flying away, torn messily off. Her cockpit exploded as her jury-rigged auto-ejectors hurled her into the night sky and out of the fight. The *Lumberjack* unnecessarily stomped on her ruined *Crosscut* just for fun, effortlessly punching a foot actuator through the downed machine's chest.

Johnny did what he could and raced in at the *Lumberjack* just a hair too late, moments after it finished off Stringer's 'Mech. Remembering a lifetime of bunkhouse yarns from Brownpants, he knew he had to get in close against the LRM-equipped machine, knowing—hoping he'd remembered correctly—that those types of missiles struck at great distances, but *needed* to strike at great distances. Something about targeting hardware calibrations, warheads arming, and angle-of-fire. He hoped Brownie hadn't been exaggerating as he closed the distance.

The first volley it fired at him burst from its chest and outright blinded him, missile contrails filling his field of vision in close and dazzling his thermoptics, too. But sure enough, they blasted off into the night sky, just barely over his head.

Johnny savagely thumbed at his firing studs and returned fire, his enemy looming so large it felt like he couldn't miss. He chipped away at it with the weapons mounted on each arm of his Hunter-class *CattleMaster*, only for a whole lot of nothing to happen in response. Against his expected, usual opponents, the pair of small lasers and trio of machine guns felt awe-inspiring and almost unfair. Against the *Lumberjack*'s hulking mass, one of the biggest 'Mechs he'd ever seen, Johnny Dozens felt like he might as well have been taking shots at it with his personal revolver. Its armor was cratered and sliced at here and there, but nothing was genuinely threatening the MechWarrior or the machine's lethality.

Wait, focus, remember what Brownie told you, he told himself as he ran to follow his internal instructions. *Angle. Turn. Throttle up. Fishhook behind them. And then: right torso, rear.*

Johnny's targeting displays and the madhouse lightshow of nighttime 'Mech combat half faded as he remembered a conversation from the very first time he'd asked the combat vet if he'd killed anyone. He'd been a curious, stupid boy. Brownpants had been kind enough to answer instead of cuff him. Years of conversations had ensued, especially after Johnny'd moved himself from the big house to the bunkhouse and joined the regulators.

"You ever find yourself in a pickle and up against a proper BattleMech, Johnny Boy," the bunkhouse veteran had said a dozen years earlier, "first off, you ask yourself what you done wrong to get into that situation."

No time for that part. Johnny throttled up, angling off to his left side. He was almost as fast as he thought he was; a few missiles flew overhead, but some savaged his shoulder armor instead. Even the misses were an eye-searing stream of dragon's breath from the otherwise-dark *Lumberjack*, spewing forth from somewhere in its barrel chest. Johnny'd never been this scared before, not staring down an angry range-bull, brawling in town, or even skirmishing with the usual Ortega 'Mechs.

Focus. Remember.

"Second, get behind the sumbitch as best you can. You'd best hope you brought somethin' to the dance that's faster than them, and you'd best practice your driving, 'cause it's tricky, and the bastard'll know you're coming to try it. But if you can, get the angle on 'em. Get behind 'em, every time. Thinner armor back there."

Almost got it... Johnny's *CattleMaster* kicked up sod as one foot dug into the ground beneath him and he turned suddenly, angled sharply, barely kept his balance as he hooked in at a run and got himself behind the looming 'Mech. *Almost got it...*

There!

"Third? You shoot for the right shoulder, right about here." Brownpants had casually grabbed young Johnny's shoulders to turn him around, then the veteran's calloused fingers had jabbed at him so hard he'd been afraid it'd bruise. "And then you close your eyes, 'cause an explosion's coming."

"What?" Johnny, wide-eyed, had asked. "Why?"

"Well, whole point of a 'Mech is to be 'bout the shape of a man, right? Arms, legs, familiar sense of balance, all that? That bein' the case, and, statistically, round about nine folks in ten, including BattleMech engineers, bein' right-handed, most 'Mechs'll pack their biggest piece of big iron in their right arm. Gunhand, see? Natural instincts creepin' in and affecting design choices. Plus aesthetics, they want 'em to look like soldiers, so soldiers'll buy 'em, right? So, right arms got big guns, as often as not. And then, simple truth is, the closer a gun is to its ammo, the cleaner the ammunition feed and easier th' internal workings and claptrap of the damned 'Mech are. So *usually* the right side of the chest is where you'll find missiles, autocannon rounds, and such."

Brownpants had nodded sagely and tousled young Johnny's hair. "So. Right torso, rear. Shoot 'em in the back, off-kilter just to the right a bit, and most BattleMechs'll go up like goddamned Sunshield Day."

Johnny *had* always loved the fireworks displays on Sunshield Day, celebrating the planet's 2761 rescue by the Royal Dragoon Regiment. Sunshield Day going off inside a bad-guy 'Mech sounded pretty good to him!

And so it was that, here, now, years later, in his first ever fight-to-the-death affair, Johnny had managed just exactly that. He *was* in a smaller, faster 'Mech than his opponent, and it turned out years of rustling cattle made you a decent hand at fast, tight corners. He *had* gotten in behind his opponent, albeit with some effort, had even handily avoided the snarling chainsaw it had tried to attack him with. He *had* gnawed through that opponent's rear armor, which *was* thinner. Thinking about his lost friends, he savagely unloaded; his paired lasers sliced what felt like a scalpel-accurate hole in the *Lumberjack*'s rear armor, and then his trio of machine guns bucked and chattered and filled that hole with a stream of hardball depleted-uranium rounds.

But there'd come no Sunshield Day fireworks. Instead, the inside of the 'Mech was...hollow? Empty? Johnny gawked down at his sensor screens, feeling betrayed. He had...he had just meticulously targeted...a... cargo bay? He sputtered, physically stunned by his disappointment.

Johnny's *CattleMaster* kept up a trot as he tried to stay behind the circling *Lumberjack* and keep at it, but the heavy 'Mech managed to turn a tighter circle. Its chainsaw lashed out and screamed as it tore the armor from the front of his 'Mech with a savage backhanded swipe from its right arm.

Johnny stared as it spun back to face him fully, glaring at the ten long-range-missile tubes arrayed across the *Lumberjack*'s torso. Its *left* torso.

"Well, shit—" Johnny Dozens managed before the 70-ton machine's other heavy arm swung and crashed into his 'Mech's chest, battering his fancy *CattleMaster* to the ground despite his best efforts.

"Brownie!" he managed after slamming to the Joshua dirt and bouncing around in his cockpit harness so hard he thought he might fall to pieces. Johnny saw stars instead of targeting arrays. He tasted blood from a split lip and felt his mouth fill with fear, not vengeance.

"Brownie, I need help!"

Brownpants was busy, though. As the *Scavenger* had opened fire on him with that murderous autocannon, he had leaped hundreds of meters away, the only 'Mech on either side that could do so. A stream of tracers chased him across the night sky and even caught up to gnaw at his *Shadow Hawk*, but it was no *Sidekick*.

Nearly triple the tiny AgroMech's size and sporting several times the armor, all of it proper military-grade stuff, he weathered the storm and started to fire back, all on the move. His PPC beam didn't lash out in a return blast at the *Scavenger*, though, nor did it gouge at the armor of the *LumberJack* looming over Johnny; the canny MechWarrior instead hammered at the remaining *Sidekick* and *Powerman* 'Mechs the Saltrock boys had brought, blasting them to pieces in just a few shots. Their armor plating might hold up to wind, rain, and the occasional range-bull, but the lighter machines were no match for the manmade lightning of a particle projection cannon. Where his attacks would have taken time and accuracy to do meaningful harm to the larger 'Mechs, they neatly tore apart the smaller ones.

In just a few shots, his *Shadow Hawk* finished thinning the field, building on the desperate successes of the first Castillo Verde regulators. Only the unexpectedly heavy 'Mechs remained.

But the unexpectedly heavy 'Mechs were plenty. As Johnny desperately fired up at it, the *Lumberjack* stomped down on one of his *CattleMaster*'s knees, and a probing, tearing slash from its chainsaw tore at his gyro. A PPC blast slammed into the heavy 'Mech after that, though, and—satisfied Johnny Dozens wasn't getting up any time soon—the *Lumberjack* turned and lumbered after Brownpants, a flurry of LRMs leading the way. Johnny was afraid their assessment was correct. He'd never tried to pilot with a busted gyro before, and he'd never had a leg this damaged. He struggled to get up, but as he did, he kept an eye on Brownie and the ongoing battle.

Again and again, the veteran MechWarrior fired his PPC from the very edges of its effective range, staying far from the heavier machines the Ortegas had brought to bear, sniping at them as accurately as he could while staying on the move. He was soundly outmassed by the surprise pair of Saltrock machines, but out-armored them individually, matched the range of their LRMs and power of their autocannon...and was a proper, combat-trained MechWarrior of the Alliance Grenadiers, who'd seen combat more times than Johnny'd seen titties. Brownie had a boxer's chance, he had a mean streak, and he had the only PPC on the planet.

Until, eventually, he *didn't*. The enemy autocannon bucked and blasted at his armor and eventually got lucky with a few hits. Their long-range missiles sailed and arced and homed in and sandblasted him. The PPC ran hot, Brownie's jump jets and constant fire exacerbated things, and soon Johnny—'Mech carefully propped up on one arm, gawking and egging his hero on—saw the *Shadow Hawk* moving more slowly and more stiffly, saw it forced to fire less often. He knew Brownie was staggering his shots, giving his cooling system time to recover, not just waiting for the standard PPC cooldown cycle.

The damage added up, though. Another burst of autocannon fire savaged the already-strained armor of the *Shadow Hawk*'s chest, then a flight of missiles blasted in and around the hole and tore apart the belly of the beast.

Brownpants fell, his *Shadow Hawk*'s arms pinwheeling almost comically as he tried to keep his balance. He looked like what he was, an oversized, gutshot cowboy going down with an off-kilter gyro and heat-seized myomers. Veteran or not, he fell, splaying out on his back in the cattle-churned Joshua dirt.

"Heh, heh, heh," the Saltrock gunhand in the *Lumberjack* chortled over the open comms, and another arcing flight of missiles slammed into the *Shadow Hawk*. A less literal kick while he was down than Johnny'd received, but the mean spirit was the same.

The *Scavenger* scuttled and stomped closer, meticulously lining up an autocannon shot that tore into the *'Hawk*'s PPC and sent arcing blue lightning pouring out of it and crawling across the 'Mech's torso as it exploded.

"Well. At least..." the Saltrock gunhand's voice crackled in their ears, drawling slowly, enjoying the moment.

Johnny, eyes wide, hammered at his controls to fire a blast of pathetic laser shots at targets hundreds of meters out of range.

"...you can say..." the *ScavengerMech* pilot drew it out.

Brownpants didn't answer. Johnny didn't know if his mentor was unconscious, dead, or just refusing to rise to the bait.

"...you tried." Ortega's hired gun chuckled as the autocannon lined up on Brownpants' cockpit.

Brownpants' *Shadow Hawk* shifted, right arm—a cowboy's gunhand—lifting. It didn't have any weapons mounted on it, though: the -2K variant he'd fled the Alliance Grenadiers with didn't have the medium laser there that other models did. No, LRM launcher empty for years and PPC wrecked, he was armed only with defiant scorn.

Brownie showed it as he meticulously twisted and shifted his hand actuator and lifted a middle finger at them.

"You boys oughta watch your sensors," he drawled.

PPC blasts suddenly seared the sky and hammered into the low-slung *Scavenger*. Four of them, claws of blue-white plasma slashing across the horizon, tearing into the militia machine and savaging it in a ruthless flurry. One penetrated a fuel tank, another raked raw energy across the ammunition stores for the autocannon—*in the right torso,*

Johnny realized!—and sure enough, they got their Sunshield Day fireworks.

"What in hell?" The *Lumberjack* turned and snap-shot a flight of ten missiles, high and away. Low and adjacent to the ground, straight-line blasts of PPC fire converged on the IndustrialMech in response. Torso half-filled with cavernous storage space or not, the blasts did the job as a second volley tore it to pieces. Six or so of the eight PPC shots hit while the 'Mech was still what could be called things like "upright" and "operational." It was Sunshield Day all over again, as the engine, the fuel tank, and/or the ammunition went off, Johnny couldn't tell which. Didn't matter. Bits of *Lumberjack* fell from the sky.

Johnny sat his *CattleMaster* on its rump, gawking, blinking stupidly. Twenty seconds too late, Brownie's advice sunk into his skull, and he looked down at his targeting and sensor display screens, cross-checking with what he saw on his screens.

"*Jesucristo!*" he breathed.

*Merlin*s. A full lance of them! Johnny'd read up on them in the *MechTech* and *Merc World* mags he paid a pretty penny for. They were huge and lethal, proper heavy BattleMechs, even bigger than Brownie's *Shadow Hawk*, each one more than twice the weight of Johnny's own *CattleMaster*. They didn't quite match the tonnage of the savaged *Scavenger* or *Lumberjack*, but they out-armored and out-gunned each of them, since *they* were, each and every one, dedicated weapons of war. There wasn't a hand actuator in sight; *Merlin*s were made to kill, not to build, repair, or labor. They were efficient, lethal, armored, and terrifying. Advancing crisply, neatly four abreast, they strode forward very nearly in perfect time with each other, moving with precision that showed training just as much as their precise volleys had.

Try as he might, Johnny couldn't make out the blaze orange logos they sported against their battleship-gray hides. Not before he got another set of sensor blips coming in at a run from back toward the Saltrock ranch house. Finally clear of the stampede, finally deciding to get involved, or both; it was the pair of 'Mechs he'd expected to see sooner, rather than later. He'd have rather seen them than the looming *Lumberjack* and *Scavenger* that had torn apart his friends, he knew that much for certain.

One of the late arrivals was a *Powerman* sporting vehicular flamers and a paint job to match, and Johnny knew it was Juanita Ortega piloting her beloved *Diablo*, as befit the princess of their rival ranch. Diego Ortega himself arrived in *La Tormenta*, his family's customized *Powerman*. *La Tormenta* had the XI-M-B variant's standard SRM-4 launchers in each arm, but some long-dead Ortega had outfitted it with a third SRM-4 rig, all lined up in the center of the light 'Mech's chest, the missile tubes aligned straight up and down like a set of buttons. The other Saltrock machines—besides the pair of newcomer heavy hitters—had been plain, bare steel, same as most of the Castillo Verde machines. Joshua didn't suffer paintjobs lightly. *Diablo* was painted as fiery as the Joshua sunset and *La Tormenta* was a gleaming white, like a dashing suit, and accented here and there with lines of a yellow as bright as gold; it was a gunslinger, not a workhorse, and it showed.

But they were still just 35-tonners, and civilian ones at that, advancing to square off against four *Merlin*s, any one of which could blast them to pieces. Beneath that pretty white and gold paint there was just civilian-grade armor, and not much of it. Ortega didn't carry himself that way, though. He stood next to his daughter, in a 'Mech just as fragile as his, and glared up at the foursome of military-grade killers without fear. They were Chihuahuas trying to stare down Rottweilers.

"You are on my property, and you have fired on my lawfully employed ranch hands. By rights and law, I can shoot you dead." Johnny recognized *Señor* Ortega's voice. No one else on Joshua, except maybe Johnny's own father, used quite that same tone.

"You can try," came back an amused woman's voice, no doubt bolstered by a steady target lock. Her *Merlin* pivoted ever so slightly, every weapon aiming down at the light 'Mech.

Another *Merlin* stepped forward one pace, though, and lifted its laser-arms to the sky in a show of peace and calm.

"No, sir, by law, no you can't." The new speaker sounded young. Johnny's age, or Juanita Ortega's. "*We're* here by law to end this feud. And I think you'll find we just did."

"Not quite," Ortega nearly started them all shooting again as his 'Mech mimicked a shrug; a shrug that ended with one of its missile packs leveled off to the side, right at Johnny's cockpit. Dozens blinked stupidly up at the missile tubes pointed straight his way as Ortega continued. "Get off my land, or you can tell your boss what happened to end his bloodline."

"Go ahead." It was the woman again, and Johnny could almost hear the smirk in her voice. "De la Cruz isn't our boss."

"*Don't* go ahead," the younger MechWarrior said, sounding to Johnny like he was shaking his head as he talked. "But…Captain Fox is right, sir. We don't work for Mr. de la Cruz."

"Then why are you here?" Juanita cut in, as sharp and unpleasant as ever Johnny'd heard her.

"Sir, Miss, I know you can't see in my cockpit, but please understand I've got here a writ. A letter from President Neil Avellar of the Outworlds Alliance, explaining that we—"

Suddenly, there was a fresh bit of commotion that almost had all the on-edge folks start shooting each other. Only this time it was—

"Aww, hell no! Ain't takin' me back!" Brownpants struggled to rise in his *Shadow Hawk*. "I ain't hangin' for no desertion, not after this long!"

"Whoa! No! Brownie, easy! I don't think—" It was Johnny's turn to wave a gun-toting arm in a desperate gesture, accidentally aiming his machine guns at his mentor even as Brownie's gyro-gutted *Shadow Hawk* slammed back to the dirt, refusing to rise.

"Who the hell's that?"

"What's he talking abou—"

"Brownie, c'mon, stand down, there's no way they're—"

"Nuh-uh! Gonna have to shoot me, sons of bitches!" Brownpants lurched most of the way to his feet, only for his 'Mech to fall over again, face down. "I ain't takin' no rope!"

"Fine, take your deserter and get off my land immedi—"

"*Pendejos*, take whoever you're here for and—"

"I ain't goin' back in no irons to let some *god-damned* Avellar string me up over—"

Another PPC blast roared out, blasting a crater in the dirt and cutting the confused radio chatter.

"Everyone *shut up*!" It was the younger MechWarrior again, his *Merlin*'s chest-mounted PPC smoking slightly. "You, point those damned missiles somewhere else. You, just power down and get out of that *CattleMaster*. And *you*, calm down! You don't even have guns! What the hell are you doing? Be still, we're not here for you! We don't even know who you are!"

Brownpants' *Shadow Hawk* froze on its hands and knees, in the middle of another attempt to rise.

"Johnny?" Brownpants asked, voice less certain than Johnny had ever heard it. The veteran was asking him what to do. Asking him for permission. Asking *him*.

"Brownie..." Johnny swallowed. What would his father say?

You're my son, he heard in his head. *We run a business.*

"Do what they say," he finally croaked out. He lowered his *CattleMaster*'s arms, digging both into the dirt. His 'Mech's engine purred, then sputtered, then died. His battery would keep the comms going for a while. "I don't know why they're here, but they ain't here for you. So let's hear 'em out."

He shifted his tone a little, speaking up. "You aren't just here to shoot, you're here to talk. So talk. Tell us what's on that letter of yours."

"You don't give orders here, *de la Cruz*." Juanita Ortega spat the name like it was a curse.

"Girl, I swear, I'll sit you down if I have to." The grouchy female MechWarrior turned one laser-arm to point away from Ortega's *La Tormenta* and down at Juanita's precious *Diablo* instead. In a way, leveling just that single weapon, the BattleMech equivalent of a sidearm, was *more* threatening. More humiliating. More confident.

For now, at least, it worked. Juanita shut up, for what Johnny thought might be the first time in her life.

"Mr. Ortega, Mr. de la Cruz, and, just, everyone else," the young, patient MechWarrior began again. "I have here a letter from President Neil Avellar. It ends this feud, this war, this whatever-it-is. You're hurting the industry of the planet, you're threatening your production, and as a result, we have been duly deputi—"

"Who are you? Who is 'we'?" Ortega cut in.

Johnny didn't blame him. It struck him as a fair question, and he was curious. With his power off, he couldn't zoom and enhance well enough to make out their logos, and in all the excitement he'd forgotten to do so earlier.

"We're Mountain Wolf BattleMechs, sir. Members of Mountain Wolf's security team, sent here by the President himself, and deputized by the unanimous vote of the Baliggora Planetary Parliament. We've been sent by Chairman Barnabas Huard, specifically, to carry out this operation within the Baliggora Province, and to put an end to your fighting. We're also here to—"

"The Baliggora Province hasn't meant a damn to anybody on Joshua in a hundred years. They don't know we exist, boy." Ortega again. Johnny wasn't sure the "boy" was necessary or wise, but they *were* standing on Ortega's land, and Johnny knew his own father'd be probably less than entirely civil, too. "So enough lies. What the hell's really going on? And who *are* you, really?"

"Sir, listen very carefully, and, please, never call me a liar again. I am Cameron O'Leary, Chief Operating Officer of Mountain Wolf BattleMechs. I'm the third child of the Duchess Olivia Rippon-Hart of Vendrell, and only son of Graf-Consort Brandon O'Leary, CEO and President of Mountain Wolf BattleMechs." The younger man was picking up steam as he went, bolstering himself with reminders of where he came from. "But right now, I'm the man heading up a lance of heavy BattleMechs that are the most dangerous things on this planet or for weeks of travel in any direction, and that's *not* counting the firepower of the *two* DropShips that also report to me. So you'd be wise to adjust your tone and posture, sir, and not to insult me again, and you'd be *really* wise to slide that target lock of yours somewhere else."

"You won't tell me what to do on—"

"I absolutely will, I have a letter fr—"

"To hell with your letter! *Jesucristo* himself couldn't write a letter telling me what to do on my own land!"

"Sir, you really need to—"

"My daughter and I will fight you if we must!"

"She's your *only* daughter, isn't she, sir?"

The silence after that reminder-slash-threat was deafening. The MechWarrior, the businessman, didn't need to say the rest of it out loud.

His right-hand woman decided to anyway.

"If you don't stand down right now, Ortega, your family will end when this gunfight does, and our jobs will get a lot easier." She spoke with the cold certainty of someone who'd killed from the cockpit of a *Merlin* before.

"Thank you, Captain Fox," Cameron O'Leary said, in a way that made his exasperated sigh quite clear. He took a moment to center himself. "But understand, sir, she's not wrong. There's no need for this to continue, and there is literally no point in you trying to continue it. It's over. If a single missile slips those tubes of yours, or her *Powerman* shows us a single thermal blip from those flamers, we will take you to pieces with our PPCs and lasers, sir, we will lock you down and roast you with flamers in close, and we will step on what's left. We won't need a single round of ammo to finish both of you off, sir. Attack us, and you won't even be a change in our armorer's inventory counts. Sir."

Johnny thought the "sir" was a nice touch.

"But if you stand down and let us finish carrying out these instructions in peace, then I swear to you, sir, *wallahi*, you and your daughter won't be hurt. Or your wife, your people, even your cattle. You just need to power down and read this letter, and you'll see you're all going to be treated fairly moving forward. Don't worry, it's in my best interest, just as much as yours, that this all go smoothly. I know you're used to having things your way, in large part because you're a rich man, but believe me, sir, your cattle are about to be worth a whole lot more if you'll just let us finish."

What? Johnny's brow furrowed. *What the hell is going on?*

"We've already talked with *Señor* de la Cruz, er, senior. He's the one who sent us this way. I'm only sorry we couldn't get here sooner. I think a few more people would still be alive." Johnny got the sense Cameron O'Leary really seemed to mean that. "I understand maybe this hasn't all been the best first impression, Mr. Ortega, but we'd rather have you and your family helping us with this than obstructing, and if you *do* obstruct, it won't be for very long, and it'll be the de la Cruzes who benefit."

Johnny watched O'Leary walk his *Merlin* forward—"Captain Fox," the woman, took a reflexive earth-shaking half step after him before she caught herself and stopped—and Cameron advanced the heavy 'Mech slowly until he was well within Ortega's missile range. Closer. Into Juanita's flamer range. Closer. Then he stood very, very still, as easy a target as any gunner could hope for. Looming over both Ortega machines, he stopped.

"But I need you to understand, sir, we're not here to save de la Cruz. We're not here to save anybody. We're here to extract you. This is a delivery job. We're bringing peace to Joshua by emptying it."

FAMINDAS
ALPHERATZ IV
OUTWORLDS ALLIANCE
19 MARCH 3034

"...and that's the situation. So, Mr. O'Leary—*ahem*—Brandon, please, think about it before you volunteer your son for this operation," Neil Avellar said, tugging nervously at his collar. To Cameron, he seemed to be a man growing accustomed to making hard decisions, and he was, this far into his presidency, catching onto the fact that *every* decision was hard. Making hard decisions might never be comfortable to him, but Cam gave him points for doing it, regardless.

"There's no need, Mr. President. I understand." Brandon O'Leary sat back in his chair opposite the President, and reached over without looking to pat his son on the shoulder. Cam jumped just a little.

"Cameron's ready. He'll handle it. As a mercantile affair, we'll fill our *Triumph*-class with the cargo, the first wave of it, at least, and our *Leopard* can be used to shuttle high-status guests and our officers. As civilians, we'll need to be deputized to keep the whole thing legal and aboveboard while keeping you at arm's reach instead of the government directly being involved. You're right. I've got the ships, I've got the 'Mechs, and Captain Fox and her people can make the time."

He leaned forward, elbows on his armrests, fingers steepling.

"But understand, Mr. President, I get it. I see what you're sending us to do. Joshua's a lost cause; I don't need your supplementary stack of papers to see it. Out of the way of shipping lanes, literally off the edge of the map, the whole world's a frog, slowly boiling. It's dying, and it needs a clean end while it can get one. It's got one thing to offer the universe, which is also the one thing you *need*, and you need it closer to home. Your people are starving, their people make food. So sure. We'll do it. We'll roll up our sleeves and see it done. We'll stare down the ones we have to, and we'll gun down the ones we *really* have to, if they force our hand."

Neil Avellar glanced at his wife; she smiled and nodded back. Brandon O'Leary stood. Cameron rose alongside him, not sure what there was left to say *after* his father had agreed to send their corporate security to, arguably, carry out something like a genocide?

"But in exchange, Mr. President, Cameron is heading up this whole expedition. This whole operation. We're not undertaking any half measures for you, sir. His will be the face they see, and the voice they hear, leading the way. Cameron will be the one offering these people jobs, if they need them, after the relocation. The ranchers will keep ranching, that's the point, don't you worry, but the rest of them, the whole planet, will be looking for a way to keep a roof over their heads, and Cameron, and Mountain Wolf, will offer them that. Personally. At our usual generous salary rates and benefits packages. We're here to build, not to take advantage. My son will make war if he needs to, but then he will make peace, and he'll get those people and their sheep and cows and whatever else into our ships and back here to the Alliance proper. *Only* our ships, and those we contract, like you want. For which we'll be compensated by the Alliance at one point five times the usual rate for shipping."

Neil paused only briefly. "One point two?"

"Acceptable." Brandon nodded and continued. *He'd agreed quickly*, Cameron noticed. *Too quickly.* He was up to something else. "You pay us one point two times standard shipping rates, you halve the remainder of our exclusivity clause, and we'll get it done. Cameron will oversee the deportation, transportation, and immigration logistics. Cameron will oversee the onboarding for anyone interested in a job. Cameron and Mountain Wolf's holdings here on-world will assist the Outworlds Alliance in housing and socialization, or whatever you want to call... all of this."

"I look forward to the assistance, and I'm sure these poor people will be ever so grateful." Rebecca Avellar favored Cameron with a warm smile, agreeing to terms in her husband's name with graceful and practiced ease. "While it is our hope that the former people of Joshua will be of great help in keeping the Alliance fed, we, of course, understand that *they'll* need food, too. And room to not just continue, but grow, their industry. We have several appropriate locations already selected, keeping these two families and their ranches far away from one another, and I can't wait to go over them with you."

"Dormandaine, maybe? I've heard it's nice." Cameron returned her smile, and meant it.

But...wait... He squinted slightly, already doing math in his head. Judging by the JumpShip recharge rates he knew they were dealing with, the distances they needed to travel, the estimated amount of people and material they'd be transporting, and the cargo capacity of their DropShips, to say nothing of the administrative side of things and the onboarding and new-hire processes needed...and...and...

How long are we staying here? Father told Mother he'd be back home to Vendrell by her birthday. There's no way he can manage that, unless...

Brandon seemed to read his son's mind. "And Cameron will be doing all of this without me, because I'm going back to Vendrell!

"Not to worry, I'll charter something, our ships will stay here," he helpfully continued, as though his individual travel requirements were going to be anyone's chief concern.

Cameron blinked as Brandon elaborated, smiling wryly. "Cameron will remain here at Stonehold Estate and head up our Alpheratz facility once this is all over. In perpetuity. I will concern myself with the rest of Mountain Wolf's interests, like shipping and distribution anti-spinward, preparing for a Vendrellian expansion since you're so graciously and unexpectedly lifting our exclusivity restriction, and other dull, political, Lyran affairs like spoiling my grandson and keeping my wife from killing me for this. In due time, I don't doubt that some of your experienced Alpheratzi employees will be moving anti-spinward and joining us on Vendrell as they're needed, but in the meantime, Cam will have plenty to work with. Good people, led by a good man."

"Our Alpheratz facility," his father had said, as though they had another one. As though this Alpheratz production line wasn't, in many ways, *all* of Mountain Wolf BattleMechs. As though it wasn't the only place in all the universe you could build a *Merlin*, and as though the *Merlin* wasn't Mountain Wolf's only offering to the 'Mech-starved armies of the Inner Sphere.

Brandon had just, in effect, given the company to Cameron in everything but name. His father was withdrawing, fleeing halfway—more than halfway, in fact—across the Inner Sphere and staying there, to live in Lyran space, with his Lyran wife, to try getting a Lyran facility up and running. The Outworlds Alliance "branch" of the company, which was to say all of the company save their shipping concerns, was suddenly...Cameron's.

Cameron, whose father had *not* informed him of any such possibility, despite the length of their flight, was, frankly, poleaxed by the news.

The Avellars were gracious enough to look away, either glancing at the star map or at each other, giving the O'Learys a moment as it all sank in.

Cameron didn't waste the opportunity, just reached out and shook his father's hand. Brandon returned it, squeezed Cameron's arm with his free hand, and shot his son a wink, as though Cam had been in on it the whole time.

Cameron's head spun; he loved his mother and adored doting on his young nephew, but a great many other Vendrellians—including his half siblings—had always made it clear to him that Cameron wasn't truly one of them, that a graf shouldn't have wed a duchess, that his father's name lowered Olivia Rippon-Hart's rather than being lifted by it. Cameron had taken that O'Leary name as he'd reached legal adulthood for a *reason*. He knew he'd never be accepted as a Rippon-Hart of Vendrell, and at times he worried he'd never be accepted on Vendrell at all. Now...here...on Alpheratz, running one of the most important businesses in the Outworlds Alliance, he'd never have to be accepted by Vendrell. Let his brother be duke someday. Let his brother be Vendrell.

Cameron would be Mountain Wolf BattleMechs.

Brandon smiled warmly, and Cameron didn't doubt for a second that his father knew all of that and more. He pulled his father into an embrace and held it. Cam couldn't find the words he wanted to say, so he didn't try. As they disentangled, Brandon gave him a confident, proud, nod. The Avellars smiled at each other, only a little awkwardly, and Brandon cleared his throat.

Then, slowly and almost formally, Brandon reached across the table and held up one finger.

"Oh, and one last thing, Mr. President. I have every confidence that Cameron will be able to do all of that while *also* receiving your enthusiastic endorsement for the upcoming elections to the Planetary Parliament of Alpheratz. Furthermore, when the *next* elections roll around, once people have gotten to recognize him—and if you genuinely believe he's handled these responsibilities well—I hope you'll consider just as enthusiastically encouraging your people to select him to represent Alpheratz in the Executive Parliament, as well."

There it is. Cameron watched as Brandon shifted his hand and turned that held-up finger into an offered handshake.

It hung over the table. Neil Avellar looked down at it, casting just the slightest look to his wife as he stood stock still. Cameron held his breath, fighting dizziness as his world took a second unexpected turn in as many minutes.

His father had just placed a tremendous amount of trust in him, given him amazing responsibilities, and was stacking the deck in his favor, all in one move. The more Joshuans he successfully, peacefully talked into relocating, and the more smoothly he handled it, the more votes he'd get. Guaranteed. And, crucially, the Parliamentary system of the Outworlds Alliance was a cumbersome beast, demanding unanimous votes for very nearly every step of legislation, including military spending. Having an O'Leary in one of those seats, while running Mountain Wolf, would give Cameron unprecedented opportunities to make certain the company and the nation stayed intertwined.

You said you wanted us to be friends, Neil. Cameron held his breath as he waited for the President's response to this last, crucial offer. *This is how we can prove to you that, exclusivity lifted or not, Mountain Wolf isn't leaving the Outworlds Alliance any time soon. Vendrell will be nice for Father to have, but Alpheratz will stay Mountain Wolf's home. I promise.*

"So. Do we have a deal?" Brandon O'Leary stood stock still, hand out across the desk. "You put some spinward respect on our family name, Mr. President, and we'll go gather up your refugees, relocate their stock, and feed your people."

Cameron stared, waiting to see how much his life would change, how quickly. There was a long pause, then the President reached across the desk and shook his father's hand on it. His wife gave Avellar a little nudge, then Neil offered a shake to Cameron.

Without hesitating, he took it. The bargain was made, the deal was done. The future secured.

Now...I just have to mercy kill a world.

CHAINS: ALTERNATE PILOTS FOR THE CLAN DIRECT FIRE STAR

WUNJI LAU

[Ten alternate pilots for use with *Force Pack: Clan Direct Fire Star*.
Ten lives, ten links.
Sins and virtues, intertwined.]

Gunnery: 3	ARAWAL	Piloting: 4

Rank: MechWarrior
Affiliation: Clan Wolf
Unit: Epsilon Galaxy
BattleMech: *Highlander IIC*

Chains, Part 1: After Aleksandr Kerensky's final assault on Unity City, Jerry Sims was one of the first to enter the long-sealed Audience Chamber. When he saw the charnel house within, his first thought was not horror or grief, but profit. His short-lived looting spree ended in execution, and his plundered keepsakes returned home. All but one: nestled in his *Highlander*, vanished with Kerensky's Exodus. For decades, fatal accidents befell every pilot of that 'Mech until it was finally decommissioned.

Centuries later, Arawal knew nothing of his refurbished 'Mech's history. His backwater raid would help the Wardens to dissuade the Crusaders from their mad rush to Terra, and he would tip the balance, bound by honor and the Way of Kerensky.

Special Pilot Abilities (Cost: 2)
- **Hot Dog:** Apply −1 target modifier for all rolls to avoid overheating effects.

"From gluttony, desolation. From dogma, dissent."

Gunnery: 3	MIREILLE	Piloting: 4

Rank: MechWarrior
Affiliation: Clan Smoke Jaguar
Unit: Zeta Galaxy
BattleMech: *Rifleman IIC*

Chains, Part 2: She believed herself doomed, but the *Highlander IIC* crashed to earth, an unrelenting giant felled by pinpricks. Surely this was proof of the superiority of the Smoke Jaguars! Even a second-line Jaguar might earn a spot in Operation Revival.

In the foe's cockpit, the Wolf pilot lay dead, but a hidden glint drew her eye. A tarnished pendant bearing the ancient Cameron Star crest—and perhaps a hint of blood in its crevices—found its way into her hand, her pocket, then her 'Mech. At its touch, an ignited anger, a rage that seemed to reach across centuries, prompted a renewed vow: her blood heritage would prove itself, and nothing would keep her from reaching Terra.

Special Pilot Abilities (Cost: 2)
· **Jumping Jack:** Reduce Attacker Movement Modifier from +3 to +1 when firing after jumping.

"Take. Us. Home."

Gunnery: 3	HALVORI	Piloting: 3

Rank: MechWarrior
Affiliation: Ghost Bear Dominion
Unit: Theta Galaxy
BattleMech: *Grizzly*

Chains, Part 3: In the rust-yards of Courchevel's Dragon's Rift, the rain-washed pendant glittered. Halvori had not expected to find such a treasure. Here, twelve years ago, the Smoke Jaguars had fought arrogantly, died recklessly. Here, she had expected only silence to accompany her indecision. Should she accept love? Abandon the warrior's path? Trade glory for one perfect desire?

At the pendant's touch, certitude crystallized. Oath-bound to wive the day she took up the bauble, she kept it near for their years of warmth and devotion. Oath-broken the day her beloved vanished in Blakist fire, she gave it to another on the battlefields of Ascella.

Then, only silence to accompany her.

Special Pilot Abilities (Cost: 2)
- **Blood Stalker:** –1 To-Hit Modifier against single enemy (+2 against all others) until enemy retreats or is disabled/destroyed.

"Family. Familiar. Loss. Too familiar."

Gunnery: 2	SLEVE SERNANDEZ	Piloting: 4

Rank: Captain
Affiliation: Stone's Coalition
Unit: Stone's Lament
BattleMech: *Grizzly*

Chains, Part 4: Caged by the Word, freed by the Stone, Sernandez gladly took up arms to end the holy war. Past forgotten, future undreamed of, he wished only to fight alongside his new comrades. Sensing his purpose, a friend passed him a gift with a strange missive: "It wants to go to Terra."

On New Home, he stood firm against onrushing shadows. His broken 'Mech, left as an epitaph; cause for lament for some, avarice for others. The Diamond Sharks paid respect to the body, but kept the trinket they found. One leap from Sol, the pendant traveled outward, Sol receding.

Special Pilot Abilities (Cost: 2)
- **Multi-Tasker:** May make an attack against a secondary target in the front arc at a +0 To-Hit Modifier and in the side or rear arc at a +1 To-Hit Modifier.

"Noble sacrifice. Needless sacrifice."

Gunnery: 4	SHONVIL	Piloting: 3

Rank: Star Captain
Affiliation: Clan Sea Fox
Unit: Fox Khanate
BattleMech: *Phoenix Hawk IIC*

Chains, Part 5: Shonvil's Bloodhouse had scented its prey across the Inner Sphere for decades. She craved not only the glory of her house's name, but also the honor of triumph in the merchants' arena. The chained Cameron Star she wore, passed to her from Sharks to Foxes, guided her hand, or so it seemed.

With every Bloodright duel, every signed contract, she neared her goal, until at last, one final decision awaited: accept one victory, or risk all for two. She lost her final Bloodright duel the same day her carefully orchestrated deal fell through. When she awoke, the star was gone.

Time to begin the climb anew.

Special Pilot Abilities (Cost: 2)

- **Maneuvering Ace:** May make Lateral Shifts. Apply a –1 modifier to Piloting Skill Rolls to avoid skidding.

"Focus and blindness are married by greed."

Gunnery: 3	VENTANNA XUA	Piloting: 5

Rank: Lieutenant
Affiliation: Mercenary
Unit: Kraken Unleashed
BattleMech: *Bane*

Chains, Part 6: Her comrades still called the Sea Fox 'Mech a *Kraken*, but Ventanna cared only that the machine suited her preference for fighting from unassailable range and that its cockpit had contained an odd good-luck charm that called to her. On the regiment's travels, she fought just well enough to escape opprobrium, always at the edge of effort.

Then, one day, as her comrades died in the valley below, she simply turned and walked away. Year by year, she cared less and less, selling her 'Mech, leaving the stained pendant behind, and vanishing into the warren-like slum blocks for the life of freedom she always sought.

Special Pilot Abilities (Cost: 3)

- **Sniper:** Reduce range To-Hit Modifiers by half: +1 for Medium, +2 for Long, and +3 for Extreme.

"'Freedom' is a strange name for fear."

Gunnery: 4	RABTEN HEILIGENBLUT	Piloting: 4

Rank: Leutnant
Affiliation: House Steiner
Unit: Coventry CPM
BattleMech: *Highlander IIC*

Chains, Part 7: He found it in a garbage can. Old, pitted, bent. Like him. He held it tight and clambered into his cockpit. He hung the trinket near. Worn, rusted, tired. Like his 'Mech.

He looked out to the burning skies. Behind him, the Whitting memorial, stone, silent. Before him, the Jade Falcons, enraged, unhinged. To the frightened few with him, he said ancient words, "How can a man die better than facing fearful odds for the ashes of his fathers?" As they stood, so they died; a rampart on which will outlive steel.

The pendant fell to earth. Steadfast, enduring, resolute. Like his duty.

Special Pilot Abilities (Cost: 1)

- **Melee Specialist:** Apply a –1 To-Hit Modifier for physical attack rolls; add 1 point of damage to successful attacks.

"Diligence is laudable for that it is seldom repaid in kind."

Gunnery: 3	RODERICK STEINER	Piloting: 3

Rank: General of the Armies
Affiliation: House Steiner
Unit: Second Royal Guards RCT
BattleMech: *Rifleman IIC*

Chains, Part 8: Seeing the remains of Whitting's defenders, Roderick knew his enemy would give no mercy and deserved only retribution. His comrades told of a charm he carried in the days following, glinting through corrosion, grasped tightly as he crafted a private stratagem, a plan by which the burden of vengeance would be his alone. His struggle was plain, his efforts to hold back his troops' fury halfhearted, his need for honor strained to breaking.

Yet, in single combat, he saved a world. In refusing unheeding reprisal's call, he perhaps saved himself. As the Jade Falcons vanished from Coventry, so journeyed the pendant.

Special Pilot Abilities (Cost: 3)

- **Inspiring Commander:** Steiner may grant the ability to re-roll a failed attack roll three times per scenario. The re-roll must be accepted.

"The honoring of diligence with restraint is rarer yet."

Gunnery: 3	**DAROSZ**	Piloting: 4

Rank: MechWarrior
Affiliation: Clan Jade Falcon
Unit: Delta Galaxy
BattleMech: *Bane*

Chains, Part 9: He had waited decades. Bided his time as his *sibmates* aged and died, in body or in spirit. Suffered the dishonors of Coventry, tight-lipped. At last, though the younger warriors grumbled, he earned his place on the road to Terra and finally perched, a proud Falcon, on the peaks of the homeworld.

Though his 'Mech burned beneath him in the northern forests, he felt no loss, no shame. After such a wait, this was enough. Terra was his, in a way, and he was now Terra's. He held out one hand, a glimmer shining through the blood. To the victor, silhouetted in tears, would go the final steps.

Special Pilot Abilities (Cost: 1)
- **Human TRO:** Add a +1 modifier when rolling on the Determining Critical Hits table.

"In persevering, the road may become the destination."

Gunnery: 3	TSENNA	Piloting: 2

Rank: Star Captain
Affiliation: Clan Wolf
Unit: Beta Galaxy
BattleMech: *Phoenix Hawk IIC*

Chains, Part 10: It is Tsenna's last day as a warrior. The battle for Terra took much from the Wolves, but more from her. Her former comrades and ascended ilKhan may mock her decision, but she knows that with the dawn of a new age, this stage of her life is over.

The laborer caste is welcoming, familial...peaceful. She abandons her 'Mech, carrying one memento, the last bequest of her final opponent. At the newly carved memorial to the Cameron family, she lays the pendant upon white marble. When she looks back, it is gone, perhaps never there to begin with.

She walks away, smiling anew, whispering, "At last, I can rest."

Special Pilot Abilities (Cost: 2)

· **Maneuvering Ace:** May make Lateral Shifts. Apply a –1 modifier to Piloting Skill Rolls to avoid skidding.

"At last, we can rest."

WARSHIP REVIEW QUARTERLY: SLS CALIFORNIA

KEN' HORNER

Namesake: Terran Administrative District
Builder: Krester's Ship Construction
Laid Down: 2682
Launched: 2688
Fate: Destroyed near Mars, 2777

Design

The SLS *California* was a *Texas*-class battleship constructed for the Star League Defense Force. Weighing in at 1.56 million tons, this WarShip spent a hefty 1,782 tons on lamellor ferro-carbide armor, making it one of the toughest WarShips ever launched. The Rolls-Royce Kraken engines gave it impressive thrust, a full G over the *Monsoon* it replaced. The hull was designed to accommodate six DropShips, with a dual set of corridors connecting them with the interior of the WarShip: one set for passengers and a larger set for cargo that led directly to the cargo bays. Three different grav decks were installed, all capable of up to 1.2 G. Typically the larger two were run at 0.5 G, while the smaller deck was set at 0.2 G to allow for a quicker transition to 0 G operations for crew needing to work off the grav decks frequently.

The *California*'s offensive load was borne primarily by energy weapons. Four dozen Omicron class-45 naval lasers were assisted by sixteen Sunspot-3L heavy naval particle projector cannons. The lasers were grouped into a dozen on either broad side and aft section, while the PPCs were in quad bays on the fore and aft sections. Four Killer Whale launchers and eight AR-10 tubes provided missile support, while a pair of massive Winchester-Boeing class-40 naval autocannons provided a huge, close-range punch. All of these weapons were tied together under the MORSAT targeting and tracking system, run by the Communal XXX computer system that also operated the Pathfinder 43CD communication system. In addition to its array of weapons, the *California* carried forty fighters and sixteen small craft.

General Capabilities

The *California* was launched after the introduction of the first *McKenna*-class WarShips in an era when offense was more desirable than defense. Ironically, with its extensive armor protection, the *California* would have been tailor-made for the Succession Wars if any had remained in the Inner Sphere after the Exodus. The *California* served as the reserve flagship for both the Seventy-First Line Squadron and the Seventh Fleet, spending less than five years total in that role when the *Golden Hind* was being refitted. In combat operations, the *California* would lead the squadron into battle while the remaining ships ideally stayed in intermediate range and removed the most dangerous opponents with combined fire. Due to the larger grav decks on the *California*, diplomatic interactions and large fleet gatherings were typically carried out on the *California* instead of the *Golden Hind*.

Deployments

The *California* spent most of its career in the Seventh Fleet, in the Seventy-First Line Squadron, but saw little action prior to the Amaris Coup. During the Periphery Uprising, the *California* was in the Magistracy of Canopus, and the squadron did not come under fire. When the Seventh was mobilized back to retake the Hegemony, the *California* was removed from the Seventy-First and assigned to lead an ad hoc 145th Escort Squadron with ships currently unassigned to any fleet.

The most notable combat action for the *California* was in the opening rounds of Operation Chieftain. The *California*, along with the *Congress*-class *Red Bluff* and *Lola III*-class *Fred T. Berry*, was assigned to provide naval support for the force assigned to liberate Zebebelgenubi. A half-dozen JumpShips loaded with an assault force assembled with the 145th on the edge of Lyran space. While preparing for the attack in the Alphecca system, Captain Angie Partridge found an old classmate, Kaptain Bethany Tannenhauser, in-system commanding the LCS *Richthofen*. Prior to the assault on 21 August, the two captains dined together.

The next day, the attack commenced, but the fleet arrived in the Zebebelgenubi system with the *Tharkad*-class battlecruiser. The ships were almost immediately engaged by the Republican defenders, led by a *McKenna*-class battleship. Formerly the SLS *Jupiter*, the rechristened *Genghis Khan* had been six months into a scheduled two-year refit prior to the Amaris coup. The Republic forces captured the *Genghis Khan* and returned it to service, but were only able to outfit the ship with a squadron of *Samurai* fighters and four more mothballed *Star Dagger*s.

The official report stated Kaptain Tannenhauser had a "brain fart" and input her old classmate's destination into her own navigation computer by accident. Upon arriving in-system, they were immediately attacked, and needed to defend themselves. The three titans engaged, and only the thick armor and two targets saved the allied forces from the formidable firepower of the *Genghis*. The fighter battle quickly went against the Republic forces, and the *Genghis* was unable to effectively abate the harassment from the smaller craft. This was exacerbated when a pair of *Stinger* LAMs landed on the hull of the massive vessel and ripped open a cargo door. The pair briefly unloaded a few salvos of laser fire inside the battleship before fleeing back to the *California*. The *California* accelerated straight at the *Genghis*, weathering a massive barrage with what little armor was left on the nose. At the last minute, the *California* banked, and a salvo of lasers and a massive NAC-40 fusillade cut through the open bay into the bowels of the battleship. Internal explosions and continued fire from the rest of the forces left a smoking hulk behind as the few remaining Republic forces retreated.

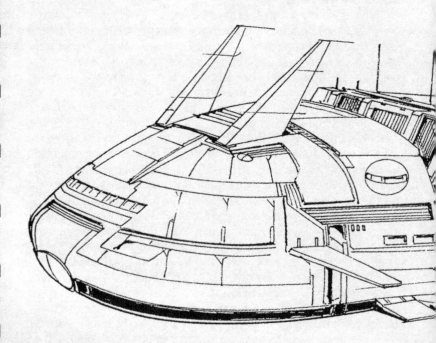

The *California*'s last engagement came in action near Mars in 2777. Assigned to escort a dozen DropShips to the red planet, the task force found itself accosted by six *Caspars*. They attempted to bypass the battleship to attack the smaller DropShips, but the *California* interposed itself between the attackers and its charges. The task force focused all their firepower on one of the *Caspars* and destroyed it. The *Fred T. Berry* then continued its mission while the *California* and *Red Bluff* occupied the attackers. The *California* destroyed two more with a flurry of laser and PPC fire before the WarShip's armor started to fail under the combined fire of the remaining *Caspars*. A furious, final barrage overtaxed the *California*'s cooling systems as the ship was destroyed, but it took two more *Caspars* with it. The last drone sparred with the *Fred T.* until it too was disabled, and the DropShips made their assault on Mars. The *Red Bluff* evacuated the survivors from the *California* and helped the *Fred T. Berry* provide cover for the forces attacking Mars.

Notes

From the *Lemuria*, the *Texas* preceding the *California*, through the next half-dozen *Texas*-class ships, the repair bays were redesigned into a massive repair bay between doors five and six. Designers expected a 12 percent increase in repair efficiency. While the return was not as dramatic, it did reduce repair turnaround. However, as shown with the *Bavaria*, heavy damage to fighters effectively clogged up doors five and six, impeding the ability to rapidly deploy and recover fighters during heavy combat operations.

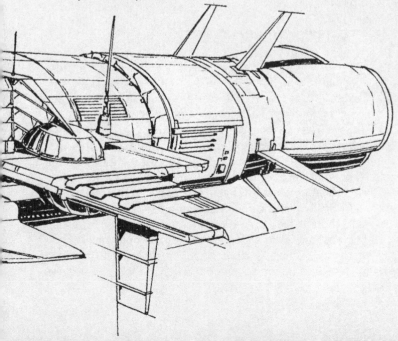

SACRIFICE OF ANGELS

DEVIN RAMSEY

"My brothers and sisters, the hope of the Star League goes with you. May your bravery never be forgotten. Good luck and Godspeed."

—General Aleksandr Kerensky
to the ships of Task Force Leonidas, 26 January 2777

STEFAN AMARIS-CLASS WARSHIP SLS *CHIEFTAIN*
NEAR MARS
TERRA SYSTEM
27 JANUARY 2777
2213 HOURS, TERRA STANDARD TIME

Whenever the crew of the SLS *Chieftain* knew they were going into combat, especially a proper furball, one of the highest-priority tasks was to safely depressurize as much of the vessel as possible before contact with the enemy. It may not have been standard operating procedure for most Star League Defense Force WarShips, but it had become standard practice aboard the *Chieftain* when the crew discovered several corners had been cut during her construction, making keeping the vessel pressurized during combat a greater risk, rather than benefit, to the crew. Preemptive decompression limited explosive decompression risk, and it allowed the ship's environmental systems to capture most—if not all—of the breathable atmosphere that would otherwise be lost when the hull was inevitably perforated. The core sections, however—such as command & control, main engineering, the medical bay, and other critical locations buried deep in the bowels of the ship—*those* remained pressurized.

One errant shot through the hull breaches any of those sections and they'll pop just like anything else, Charlie mused, lost in his own scattered thoughts as he rested on the cusp of consciousness. *Still, the captain's doing the best he can with what he's got.*

For damage control personnel aboard a WarShip, such as Petty Officer First Class Charlie Evans, technician's mate, their stations were placed all over the ship, and they had to be ready to respond to an onboard emergency anywhere. So they suited up and waited for all hell to break loose.

Every crew member's focus had to be on doing their job to the best of their ability to maximize the chances of survival for their crewmates, knowing they were all doing their damnedest to return the favor. Despite this, whenever the fighting got really bad, the unspoken hope everyone shared was for one of two outcomes: survival or a quick death. *Sounds horrible in so many words, but it's just a fact. Suffocation from a suit breach isn't exactly a pleasant way to go, and there are so many worse alternatives.*

With this mission, however, Charlie's hopes were a bit different than the norm. In fact, just about all aboard the *Chieftain* were united in a single hope. It mattered not how quickly or slowly everyone aboard died; all that mattered was how much they could achieve before they inevitably expired.

And it *was* inevitable. Forty ships, led by the *Chieftain*, had been assembled with all-volunteer crews, all of whom shared this same dreadful sentiment. All of this was just so the rest of the Star League Defense Force fleet, beaten and battered as it was, could be given a chance at liberating Terra from that bastard who managed to turn the Star League on its head: the "Usurper," the fat Genghis Khan-wannabe, Stefan Amaris.

It was a point of amusement for the *Chieftain*'s crew that she was a captured WarShip named after the Usurper himself—a *Stefan Amaris*-class battleship. Originally slated to be christened the RWRS *Terens Amaris*, this powerful vessel and another like her were still under construction when they were taken by the SLDF. Recognizing the potential of these valuable assets, General Kerensky had ensured that both ships were completed—but instead of serving Amaris' Rim Worlds Republic, they had SLDF banners painted on their hulls. As a result, the *Chieftain* and her sister ship, the *Vengeance*, were two of the newest vessels in the fleet. Unfortunately, the *Vengeance* was now just a memory, and the *Chieftain* had already seen enough action to look nearly as worn out and beaten down as the rest of the fleet.

Hell, the *Chieftain* had even managed to have an entire military operation named after her—at least, the crew liked to think it was—when the SLDF had started retaking the worlds that had once flown the flag of the Terran Hegemony. The core worlds at the center of the Inner Sphere. The worlds that made up the heart of what was once the Star League.

Now, with the SLDF poised to finally liberate Terra from Amaris' grasp, the *Chieftain* had become the lead WarShip of Task Force Leonidas. No two ways about it, this was a suicide mission, but one undertaken for the sake of the entire Inner Sphere. The fleet of *Caspar* drone WarShips protecting the Terran system had to be drawn away from the planetary approach vectors, opening the door for the rest of the SLDF fleet. It had been learned that the specifics of the *Caspars'* tactical programming dictated it would take at least thirty hostile WarShips in-system to draw the drone fleet away. Fewer than that, and only a fraction of the massive *Caspar* fleet would change its priority to converge on the threat. The forty ships of Task Force Leonidas would ensure that at least thirty successfully made the risky jump to a pirate point.

It seemed the cruelest joke of all that the SLDF fleet now had to overcome the very machines created to ensure no one could ever threaten Terra. All of this because Stefan Amaris had expropriated the Star League from within, and was now using Terra as the seat of his power.

An alarm roused Charlie back to consciousness. "Action stations, action stations. Set condition one throughout the ship. This is not a drill." The XO's voice had long since lost its crispness and excitement from the previous day, when the mission began and Task Force Leonidas had jumped to the Terran system—and straight into hell.

Charlie's eyes opened to the underside of the bunk above him as he stirred. He had passed out in his suit. *If you must sleep in a combat zone in space, doing so in your personal atmospheric suit is generally a wise choice, so long as you remember to plug your suit into the charge and air supply ports by your bunk!* He remembered his drill instructor's words like they had been yelled at him yesterday. They had already saved his life more than once.

Despite her best attempts to mask it, the XO sounded like Charlie felt. Utterly exhausted. His body felt like lead. After twenty-plus hours of near-constant scrambling to repair and keep different critical ship's systems running during and between engagements, he had resorted to taking one of the distributed stim pills. After roughly eight more hours he had crashed out hard, forcing him to get some rest during a lull in the fighting. The wall-mounted chronometer told him it had only been about three hours since he lay down.

When he failed to immediately react to the alert, a passing crewmate—Amber Beauregard, a member of his damage control team—slapped his shoulder, causing him to jerk slightly, confirming life. Smiling down at him, she looked a lot more energetic than Charlie felt, but the black lines under her eyes were darker than ever, and she looked almost pale. There was no question her energy was stim-induced. The tremble in her hands as she exchanged a thumbs-up with him before moving on was a dead giveaway.

Charlie hated the idea of popping another pill, but by this point, counting on adrenaline alone was a lost cause. The human body was never meant to deal with constant stresses over such an extended period, but such was war. Besides, at this point, everyone aboard the *Chieftain* knew how this was going to end.

No reason to hold back now.

As had been drilled into him through years of constant fighting, he checked the comm device on his wrist for breathable atmosphere—as if the other members of the crew walking around the room in various stages of suiting up weren't enough to make its presence clear. After an instinctive stretch that resulted in pleasant pops throughout his sore body, he unbuckled the strap holding him to his bunk and disconnected his suit from the wall. He then twisted his helmet to the side to pop the seal and took in a breath of "fresh" air as he removed the helmet. The air carried a strong scent of burned electronics, the sickly-sweet smell of spilled hot coolant, and the stale odor of sweat.

Topping it all, however, was the scent of blood mixed with cleaning agent.

The crew bunk rooms had been temporarily converted into a triage facility after an inner hull breach in the medical bay about six or seven hours earlier. Fortunately, the damaged facility had been restored shortly before Charlie came here to rest, but there was still blood on the deck from the wounded and dying who had ended up in the makeshift medbay. Someone had clearly started to clean the deck at some point, but judging from the remaining mess, they had been interrupted.

Like many others present who had used the reprieve from battle to get desperately needed rest before they started making horrible, exhaustion-induced mistakes, Charlie was rising far slower than was normal for a ship-wide alert. The occasional murmur aside, almost no one was talking. Everyone was just going through the motions by this point. It was not that everyone was resigned to their fate and just dragging their feet—though surely some were—everyone was so fatigued it was simply the best they could do.

A familiar thrum began to vibrate through the *Chieftain* as her engines slowly ramped up, the increased acceleration resulting in artificial gravity—or "thrust gravity," for short—building to what felt like a little less than 1.5 standard Gs.

Charlie cautiously rose from his bunk with a groan, allowing a moment to calibrate himself to his new "weight," then opened his personal locker. He gazed longingly at the holograph of his wife and son standing with him, all happy smiles, while he took a swig of water to down a stim. He sighed softly as he lowered the water bottle from his lips before taking a deep breath through his nose to fill his lungs fully, despite the unpleasant odors. Shaking his head sharply twice while opening his mouth wide to induce a yawn, he managed to get some natural tears to wet his dry eyes.

Charlie found himself staring at the blood-stained deck, thinking of his family. *Even more blood on—*

A loud *clang* from someone dropping something metallic on the deck elsewhere in the room startled him, breaking his train of thought. With a tiny surge of angry energy, he snatched the holograph of his family from his locker and stuffed it into one of his suit's pockets, pulled out his toolkit, and slammed his locker shut. He quickly checked to make sure everything in his toolkit was in order and all his other supplies were located correctly on his suit.

Satisfied, he refilled his suit's water supply and swapped out his life support pack. Without thinking, he deposited the used unit to be inspected and serviced, then paused. He let out a snort when he remembered that the servicing station for the packs had been obliterated ten hours ago. *Old habits...*

He donned his helmet once more. The seal around his neck clicked reassuringly, and the suit's life support system auto-engaged. "Proxy comm check, one-two," he called.

A chorus of replies from other fully suited people in the room answered him. Unless otherwise selected, the suit-comms functioned in a proximity mode that effectively simulated talking as if unsuited. It was convenient, and it helped the crew to feel more comfortable.

He checked his chronometer and muttered a curse. It had taken him more than four minutes to do what should have taken less than two. Directing frustration into action, he grabbed his toolkit and exited through the airlock into the corridor outside, then headed to his station near the stern of the ship. Halfway there, his stomach growled, causing him to realize he hadn't eaten anything in twelve hours. He muttered another curse, wondering how he had managed such a blatant oversight. Sipping some water was all he could do about it, now.

The body language of most nearby told him he was far from the only one struggling. Although part of him found this comforting, more than anything he was alarmed. *Bloody hellfire, if everyone else is in the same state, we're already dead!* A bit more energy dribbled into his body. Whether it was adrenaline, a bubble of fear, or the stim kicking in, he could neither tell nor care. He was just grateful it let him move faster.

The ship began to shudder with increasingly frequent hull impacts and outgoing weapons-fire. Seconds later, the *Chieftain* bucked from a direct impact up near the ship's bow. From the feel of the impact, it was most likely an aerospace fighter crashing into the ship.

It was pure luck Charlie had just grabbed a railing after releasing another to turn from one corridor to the next. Nevertheless, he lost grip on his toolkit as he faceplanted into the nearest bulkhead. He mumbled incoherent curses as he quickly picked his toolkit back up, grateful it hadn't popped open and emptied itself all over the deck.

At least the surprise impact seemed to finally wake him up.

"Anybody hurt?" someone called out. Everyone in sight paused for a moment to look around, searching for anyone who looked injured and listening for any replies. Those who had fallen were giving thumbs up to indicate they were fine as others helped them to their feet. After a couple seconds of silence, the same voice piped up again, "Alright, get to your stations!"

"Yes, sir!" Charlie and everyone else in the area answered automatically without any knowledge of who or even what rank the individual was.

Charlie soon reached his damage control station: station forty-four, near the starboard engine—engine number four. He exchanged greetings with Hank Childers, Klaus Schumacher, and Amber Beauregard. He turned to greet Benjamin Takei, usually the most punctual of their team, only to remember the Draconis Combine native would never report to his station again. It was just the four of them now.

Three days ago, before Task Force Leonidas' final preparations for the jump to the Terran system, Charlie had mentioned his amusement that their ship number, engine number, and damage control station were all made up of fours. Takei took that moment to point out that the number four, though a different word altogether, was pronounced the same as the word for "death" in Japanese. Clearly sensing the soured mood, Takei then cheered up the rest of the team by sharing a bottle of *sake* he had been saving. What followed had been a great time, just five friends, brought together from totally different walks of life, sharing stories and reminiscing.

Two days later—not even twelve hours ago—Takei had died when something substantial struck the hull. The ship's tough armor didn't breach, but the impact had smashed that spot of the hull inward so badly, it completely crushed the corridor he'd been passing through, killing him instantly. Part of Charlie wished he could have traded places with Takei. Partly because it grieved him that his good friend had died right before his eyes—but also, selfishly, because the death had been so instantaneous.

Charlie rested a hand on the top of Takei's seat. He wondered what Takei would say, now that there were just four of them left alive on the team.

After a short moment of silence, Beauregard's gentle voice filled Charlie's helmet as she put a hand on his shoulder. "He's in a better place."

"I know, it's just—"

His reply was cut off as a severe impact nearby caused the ship to buck sharply to the side, knocking them all to the deck as the overhead lights cut out, leaving the room faintly illuminated only by the damage control board's displays for a second before the emergency lighting engaged.

Even as everyone was saying they were all right, the deck started vibrating unusually. The vibration built for several seconds, then suddenly stopped. At the same time, the thrust gravity significantly weakened to what felt like just under one G, which meant the ship's acceleration had been greatly reduced. The four of them exchanged worried glances before looking at the damage control board. Seeing red lights popping up in the display for their section, they immediately scrambled to their feet.

"Damage control to starboard engine!"

Charlie, Schumacher, and Childers were already out the door and into the corridor, toolkits in hand, before the XO had finished giving the command. Meanwhile, Beauregard remained behind in the damage control room, having tied herself into the suit comms of the three mobile team members to provide support. Her reply from the damage control room was crisp, "DC four-four responding!"

Seconds later, the three entered the forward compartment for the starboard engine and collectively cursed as they took in the sight. The entire compartment had been blown wide open. The ship's thick hull had not just been breached, but savagely ripped away, exposing the entire section to space. It was a grim reminder why so much of the ship was depressurized prior to entering combat. It also left the compartment seemingly illuminated almost as much by the intense fighting outside as the remaining emergency lights inside.

There were casualties. There were supposed to be four engineers in this compartment and two in the next. Seeing the carnage before him, Charlie was suddenly grateful for his empty stomach. He was also glad he did not know any of these engineers personally.

Two motionless bodies were on the deck, with far more than just their suits shredded. Two others were desperately trying to free a third, a struggling woman pinned to the inboard bulkhead by a warped piece of exterior hull that had been ripped free and hurled across the compartment. A burst of dazzling particle projection cannon fire outside drew his eye to the hull breach, where he spotted a dismembered arm wrapped up in a ripped wiring harness near the edge of the giant hole in the ship. Unfortunately, that accounted for all six.

"Evans here. The forward compartment's breached. Two confirmed dead, one is...mostly missing. Fair to say that one's dead, too. One engineer is pinned and likely injured, but alive. Two engineers, presumably from the next compartment, are trying to free her. We're assisting," Charlie reported to Beauregard as he and the others quickly moved to help free the trapped woman.

"I'm losing air! I'm losing air!" She cried out repeatedly, flailing about in a panic as the others tried to free her. There was indeed air flowing from somewhere, made visible only by the red-tinted vapor escaping her suit with it, but none of them could see the source. It was concealed by the big chunk of dislodged hull armor pinning her against the wall.

"Evans, I've gone ahead and—" Beauregard began.

"Wait one," Charlie interrupted.

"Hang on! We've got you! Stop flailing, or you'll rip your suit even more!" Childers shouted at the panicking, trapped woman, grabbing her hands to steady her.

Looking over the shape of the panel, Charlie quickly did the math, then told everyone else where to grab onto the heavy panel before grabbing it himself. "All right! On three! One, two, three!"

All of them pulled in unison. The mass of jagged metal budged slightly, then stopped. Even with the reduced thrust gravity aboard the ship, it was heavy as hell.

"Again!" Charlie shouted. Everyone tried to better brace themselves for slightly increased leverage. "One! Two! *Three!*"

This time it shifted more, moving just enough for the engineer to slip out and collapse to the deck.

The large rip across the engineer's thigh was immediately visible. A fair amount of blood was escaping with the pressurized air, lightly splattering over everyone else. She was doing the best she could to try to cover the tear in her suit and reduce the volume of escaping air to little avail.

"Hold it together so I can patch it!" Charlie opened a pouch on his belt and pulled out one of his two suit patches. Kneeling, he stripped off the adhesive backing and carefully applied the patch over the tear, quickly patting it down. He repeated the process with his second patch when the first didn't cover the entire tear. Mercifully, that stopped the leak. He made a mental note to grab more suit patches from the supply cabinet as soon as he was done fixing whatever needed to be fixed.

Charlie made eye contact with the hyperventilating engineer while placing one hand atop hers and another on her shoulder. "Hey! *Hey!* You're all right..." He read her nametag. "...Williams. Calm down. Slow breaths. You're okay. You've still got..." He checked her forearm for her air supply readout. "...about twenty minutes' worth of air left. You'll be okay, so long as you don't gulp it all down here and now."

He felt a hand on his shoulder. The room was illuminated with a strobe-like effect from a volley of missiles zipping by outside as he looked up to Schumacher standing over him. The tall Lyran spoke softly, "Evans, we don't have time for this. The *Chieftain* is already down to three engines. She'll not survive long on two, now."

Charlie looked from Schumacher to Childers and the other two engineers, and then he remembered he had told Beauregard to stand by. *What the hell are you doing, Charlie?!* He had let the sight of a crewmate in distress take his focus off the real task at hand—saving the ship. He hoped the delay hadn't doomed them all. "DC four-four. Evans here. Sorry, Beauregard, we had an engineer in distress. Go ahead."

"I registered a severe drop in hydrogen pressure to the starboard engine, so I cut the pumps. How bad is it in there?" she asked.

The damage was severe. The entire starboard side of the compartment and then some was just *gone*. Wreckage was scattered all over the deck, and several damaged consoles and conduits were sparking. Charlie immediately spotted the cause of the hydrogen pressure drop Beauregard had mentioned. Not far from the breach, two of the engine's hydrogen lines were damaged and vapor was visibly escaping—though the pressure was already rapidly dropping with the pumps shut off.

"It's...It's a wreck down here. Do me a favor and cut power to the central and starboard side instrument panels and lighting for this compartment. Missing parts don't need power anymore, and the last thing we need is to touch a live wire." He motioned to Hank. "Childers, give me a hand patching up these hydrogen feeds."

While he waited for Beauregard to acknowledge, he stood up and retrieved a pair of pressure pipe patch kits from a nearby storage locker that was fortunately still intact, though the door had been smashed and partly ripped open. He handed one of the repair kits to Childers, then quickly read the names on the uninjured engineers' suits—Samuels and Jameson—and turned to Schumacher. "Looks like the deck is still mostly intact, but take Jameson and check the next compartment for additional damage." The vast majority of the engine was under the deck they were standing on, and they needed to make sure there wasn't more extensive damage below.

Schumacher nodded curtly before heading down, engineer in tow.

Beauregard came back a few seconds later. "All right, that's done. What else?"

"It looks like the damage is localized mostly to this compartment. Waiting on Schumacher's report—"

Schumacher piped up. "Damage seems generally contained to the forward engine room. Very little down here." He paused, then groaned softly. "Though it seems we'll need to fix a thing or two. Couple-few minutes, tops."

"Anything you need me to do?" Beauregard asked.

"*Nein*, it's straightforward enough, though Jameson will require my help." Schumacher sounded confident, and that was good enough for the rest of them.

Samuels, the other uninjured engineer, piped up from a barely functional diagnostic console. "Between the severed control signal and the drop in hydrogen pressure, it looks like the engine shut down automatically." He glanced at the wrecked consoles to either side of him. "Unfortunately, with so little working around here, I'm a bit limited in what I can see. I could use some help with diagnostics."

"You get that, Beauregard?" Charlie asked.

"Yeah, I got it. He's right. The engine's completely powered down. From what I can tell from here, the primary control circuit's shot. Good news is at least part of the backup circuit is still working, because I'm getting status info from the engine through that. However, by the looks of it, none of the commands are being received by the engine through that channel, either. Damaged electrical connection?"

Just as Samuels nodded at Beauregard's assessment, the ship was struck heavily, not far forward of/above the breached engine compartment. The room lurched violently to the side, throwing everyone to the deck, as roughly a dozen small pieces of debris rocketed into the compartment from outside, mostly lodging themselves in the deck, followed by a sizeable chunk of ruined hull floating past and away. It was a chilling reminder to everyone that the ship was still in the middle of a pitched firefight.

Charlie looked around the room after getting back up to his knees. Samuels and Williams seemed to be moving just fine, and he didn't see any visible signs of further suit breaches among them. "Everyone okay?"

The three engineers and Schumacher replied. Childers did not. Charlie turned around to see Childers motionless on the deck, facedown, atmosphere escaping rapidly where his helmet's visor should be. "Childers?!"

Silence.

"Hank!" he shouted as he leaped over to roll Childers onto his back. He immediately knew Childers would never reply. His face was unrecognizable, a piece of debris having punched straight through his visor and deep into his skull.

"*Shit!*" Charlie howled in anger and frustration.

"What?" Beauregard asked, alarmed.

Taking a deep breath and blinking away the tears trying to form, Charlie answered with a sigh. "Childers is gone. He's dead."

"*Scheiße!*" Schumacher hissed from the next compartment. Beauregard was silent.

Seeing Samuels and Williams suddenly standing still and looking dumbstruck, Charlie growled at them, "Hey! You two! Get the engine's controls restored! I'll fix the hydrogen lines! *Go!*"

The angrily barked command seemed to shake them free of whatever fog had descended over them, and they scrambled back to work, though Williams was understandably limping and moving slowly. Part of him wondered if he should have recommended a tourniquet.

As Charlie returned to repairing the damaged hydrogen lines, the *Chieftain* shifted sharply around them. She had been struck somewhere along her port-side aft, likely around her long-dead engine. *At least no more harm can be done there,* he thought, grateful he'd managed to keep his feet under himself this time.

Between the various impacts and the helmsman's attempts to rotate and pivot the *Chieftain* using her remaining maneuvering jets, the ship was constantly moving in unpredictable ways. Despite this, it took him less than a minute to get the first wrap-around pipe patch placed and latched together, as well as clamped down at both ends, thanks to the electric impact gun from his toolkit. "One line fixed, one to go."

The ship suddenly lurched hard forward—upward, from their perspective—nearly dropping everyone to the deck once more and forcing Charlie down to his knees. Then he felt something that made his blood run cold. The constant thrumming vibrations of the ship's remaining engines stopped altogether, and he suddenly began to feel weightless at the same time.

"What the hell is going on, Beauregard?!" he yelled as he scrambled for a handhold on the deck. Failing to find one, he instinctively engaged his magnetic boots to anchor himself as the scrap scattered all over the deck started to slowly rise, no longer held down by the force of the ship's thrust.

"Engines one and three just took a direct hit! They're...they're *gone!*" she exclaimed, stunned.

With engine two long-dead many hours ago, the loss of engines one and three meant engine four was the *Chieftain*'s only remaining intact engine, and even that was assuming—"What about four? Any of the readouts you've got showing additional damage?"

A projectile of some kind struck a piece of the bowed-out hull at the edge of the breach, ripping it clean off and sending debris darting across the room. A palm-sized piece of shrapnel sliced cleanly through the very tip of his right boot, taking just a bit of rubber with it as it buried itself in the deck plating.

Charlie took a slow step back and stared for a few seconds in stunned silence before noticing out of the corner of his eye that Samuels had stopped moving. He was still rooted to the deck by his magnetic boots in a roughly standing position, but debris had visibly claimed him as well, as his body was no longer in one piece. "We've lost Samuels."

"Understood," Schumacher said through clenched teeth, physical exertion in his voice.

A moment later, Beauregard spoke up. "Good news is engine four appears to be intact, bad news is we still don't have control over it."

Before Charlie could mutter a curse, Williams spoke up in a very winded-sounding voice. "You should...have it now."

"Checking! Stand by," Beauregard replied.

"Williams, where are you?" Charlie asked as he realized she was nowhere in sight, and it sounded like she was on the verge of passing out.

"Service crawlspace... Suit ripped again..." She sounded like she was straining to verbalize anything, and her voice was getting weaker with each word.

He was pretty sure he knew where this was going. She'd had relatively little air in her suit as it was. "How bad?"

"Bad." It was a miracle Williams' microphone picked up her voice at all, it was so quiet. "Keep..."

He listened intently for a few seconds, waiting for something, *anything* more, but there was nothing. "Thank you, Williams. We'll take it from here." He desperately wanted to smash something or even scream, but there was no time for it. Giving up on the search for the kit Childers had been carrying, Charlie retrieved the last pressure pipe repair kit from the locker while he waited for Beauregard to confirm the control fix had done the trick.

A cold chill ran down his spine when he looked back and realized where he would have to position himself to make the second pipe repair—right on the edge of the massive hole in the hull. He swallowed dryly as it occurred to him for the first time since entering the compartment that, despite being technically inside the ship with mag-boots, everyone should have been using safety tethers this entire time because of the hull breach. He quickly pulled out a tether from a larger pouch on his belt and clipped it to a dedicated ring built into the deck. "What's the word, Schumacher?"

"*Alles gut* here, but we should stay to monitor the fixes during engine startup." Schumacher sounded relieved. Clearly whatever needed fixing had turned out to be more of a handful than he thought it would be. At least it had been quick.

As Charlie grabbed the now-floating pipe repair sleeve and clamps, Beauregard came back with, "All right! Whatever she did, the backup control circuit's fully restored. How long before we have hydrogen?"

Squatting down into a position where he was nearly straddling a part of the jagged, ripped-open hull, Charlie began wrapping the repair sleeve around the pipe. "Give me sixty seconds, then fire it up." He latched the sleeve together and started to slip the first clamp over one end.

"Understood."

Charlie nodded at her reply, threading the bolt into the first clamp. Fumbling with the impact gun was already a bit of a challenge with the suit's gloves, but it hadn't presented too much trouble during the first pipe repair. This time, with the unusual angle he had to hold himself at to keep his mag-boots in contact with a surface to anchor himself, combined with the lack of thrust gravity and the ship still jerking around from repeated impacts, it was proving more difficult than expected. After nearly ten seconds of fumbling, he managed to get the impact gun's socket onto the bolt head. With a long pull of the trigger, the bolt tightened down rapidly and clamped shut one end of the pipe patch.

It was when he reached for the second clamp that he realized, during the moment he had focused on getting the gun onto the bolt, the other clamp had disappeared. His heart skipped a beat as he saw it floating away from him, out into the great beyond. "Oh, *shit*!" he cried out, immediately disengaging his magnetic boots and leaping out to grab it.

"What's wrong?" Beauregard called.

His hasty attempt to grab the clamp only resulted in clipping it with the tip of one of his fingers, sending it spinning with increased velocity. It was still moving slightly slower than he was, so he got a second chance to grab it, this time bouncing it back directly toward his head. He instinctively swatted both hands against his helmet's visor hard enough he was surprised not to see it crack. He breathed a sharp sigh of relief as he glared at the heavy clamp right in front of his face. He quickly got a firm grip on it with one hand and reached for his tether with the other.

"Evans, what's wrong?!" Beauregard repeated.

"Nothing, it's fine," he answered as he pulled himself back inside, landing a couple seconds later and re-engaging his mag-boots.

A sharp explosion sent a shudder through the deck just as he swiftly repositioned himself to finish the repair. As he removed the bolt from the clamp so he could slip it over the open end of the pipe patch, he realized he was cutting it too close. "Just give me fifteen more seconds!"

There was no reply.

"Beauregard, do you copy? I need more time!" he called, worry taking hold as he set the clamp in place.

Silence was the only reply.

"Beauregard?! Amber!" he called out, fumbling the bolt. "Schumacher, can you hear me?"

"*Ja*, but I don't think she can. Beauregard, do you read?"

With nothing but deafening silence answering them, Charlie felt panic begin to grip him.

He managed to get the bolt threaded, but just as he did, he felt a shudder through the pipe. To his horror, pressurized hydrogen began to pump through the pipe with extreme force, blasting out through the open side of the sleeve. The repair sleeve started to shift slightly, the pressure beginning to move it along the pipe. If it moved too far before he clamped it down, it would never seal.

Grabbing his impact gun, he hastily tried to get the socket seated onto the big bolt, but missed. Much to his relief, it slipped snugly over the bolt head on the second attempt. He immediately squeezed the trigger with all his might and held it.

A cluster of small, fast-moving objects at the edge of his vision caught his attention. They rapidly grew closer. He cursed inwardly as he realized what they were. Enough of them had flown by earlier.

He felt the gun torque hard against his grip, the bolt clamping the sleeve shut just as the wave of long-range missiles struck the hull aft of his location. At least one hit close enough that he was caught by the edge of the blast. In a flash, he was hurled from the ship, his tether instantly snapping.

It took him a moment to get over the shock, his surroundings having gone from dimmed compartment lighting to a blinding flash to the black of space. However, once his vision cleared, he began to see the flashy commotion of battle all around him once more.

The *Chieftain's* last remaining engine flared to life, the ship slowly beginning to accelerate forward, leaving Charlie behind. He knew then that his repairs had somehow held—and so had everyone else's.

As he floated out into open space, his final duty fulfilled, Charlie clutched at a dull ache that began to form in his side. He looked down to discover a sizeable tear in his suit. He covered it with his left forearm and hand, managing to slow but not stop the escaping air. Along with the air, there was a significant amount of blood bubbling out over his glove. With a chill, he realized he had no suit patches left. Looking down farther, however, he knew it would not have mattered. There were multiple suit breaches from shrapnel, with red-colored vapor slowly seeping out through several of them.

"Well...shit," he whispered. He was finished, but he had made it count for something. There was nothing more he could do.

He pulled out the holograph of his family with his right hand and smiled sadly at the image. *Even more blood on Amaris' hands*, he finally finished his thought from earlier.

At the end of 2766, Charlie's wife Maria and their son Paul had been on Terra with his sister, Jennifer, spending time with Charlie's parents while visiting Rome. Charlie was not religious, never had been, but

Maria had been raised Roman Catholic, and she had insisted on Paul seeing the home of her religion. As Terra was literally the safest place in the Inner Sphere, and he knew it would make her happy, Charlie saw no harm in it. Besides, Paul loved ancient architecture, and seeing the Sistine Chapel would surely be a highlight of his teenage years. Charlie had wished he could have gone with them, but duty called. At least Charlie had been smart enough to get the one quick holograph of the three of them together.

That was roughly eleven years ago, and it was the last time Charlie had received any word about them—until two weeks ago, when he got a message from Jennifer. It had taken more than half a decade for the message to find its way to him, and Charlie could only guess at the journey it had taken. He only knew it was a miracle to get news from Terra at all—even news several years out of date. Like anyone else in his position, he had been overjoyed when presented with a message from his family.

However, the news was...

He wished he had paid closer attention to the sadness in the intelligence officer's voice when she had handed him the message. He had thought it was jealousy on her part. He couldn't have been more wrong.

It turned out that Charlie's family had all been trapped in Rome with his parents when Amaris seized power. When Amaris' lapdogs, the Greenhaven Gestapo, attacked the Papal States in 2770, they had sacked Rome for some quick cash. Maria, Paul, and both of Charlie's parents lost their lives just because they happened to be passing near a hunger-strike demonstration on their way to a shelter after Charlie's parents' home was destroyed. His parents were crushed underfoot by a Gestapo 'Mech, while both Maria and Paul had been partially buried under rubble when a building was felled by the same 'Mech.

Jennifer had been forced to watch them slowly die as she stayed with them—barely resisting the urge to run away—and managed to keep them company, all while cradling her own badly broken arm.

Adding salt to the wound, the message he received from Jennifer had not actually been sent by his sister. A scavenger with a conscience had discovered her noteputer on a corpse and found several messages waiting to be sent. The individual had apparently been burdened by hundreds of messages like this, gathering them until a chance to finally send them off presented itself.

When Charlie opened that message... In that moment, his world imploded. Any hope of seeing his family again had been shattered. He hadn't really cared about the politics of the war. He had just wanted to see it come to an end so he could be with his family. He had been fighting for over a decade with just that one goal keeping him going.

Something in him had snapped.

It suddenly felt so very personal.

He was unsure if it was some part of his mind desperately latching onto another form of motivation or just because he wanted revenge—or both—but his new goal was single-minded. Stefan Amaris, and those who supported him, had to pay. Charlie did not care if it was by his hand or another, he would do anything to make sure it happened.

So, when the call for volunteers for Task Force Leonidas was sent out, Charlie immediately replied, only to discover the ship he already served on was going to be leading it.

The bright flash of an SLDF WarShip exploding nearby drew his gaze away from the *Chieftain*. He realized with a deep pang of sorrow that it was the SLS *Maloo*, a *Kimagure*-class cruiser. Charlie had been assigned to the *Maloo* for nearly a decade before being transferred to the *Chieftain*. He had many fond memories of that ship. And now she was gone. Worse still, he couldn't spot any escape craft near what was left of her. He hoped he was just too far away to see them.

Charlie turned his attention back to the *Chieftain*. The once-proud WarShip was shot to hell and gone. More than half her hull was ripped wide open, and coolant was bleeding into space from burst heat sinks all over the ship. Flames were belching from deep inside where several pressurized sections of the vessel had been breached and were venting atmosphere into combustible fuel sources.

She was dying. No two ways about it, the poor girl had simply taken too much, and had reached the point of no return. And yet, as though powered by the sheer willpower of her crew alone, the *Chieftain* pushed forward.

A thrill of mixed pride, horror, and sadness filled him as Charlie watched the *Chieftain* fight on, her last engine throttling up to maximum. She destroyed another drone WarShip as her starboard guns fired their last, an internal explosion rippling down her starboard side and destroying what little recognizable hull remained.

Then he saw it. Another *Caspar* drone WarShip on an intercept course with the *Chieftain*.

No, he realized with a start, *the other way around*. The *Chieftain* had put herself on an intercept course with *it*!

He barely had time to comprehend what was about to happen before the *Chieftain* rammed directly into the middle of the *Caspar* drone. For a split second, the two tremendous ships merged into each other, the two giant masses of metal mangling one another before the drone vessel's keel snapped under the force of the impact, the automated WarShip breaking in two. Even broken as it was, the *Caspar* WarShip continued to fire relentlessly, not caring that it had been literally snapped in half.

For the briefest of moments, it seemed like the *Chieftain* would simply keep going, as though even that horrible collision would not break the giant vessel. But then a small flare of light aft of the impact zone became visible. Three more flares rapidly dotted down the ship's spine as they grew in intensity—before a near-blinding flash took the place of the *Chieftain* as she violently blew apart as she passed between the halves of the bisected drone ship.

The explosion quickly faded, allowing him to see the results. His eyes widened as he watched the two halves of the wrecked drone vessel tumble away, propelled in opposite directions by the exploding *Chieftain* between them. One half kept going, with nothing visible in its path. The other half, however, smashed straight into yet another *Caspar* drone—the same vessel that had destroyed the *Maloo*, no less. The ship maneuvered to avoid the collision, but its aft quarter was struck hard. The impact crushed the drone's engines and must have struck an ammunition magazine, because a split-second later the aft section of the vessel detonated.

A small piece of debris smacked into Charlie's face shield, cracking it, and startling him. With that, all nearby was suddenly calm. Though there were still distant flashes of the continuing battle elsewhere, most of them were barely larger than the stars that filled the void around him.

He began to feel dizzy and weak, and he was already completely numb. The stars and flashes of light faded from sight, leaving him with nothing but the dimming image of the glowing holograph in his hand. His air supply was nearly gone, but the combination of severe trauma, blood loss, and exposure was killing him even faster.

Well, Maria, you were the one who always said you believed in life after death. I never really believed it, but... Hell, if it turns out you were right all this time, I hope I see you and Paul real soon.

The holograph slipped from his grasp as his consciousness joined the inky black space all around him.

UNIT DIGEST:
TARANTULAS BATTALION

ZAC SCHWARTZ

Nickname: The Goliath Birdeaters (3129) / Tanaka's Tarantulas (3152)
Affiliation: Wolf's Dragoons
CO: Major Emily Tanaka
Average Experience: Veteran/Fanatical
Force Composition: 30 BattleMechs, 30 Zibler hovertanks, 150 Elementals, 20 aerospace fighters
Unit Abilities: Tactical Specialization/Attack (see p. 87, *Campaign Operations*)
Parade Scheme: Crimson with cyan highlights

UNIT HISTORY

Tarantulas Battalion began as part of an experiment conceived by General Siena Cameron of Wolf's Dragoons. Raised on Arc-Royal in 3129, they were second in a series of striker battalions: smaller, more flexible formations built to accomplish objectives where a regiment would be overkill. Conceived as a force mixing battlesuit-toting OmniMechs with hovertanks and close air support, they proved highly effective against the Jade Falcons during their years on that front. When Cameron retired, Thomas Brubaker, a member of the Spurs movement that favored the Dragoons leaving their longtime Lyran employ, assumed command. The strikers soon found themselves thriving in a new environment: the rough-and-tumble chaos of the Draconis Reach.

Major Evan Rochelle, the battalion's pugnacious first commander, led the Tarantulas to glory in the Draconis Combine's employ. As the Dragoons swept across the Reach during the late 3130s, the Tarantulas were at the tip of the spear. From their capture of Marlowe's Rift's capital Ashoka to breaking a battalion of the Tenth Avalon Hussars on Misery, they were Wolf's Dragoons' ace in the hole time and again. Rochelle preferred leading from the front, with his *Linebacker* often seen in the thick of battle.

Unfortunately, this instinct served him poorly during the Battle of New Avalon in 3146. Leading a charge against the vulnerable flank of the Second Robinson Rangers, Major Rochelle's battalion savaged the Davions, but at the cost of their hard-charging commander's life. A former captain from Wolfsbane Battalion, Eric Gamble, assumed command. Under Major Gamble, the unit's tactics shifted toward an emphasis on hitting their opponent from unexpected directions. They hardly had time to hone this new playbook, however, as the Combine began shifting the Dragoons to garrison posts in the deep salient known as the Dragon's Tongue. Soon, conflict with their employers arose, then the Clan Wolf emissary, Marotta Kerensky, arrived on Parma and convinced the Dragoons to exercise their escape clause and travel to Terra to fight Malvina Hazen's Jade Falcons.

The Tarantulas and Wolfsbane Battalions, stationed on nearby Monroe, didn't learn of the "training accident" on Parma until a JumpShip arrived a week later, with orders from Brubaker to pack up the Dragoons' dependents and escort them to Savannah, in the Free Worlds League. In a fit of cosmic coincidence, Monroe was also garrisoned by the Ryuken-*san*, descendants of the brigade first trained by Jaime Wolf's Dragoons. The Ryuken, mistakenly believing the Dragoons were simply abandoning their contract, moved to stop them. But Majors Gamble and Castle had anticipated this and expertly intercepted them with a double envelopment that led to their swift surrender.

Kerensky's offer proved to be a poison pill: the Falcons were stopped, but at a terrible cost to the Dragoons. Eighty percent of the brigade lay dead on Terra, and the ilKhan cast the survivors aside, leaving them to limp to the rendezvous at Savannah. Tarantulas Battalion and Wolfsbane Battalion were now their only combat-effective forces. Their new commander, Colonel Hack Kincaid, reoriented Wolf's Dragoons around a single, burning desire: to see Alaric Ward brought low.

Securing an arrangement with Captain-General Nikol Marik that gave them funding and a base of operations on the abandoned world of Ilion, Kincaid immediately set to work making trouble for Clan Wolf. In July of 3151, a sizable Dragoons flotilla jumped to New Olympia, dispatching Tarantulas Battalion to the surface. The Allison MechWarrior Institute now produced *sibkos* for the Wolf Empire Touman, and the cadet Cluster eagerly accepted the mercenaries' offer to meet their opposite number in battle on the following day. Once battle was joined, Major Gamble sprung his trap: thirty purpose-configured Ziblers streaked out of hiding and hosed down the cadets' BattleMechs with white-hot

plasma. With so many cadets piloting outdated 'Mechs lacking modern heat-dissipation systems, most of the Cluster was crippled or disabled outright. Their mission accomplished, the Tarantulas collected the cadets, instructors, and their 'Mechs as *isorla* and departed.

To capitalize on their initiative, the Tarantulas moved on to nearby Campbelton. Flush with confidence from their victory on New Olympia, they were unprepared for what awaited them. Upon debarking from their DropShips outside the capital of Atholville, they were immediately hit by barrages of Long Tom artillery, followed by rotating hit-and-fade attacks by two Supernova Binaries. Major Gamble was badly injured when his *Vulture* was swarmed by Wolf Elementals, and Captain Norton of Bravo Company was killed by a direct cockpit hit from an artillery shell, with Bravo taking heavy losses. With Dragoon lives at a premium, the ranking officer, Captain Haya Tetsuhara, elected to withdraw.

With the Dragoons using their *isorla* cadets and the mountain of salvage from Terra to rebuild, Eric Gamble was transferred to command a battalion of the reconstituted Epsilon Regiment, and Captain Tetsuhara was promoted to command the re-formed Zeta Battalion. This left the

Tarantulas to serve under newly minted Major Emily Tanaka, former captain of Alpha Company. Tanaka was a lance commander only two years prior, and has struggled with the challenge of leading such a large force. While they rebuild and wait for their next assignment, Tanaka has been putting the Tarantulas through their paces on Ilion, conducting as many intramural simulated battles as she can to get more practice managing an entire striker battalion in the field.

COMPOSITION

When the Tarantulas were assembled in 3129, they followed the template set by General Cameron: three Stars of fast heavy and assault OmniMechs, three Stars of Elementals, fifteen hovertanks, and a wing of aerospace fighters. Transportable by a single *Odyssey*-class JumpShip, the striker battalions could engage in the kind of rapid planet-hopping campaign the Blackout had made so difficult to defend against. The lower proportion of 'Mechs on the battlefields of the 3130s meant few opponents could defend against these attacks.

By the 3140s, the paradigm had shifted. With 'Mech factories coming back online across the Inner Sphere, the Dragoons had to up the ante. Like their sister battalions, the Tarantulas doubled their ground forces, expanding to the size of a full Clan Cluster. Still backed by a fighter wing, the unit's upgrade to larger DropShips allowed them to use the same JumpShip, retaining their strategic flexibility.

INFAMOUS ARMS DEALERS

ALEX FAUTH

OvKhan,
*   I acquired this report during one of my own investigations and thought it might be of interest to us. While we may be big fish, it is also a vast ocean, and we would do well to know who else we are swimming with. These groups may be threats to our profits, but the potential exists to turn them into opportunities.*

—Watch Agent Shawn, Gamma Aimag, Tiburon Khanate,
1 June 3151

DAVID BOTTEGER

A self-made man, David Botteger made his fortune preying on the uncertainty caused by Gray Monday and its aftermath. Getting his start selling small arms to fearful homeowners and operating out of lawless Free Zones, Botteger saw his business bloom as the Lyran Commonwealth's economy faltered and the HPG blackout saw no sign of ending.

When the Commonwealth was ravaged by the Jade Falcons and the Wolves, Botteger stepped up his business, selling weapons to everyone from planetary governments to merchant crews. His biggest break came when he was able to make contacts within the Lyran Commonwealth Armed Forces, and began supplying line units Tharkad could not afford to look after. The recent aggression by the Hells Horses and Rim Territories has only helped to further expand his markets, with fear of the aggressive Periphery realm serving as a strong incentive.

Presently, Botteger presides over a business empire that stretches across the coreward Commonwealth, and he has recently begun making inroads into the Hinterlands. His operations are largely focused around selling small arms and other "civilian" equipment such as armored cars and the like. Aside from those military contacts, his biggest areas of growth have been in planetary militia units and private security firms.

Entirely unsubtle, Botteger revels in his newfound wealth. He maintains a palatial estate on Adelaide stocked with fine foods, elaborate furnishings, customized luxury vehicles, and a menagerie of exotic creatures, all surrounded with his own personal security force. He maintains a high profile, clearly enjoying the publicity without being afraid of the consequences of his actions. All of this suggests he may have powerful backers or, at the very least, some very pliable allies.

MANTISTIQUE AND ASSOCIATES

For decades, the planet Wilkes remained an independent world within the former Free Worlds League, a situation Mantistique and Associates took full advantage of. The group set up shop during the Jihad, when they, out of common desperation, sold low-quality weapons to terrified clients throughout the League. After the nation's collapse at the end of that conflict, they took advantage of Wilkes' independence and lack of federal regulatory oversight to produce and sell weapons across the former League.

Unashamedly profit driven, the company used the often-chaotic situation among the former League's independent worlds to their fullest advantage. They would gladly supply both sides of a conflict if the money was good, and showed no concerns about dealing with pirates. It was not uncommon for raiders armed with Wilkes-made weapons to face militias also using weapons from the same supplier. For their part, the Wilkes government turned a blind eye toward the trade, the result of both hefty bribes and the benefits the lucrative sales brought to the economy.

Wilkes' rejoining the League in 3151 has been a blow to the company. The reborn League brought a measure of stability to the region, which cost them many of their buyers. Meanwhile, the greater oversight of the new League compared to its predecessor does not bode well for the company's practices. There are rumours circulating that they are considering relocating to the Magistracy of Canopus or even the Marian Hegemony rather than risk being called to account.

SMYTHE-JONES FAMILY

The Smythe-Jones family did an excellent job of hiding their operations through an innocuous front operation. It is only with the collapse of the Republic that the full extent of their arms network has come to light.

Operating since at least the turn of the century, the Smythe-Jones family hid their dealings under the cover of the Tharonja's chain, a popular restaurant franchise that had branches across the Republic. Under the cover of their legitimate operations, they moved weapons, munitions, and more, selling to any parties they felt they could trust to remain discreet. It is now known they were dealing with Jacob Bannson before the Blackout, and it is believed they had a hand in arming many of the smaller groups that rose up in its immediate aftermath. However, they also carefully managed their business assets to create enough deniability between the two sides of the organisation that they could "burn" the arms dealings if needed and continue to profit off Tharonja's as an entirely legitimate business.

By pure happenstance, the leadership of the family business was outside Prefecture X when the Fortress Walls went up. While they took a hit on losing the literal core of their empire, they were able to continue operating both their legitimate and criminal dealings as the Republic crumbled, profiting off the continually escalating conflicts around the former nation. Under the current leadership of Rainbow Smythe-Jones and her wife (and reported head chef) Leanne, the family has established solid toeholds in all five Successor States.

SHINJI "SONNY" HIKORI

Shinji "Sonny" Hikori had supplied pro-Combine groups (such as Combine Now!) within the Republic before the Blackout, although this seemed to have stemmed less from any sense of patriotism and more as a desire to profit from their dissent. The events that followed Gray Monday saw him operate more openly, as he became a supplier to the Dragons' Fury in their efforts to reclaim worlds for the Combine. Hikori's agents helped to arm militia units and Combine "citizen's brigades," helping to stoke ethnic violence within Republic worlds.

While he was a supporter of Duchess Tormark, Hikori's organization wasted little time in switching sides in the aftermath of the failed Nova Cat uprising. His agents continued to supply pro-Combine groups within the former Republic, while also expanding operations into the Draconis March. As the tide has turned against the Draconis Combine Mustered Soldiery, Hikori's agents have helped to provide weapons to the newly raised *ashigaru* units, a move that is as much about patriotism as it is about profiting off a desperate situation. While many may protest this blatant profiteering, right now, few will refuse weapons at any price.

In many ways, Sonny Hikori is more interesting than his own organisation. Previously he was known to be flamboyant and openly flaunting his wealth, but that changed suddenly in the aftermath of the failed Nova Cat revolt. There has not been a single verified sighting of him since then, but nonetheless, his organization continues to act as if he were in charge. His agents go to meetings aimed at implementing his directives, but they don't seem to interact with him directly. This leads to the question: Is he still running the show, or has somebody else seized the reins of his organization?

DROZ ARMS

Founded by a pair of brothers around the turn of the century, Droz Arms established itself selling weapons to worlds on both sides of the simmering conflict between the Taurian Concordat and the Calderon Protectorate, as well as those that had been left abandoned between. The group marketed themselves carefully, playing to the two strongest sentiments of Taurian culture: the rugged frontier spirit and the perpetual fear of Davion invasion. This careful manufacturing of their image allowed them to sell everything from pistols to reconditioned *Quasit* MilitaMechs while still maintaining the illusion of being a family-owned company.

The effective collapse of the Concordat during the 3120s created a wealth of new markets for the company as they continued to adapt to changing circumstances. As each world declared independence from the Concordat, the company was there to sell weapons to help protect that newfound freedom. Agents from the company could be proudly independent and self-reliant on one world and then aggressive Taurian patriots wanting to see their nation reclaim its lost territory on the next. The then company president, Marius Barrault, once joked that Protector Urratia was their best salesman.

For the moment, the company's biggest concern is the growing rapprochement and planned reunification between the Concordat and Protectorate. A stable, reunified Concordat able to reclaim many of its presently independent worlds would be a major blow to the lucrative markets Droz Arms has spent decades cultivating.

LONE WOLF AND FOX

BRYAN YOUNG

PART 4 (OF 4)

CHAPTER TWENTY

LEOPARD-CLASS DROPSHIP *WILD COYOTE*
ZENITH JUMP POINT
ALYINA
ALYINA MERCANTILE LEAGUE
1 NOVEMBER 3151

Bugsy Heidegger was getting too old for this.

Trying to maintain a mercenary screen on four planets spread across the Alyina Mercantile League with the Lone Wolves was hard enough, but throwing their AML Militia and a whole bunch of other hotheaded mercenaries into the mix was just trouble.

And as Major Hendrix McHale—the second-longest-serving MechWarrior in the Lone Wolves—was explaining to him across the vast distance of space before he jumped to a different sector to oversee, it was difficult to just keep track of what the hell was going on, let alone make decisions.

"You're gonna need to say that again," Bugsy said, then waited for the signal delay to reach Alyina and the response to bounce back. He floated in front of the screen, waiting for the *Wild Coyote* to connect to the JumpShip so he could continue his tour of the engagement zone and make adjustments as necessary.

McHale stood there on a dodgy video feed patched in from AML Headquarters in New Delhi. He'd been left in charge of Alyina while Bugsy had gone to Butler and the other planets to ensure compliance with the contract and defense against outside forces. McHale hadn't been with a larger unit, he had his own 'Mech, an *Archer* he'd painted in Lone Wolves blue and orange. Standing there on the video feed, he wore the dark red and black uniform with Lone Wolves patches common among those who weren't part of a larger unit like the Foul-Tempered or the Fox Patrol. The poor reception made McHale's dark brown skin almost wash out the details of his handsome face, but Bugsy made up the rest from his memory.

"She wants to void all of the contracts," McHale said finally, his mouth slightly out of sync with the audio.

"That's what I thought you said, but that doesn't make any sense. Why would she wanna do that? We signed for six months, and we're the best chance she has to defend against the pirates that keep attacking and Jiyi Chistu's Jade Falcon remnants on Sudeten if they decide to attack."

Bugsy bit his fist, waiting on the long lag between communications. He couldn't jump until he had whatever this situation was taken care of, and he already felt like he was behind schedule.

"Yeah, well, there was an attack last night. Bad one. Some mercs cracked open a jail and their vault and made off with some booty. Why worry about pirates when the mercs are going to steal your shit anyway?"

Just hearing the words was enough to enrage Bugsy Heidegger. He wasn't prone to getting mad, but if there was one thing that pissed him off, it was the unprofessional behavior of certain merc companies outside his control.

"Who was it? Tell me when you reply, but it doesn't matter, I'm sure I have a guess. It was the Tread of Doom guys, wasn't it? I knew that damn tribunal was gonna go south for us. But here's the thing, do you need me to come back? I can get back planetside and talk to her, or you can do it. Do you think you can handle it? I can tell you exactly what to do and what she's gonna wanna hear, but whether you pull it off or not is entirely up to you."

Bugsy would've loved to tap his foot against the deck plating as he waited for a response, but his foot just sort of floated there, and the effort to tap it against something would've been beyond annoying.

Finally, McHale started again. "You got it in one. Tread of Doom. And I think I can handle this. To be honest, I think it would be worse if you were to come back and not deal with the rest. But yeah, these Tread of Doom guys, real edge-runners, didn't like the result of the tribunal. They blew up the prison and let hundreds go to get their one guy. And then they got away with one of the smaller vaults from the Depository and hightailed it outta the system. Had a JumpShip at a pirate point to escape. No idea how they arranged that, but they're long gone now, which is all the better. But that doesn't mean she's not pissed."

"I think we can work this out just fine, but you're going to need to play it straight with her. Don't get angry, just talk her through it. Here's what we're gonna offer her..."

CHAPTER TWENTY-ONE

ALYINA MERCANTILE LEAGUE HEADQUARTERS
EXCHANGE PLACE TOWER
NEW DELHI
ALYINA
1 NOVEMBER 3151

Syndic Marena sat opposite Major McHale of the Lone Wolves at her desk in her office at the top of the AML headquarters. The wreckage of the jail and the Jade Depository had stopped flaming, leaving tendrils of black smoke as nothing but a faded memory, but she could still see it clearly. The Tread of Doom incident angered her, and the news of the pirate attack on Butler had soured her feelings even further.

She was not one given to rage, but her frustration had done nothing to help her mood and tact. She'd had an easy time with Major Heidegger; he was a shrewd negotiator and she respected that. But he was off-planet, doing the job she'd contracted him to do, and here was someone else in his stead.

Major McHale seemed much more nervous than Heidegger. Like he wasn't comfortable negotiating, but Marena's mind was practically made up. It wouldn't matter because there wasn't much to negotiate.

"After this," she said, "why would I not simply cancel your contracts and the contracts of all of those mercenaries who came here and send you all packing up to Kandersteg and Galatea and whatever other nests you all call home?"

McHale cleared his throat. "Well, uh, for one. I think it would leave you in the same position you were in before we got here. Open and exposed, vulnerable to attacks."

"Are you insinuating the Lone Wolves have made no headway in training the militia?"

"We have, but it takes more than a couple months to train MechWarriors up, and to train anti-BattleMech infantry, even longer. A lot of nerve that goes into that."

Marena knew he was right, though she was loathe to admit it. And they still hadn't found the source of the leaked information that allowed pirates to come and start taking their 'Mechs willy-nilly. And to McHale's credit, the Lone Wolves hadn't started any trouble. They had arrived first and remained most professional. It was the units that had been brought in by her merchants that had caused the problems. The Lone Wolves were disparate in their makeup, sure, but they answered to one person she could negotiate with.

"How do you propose to remedy this?"

"I'm not sure there's anything for the Lone Wolves to remedy, per se. It wasn't one of ours who got into a drunken scuffle and threw a tantrum that cost you two buildings, three Elementals, and a lot of egg on your face. But I can make some recommendations."

"I am nothing if not willing to listen. What do you propose?"

"So, I spoke to Major Heidegger about this very thing, and I think instead of canceling the contracts as you said was your intent, we can modify them to add some protections. Some of the other commands may bristle a bit, but the Lone Wolves, who I think is still your single largest source of protection, would be willing to go along. So, if you wanted us to fulfill the rest of our contract, we're here."

"You are very convinced I still need you," she said. She was mostly convinced of it, too, but there was no advantage of telling him that.

"Well, the news from Butler makes that fairly apparent, doesn't it?"

That caught Marina's breath. She hadn't known he'd heard about Butler. The news had come in during the chaos of everything else. The Light of Heaven—another mercenary unit Marena had contracted with—had driven off an attack there. The identity of the attackers had not been positively confirmed, but the fact they had been fielding Jade Falcon 'Mechs of the same models and numbers that had recently been stolen from Factory Zone 4 gave everyone a good indication of where the attack had come from. The Light of Heaven, stationed at the capital—Smithfield—had repelled the attack with some losses, but had done so admirably. It didn't seem as though the pirates expected them to be so well-defended. But wasn't that bargaining power of her own? She could afford to cut all the mercenaries loose and float on the appearance of defense after these rebuffed attacks rather than actually have the strength.

A bluff.

A very dangerous bluff, but a bluff nonetheless.

"The attack on Butler was regrettable, and I am grateful it was repelled, but they've probed our defenses and not found them lacking. It would be easy enough for them to realize we are not a soft target."

"I don't think you believe that any more than I do. But here is what the Lone Wolves propose: we'll cover the rest of the mercenary units, and any damage they incur outside the scope of duty, using our line of credit. That way, we'll keep them in line and if there's a problem, we'll collect. The other mercenary commands will probably find this a lot easier to swallow than another tribunal."

Marena thought on that for a moment. It would certainly take pressure off her, and allow her to focus on finding those responsible for betraying her and preventing her from expanding her reach. Ultimately, she decided it was better than nothing, with one caveat.

"Only if we renegotiate each contract, and they will all includes language that increases the punishments for malfeasance on the order of the Tread of Doom. I want peace in Alyina; I do not want warriors running roughshod in the streets. I do not want them running anything, to be quite frank."

"I get that," McHale said. "And I understand completely. I imagine it's hard, what with all the attitudes of the people caught in the transition. I can't imagine being a caste member in a Clan is easy; I can't imagine having all of that torn asunder pretty quickly is any easier. I think your terms are agreeable and reasonable, and the Lone Wolves would be happy to abide by them. I can't speak for the other unaffiliated or self-affiliated merc units, but you'll have to negotiate with them separately anyway."

McHale stood and offered her a polite smile, holding his hat in his hands. "If you want to draw up the paperwork, I'm authorized to sign it in the absence of Major Heidegger, and then I'll leave you to get to the work of organizing the others."

Marena didn't like how satisfied he seemed. It was too easy a negotiation for both of them. As though he and the major had planned all of that. It would make sense. She knew Heidegger to be competent, and the terms they'd outlined for each other were really the only ones that could convince her to continue having the mercenaries defend them.

"I will see to it that you receive the contracts immediately, and I hope there will be no lapse in your service. You are quite right—the Lone Wolves have been the most professional part of this entire endeavor to date."

McHale put his cap on and nodded. "We would very much like to keep it that way, Syndic."

As he was leaving, Syndic Marena realized there was one more problem she was left with, and if the Lone Wolves were so professional,

maybe Major McHale could help her with that as well. "Actually, stay a moment longer, Major."

"Syndic?" McHale turned around, confused and pleased all at once.

"Indeed. I have one other matter I believe you can help me with."

He smiled broadly. "Anything you need."

CHAPTER TWENTY-TWO

AML MILITIA TRAINING COMPOUND
CORLEONE
MONTESSORO
ALYINA
ALYINA MERCANTILE LEAGUE
2 NOVEMBER 3151

Katie Ferraro felt everything was falling apart except the ankle actuator assemblies on Arkee's *Quickdraw.* Grateful something was working out, she had thrown all her time into getting the 60-ton 'Mech back into working order.

With both hands full tightening a sheet of armor back into place on the leg, she called back for help, "Frankie, hand me that spanner, would you?"

"Frankie isn't here, Captain," came Misha's voice.

Disgusted with herself, Katie had forgotten.

Frankie had resigned.

How could she forget?

Misha was the young apprentice technician they had been training closely—and she was nowhere near ready to be a replacement for someone like Frankie Fischer.

"Oh. Right. Would you hand it to me?"

"Sure thing, Cap."

Katie cursed at herself. She had wanted these parts, and she had wanted an XO, and all she could think of was how great Frankie would be at it, but she never once stopped to think about how Frankie might feel about it. She didn't even need to think about it. Frankie *told* her how they felt about it. But Katie had railroaded them into it anyway.

Scarecrow—her mentor and adopted father—had always said some tripe like great leaders never asked to be leaders, they had greatness thrust upon them. Katie honestly thought she was thrusting greatness onto Frankie. But maybe some folks didn't want greatness.

Maybe they just wanted to work on 'Mechs and fly ships without all the extra responsibility.

Cranking the torque spanner in the wrong direction at first, Katie almost lost the whole piece of armor and sheared the last bolt, but she was able to catch it and get it set straight. The mounts and scaffolds for the armor helped. It wasn't like she had to hold it all by herself, it was strapped mostly in place already. She just needed to keep it level.

Katie wondered where Frankie was.

They could always be found in the 'Mech bay if there were no specific assignment. What would they be doing without a 'Mech bay to hang out in?

That's when Katie realized she didn't know a whole lot about Frankie. They talked all the time and were great friends, but it seemed like all they talked about was 'Mechs. They had once spent an entire night—literally the entire thing—talking about the intricacies of a gyro assembly on the *Kit Fox.* No one could talk 'Mechs with her like Frankie. Maybe she needed to find a balance between her relationship with Arkee and Evan—which had seemed almost like they were her older brothers who still let her call the shots—where she knew intimate details of their personalities.

With Frankie, the sum of their personality could be described as "hyper-competent 'Mech tech and fun to be around." She'd gotten to know Rhiannon and Dexter a little better sometimes, but they just seemed to have heads full of other things. Because she was so close to Arkee and Evan, she seemed to relegate them to lesser duties under the guise of seniority. Yes, Arkee and Evan had been with the Fox Patrol longer and, yes, they had both been granted the rank of sergeant, but Corporals Rhiannon and Dexter were actually more seasoned veterans on the command couch.

Meditating on the reconstruction effort of the *Quickdraw* gave Katie time to think about her failings, but no solution presented itself. Just more soul searching.

Running a mercenary outfit was harder than she had ever realized, even though she'd been doing it for years. Things had been charmed to this point, but this relatively easy milk-run assignment had challenged her the most, and she didn't like that.

"Hey, Captain," Misha said from behind her.

"What is it, Misha?"

"There's a message coming down for you."

Katie hadn't even heard the sharp tone of the comm system, she'd been so lost thinking about her own shortcomings. "What is it?"

"Corporal Ramirez is upstairs in the office and needs to speak to you."

"Tell her I'll be right up," Katie said. But some part of her knew it would just be one more thing to add to the pile of her misery.

That's just how it was running a mercenary company, right?

CHAPTER TWENTY-THREE

AML MILITIA TRAINING COMPOUND
CORLEONE
MONTESSORO
ALYINA
ALYINA MERCANTILE LEAGUE
2 NOVEMBER 3151

Rhiannon Ramirez turned when she heard the door open.

Her CO, Katie Ferraro, started bluntly. "What's exploding?"

"What makes you think something is exploding?" Rhiannon found Katie to be her opposite in many ways. Where Rhiannon was tall, Katie was shorter. They both had coal black hair, to be sure, but Katie's was done up in a sloppy bun, pinned back with a pressure gauge, and Rhiannon made sure hers had been brushed and feathered appropriately. Whenever Katie found optimism, Rhiannon found darkness. Whenever Katie found that same darkness, Rhiannon had a cool sangfroid that helped get them through.

It's part of why she thought they helped make up the composition of a pretty good unit.

"That's just how things have been going around here. Has Arkee talked to you?"

"No. What's up with Arkee?" Rhiannon caught herself. There really were more important things to worry about. "Table that for now, actually, Captain. We have a message from the Lone Wolves, directives straight from our employer, Syndic Marena."

"Oh, is that all? That might actually be good. I think we've been sitting around too much for this whole job."

Katie traipsed through the room like a proper grease monkey and collapsed into her chair hard, the weight of her exhaustion written easily in her poor posture and tired eyes. She was probably the youngest member of the Fox Patrol, but carried the most weight. After all, she had founded the whole thing.

"Yeah, there wasn't anyone here, so I took the message."

"The *Quickdraw* needed fixing," Katie said, and had all the grease marks and scuffs on her clothes to prove it.

Before Rhiannon could take a seat of her own or even continue, a knock on the door interrupted them. Katie heard it and sighed, looking right at Rhiannon as though she were asking for help.

"Enter!" she shouted.

The knob twisted slowly, and in walked a guy Rhiannon had never seen before. Meek in posture, wearing nurses' scrubs. He looked like one of the locals, with skin a few shades darker than hers and a tousle of curly black hair above a kindly face.

"Nurse Dev," Katie said, welcoming him.

Rhiannon wondered what Katie would need a nurse for, and then assumed it had something to do with Evan.

"Captain Ferraro," he said with the hint of an Alyinan accent. "I was wondering about that job opportunity."

Katie looked around nervously. "Listen, Dev, I think it would be a good fit, honestly, but I'm not sure if we can afford to take on a ship's medic at the moment."

Rhiannon noticed Katie's gaze shifted to her, then to her desk, then back to Dev, as though she were evading something.

"We still have a few months left on our contract," Katie continued, "so we're not going anywhere. I'll let you know for sure by the time we pull up stakes. I just don't know if the math makes sense or not yet."

"I understand," Dev said, nodding and smiling at her. "Just the chance at getting to take off into the stars with such a storied group would make my life complete."

"It is a pretty great life," Katie admitted. "But there's a lot of bolts to tighten down here before I make a final decision."

"Of course."

"I'll let you know."

For all of his politeness, there was a softness in the nurse's eyes Rhiannon almost thought were tears. But she opted not to say anything. It was better to say nothing and stay on the sidelines. She had no idea what the play was or what the issue was. She *did* know the Fox Patrol was always scraping by, so an extra mouth to feed was always a big gamble, but a unit medic wasn't a bad idea at all. Especially in the light of Evan's recent injury.

Head hung low, the nurse shuffled out of the office and Katie groaned. Once he was almost probably certainly out of earshot, she looked back up to Rhiannon. "I really hate dealing with drama."

"Drama? I can't imagine anyone opposing a company medic."

"Then you would be wrong."

"Is he, like...charged with malpractice on Alyina or something?"

"No... Arkee thinks he's after Evan. I don't know if I should be saying anything about it if he hasn't said anything about it, but the nurse there took care of Evan in the hospital, and now Arkee thinks they're sneaking around behind his back."

Rhiannon furrowed her brow. "Oh. Wow. And he wants to come with us when we pull up stakes?"

"Seems so."

"What are you going to do?" Rhiannon couldn't help herself. Yes, the message was important, but this felt important, too.

"Arkee asked me to leave him behind, but I'd already told him I wanted him, based on Evan's recommendation. I had no idea this was all brewing in the background until Arkee came to me."

"Ah." Rhiannon let that all cycle through her head. Arkee and Evan were part of the foundation of the Fox Patrol. She couldn't imagine what it would be like for them to be fighting. Or, worse yet, separated. Part of what made them such a great team of MechWarriors was their chemistry. And she genuinely liked them both, she didn't want to see them hurting. Least of all because of each other.

"So, what's the message?" Katie asked, snapping Rhiannon from her thoughts.

"Oh, right. That. I took the liberty of pulling up the details on your noteputer." Rhiannon pointed to it on the desk. "It's largely a secret operation, and not all the details are there, but enough to put together a picture. The long and the short of it is that we're to be expecting an attack and planning an ambush."

"Great. And I still don't have the *Locust* ready."

"Where's Frankie? Surely they can help?"

"Does news travel that slow around here?"

"Dex and I have been training the militia. I feel like we've been completely cut off from the rest of the group for like a month."

"Frankie resigned."

That news hit Rhiannon like a shot from a Gauss rifle. *"What? Why?"*

Some would say Katie was the glue that kept the Fox Patrol and its 'Mechs together, and in a lot of ways that was true. But she was more like one half of an epoxy, and Frankie was the other half.

"I, uh...named them the XO. They did it for a little bit, got me all the parts for the *Quickdraw*, and then resigned after. Completely. I haven't been able to track them down since."

"You named them executive officer? Did they *want* to be the XO?"

"No. Who wants to be the XO?"

"No one *wants* to be, but you have to at least find someone willing."

"Are you willing?"

Another shot from the Gauss rifle. *"What?"*

"Seriously, Rhiannon. I'm desperate. I think you'd do a great job. And it's something we've been missing for a while. I don't want to force it on you like I tried with Frankie, that was a mistake. But...would you consider it?"

Rhiannon really had no idea what to say. She was a MechWarrior. She didn't know the first thing about being an XO.

Katie leaned forward in her desk. "Listen, if nothing else, what if it's temporary, and if you find you like it, great, we'll stick with this, but I'm desperate. This ruse we need to pull isn't gonna to be easy, and I need to get the 'Mechs together and in fighting shape and I know that's *not* something you can do. You're street smart in ways I'm not, and I know that, too. You saved my ass back on Galatea and I've never forgotten it. You know everyone, you get along with everyone—except maybe Dexter..."

"Actually, he and I have been getting along quite well on the assignment. I think he's grown up some."

"Even better. Think about it, though. I need the help. Maybe you can convince Frankie to come back. Maybe you can get me the parts for the *Locust* and maybe, just maybe, we can be ready for this attack before it happens."

Rhiannon didn't know what to say.

But if it kept the Fox Patrol together and functional, there was only one thing she could say. "We'll try it. Just temporary, like you said. Just to get us through this."

The worry on Katie's face melted away and she smiled wide again, full of that optimism she often had far too much of. "Thank you. You won't regret it."

"I hope not."

Katie glanced at the briefing on the noteputer. "It looks like we've got a week to get this put together. Do what you need to do."

"Will do."

"And see about getting Frankie back. We're thoroughly boned without them."

"I'll see what I can do, Cap'n."

Katie quickly rose from her seat. "Perfect. I'm going to go finish up the last few things on the *Quickdraw* and see about the *Locust*. There's a list of parts in the noteputer. You can use my office as yours as long as you like."

And before Rhiannon could ask another single question, Katie was gone. Right out the door.

Somehow, Rhiannon had the sneaking suspicion she was getting the raw end of the deal.

CHAPTER TWENTY-FOUR

**AML MILITIA TRAINING COMPOUND
CORLEONE
MONTESSORO
ALYINA
ALYINA MERCANTILE LEAGUE
9 NOVEMBER 3151**

Arkee slowly climbed up to the command couch of his *Quickdraw*, trying to distract himself with every meter he ascended.

He was about to go into battle with Evan. They were to lie in wait in the 'Mech bay while the rest of the Fox Patrol went out on maneuvers, far enough away to make it seem as though pirates could attack the base and steal the broken 'Mechs for spare parts, supplies, and anything else they could find. There were whispers that the pirates still hiding on the planet were getting desperate and Montessoro was lightly defended, making it a convenient target for their resupplies and then someone higher up would be fed just enough information for someone to know who was leaking it.

Based on the information in the wild, the AML training compound they'd been stationed at made the most sense. Apparently, stories had gone out that his *Quickdraw* and Evan's *Locust* were out of commission. That was no secret, Katie had been complaining loudly about it to anyone who would listen, which was her way of trying to ask for spare parts without asking for spare parts.

Frankie had gotten the parts for Arkee's *Quickdraw* before taking off, and no one had seen them since. Somehow, under the cover of night, Rhiannon had organized the delivery of enough parts to replace most of the *Locust*'s cockpit and get it back up and running. Katie had been working day and night to get both 'Mechs back to proper working order while Rhiannon started calling shots, and Arkee didn't know if he liked it or hated it.

He felt like he had bigger things to worry about.

Life-or-death things.

The sanctity and strength of his marriage.

The love of his one true soulmate.

The security that came with being loved and cared for.

Arkee crawled into the cockpit of his *Quickdraw* and it felt like being back with an old friend. It had been too long since he'd been inside. But with that old friend came tortured memories. Strapping on the neurohelmet and plugging the leads onto his head, chest, and cooling vest that would help him pilot the 'Mech and keep track of his vital signs, Arkee could only think of all the conversations he had in that very space over the comm with Evan. Not even during their time with the Fox Patrol. Before then. When they were still scrapping in the galaxy, just them against the world. Before they were dating. Before they even knew they were interested in each other.

Sitting there in the *Quickdraw* was the first time Evan let slip that he might have liked Arkee. They were mid-battle. Their third engagement, and Evan just couldn't hold it in, he guessed. Butterflies beat wings in Arkee's chest, and he couldn't believe it.

But now, all he felt was dread and insecurity. Evan was drifting away, and there wasn't anything he could do about it.

"This is Fox Three, Fox Two, do you copy?" Evan said over the comm.

"I copy, Fox Three," Arkee said.

He felt in no mood for laughter or jest like the old days.

It was all business.

"Just doing a comm check," Evan said. "Standing by."

For both of them.

Arkee wondered if Evan realized how much he was hurting. If it ever even crossed his mind why Arkee might feel tender and sad.

Katie's voice, exhausted and bedraggled, came over the comm next. "This is Fox Leader with Foxes Four and Five. We're in position and leaving the command area now. Just be sure to keep your 'Mechs cool 'til we get word they're moving in. To reiterate, since you both seem a little preoccupied, the AML Militia infantry is serving as spotters and will let us know what's going on, but they will not attack until you make your move. Understood?"

"Understood, Captain," Arkee said, then Evan followed, echoing him on the comm.

Katie's voice disappeared, and the only thing left was the dead silence of a quiet 'Mech.

Arkee tried to keep his focus aimed at the control console, lit dimly in battery mode so the engine wouldn't be completely online, to give the appearance the 'Mech was dead. He didn't like the idea of being bait, but it was what it was.

On his screen, across from him in the bay, was Evan and his *Locust*. He must have been looking right back at Arkee.

Arkee *felt* it.

He closed his eyes, and, in a flash, he saw Dev's hand on Evan's.

Arkee's eyes opened, and as much work as he'd done trying to calm down, it all disintegrated.

"I love you," he said.

But he knew the comm wasn't on and Evan wouldn't hear him. Probably not even if it was on.

They say waiting is the hardest part, but Arkee felt the not-knowing might have trumped it.

The comm sputtered to life, and Arkee hoped it was Evan apologizing and coming back, but that wasn't the case. "Fox Two, this is Alyina One, do you copy?"

Alyina One was former Clanner infantry, commanding a tank now. He wanted to say her name was Bayani. It was the one Rhiannon had beaten the hell out of. He could tell because she still sounded nasally from her healing broken nose.

"This is Fox Two," he said quietly.

"We have some unusual readings at the moment. Fox Leader and their team are still inside the perimeter, but there's something on the jungle side spiking readings. Sending telemetry to you now."

"Good. Keep an eye on it. You never know when something unexpected is going to happen," he told her as much as himself.

"*Aff.*"

Arkee looked down at the topographical map on his display, looked around at the lay of the land, wondering where they would come from.

You could never tell which direction an enemy would come from.

"Fox Three," Arkee said tentatively on the comm. "All systems go over there?"

"I think so," Evan said.

"How's the ol' *Locust*?"

"It's fine, I think. Won't know for sure until I get there."

Words formed in Arkee's throat, and he tried so hard to say them. "*I miss you*" was what he wanted to say, but couldn't.

While it was true they still slept in the same bed every night, albeit with backs turned to each other; Evan had come to their room dutifully night after night, with no other plans. It wasn't like Arkee could accuse him of being out cheating all the time. It was the occasional trips to the bar by himself. Or when they were separated by duty, and Arkee saw Dev hanging around the compound that he worried. Arkee knew how much he and Evan would sneak into any private space they could find to mess around when they were first dating.

Is that what he and Dev were doing?

"I miss you," he tried to say again.

But he couldn't before the comm sounded again and his map lit up.

"Fox Two, this is Alyina One. Fox Leader is outside the engagement zone, and we have confirmed movement in the trees. Sending telemetry."

The way it looked on Arkee's map after receiving the new data, they were going to cut a straight line from the trees to the warehouse he and Evan were waiting in. It made sense. They probably had some hovertrucks and sleds, too, ready to haul away everything they could get, same as they'd done in New Delhi.

"Stay focused then, keep your eyes open, and remember: *don't* make a move until they come this way. We don't want to scare them off until they've gone past you and we can clamp them in a pincer."

"*Aff,*" Alyina One said, as though they hadn't gone through the plan a dozen times.

Arkee cursed himself. Everything out of his mouth was the wrong thing.

He didn't *want* to be like this; to feel like this. He wanted to be happy Evan was alive. He wanted to be happy they could go into a 'Mech fight, side-by-side once again in the 'Mechs they'd met in.

But all he could do was fumble.

His hands were slick with sweat against the controls.

The heat hadn't even risen in the *Quickdraw.*

Get it together, Arkee.

"This is Alyina One. We have visual on the enemy. There is one *Ion Sparrow* emerging—scratch that, two *Ion Sparrow*s coming from the brush. It looks like a convoy is coming behind them. I count three so far."

The little red dots on his map matched everything she called out from the field, hidden and safe from their little tank-sized foxholes.

"Fox Three, are we good?" Arkee asked.

"I hope so, Fox Two. We are from where I'm sitting."

"I hope so, too."

"They are crossing the field, Fox Two."

"I see it." Arkee watched their red dots crawl across his map like ants, crossing the road and coming closer to the warehouse.

"They're almost in, Fox Three."

"I see it, Fox Two."

"We can do this together," Arkee said. Almost like a question.

"I wouldn't have it any other way, babe."

Arkee heard the hope in Evan's voice, and for the first time in a long time, it lifted him.

Maybe he could get through it.

The *Ion Sparrow*s edged closer to their 'Mech bay, on the other side of the closed doors.

"Light it up, Evan," Arkee said, bringing his own *Quickdraw* roaring back to life. He edged his 'Mech forward and pivoted left toward the door, watching Evan pivot likewise toward the door in his *Locust.*

With magres sensors, Arkee could actually see the *Ion Sparrow*s through the door. They were small, 20-ton 'Mechs like Evan's *Locust*, but much more vicious. With a partial-wing design and jump jets, they were fast harassers and scouts, making them perfect for a mission like the smash-and-grab they thought they were on. With medium lasers and anti-personnel Gauss rifles standard, they were deadly in battle—much more so than Evan's *Locust*, though he could slightly edge them out on speed.

"Alyina One, this is Fox Two. You've got a clear shot! Open fire!"

"*Aff.*"

Arkee saw their blue dots appear on the map as they came out of hiding. Although his viewscreen only showed the images directly around him in the warehouse, he saw the red heat of Evan's 'Mech next to him and found himself comforted by that.

"Opening fire," Alyina One called out.

And their distraction was enough that the *Ion Sparrow*s turned around to face the tanks, figuring they would be easy targets, not realizing the threat was now at their back.

"Open the door," Arkee called on the comm, and the techs responsible for that part of the plan went to work.

The 'Mech bay doors slowly opened, revealing a smoky fight in front of them. In the time it took the doors to open, the pirate *Ion Sparrow*s had already taken a crackling salvo of missiles, but they had reduced one of the Ares tanks to nothing more than a smoking hole, thanks to a lucky hit from one of their Gauss rifles.

Arkee didn't want to spend the time thinking about how many of the AML folks might have died already, for a stray second, he wondered if the nurse might have died, but he knew that wasn't even possible. There was no way he was out there with the tank crews, though Arkee could just imagine it: that damn nurse walking the battlefield like a modern-day Erin Hunnicutt, healing the sick and taking care of everyone before dying like a goddamn martyr, beloved by everyone.

"We've got a shot," Arkee said, trying to focus back on the battle. And there indeed, the *Ion Sparrow*s had shown them their backs.

Easy targets.

Stepping forward, Arkee fired all four of his lasers at the closest *Ion Sparrow*, boiling armor off the back of its torso and clipping one of its wings in half. A solid hit, but not a knockout blow.

Evan took the other *Ion Sparrow*, cutting across its back with his laser and chewing into the softened parts with his machine guns.

For the sparest of moments, Arkee felt a rise of panic blossom in him. It didn't matter what 'Mechs they were facing off against; they were a mismatched pair, a light and a heavy, with not enough firepower between them to take anything down definitively. Why had they even *made* a *Locust* so squishy? But Arkee caught himself.

They were the Fox Patrol.

No matter what was happening between them, they could get the job done.

The *Ion Sparrow*s must have realized they were being fired on from both directions because, instead of returning fire at the tanks or turning to return fire on Arkee and Evan, they jumped into the air, vanishing momentarily.

"We gotta push it," Arkee said. "Gotta catch 'em."

"On it," Evan said.

Evan, in the lighter, faster 'Mech, left Arkee behind quickly. He made it out of the 'Mech bay and into the field before Arkee even had a chance to emerge. Arkee's steps were tentative, he still wasn't used to how the *Quickdraw* was walking since the ankles had been replaced. It was sticking in places, and he couldn't tell if it was because it was a rush job on Katie's part or if he just had to get used to it all again.

By the time he passed the door of the warehouse, the *Ion Sparrow*s had landed and reset their facing. They were no longer caught in the middle of a kill box, but had repositioned themselves to take shots at the tanks or the 'Mechs pouring out of the bay. Thanks to their convoy, they couldn't just abandon their position in retreat.

"Alyina One, this is Fox Two, start taking out the trucks. Fox Three and I will take care of the 'Mechs."

"*Aff.* We are on it."

"Fox Two, this is Fox Leader," Katie's voice came over the comm. "We're on our way back, but something tells me you'll be done with this before we get there."

"That's the plan, Cap'n." Arkee just hoped it really worked out that way.

"Keep up the heat. We'll be there soon."

"Aye, aye."

Arkee pivoted his *Quickdraw* for a clear shot at one of the *Ion Sparrow*s. Before he could get a shot off, though, both enemy 'Mechs turned to him. Their lasers flashed, searing the front of his *Quickdraw*. The heat in the cockpit matched the panicked warmth in Arkee's middle, convinced this was the last time he was going into battle, the last time he would see his husband, the last time he would breathe the air of the world. Peppered with the metal flechettes from their anti-personnel Gauss rifles, the armor on the *Quickdraw*'s right arm cracked.

Again, it was like Arkee could feel it coming for him. As though the damage to the 'Mech was hurting him. Maybe it was a trick of the neurohelmet, or a side-effect of caring too much.

All he knew was he had to pick up from this, it didn't matter how hurt he got. He had a job to do. He'd sworn an oath. He'd agreed to the terms. He'd said "I do."

"Evan, I love you," he said finally.

"I love you, too, Ark. But aren't we both a little busy right now?"

As he said that, Evan's *Locust* took another shot at one of the *Ion Sparrow*s. He hit it with everything he had, but it looked as though it hadn't done much but cook off some of the armor just below the cockpit on the bird-like 'Mech.

Arkee fired his lasers and launched a salvo of missiles. The lasers missed, but the missiles scattered across the front of the closest *Ion Sparrow* in a cascade of explosions, but still not enough to bring the damn thing down. They were a lot sturdier than Evan's *Locust*, that much was clear.

The *Ion Sparrow*s lifted away in a gout of smoke and plasma as their jump jets activated. Tracking them along the display screen, Arkee saw them heading toward the convoy, the AML Militia tanks, and Evan.

"Be careful, Evan," Arkee said.

"Arkee, I'm always careful. We can talk about all this after we take these guys down."

"I'm just... I'm sorry. I should learn to trust you more."

"I'm sorry, too."

The *Locust* pivoted and aimed itself right at the farthest *Ion Sparrow*, which had landed in such a way as to put itself between the convoy and the tanks, almost as though it were completely ignoring the 'Mechs.

The other *Ion Sparrow* landed between Arkee and the convoy, as though they would be enough by themself to keep the *Quickdraw* from hampering their escape.

Arkee opened fire at the *Ion Sparrow* and connected with his four lasers, cremating the armor before the missiles brought it home on the inside, peppering the internal systems with starbursts of explosive fire.

Watching the *Ion Sparrow* fall, Arkee felt relief wash over him. They were going to be okay. The pirates had walked into their trap, and they were all going to walk out of this with their lives. Then he'd have a chance to be able to reconcile completely with Evan. That's what Evan deserved.

Glancing at the convoy—a string of half a dozen hover sleds, trucks, and trailers—he noticed a puff of smoke. Then another. A third.

They were firing rockets at Evan's *Locust*. One of them even managed to hit.

"I'm taking fire from the convoy!"

"I see it. Focus on them, I'll take care of the *Ion Sparrow*. Alyina One, split fire between the 'Mech and the trucks."

"*Aff!*"

Arkee knew the jump jets on his *Quickdraw* were dodgy and he reserved them for only the most special of occasions, but saving Evan's life seemed worth it. Zooming up and covering the distance between himself and the engagement zone was not a feeling he enjoyed. The pit of his stomach getting tugged down into the bottom of his waist was not his favorite feeling. He didn't like heights at all, even from the inside of a 'Mech, and the descent had a way of making him sick, but here he was.

He landed hard. An alarm sounded and the *Quickdraw*'s ankle joints groaned. Reminding himself that the repairs *had* been hasty, he knew he had to end this fast or he was going to end up flat on his face, just like last time.

Chaos spread across the field of engagement. The convoy continued firing at Evan, the militia splitting their fire between the convoy and the *Ion Sparrow*. The *Ion Sparrow* was still gunning directly for Evan, since he was the closest to the convoy. Then Arkee added to the light show with his own emerald-green lasers, lancing at the *Ion Sparrow*'s exposed back. They sheared off a chunk of its other wing and melted armor into slag there.

He fired his missiles once more, launching them right over the convoy. Most of the salvo missed, exploding in the distance, but those that hit staggered the *Ion Sparrow* forward. Not enough to take it down; the damage must have been diffuse enough to let it keep its integrity, but only just barely.

Instead of turning, it kept firing at Evan.

Arkee held his breath, watching the *Ion Sparrow*'s turquoise lasers slash the air in Evan's direction, but they missed the *Locust* completely. Then they fired their Gauss rifles—two of them packed together in one arm—and Arkee found himself screaming.

The bursts of AP Gauss shots smashed right into the actuator between the *Locust*'s leg and cockpit, dropping the leg to the side.

Unable to stand without both legs, Evan's *Locust* crashed to the ground. Hard.

"*Evan!*"

The remaining two militia tanks fired their missiles and they peppered across the front of the *Ion Sparrow* and across the convoy, but Arkee saw nothing but red.

"Arkee, what's going on?" came Katie's voice across the comm.

But he had nothing to say to her.

He marched forward, right for the convoy and the pirate in the *Ion Sparrow*. The pirate, surely understanding the danger they were in, immediately took to the skies again. Arkee's eyes scanned across his viewscreen and the topographical map on his console, and he knew exactly where the *Ion Sparrow* was heading. At the point where they were defending the convoy from two directions, the tanks and the *Quickdraw*, they had two options. Their first would be to close on the tanks and eliminate them quickly, though the tanks were much less of a threat to their comrades. The other choice was to land behind the *Quickdraw* and hope the Gauss rifle and lasers were enough to put the dusty old 'Mech out of commission.

Arkee staked his life on the latter and turned the *Quickdraw* around, adjusting the facing so he would catch the *Ion Sparrow* as it landed.

He clenched his jaw as the *Ion Sparrow* landed, true to form, right there in front of him.

He depressed the firing studs and launched everything he had at the pirate 'Mech. Lasers lashed out violently; missiles exploded in a bright cascade across its armor.

And then it was no more.

It had taken enough damage to simply fall forward, unable to stay up any longer.

Arkee turned back toward the convoy, ready to annihilate all of them as well, but Katie, Nicks, and Ramirez had arrived by that time to cut off their escape.

He allowed himself enough breath to talk, but only just. "Evan, do you read me?"

No response.

"Evan, you come in right now, or I swear to God I will come down there and kick your ass."

But still nothing.

And Arkee thought hope to be lost.

A voice squelched over the comm. "Ark...?"

"Evan?"

"Yeah... I need you to relax. I'm okay. I don't think anything is broken."

Elation filled Arkee like air in a balloon until he was ready to burst from his eyes in the form of tears. "You beautiful bastard. Don't you ever worry me like that again."

"I'll try. Now will someone get me outta here? I can't open my hatch..."

"We'll finish the mop-up operation," Katie said, "and we'll be there to get you. Just hang tight. And I hope this is the end of these ridiculous problems you two are having. You both love each other, and if this doesn't prove it, I don't know what does. Now get over to this convoy, Arkee, and let's finish this up."

Arkee blinked the tears from his eyes and smiled wider than he had in a month. "Sure thing, Cap'n."

CHAPTER TWENTY-FIVE

SAFDARJUNG SPACEPORT
NEW DELHI
ALYINA
11 NOVEMBER 3151

Syndic Marena sat in the spaceport conference room, surrounded once more by all of her chief merchants—at least those who were on planet. Merchant Claudio sat across from her. Merchant Helen sat to his right. Merchant Li was there. Merchant Julio. All of them.

Posted at each corner were Elementals in militia uniforms, all of them loyal to the AML without question. No one commented on their presence; security was always paramount.

Sitting at the head of the conference table, she felt their anxiety, palpable in the air like the swarms of bugs that used to prey on the citizens of New Delhi. But, like they'd dealt with those venomous mosquitoes, so too would she deal with her business here.

"You are all wondering why we've called this meeting."

Their heads all bobbed up and down, nodding. Some murmured to each other. There was a dozen of them there, all told, and the table was quite large. It made her happy to see them all there, dressed in their blue-and-silver merchant uniforms. But she regretted what she had to do. She regretted what they had *forced* her to do.

"We have a problem on Alyina. A problem I am doing everything I can to solve. That isn't to say we don't have many problems. To be frank with you, our problems are legion. But you all know that. This particular problem, however, might be one of our most pressing."

She scanned their faces, each one of them in turn, wondering if they would guess her intent. If they knew that she *knew*.

"Pirate attacks have been endemic here. They have harassed us across all the worlds of our holdings. They have threatened us here in the capital, they have threatened us across the other nine landmasses and island systems on the planet of Alyina. They have eluded us every step of the way. We have had to bring mercenaries into our home and within our borders to defend us because our militia is not yet strong enough to defend ourselves. We've made many compromises, and I have made many mistakes."

Marena rose from her chair and walked slowly around the room as she spoke. "It should come as no surprise that the pirates marauding us have had a source inside the Alyina Mercantile League, telling them where and how to hit us."

Not a single one of them batted an eyelash. None of them looked concerned in the slightest.

All the better, Marena thought.

"We assumed for a long time that the source of the information was someone from the former warrior caste, disgruntled by the new way of things here. Those fears were shared by many of us. Learning to be merchants without the oppressive boot of warriors on our necks is difficult work. What surprised me was not that we had someone working against us to prevent these needed changes, I expected that. Change is difficult. But I put into motion a plan that would reveal the identity of the leak. We offered specific details through specific channels and set an ambush."

Marena reached the head of the table again and paused to look at each of them again. She wanted them to struggle with the tension and anticipation. "What truly surprised me was that this person, the source of much of the intelligence the pirates acted on, is sitting in this very room."

Gasps came from around all edges of the table.

"That's impossible," Merchant Claudio said. "All of us here are completely loyal to the AML. We're all merchants here..."

"Be that as it may, Merchant Claudio, someone has betrayed us."

Merchant Helen motioned with her hand. "Tell us then. Who would do this?"

Marena locked eyes with Merchant Julio. He had done his best to stay unassuming, out of the way, and off her radar, but his part had been laid bare.

She didn't have to say a word, let alone his name. He withered beneath her glare. As soon as the other merchants realized she was staring at him, every eye in the room became glued to him.

"I had to," he said finally, practically melting beneath her stare like ferro-fibrous armor liquified by a heavy laser. "I had no choice... It was our way of life..."

"Spare me your excuses, Julio." Marena wondered where that hot feeling of outrage in her chest had gone. It had been replaced with something much colder.

Unfeeling.

A frigid coldness.

And she knew *that's* what power felt like. Coming back into control of everything she had worked so hard to build. This was the first step of many more she would have to take to ensure the long-term viability and survival of the Alyina Mercantile League.

And that anger she thought would be there once Julio had confessed was completely...absent.

This was *necessity.*

He looked desperately around at the others. "It was just business; you would have done the same in my position..."

Marena nodded to the Elementals. "Take him."

As they closed in on him, Julio looked right up to Marena. "It was the only way to force your hand..."

The Elementals gripped him by the shoulders and stood him up, ready to drag him as he pled for his life with a new bluff.

"You wouldn't have hired the mercenaries if it weren't for their threat! I did it for *us*. Can you not see it?"

As the Elementals dragged him out of the door, Marena did not give him the satisfaction of a response. Nothing he said mattered.

Only the Alyina Mercantile League.

The door closed.

And Marena was alone with her Merchants.

Those she had still deemed loyal.

Looking around, she met each one of them in the eyes. "Know this. He will be sent to a tribunal for sedition and treason. They will find him guilty—the evidence is incontrovertible—and he will be put to death. This is the price of betraying the Alyina Mercantile League to her enemies. Am I understood?"

They remained there in silence, unsure of how to respond.

That is, until Merchant Claudio nodded in support. "*Aff.*"

"*Aff,*" the rest of them echoed around the room.

Hearing their assent felt right. And good. "Excellent. Now, we have more pressing things to worry about. Like what we do about ferreting out the other malcontents, and what worlds we can fold into our holdings to stand strong against all who would take everything from us."

"*Aff,*" they all said again.

Louder.

Stronger.

Together.

Yes, Marena thought, *the Alyina Mercantile League will flourish, indeed.*

CHAPTER TWENTY-SIX

THE CONQUISTATORE
CORLEONE
MONTESSORO
ALYINA
ALYINA MERCANTILE LEAGUE
11 NOVEMBER 3151

Katie was told the Conquistatore was the place she needed to go, and as soon as she walked in, she understood why.

Well, there were two reasons. First were the dazzling murals across the walls of so many of the great 'Mechs throughout history. A *Marauder* battling a *Catapult* on a lava planet. A pair of *Locust*s zooming across an *Atlas* about to obliterate them both. An *Archer* in black and red, bowing to a flat-red *Warhammer* against a color-streaked sky. Each of them was wreathed in gilded paint that reflected the warm light of the place. It was exactly the sort of place she would love to spend time in, if she'd known of its existence.

The second reason Rhiannon told her to go there, she could only assume, was in the booth right below the mural of the *Archer* and the *Warhammer*. There sat Frankie Fischer, nursing a beer. They were wearing generic work coveralls, smeared in grease. They must have picked up a job somewhere.

It stabbed at Katie, thinking of Frankie sitting there, drinking alone and hurt because of what she had done. Frankie was part of the family, and that wasn't how you treated family. *I should have known better.*

She stepped over to the bar and asked the bartender what Frankie was drinking—Guerriero Meccanico, the bartender called them—and ordered two more. With a pair of frothy wheat beers in frosty mugs in hand, Katie approached Frankie's booth. "This seat taken?"

Frankie looked up, and Katie could tell from their face they weren't exactly excited to see her.

She slid the beer across the table as a peace offering to Frankie, who shrugged. It wasn't permission, per se, but they didn't throw the beer in her face either, so Katie would take it.

She sat down and sipped her own beer, finding it had a citrusy tang.

"Listen," Katie said after a long moment. "I want to say I'm sorry."

Frankie lifted their first glass of beer and chugged it in one breath. They placed the empty glass down, picked up the one Katie brought, and tipped the glass to her, almost as if in salute. "I bet."

"I get it if you're still mad at me."

"How'd you find me?"

"Ramirez."

"Of course."

"She's taken on the role of XO in the unit. At least for now."

"That's what she said." Frankie took another swallow of their beer. "She send you here?"

"Yes. But I think it was to look at the murals."

Frankie looked up at the *Warhammer*, almost staring into the detail of the House Kurita logo emblazoned on it. "Yeah, that's very much your speed." They looked back at Katie, locking eyes with her. "What do you want?"

"I didn't come to beg or bother you. Naturally, I want you to come back to the unit, though. But mainly I saw you and just wanted to apologize. I screwed up, and I feel awful about it."

"What is it, exactly, you feel awful about?"

"Railroading you. It wasn't fair, and I shouldn't have done that. I should have respected your wishes. But I was desperate. I just want this unit to function well, and I think I can do or say anything that pops into my head to make it happen. I just want to keep this unit together because I *love* this unit. I love everything it's become. But this unit doesn't mean anything without the folks that *make* it the Fox Patrol. And we couldn't be the Fox Patrol without you any more than we really could be without Arkee or Evan. Or even me. You're part of this now... and it feels wrong to not have you around."

"So you're saying you should have listened to me?"

"Always."

"And respected my agency?"

"Definitely."

"And should never have tried to make me XO?"

"Never."

Frankie narrowed their eyes and pursed their lips. They thought about something for a moment, then brought the beer to their lips once more. They took a long, slow drink of it and smacked their lips when they put the mug back down on the table.

They belched and wiped their mouth. "Apology accepted."

Katie felt the weight of her guilt lessen instantly. The tightness in her shoulders eased and she could breathe again. She sipped her own beer again as the pair of them sat there in silence.

They drank.

And drank.

Until Katie finally said, "You *are* coming back, right?"

Frankie grinned. "'Course I am. But I swear on the soul of the first *Mackie* if you ever pull shit like that again, I won't just resign, I'll burn everything down with me."

Katie smiled. "That sounds fair enough, Frank."

"Good. And don't think I don't mean it."

"I know, Frankie. I know."

CHAPTER TWENTY-SEVEN

AML MILITIA TRAINING COMPOUND
CORLEONE
MONTESSORO
ALYINA
ALYINA MERCANTILE LEAGUE
12 NOVEMBER 3151

Arkee stared out the window in the mess hall above the 'Mech bay, looking at the scorch mark on the field where he'd almost lost his husband again. He'd barely touched his lunch.

Evan was talking, but he couldn't quite focus on it. All he could think about was how much of a jackass he'd made himself out to be.

"—you hear me, Ark?" Evan said, and Arkee finally registered it.

"Huh?" He turned to Evan, sitting across the table. He hadn't touched his lunch either.

"I said I'm sorry."

"I know." Arkee looked down at his own food, unable to make eye contact with Evan. It was something Evan had brought him, a local dish. Curry and pasta with a spicy sausage in it. He pushed it around with his fork. It smelled amazing, but he wasn't sure he could eat anything.

"I don't want to cause you any problems. And I don't want to make you feel like I'm anything less than faithful to you."

"I know you don't."

"That's why I told Katie to forget bringing Dev on as a medic. If he's gonna cause you that much heartache, I'd rather we leave him here and pretend he never existed."

Arkee looked up at Evan, searching his face for truth. "You what?"

"I told Katie to forget about the whole thing. It was a terrible idea anyway."

"Ev...I think I'm the one who owes you an apology."

"What for?"

"For being a jealous idiot. Dev was your nurse. He was supposed to take care of you. This is all my insecurity. I wake up every morning thinking you're gonna find someone better than me and that's going to be it. You'll be done with Arkee Colorado, and I'll have to find someone else. You're gonna realize how much I'm the worst."

Evan smiled softly. "You have no idea how much I love waking up every morning as Mr. Colorado."

"But the point is this: I should trust you. You love me, right?"

"More than anything."

"And you're faithful?"

"Completely."

"Then why should some nurse get me so insecure?"

"He shouldn't."

"Then that's something I need to work on. That's on me. I'm gonna to tell Katie if she wants to bring Dev on as a medic, that's her prerogative. She won't hear a peep out of me."

"I'll let her know you said that."

A sudden flood of concern flooded into Arkee's chest. "It's not like we'd have to hang out with him or anything..."

"You'd never have to see him if you didn't want to. Only if you were wounded. Which is the only reason I thought he might be worth recruiting in the first place. I couldn't bear the thought of you not having someone like Dev to help nurse you back to health for me if you got hurt."

Arkee blinked. "Really?"

The only reason Arkee could imagine Evan wanting to bring Dev along as a Fox was because he'd found someone new. He never thought *he* could've been the reason for it. "I'm sorry I'm such a jackass, Evan."

"Can you apologize to me for that, too?" a voice said, interrupting their conversation.

Sheepishly, Arkee looked over to see Rhiannon standing there. He wondered how long she'd been there, just listening to the two of them.

"I hate to break up this little make-up session, especially since I need you two to be on better terms like, yesterday, but I have some good news, and I want you both to hear it."

Arkee looked back down at his plate of food, but Evan looked right up at her. "What's going on?"

"I was able to negotiate some salvage rights with the Alyinans."

Evan brightened. "You're gonna be able to get the parts to fix my *Locust* again?"

"No."

"I thought you said this was good news."

Rhiannon smiled cruelly. "We don't need your *Locust* anymore. It's old and obsolete."

Arkee felt a knot of anger rise in him, and suddenly Rhiannon didn't seem very friendly. "Are you making fun of my husband?"

"No. They're letting us salvage the *Ion Sparrow*s from your last engagement and got us access to other spare parts. Congratulations, Evan Huxley, you just got an upgrade."

Confused, Arkee looked over to Evan, who had the biggest grin on his face he'd ever seen.

"I'm getting a brand-new Clan 'Mech?"

"Well, brand new-ish," Rhiannon said. "Remember, you two did beat the hell out of the two, so Katie's gonna have to piece 'em together into one new 'Mech. Sorry again."

Arkee thought Evan was going to cry.

"Rhiannon, my *Locust* was two hundred years old. This *Ion Sparrow*, beat-up though it might be, came off an assembly line *this* year. What can I ever do to repay you?"

"You two can knock it off with these marital problems. We got work to do."

Arkee tried not to think about the fact that the *Locust* was the one he'd met Evan in, and all the sentimental baggage that came with it. He smiled weakly. "Sure thing, Rhiannon. I'll do my best."

He looked over and all the weakness he felt faded in Evan's eyes. He really did love that man, and he knew in that moment he would walk over hot coals or fight a *Kodiak* in a *Locust* for him. "As long as you're happy, babe."

The indentation of Evan's dimple as he smiled filled Arkee with everything he needed.

The rest would be okay, and he knew it.

EPILOGUE

SAFDARJUNG SPACEPORT
NEW DELHI
ALYINA
15 FEBRUARY 3152

Syndic Marena watched with pleasure as the DropShips rose from Safdarjung Spaceport, their engines burning bright in the sky, shooting stars against the dark Alyinan night. With those DropShips left far more of her problems than solutions. It was an easy decision to send away all the malcontents and would-be warriors who wouldn't play by the rules of the new order that she'd spent the last few months rounding up into the stockades. It would be far cheaper to make them Jiyi Chistu's problem, and she could dress it up as a "gift." He wanted to play Khan, so he could take all of those from Alyina too stubborn to get with the program.

It also made it far easier to send a few "malcontents" loyal to the AML along with those unruly troublemakers to integrate with them on their way to Sudeten. They would blend in and be the perfect spies. The information they sent back to her would be vital in her attempts to keep the Mercantile League on the top of the food chain in the former Jade Falcon Occupation Zone.

"It is a shame about the Lone Wolves," Merchant Li said, standing at her side.

"A necessary loss," Marena said, watching the mercenary unit's ships head toward the JumpShips alongside those she had dispatched. "They did what they were supposed to do. And, as Major Heidegger said, this deployment had been too quiet for their tastes, which meant they did their job. They got their pay and their 'Mechs and, as he said, they could find somewhere more lucrative. What merchant could begrudge a businessperson such a sound decision?"

"They were simply the most honorable of the mercenaries brought to our holdings. Those that are staying are a little more...rambunctious."

"And there are clauses in their contracts that allow us to keep them under control. It's not the most ideal, but it will work out."

"I defer to your wisdom, Syndic."

Marena watched the DropShips grow smaller and smaller until their thrusters were indistinguishable from the stars. Then, she turned back to the spaceport building and marched toward it.

Merchant Li followed her, ready to take any orders she offered.

"Summon the head of the Militia to me."

"Star Colonel Margolian?"

"*Aff.* We have much planning to do."

"Yes, Syndic. Thy will be done."

Marena smiled. Everything was going to work out just fine.

LEOPARD-CLASS DROPSHIP *OGAMI ITTO*
ALYINA
ALYINA MERCANTILE LEAGUE
15 FEBRUARY 3152

Most of the time, Bugsy Heidegger was glad he was in charge. He got to pull things together, he got to pick the jobs and recruit new folks. Sometimes they worked out—like the Fox Patrol had—and sometimes they didn't work out.

And sometimes, Bugsy Heidegger wished he'd never even heard of the Lone Wolves.

"I understand, Jules—"

"Julian. And that's Colonel Ellison to you, Major Heidegger."

Bugsy tried not to look too harried or annoyed, but such was his plight, strapped into a chair on the bridge of the *Ogami Itto*, listening to the CO of the Foul-Tempered bitch about being between jobs on the viewscreen. "Of course, Colonel. But I'm saying this is a rich opportunity."

Ellison looked angry, as he always did, strapped into a chair on his unit's DropShip, the *Black Mood.* "You said that about our most recent post, too. And the most we fought against were insurgents *we* trained. We need action, Major. Well-paying action. That's what the Foul-Tempered crave."

"Major, let me tell you: we're heading to Sudeten. You know anything about Sudeten?"

"Only what you put in your briefing."

"So, you know it's a hot spot of trouble. We're dealing with what seems to be a whole new breed of the Jade Falcon Clan, and they're gonna need all the help they can get, at least according to the intel I got."

"Clanners don't hire mercenaries."

"That's what you said about the Alyinans, and that worked out well enough. Didn't it?"

Ellison considered that. "Hm."

"Trust me, we'll find all the action we can handle on Sudeten, and we'll make plenty of money on the side. And besides, maybe we can get some more Clan 'Mechs in trade, too. Wouldn't that be a sweet deal?"

"This had better work, Major. Or the Foul-Tempered will no longer find working with the Lone Wolves tenable."

"I'm sure it'll be fine," Bugsy said, knowing maybe it would be even *more* fine if the Foul-Tempered left.

"Listen, we're coming into some interference," Bugsy lied. "I'm gonna have to let you go..."

"I'm not getting any interference," Ellison said, unamused.

"No, it's all on my end? In any case, I'll see you planetside, Colonel! We're not gonna miss our door of opportunity. Take it easy out there, and we'll have a great time."

Bugsy clicked off the monitor and sighed.

Sometimes he found it exhausting having to put on that act all the time.

But he was doing what he loved.

And that was all that mattered.

CONFEDERATE-CLASS DROPSHIP *FOX DEN*
ALYINA
ALYINA MERCANTILE LEAGUE
15 FEBRUARY 3152

Floating weightless in the DropShip's common room, Katie Ferraro couldn't wait to find out where they were going next.

"What'd you think, Captain?" Dexter Nicks asked her, looking out the window at the small dot that had become of Alyina.

"What do you mean, Dex?"

Dex waved a hand to the rest of the crew, floating in various spaces, clinging on to the walls across the room. Arkee and Evan laughed in one corner at a joke no one heard but them. Rhiannon and Frankie were having a conversation in another, probably talking about parts and supply lines and what they were going to do for it when they arrived on Sudeten. Misha and Dev, the newest recruits, nervously gripped the handholds, side-by-side, green with space sickness. "I mean, this. All of this. What you've built. What do you think?"

"I think we've got our best days ahead of us, Dex. I screw up. I screw up a lot. But we always manage to come back together."

"And you think sticking with the Lone Wolves is our best bet?"

"For now. Not forever. They're a stepping-stone. We'll get to where we want to be eventually."

"And where do you want to be, Captain?"

"Me? I want us to be the best damn merc unit in the Inner Sphere."

Dexter laughed.

Katie laughed with him.

But despite the laughter, she was serious.

They would be the best damn mercs in the Inner Sphere. And one day, in a place like the Conquistatore, there would be a mural with a *Kit Fox* on it, decked out in Fox Patrol livery, leading the charge in some decisive battle that would mean something for the people of the Sphere.

At least that was her dream.

And in Katie's experience, dreams were meant to come true.

MYSTICAL 'MECHS AND GIANT MONSTERS

JAYMIE WAGNER AND JAMIE KAIJU MARRIAGE

Excerpts from *Mystical 'Mechs and Giant Monsters: Kuritan Outlooks on Enemies and Allies through the Medium of Popular Entertainment from 2915–3145*, by Professors N. Yuka and J. Raketen, New Syrtis University Press (3151).

THE EVER-SHIFTING FOXES

Though the people of the Draconis Combine began with a pastiche of Chinese, Korean, and Japanese myths from which they derived their own mythology—particularly in the role and importance of the Dragon—they took a curious approach to certain shared elements from those roots, often acknowledging only one or two particular aspects at any given time.

A rare exception would be the role of Fox Spirits, particular in the *tokusatsu* and *sentai* genres.

Where a number of series produced from 2620–2990 simply cast fox spirits such as *Gumiho* and *Kitsune* as honorless enemies or hapless buffoons to be defeated by the various hero teams, the close of the twenty-ninth century and dawn of the thirtieth saw them positioned more and more frequently as "honorable adversaries" or sometimes even anti-hero characters, much more in line with the rare appearances of the *Tengu* or allusions to Chinese mythology, such as the popular "rival heroes" of the 2800s who were reimagined versions of characters from *The Journey to the West*.

By the mid 3050s, the heroes of *Gusoku Sentai Kyoryoku* would even be assisted from time to time by the *Bangai Hīrō* "Victorious Nine," a battle-armored hero who possessed nine fox-like tails that expanded from their suit to create gusts of winds or flame in battle or to cast powerful magical spells that could do anything from healing the team's wounds to dismissing illusions.

The series finale, *Battle for Love of Our Home! KYORYOKU!*, would see Victorious Nine perform a heroic sacrifice of their magical powers to dispel the powerful illusions of the Smoke Bear Army that had kept their great battle fortress "Shrouded Claw" hidden even as it bombarded the world of Neo Samarkand. Interestingly, the character's fate was left deliberately ambiguous, so he could potentially be brought back for movie or "Great Battle" projects, such as the very successful *Kyoryoku Gosuko tai OmniRanger* of 3062.

By the late 3080s, however, the trend had begun to reverse itself. Signs of honor and nobility from fox-themed characters would fade over time until the trends of the late Star League and early Succession War eras had returned in full force by 3130, where the forces of the "Republic of Greyfox" and their "Imperator Ishi Noivad" would be the primary antagonist for the new *GattaikenRanger* team.

WHEN THE WEREWOLF STRIKES

The artistic expression the creation of shows within the *Tokusatsu* medium provided often proved a blessing for the creators of shows such as *Fight, Fight, Super Kamishibai* (3011–3018) who, due to governmental oversight of their production, had been advised not to portray any specific major Inner Sphere House directly as the antagonist for diplomatic reasons. This required the writing team to choose their villain of the week with caution.

For an *Eiga-toshi* creative studio that had developed its following from the production of giant monster movies, this was not the creative barrier many other production houses considered it, but a brilliant inspiration to their art—a fact made apparent when their first season was completed in a mere three months of shooting.

For a prime example of this use of creative freedom, we can closely examine the episode translated as "Werewolf Terror" (s03e17). In this episode, the titular werewolf is a lone *Atlas* BattleMech terrorizing a remote village, painted in an over-the-top monstrously wolfish paint scheme, but in the traditional blue and white colors of House Steiner. The episode, with a message of power through working together even against the strongest of foes, culminates in the *Super Kamishibai* lance taking down the *Atlas* with their signature "Super Mega Alpha Strike" attack from the overstrength lance of individually colored light 'Mechs.

As with all episodes that attempted to work around diplomatic censorship, the *Atlas* pilot ejects from their 'Mech at the resolution of the fight to avoid any kind of origin indicators such as accent. The pilot would return during the final season of the series, as they had proven a fan favorite, especially in those regions that straddled the Combine and Commonwealth border, where much of the populace had seen their share of *Atlas* BattleMechs leave their mark on the cities and farming communities they called home.

THE MONSTROUS METAPHOR

When it comes to using artistic expression for a society with an unending conflict cycle, few examples are more potent than using *kaiju* (giant monsters, strange or otherworldly creatures) in films as a dramatic representation of often unimaginable terrors during times of war.

The atrocities performed by various factions of the Inner Sphere and beyond, depicted as the most monstrous of cinematic creations, are central to these films as the underlying understanding that humanity itself is the root cause of these monstrosities, either as the tool for its creation, such as the use of nuclear or biological weaponry, or as a direct response to those atrocities, seeking vengeance on behalf of the victims.

One of the more interesting examples comes from the 3053 film *Tokegegon vs. Star Jaguar,* produced by Hanshin studios on Pesht as a response to the destruction of the city of Edo on Turtle Bay by Clan Smoke Jaguar (3050).

The film begins as the titular monster is roused from his slumber under the seas of Turtle Cove by the launch of an "Invincible Automated Protector" robot that malfunctions during testing of its prototype "Triple X" Fusion Engine and disappears into space. A century after Tokegeon has been driven back into slumber beneath the waves in the previous film, the Star Jaguar robot returns to the planet. Still malfunctioning and refusing to acknowledge attempts to deactivate or disarm, the robot crashes into its former launch site—now the present-day city of Kyokyo—utterly destroying it. Still functional, if damaged, the robot begins to "patrol" the countryside, the now breached reactor in his core leaking deadly radiation.

With no other viable options, the president of Yayoi orders the Turtle Cove Defense Force to set off a bomb that will reawaken Tokegeon and draw Star Jaguar to the area, hoping to contain the risk of further contamination at the cost of potential future attacks from the beast.

Much of the defense forces trying to secure the perimeter of Turtle Cove are destroyed, but Star Jaguar is eventually defeated by Tokegeon, the kaiju's Nuclear Frost Breath rendering Star Jaguar's impenetrable armor brittle enough to be smashed apart by conventional fire support and the monster's own claws and tail.

There is no celebration or great fanfare as the victor sinks beneath the waves. Instead, a slow pan of the radioactive desert that had been a green and thriving metropolitan landscape is shown to the muted strains of a mourning ballad as the credits begin to roll, eventually fading to a white screen and black characters.

PLANET DIGEST: ZATHRAS

ALEX FAUTH

Star Type (Recharge Time): K1V (192 hours)
Position in System: 4 (of 8)
Time to Jump Point: 5.18 days
Number of Satellites: 2 (Zathras Alpha, Zathras Beta)
Surface Gravity: 1.03
Atm. Pressure: Standard (Breathable)
Equatorial Temperature: 22°C (Temperate)
Surface Water: 55 percent
Recharge Station: None
HPG Class: None
Highest Native Life: Mammal
Population: 12,525,000 (as of 3150)
Socio-Industrial Levels: D-D-B-D-C (3150)
Landmasses (Capital City): Zelenodolsk, Zhashkiv, Zolotonosha, Zorivka (Zastavna), Zvenyhorodka

First settled in the late 25th century, Zathras had plenty to offer its initial colonists. A cool world of sweeping plains, broad tundra, and rugged mountains, its Terra-like conditions and minimal need for terraforming or advanced life-support equipment made it ideal for settlement. The planet's native megafauna proved to be ultimately beneficial, as the Zathran Dzahn (a massive, herbivorous woolly mammalian hexapod) could easily be tamed and used as a beast of burden. Soon the creatures could be found hauling cargo and supplies across the world's expanding colonies.

Incorporated into the Magistracy of Canopus soon after its founding, Zathras remained isolated within the nation. Initially, Zathras was an agrarian world, with small settlements and massive sprawling farms across three of its five continents. It was lightly settled, with much of the population living in small farming communities. The planet offered very little resistance to Star League forces during the Reunification War and was easily conquered with minimal damage to its farms or people.

The Star League era brought a change of direction to Zathras, after surveys found vast resources of valuable ores hidden beneath the surface and not accessible to the early colonists. Overnight, mining became the planet's key industry as companies took advantage of new technologies to exploit these finds. New cities sprang up, with the world's society quickly coming to be dominated by mining magnates who grew fabulously wealthy off the bounty Zathras offered. While bound by the Canopian system of non-hereditary nobility, many of these magnates simply bought their way into power through their growing wealth and influence, ensuring that their families would continue to hold positions of power for generations to come.

At first, Zathras weathered the fall of the Star League by exporting minerals to the rest of the Magistracy. However, as the Succession Wars dragged on, the world was stripped of its defenses to help shore up other borders, leaving it increasingly isolated. Pirate raids became a common threat, with the Zathras planetary defenses stretched thin to try and protect the vital mines and population centers. In 2899, a raid devastated the city of Zaitseve, with the pirates carrying off massive stores of valuable minerals and numerous prisoners, including one of the wealthier magnates. When the Magistracy Armed Forces didn't respond to the attack, the Zathras government declared independence in protest, thinking it was better to stand on their own than be subject to an increasingly indifferent Canopian government.

Wasting no time, planetary governor Nanaz Jalali declared herself to be the Empress of the Empire of Zathras, even though that empire existed in name only. To prop up her rule, she created a system of hereditary nobles, essentially gifting the world's wealthiest mining magnates with titles in exchange for their loyalty. Canny trading of mineral reserves allowed the newly formed empire to hire mercenary forces to help protect its holdings against further raids, as well as any efforts by the Canopians to reclaim their world (even if the latter was unlikely).

The next century saw the evolution of a distinct imperial culture among the world's ruling elite as they cemented their place in power. Lavish displays of wealth became a common occurrence, as many of the nobles sought to outdo each other in showing off their power. Massive galas, festivities, parades, and other events became key parts of the social calendar for the nobility, as each sought to not only demonstrate their own capabilities, but also maintain the favor of the ruling Empress.

Meanwhile, living conditions elsewhere on the world faltered. Now cut off from the larger Canopian economy, the average person's quality of life deteriorated as technologies failed and the economy grew stagnant. The planet's agricultural output was being spent on supporting its own population, but much of the wealth that came from its minerals was either spent on hired mercenaries or ended up in the pockets of the elites. While farming and mining remained principal industries, there also emerged a privileged class that attended to the nobles and their extravagances. The Empress' official imperial hairstylist was one of the best paid positions on the entire planet, and those in her retinue lived well for little effort.

The early 31st century was a time of growing ambition, even as much of the planet remained impoverished. Empress Aydin II had decided her "empire" needed to be one in fact as well as name, and had dreams of creating an interstellar nation. She set her eyes on Aquagea, a nearby world that had been abandoned by the Free Worlds League following a brutal civil war and independence campaign in the previous century. To her, it represented an ideal first conquest for the Zathras Empire, and she began drawing up plans for an invasion.

While the original plan had called for an invasion as early as 3022, the combination of hiring mercenaries, the Fourth Succession War, and the Andurien Secession all delayed the launch until 3040. The grandly named Zathras Imperial Expeditionary Force (a mixture of conventional and mounted infantry supported by some low-end mercenary units) found little opposition when they made landfall. With Aquagea's cities destroyed during its recent independence struggle and its population little more than scattered farmers, the ZIEF easily "conquered" the planet in a matter of weeks.

Zathras' elites congratulated themselves on their victory and expected to soon revel in their newfound colony's wealth. Instead, they found the ZIEF soon caught up in a grassroots insurgency from a population that had no desire to lose the independence they had fought for a century ago. To make matters worse, it soon became clear Aquagea had little to offer otherwise. Its ruined cities had been plundered for anything of worth long ago, while the population were little more than subsistence farmers. As if that wasn't enough, the ZIEF's supply bases also were targeted by pirates who saw ample opportunities for plunder.

Far from building an interstellar empire, the conquest of Aquagea had turned into a deadweight that had drained resources for no actual benefit. In 3070, Empress Aydin III ordered a "strategic realignment of Imperial assets," withdrawing all forces from Aquagea and essentially leaving the world independent. Any further dreams of conquest were put on indefinite hold as the Imperial leadership tried their best to put any sort of positive spin on the debacle.

However, the situation further deteriorated as several key mines that had provided Zathras with its main source of wealth had played out by the end of the 31st century. The economy faltered as exports dried up, with many of the ruling nobles now seeing their own fortunes failing. Many were forced to cut back on their extravagances (for example, the official 3120 Empress' Birthday celebrations featured only a dozen dancing Dzahns) while some saw their holdings collapse under their own weight. As the mineral wealth dried up, so did the planet's main source of income for hiring mercenaries to protect it against pirate raids.

In 3148, a pirate band carried out a series of savage attacks across the Zhashkiv continent, burning croplands and destroying transport links, and hampering the ability to distribute food. With the risk of famine a real possibility and the economy on the verge of collapse, Empress Parivar made the unprecedented move of reaching out to the Canopian government, looking for some form of aid to help feed her people (while also ensuring that she stayed in power). The reply from the Canopian emissary was simple: if Zathras rejoined the Magistracy and gave up its imperial ambitions, then it would help rebuild the planet's economy and infrastructure, especially the damaged transport hubs.

This offer sparked considerable debate within the nobility, with many wary of what conditions the Magistracy might impose on them and others concerned they would lose their power. Still others were more accepting of the situation, knowing anything was better than famine. Some also questioned the precision of the pirate attacks and the convenient offer of Canopian aid. Countess Sofia Cosmidi put it best when she stated, "Either we give up our freedom or we starve. Either way, bad for Zathras." Eventually, Empress Parivar accepted the offer, with the world formally rejoining the Magistracy at the start of 3152.

Immediate food aid brought needed relief to the population and was a precursor to other steps. Several Canopian companies have become interested in helping to redevelop the world's fallen technological base and decayed infrastructure; although, so far these efforts have been more exploratory than anything else. However, the ruling nobility is concerned with the idea of outsiders interfering in an economy that had effectively been a closed shop they could exclusively control. An even bigger looming issue is the reintegration of the planet's leadership into broader Canopian society, as the two now have completely incompatible systems of noble titles and peerage.

The fourth planet from its sun, Zathras sits on the edge of its system's habitable zone. The world is cool, with extensive ice caps helping to keep overall temperature down. Geologically the world appears to be old, resulting in tectonic stability with much of its mineral wealth being originally well-hidden below the surface. Three of its five continents are inhabited, with the last two being largely covered in sheet ice.

While not compatible with Terran biology, the native wildlife is mammalian in nature, with six limbs being the norm. The Dzahn was a boon to early settlers, but the savage Tyhr represented such a threat that hunting parties were formed to keep its population at bay.

Originally, much of the surface was dominated by sweeping grasslands, deep forests, and tundra, punctuated by a few old mountain ranges. However, several centuries of poorly regulated, deep-cut mining has left massive scars across parts of the planet, resulting in rivers and soil heavily polluted by runoff. While many of the mines have been exhausted, those still active are run with minimal oversight in an ever-increasingly desperate effort to wring every last drop out of them, getting blood from the proverbial stone.

Most of the population lives in small towns scattered across the three habitable continents, and is mostly engaged in farming or mining. The average technology level is low, comparable to the early twenty-first century at the best of times. Use of Dzahn for transport and agriculture is commonplace, aided by their hardy natures and comparatively placid temperament. Education is usually poor, and literacy spotty at best.

Conversely, the cities contain grand estates built by the nobles, the most opulent of which is the Empress' palace in the capital of Zastavna. The cities are generally more technologically advanced and have a higher standard of living, although they also have been in appreciable decline for the last half-century. While the administrative functions needed to run the planet occupy a good part of the workforce, a substantial part of the urban population exists to support the planetary nobility and their lifestyles. In the cities, nobles throw lavish festivals for themselves, flaunting their wealth. Behind the scenes, these galas are often hotbeds of intrigue as the nobility attempt to curry favour with the Empress and engage in their own rivalries.

TERRAIN TABLES

Zathras' terrain is largely Terra-like, and as such, it can use standard mapsheet tables. The **Tundra** (see p.38, *Tactical Operations*), **Deep Snow** (see p. 39, *TO*), **Ice** (see p. 48, *TO*), **Snow** (see p. 58, *TO*), and **Extreme Temperatures** (see p. 60, *TO*) rules can be used to further simulate planetary conditions.

OF THE DUST OF DREAMS

DAVID RAZI

FREIGHT OUTPOST SIX-EAST
LONDERHOLM VI
KERENSKY CLUSTER
12 AUGUST 3071
1830 HOURS

Under swirling torrents of gray dust that filled the night sky, the starport was alive with activity. Orders from unseen loudspeakers echoed across the tarmac as primeloaders and maintenance crews intertwined around the feet of the grounded DropShip. Passengers left the small tarmac and headed for the single structure of the starport for processing.

Inside, Technician Aneikas stood at the processing station as the man behind the counter verified her transfer details and another man stood over his shoulder, eyeing her intently.

The clerk slapped her data card into the side of his yellowing terminal. The green glare of the screen washed over his face as he looked back up at her silently.

"Technician Aneikas, transferring from New Kent," Aneikas said as she reached for the card being passed back to her.

The second man snatched the card first and pocketed it. "Everything checks out," he said to the clerk with a smile.

"*Aff*, sir," came a casual reply.

Aneikas wondered at his interest in her, expecting he was a security officer and she'd committed some as-yet-unknown offense.

"Excellent, we need her right away," he said, guiding her away from the desk.

The clerk moved on to the next transfer.

"Head Technician Remont," the man said to her, "this way, please."

Aneikas glanced over her shoulder at the other technicians being processed and led to their posts. Slowly, she picked up her small bag of personal effects and followed the man around the counter and down a hall to the service corridor.

They walked ever deeper into the underbelly of Six-East, past laborers toiling away, over grated floors opening to massive cargo conveyers, and finally through a bulkhead that opened onto a gantry overseeing generators and pumping equipment, the beating heart of the facility.

Remont opened the door to an office, gestured her inside, and shut the door after glancing either way down the hall.

The steel walls were covered with shelves, filled with manuals and reports that looked older than the base itself. As the door closed behind her, Aneikas held herself at attention. With her arms held firmly at her sides, she picked at the seam of her pant leg as she tried to keep her breathing steady. Pulled from a posting on an important world to a distant rock and separated from her colleagues, Aneikas figured she'd definitely upset someone of considerable import.

Then his eyes were on her, and his face was awash with familiarity as he leaned back in his chair and observed her, smiling in disbelief.

"Sir—"

"Remont, please," he said, slowly coming to his feet and cupping his jaw.

"You are the head technician on planet, *quiaff*?" she asked, turning back from the door as it closed behind her.

"*Aff.* I require that your unique qualities be put to work immediately." His words seemed carefully chosen as he explained to her.

"All due respect, sir, I was not aware I had unique qualities."

"Allow me to disillusion you of such thoughts," he said with a curious smile as he led her into the adjoining room.

The lights were off, but a set of chairs was in the middle of the room, and she sat in the one he gestured toward. A form was barely visible across the room, and Aneikas' heart raced as she realized this curious interview by her superior seemed to be irrecoverably careening toward criminal acts.

Then the door closed and the light came on, and her heart almost stopped completely.

Sitting in a chair in the corner, Aneikas stared back at herself.

"Hello, sister," the reflection spoke, her smile not reaching her eyes.

Remont walked around the side of Aneikas and leaned against the wall, looking slowly from one woman to the other. Like any other Trueborn raised in a *sibko*, he was no stranger to seeing *sibkin* who looked very much alike, even well into adulthood, but never before had he seen two people who were truly identical.

"Hello, Odraz," Aneikas said at last. "What is a noble Coyote warrior doing down here with us mere technicians?"

"You are still angry with me, *quiaff*?"

Aneikas bit her tongue as she looked across at her sister. For their entire childhood, in a farming village in a distant corner of the Coyote homeworld, they had dreamed the forbidden dream of becoming warriors. Then came the fateful day when Clan Coyote allowed for a significant increase of Trials of Position for the front-line service of freeborns, children born not of the precision of the scientist caste's machinations, but of woman, with the randomness of nature at the helm. A randomness that gave their mother a pair of identical twins, equally strong, fast, determined, and utterly inseparable. Until the day one made their dream a reality, while the other woke up, and could scarcely remember the dream at all.

Thoughts of their youth vanished into the dust of the past as Aneikas answered her twin. "*Neg*, I'm over the loss," she said, forcing a cordial tone. "It's just that we haven't seen each other since then. I'm happy I get to contribute to the Clan as a tech. I'm good at it, even if..."

Her speech trailed off as she stared across the room at her sister, who looked down at her nearly pristine, gray warrior's jumpsuit, with clear MechWarrior insignia, before looking back at Aneikas' faded gray boiler suit that had seen more than its fair share of use.

Aneikas caught Remont staring and cocked an eyebrow at him. "The resemblance is still quite shocking," he said.

"Surely you didn't come all this way to gawk at your sib?" Aneikas asked before looking back at the head technician.

"All the way from the barracks, you mean? I am stationed here as well."

"Oh..." Aneikas managed to choke out, trying to hide discomfort as indifference.

"I had you transferred here," Remont said, clearing his throat. "I called in a favor to make use of your experience with repairing ProtoMechs."

"There's got to be a dozen people better trained right here in the Londerholm system," Aneikas said, alternating her questioning eyes between her two interrogators. "Why do you need me?"

Odraz caught her eyes and held them with her own.

"I am pregnant."

The dull thrum of machinery and workers through the concrete walls died away completely as Aneikas' heart skipped a beat and she held her breath. The words replayed in her head as she checked for some kind of mistake.

"You will take my place and assume my identity," Odraz said to her unresponsive sister. She leaned toward her. "Anei!" she barked, snapping the technician back to reality.

"Odry, how could you..." Aneikas asked, anger threatening to color her tone.

"I am not sure. I think my implant faulted. It happens sometimes," Odraz explained with a shrug.

"Not how *did* you, how *could* you?!" Aneikas spat out. "You took—" She stopped herself.

"I took? Took what, Anei?"

"You know what," Aneikas seethed.

"I won the Trial of Position fairly, by Clan law. What I took was rightfully mine."

The memory replayed before Aneikas' eyes as it had a thousand times before. Two sisters darting through the trees, together, unwavering until the end, when only one could prevail. Two hunters bearing down on the last cadet left before their bond would be broken. Two sets of eyes watching him struggle to keep going, unaware he was about to be overtaken. One sister breaking their truce early, guaranteeing victory for herself.

"And after three years, you're just done with it now," Aneikas said softly.

"I want this, Anei," Odraz said, holding one hand on her still-flat stomach. "I never thought anything would be more important to me than becoming a warrior, but...everything changed when we found out."

Remont stepped forward. "I...snuck a pregnancy test from the worker dormitory. We...were both very surprised."

"I bet," Aneikas said, grimly.

The tension continued to thicken the air, a miasma pulling the breath from each of their lungs. There was no question as to the severity of the proposition. A civilian replacing a warrior was not simply illegal; to even discuss it was grounds for investigation by the Coyotes' paramilitary police, at best.

To be given a second chance to be a warrior, charging into battle, chasing glory—it was intoxicating. But always there was the Trial of Position. The dream Aneikas could not fully awaken from, that threatened always to overwhelm her in a fugue of bitterness.

It would be all too easy to report this to command, to take from her sister what she now desired most. Death for the fetus, Abjuration for the parents, or worse.

To accept the offer, however, could mean death for them all. Daring to break the sacred order of the castes was a crime of the highest order.

But to taste the life of a warrior...

Aneikas looked intently at the mixture of subdued anxiety and hope that colored the technician's face. A look she'd spent the last three years hoping to see on the face of her own mate.

Then she looked at Odraz, the other half of her childhood that had betrayed her and been cut from her life, gazing back with the same dark eyes as her own, eyes that gave nothing away. Except this time, they were different.

Finally, Aneikas took a breath.

"When is your next medical exam?"

Odraz held her expression, but her tone softened slightly. "I had it moved back to next week. It will not be long before I start to show." She stood slowly and took a step toward her sister. "Anei...I know this is a *lot* to ask...but I am not going to let them take my baby."

"You know I have to do this, Odry," Aneikas said distantly as she stood.

The two conspirators looked back at her with equal measures of relief and happiness.

"Well," Remont said, trying to maintain his composure. "I will get my equipment."

It had been three long Terran-standard years since the trial that saw Odraz rise from her beginning as the freeborn child of a laborer couple, and life as a Clan warrior was not easy. Her body was pocked with small scars they would have to replicate on Aneikas and keep hidden long enough to heal. Cropping her long, dark hair to Odraz's shorter length was easy, and thankfully Aneikas' strenuous life as a BattleMech technician, coupled with her personal regimen upheld from her bid for warrior training, kept her fit enough to pass for her sister at a glance.

Londerholm II was home to millions, a breadbasket world on the edge of Clan space, and defended by an entire Cluster of Coyote warriors, but its star was also home to Londerholm VI. Home to a skeleton garrison of five warriors, it had few inhabitants. Its off-kilter ellipsoid orbit saw it and Londerholm V jockey for fifth position in the system.

Currently, it was VI's winter; a twelve-month stretch in sixth position that meant cold days and colder nights, but less intense windstorms. Private quarters were perhaps the only luxury offered on the near-frozen ball of rock. The facility named Six-East was primarily for the storing and shipping of quartz and other minerals, and Six-West, where the three other warriors were stationed, was a small quartz mining operation in the mountains that doubled as a venue for testing

ProtoMech mobility. Details on both were in a set of notes prepared for the inevitable exchange of identity, and went into dizzying minutia.

Aside from basic protocol and profiles on other warriors, Aneikas didn't know what else to expect, but every aspect of Odraz's routine was listed. If the plan worked, at least there would be ample time to study it.

"Everything you need to study is in your quarters," Odraz said.

"I don't know why I couldn't review all that for a few weeks first," Aneikas said back, fastening her sister's uniform closed.

"You would do well to clean up your speech, MechWarrior," Remont said with an air of disappointment. "Your sister always makes it a point to avoid contractions."

Odraz sighed. "You used to be so good about that."

"So did you," Aneikas said, glaring back.

"I'm getting into character."

"Anyway," Remont interrupted, "the exchange is best done now, before anyone has a chance to familiarize themselves with the new personnel, namely you. Your sib will be transferred as you to Six-West, where we are running tests on ProtoMechs."

"I spent some time learning ProtoMech designs over the last couple weeks, but I expect I'll be moved to something more mundane," Odraz said, looking at Remont.

Odraz approached and held a mirror at arm's length, alternating her gaze between her own green eyes in the reflection and her sister's, a smile tugging at her lips. They both knew the reality that lower castes rarely interacted directly with warriors, and they looked so alike none of them would question it for a second. The real problem would be interactions with other warriors.

Remont mentioned the time, and they all collected their respective things. Leaving Odraz behind, with barely any acknowledgment from her, the two technicians left for the warrior barracks.

Aneikas would spend her days defending Six-East, which she tried to observe every detail of as they walked toward the "barracks," the one hallway of the living quarters where warriors were assigned. The walk there was almost entirely silent, despite the continuous work being done throughout the base, even at such a late hour. Her body was moving through the corridors as though in a dream, her mind trying to process everything that had happened and keep from seizing up.

They ascended a steel stairwell into the intersection between the central wing and the living quarters. His voice quiet as assorted civilians walked past, Remont reminded her of the notes she had left herself in her footlocker, and gestured with his head past the doors to her private quarters.

She nodded farewell and assumed the confident stride of a MechWarrior to the best of her ability, reminding herself to not make friendly eye-contact with lower-caste workers as she passed.

Inside her room, beneath the cold halogen lights, she patted the sweat from her palms onto her jumpsuit and walked to the bed, head swimming. As she lay back, sore from the day of travel and hours with her benefactors in the engineering section below, she felt a curious bit of disappointment. The bed was firm. Uncomfortable, even. It was just like the beds she'd slept on throughout her career as a technician. The room was dank, the air was stale. It occurred to her then how rough the fabric of her uniform was. Her breathing slowed as she tried to compose herself. She'd need to go over countless notes to be prepared for the coming months. She pulled herself to her feet and retrieved the notes. She would start with personnel and continue until fatigue forced her back to the relative comfort of the bed.

Bolting upright in the pitch blackness, Aneikas had been woken by the sudden change in lighting, and started to feel for her bedside light before remembering she was no longer in her usual room. A harsh, white emergency light aura revealed the room to her as she pulled herself out of bed, trying to not let panic set in. Investigation was her only recourse.

Her boots clanking down the metal grates of the hall were drowned out by chattering work crews until she reached operations. The emergency lights betrayed the smoke and dust hanging in the air of the base's ever-struggling air filtration system. The tones of a restarting computer stuttered in the background.

She panned calmly over the room, trying to recognize anyone from her notes, picking out only Remont, sitting with his fingers against the bridge of his nose, before a voice demanded her attention.

"Sleep in your uniform?"

She swiveled her head to the right, where a man with MechWarrior rank insignia adorning his lapel sat on a desk, drinking from a mug as he looked at her.

"Misaki...*neg*, I, uh...what happened?" she asked, trying to avoid attention from anyone else in the room.

His response of shrugging and returning to his drink was interrupted by rising tempers across the room.

"It is your job as head technician to keep this station functioning!" came the older woman's voice.

"Which I cannot do if your scientists keep straining our capabilities," Remont replied, clearly tired of what was assuredly a frequent discussion.

In her peripheral vision, Aneikas saw Misaki watch her, malaise and curiosity coloring his eyes, her inaction drawing him in.

"Sitrep?" she called out, feigning confidence as best she could.

"Reactor surge," Remont said, turning to face her. "Anything connected to the main lines probably got erased. Good morning, MechWarrior Odraz." He stood, approached the terminal in front of him that had completed its booting cycle, and drew up his crew radio. "Try it now."

Unseen workers rushed to comply, and the lights flicked back on. Computer screens switched from black to solid green as they loaded their programming.

Aneikas had been warned about the older woman. The head scientist on-planet, Urima, was well into her forties, and had seen many come and go while she toiled away on Londerholm VI. She and Remont continued arguing over the blackout and whose fault it was. None of her team had overloaded the system, but he'd told them for weeks it was only a matter of time before something fell apart.

Misaki rolled his eyes at them and hopped off the desk to leave. "Come on. Breakfast."

"MechWarrior Odraz," Remont called out as she turned to leave, "I may have some bad news."

Directly below main operations control, the 'Mech bay was deep, built half into the mountainside to account for the limited real estate in the valleys of the rocky planet. Armor cutting saws and welding equipment rang out a cacophony that could reach throughout the base when the wind settled.

Remont led Aneikas past crews assembling curious-looking sets of weaponry and resetting diagnostic equipment to the foot of a gantry holding a towering hulk all her own; a *Clint IIC* in the black and blue mottled camo of Clan Coyote's Rho Galaxy. She had piloted several of these over the years, shuttling them between DropShips, repair gantries, and the like, but this one would be hers, and the severity of that loomed over her with equal stature as the machine itself.

"Your *Clint* was connected to the main to update the DI computer. All of the firmware is fine, but the memory was wiped. Including your brainwave pattern for the neurohelmet, which, I'm afraid, was also linked for a maintenance check."

She turned to him, trying to find the words before leaning in. "Why didn't you tell me?"

"I was going to swap the files last night, but I could not get to the administrator terminal. I had to improvise," he replied in a low voice. "Get used to surprises, Odraz."

She clenched her jaw and looked away from him.

"Into the cockpit, please, MechWarrior," he announced loudly. "Let us begin the recalibration. There is a vomit pail on the gantry you can use if necessary."

It was midday by the schedule they kept synchronized with Londerholm II, but the sun was still continuing its climb through the morning sky, pink and low, barely visible over the jagged peaks. The distant sun's faint light kept the equatorial base Six-East at a brisk ten degrees Celsius with the constant wind, but unpleasant weather would not delay a patrol. Over the last couple of years, banditry had become rampant, and so patrols, even for small operations like those on Londerholm VI, were increasingly necessary.

The *Clint* walked through the canyon slowly, each footfall hinting at the trepidation of its pilot. With her neurohelmet recalibrated, "Odraz" had taken her BattleMech out on patrol to ensure everything was working normally.

The wind faded briefly as she stepped carefully up a hill, and the valley before her, and the steep blue peaks beyond, caught Aneikas' eye. The red rock of the lone satellite, Londerholm IIa, hung above them, completing an image made all the more beautiful through the glass of a 'Mech's cockpit. She had goosebumps, and not from the chill of the coolant coursing through her vest.

"You're skylining yourself, Odraz," Misaki said in her ear.

"Right." She turned carefully on the rocky terrain and started back down the hill, easing back on the throttle every couple of steps.

Misaki's *Savage Coyote* bounded through the narrow valley below with familiarity in every move. "Off your game this morning."

"My...balance is still off a bit," she replied, shaking her head at her loss of composure.

"Well try to remember there are bandits out there," he said with a sigh.

"And you try to remember—"

Her words were cut short as the rough terrain gave way, and her left leg slid out from under her. She gasped sharply as the *Clint* jerked to the side, and the ground rushed toward her. The clash and rumble

of the impact enveloped her momentarily, but laughter soon replaced it. She coughed as she caught her breath from the impact against her five-point harness, forcing her clenched hands open and off the controls. Her eyes opened to find flashing red flooding the cockpit, and a pair of metal feet just beyond her canopy.

"Very graceful, Odraz!" came Misaki's voice between laughs. "Think you can stand?"

She sighed deeply and pried her fingers off the controls while wishing her sister had been stationed on a smoother planet.

The remainder of the patrol was uneventful. Aneikas tried to keep focused, but could not help eying every slope and incline with added apprehension. A few hours later, they found themselves passing back through the perimeter of the base, and into the 'Mech bay.

Sore and embarrassed from the patrol, she eased herself onto a bench in the pilot locker room after having backed her *Clint* into its cradle just minutes prior.

Misaki strolled in, sweat-drenched in his pilot togs of coolant vest and cutoff shorts, but somehow immune to the cold. He got some water and smiled at his teammate.

"You look like you tried to wrestle a bog weasel," he said between drinks.

"I forgot how awful that feels, taking a fall," she said, trying to retain composure.

"Even after we fell down that canyon last month?"

She paused and looked away. "That was only a month ago, *quineg*?"

"We're still on for sparring, though."

"We... *Aff*. Of course!" she said.

"You forgot. Every third night?"

"I apologize. I...I made plans to spend my off time with our head technician tonight."

"Not surprising." He rolled his eyes at her.

"We can reschedule—"

"It's fine, Odraz. Forget it." He tossed his spent towel on the bench. "Is that why you were late this morning? You've been a bit off."

"*Aff*, we were...up late."

He gestured as if to say that explained everything.

She was taken aback. "That bothers you...because he is Trueborn, *quiaff*?"

"Why are you always so formal?"

She stared back at him for a long moment, unsure how to respond. "I try to be more than I am."

He sighed loudly. "Well, no matter what, we're still freebirths. Don't forget that. He won't."

The noise of the 'Mech bay and its repair crews tending to her damaged *Clint* faded away as she sat and stared at the wall. She left to meet with Remont.

In her private quarters, Aneikas and Remont pored over the notes left by her sister.

"Your Star Commander, Levi, expects daily updates. Text is acceptable. Examples of previous reports are best referenced for their typical composition," he said, stacking some papers across from Aneikas, who looked off absent-mindedly.

"What kind of a warrior is she?" she asked finally.

He froze momentarily before delicately answering, "It is not the place of a technician to..." He caught her impatient gaze. "Odraz is professional...determined..."

"But?"

"But she did get sent to Rho Galaxy. Assigned to largely noncritical posts..."

"Maybe if I were Trueborn, I would have had better opportunities to prove myself."

"Maybe if you were Trueborn, you would still have ended up a technician such as myself," Remont said, becoming a bit worked up. "Which is not so bad."

"It is for me."

"How fortuitous, then, that you have had a second chance." He looked away and sighed "I thought you were happy with your life."

"I lied. I thought raising my own children for the Clan might help, but I never got the chance to do that either," she said, wincing at the memory.

"You never reproduced?"

"My mate died earlier this year in a labor accident. I still haven't been assigned a new one, since there weren't many of us at my last post." She sighed. "We tried for children, but...I think about him often. He was so quiet when we met, but he could always make me laugh when we were alone." Aneikas stared off into the distance, eyes unfocused. "I think I loved him."

"You sound like coffinmates," Remont said derisively.

"Aren't you and Odraz?"

His eyes widened as he considered the question.

"How are you two together, anyway? A warrior and a technician? That must raise some eyebrows."

"We...expected opposition," he said slowly, "but it seems others turned a blind eye to it. This is a small base, with a short roster."

"I meant how you came to *be* together," she said, resting her head in her hand. "Is it just because of the 'small roster'?"

"No," he said with absolute certainty. "I care for her a great deal."

"I should hope so. She's having your baby. And putting a lot on the line to do it. And so am I. If anyone finds out, the Trials of Annihilation will be immediate."

"The way things have been going lately? A trial if we're lucky. But they would probably simply execute us on the spot."

The silence of the room became oppressive as they sat unspeaking, drinking in the gravity of their situation.

"What did you mean when you said you 'had' to do this?" he asked. "You two had not even spoken in years."

"She's...family." Aneikas shrugged, with a thin smile. "It's what freeborns do."

"She stopped you from being a warrior."

"But I will not stop her from being a mother."

Her words hung between them, the hum of the struggling ventilation in the background.

Remont finally cleared his throat and stood. "We should get some rest. I will see about getting a rudimentary simulator sent in for you." He was about to say more but closed his mouth, disappearing through the door, leaving only the muffled clang of his boots on the hall plating as he left Aneikas behind.

It would take months to improve her skills to acceptable levels. Fortunately, her illustrious station on Londerholm II would afford her ample time.

FREIGHT OUTPOST SIX-EAST
LONDERHOLM VI
KERENSKY CLUSTER
28 DECEMBER 3071
0810 HOURS

The command room was filled with the casual day-to-day of running a secluded outpost, winds whipping past the windows, condensation running down them to pool on their corroding sills.

Misaki leaned against a terminal with a hot mug of quillar tea in his hands and watched his starmate stare into a small monitor. Flickering back was the image of a bearded man in a ProtoMech bodysuit, sneering casually.

"Your gripes are noted, MechWarrior Odraz, but we are not getting replacement warriors any time soon."

"*Aff*, Star Commander, but these bandits have gotten bolder, and there is simply too much planet and not enough of us. They are obviously being resupplied from somewhere." She sipped her own morning mug of tea, knowing her concerns would be, as usual, dismissed.

"With this terrain, tanks are useless up here—"

"Tanks are useless everywhere," Misaki offered.

The commander glared at him briefly. "—so Cluster command will not be reinforcing us. Make do."

Their commander was replaced by the Clan Coyote emblem, and Odraz shut off the monitor.

"I hate that guy," Misaki mused as he sipped his tea.

"He does not care much for us either," Odraz replied, catching glimpses from nearby scientists and technicians trying to eavesdrop on warriors. "Early spar?"

A corner of the 'Mech hangar, beside the pilot lockers, was kept clear for weight training and sparring, as the base did not possess a gymnasium of any kind. Grunts and heavy breathing were drowned out by the techs' machinery. Odraz and Misaki circled each other, striking quickly and blocking quicker, both preferring speed over power. She grabbed his leg as it swept up and slammed into her ribs, twisting it to lock his knee.

"I guess your dry spell's over," he grunted.

"Maybe yours is starting!" she said, smiling before launching him backward, moving in to land some blows.

Misaki caught movement out of the corner of his eye. "Hey, your lover is here!" he jabbed.

"What?" she said, wheeling her head around. A leg swept into her ankles and dropped her to the mats. She locked her knees around his leg and heaved him over to roll, but they both were stuck in place, panting loudly, neither gaining advantage over the other.

Remont waited patiently for them to admit to a draw before he walked off with Odraz. "I thought you might be interested in our latest crew rotation," he said, passing her a manifest.

"Finally getting a second physician, *quineg*?" she said with little enthusiasm.

"Actually, the departures might be more notable." He ran his finger down the side of the list.

"Aneikas, outbound…" she read quietly.

"Seven months pregnant, not much good in a ProtoMech hangar," he said, grinning.

"Is that the real reason?"

"*Neg*, she just is not especially good with ProtoMechs," he said quietly.

"What a shame that you transferred her all the way out here, then," Odraz said, raising an eyebrow.

"They should be arriving on the hauler. It is unfortunate you cannot see her off."

"Indeed...I have not seen her since...then," she said, forcing a bit of a smile. "Any idea who the father is?"

"Oh, some merchant on New Kent, I think."

"Well. You know what they say about merchant libidos."

"I really would not."

"Nor would I," she said, a grin tugging at the corner of her mouth.

"Normally the Fertility Council frowns on unsanctioned reproduction, but they have no genetic concerns in this instance." He paused and sighed. "She will be sent to Londerholm II for light duty...I was... considering transferring there myself someday. If a post becomes available, that is."

"Maybe I can transfer out of here myself, someday," she offered with a hint of envy.

"The way things have been going on other worlds, I would not be surprised," he said. Word of deployments elsewhere seldom trickled down to civilians in distant outposts, but the Kerensky Cluster had become a conflagration of combat and animosity in the last couple years. Temperate worlds like Londerholm II may have been more pleasant to live on, but they were also much greater targets. All the more worrisome by the decreased civility of inter-Clan combat of late.

"Odraz!" Misaki's voice called out from the gantry to the hangar control room. "Get up here!"

Their eyes met as a klaxon sounded throughout the base.

The door to command slid open, revealing a room of people with eyes locked onto a screen depicting the outer perimeter of the base. Odraz and Remont walked up beside Misaki, who leaned over the terminal. Head scientist Urima held her hand to her face in thought, her eyes darting up to Odraz only briefly when she walked in.

"Sensors only caught them at the ten-kilometer mark," Misaki said over his shoulder. The red lights dotting the screen washed his face in an upsetting glow. A full Star of contacts was slowly but ceaselessly approaching from the northwest. The scattered dots flickered in and out, signals obscured by the ferrous canyons.

"Raise the Star Commander," Odraz said, reaching for the comm terminal and hitting the emergency call switch to the other complex. "We can hold them off until..." She let her words trail off.

"Until what?" Misaki finally said. "Until they cross thirty kilometers of jagged rock without a DropShip? It'll take them an hour to get here!"

All eyes fell on MechWarrior Odraz as she held the comm terminal headset, the outgoing signal remaining unanswered.

"Remont, get our BattleMechs ready, we will meet them head-on," she said almost running out the door, Misaki in tow after draining his mug.

The hangar flew into a frenzy as they ran to their 'Mechs. As she scaled her *Clint*, Odraz saw Urima on the hangar gantry, watching her.

The two warriors made best speed over rolling crags and past jagged columns to meet the incoming threat. They had still not gotten a response from the Star Commander, but they couldn't wait for his orders. They would engage the threat directly, as far from civilians as they could manage.

No sooner did they see the enemy than they came under fire.

"Where in the Great Father's name did they come from?" Odraz yelled over the sound of pulverized rock as missiles struck the cliff face in front of her. She swung her *Clint* out and fired her autocannon, pellets of submunitions tearing into the shoulder of the ancient *Thorn*.

"Bandit leader," she yelled over her radio, "identify yourself and face me!"

There was a delay as autocannon fire darted into the canyon walls around her, narrowly missing her cockpit.

"Coyote MechWarriors," a woman replied, "this is Star Commander Ifreann of Clan Ice Hellion. This is our declaration of a Trial of Grievance over your offending presence on this planet."

"This...This is MechWarrior Odraz of Clan Coyote!" Odraz replied, overcoming her surprise. "For what reason do you—"

"Our Circle of Equals shall extend from this ridge to the far side of your mining complex."

Odraz froze momentarily the Hellion's words.

"*Zellbrigen* will not be observed." The radio went quiet as more autocannon fire struck Odraz's shoulder.

"*Stravags!*" she yelled, raising her own autocannon and firing into the oncoming 'Mechs. "This is too damn far, even for them!"

"Everything's been going to hell, even on this dead rock!" Misaki shouted in response. His scorched *Savage Coyote* backed against a wall as emerald lances slashed through his left pauldron.

"Then we'll teach them their place!" Odraz huffed through clenched teeth as she slammed her feet onto her jump jet controls. She lurched up over the shallow ridge and watched as her pulses of green light stabbed at an approaching *Locust IIC*. Molten beads splashed onto the dusty canyon floor and the 'Mech slid haphazardly behind cover. Lost in the moment of firing, Odraz felt her *Clint* come down hard on its left leg, and her armor diagram lit up.

"*Savashri!*" she cursed, trying to focus. What the Hellions wanted was immaterial. The Coyotes had shared the Londerholm system with them for years. The Hellions had come for a fight, as they had many times before.

"They keep pushing us south, we're cut off from the base!" Misaki puffed through clenched teeth.

"Luna Four!" a static-garbled voice shouted in her ear. "This is Six-East, are you there?"

"Six-East, Luna Four, go!" she yelled, limping her 'Mech back and darting her eyes to either side of her cover.

"Six-West is overrun," came the voice, nerves creeping in. "Please advise."

Odraz froze, skin slick with sweat, head swimming, hands aching as they clenched the controls, until an azure blast pounded the rock beside her, scattering debris and molten rock across her *Clint*'s right side. She snapped back into combat, swinging her torso to the left to see the *Locust* dart by once again. The *Savage Coyote* stepped out between them and leveled its arms.

"Odraz, retrograde!" Misaki yelled as he delivered an alpha strike into the fleeing light 'Mech.

She watched the burned husk of the *Locust* grind to a halt against a pile of gray stone, satisfied it presented no threat, before swinging back around to find a *Rifleman IIC* ponderously descending the cliffside. Brilliant blue lances from its remaining arm sliced into Misaki's torso, severing critical power lines and dropping his right arm dead against the *Coyote*'s side. Skylining behind the *Rifleman* were two more chassis Odraz couldn't identify in the swirling dust. Then a third. She spewed the last of her cluster rounds into the ragged formation, desperate to find a gap in their armor, but to no perceptible avail.

"Let's go!" she said, jump jetting back over the rock formation behind her.

The wind started to pick up, dust and rocks hammering them like sideways hail, as Misaki came about and ran, passing her by. Metal shrieked and the rock face between them lit up as a shot ripped through

his back armor and triggered an eruption of unspent missiles that reached out behind him like a robe of fire caught in the wind. His yells filled the comm as his 'Mech staggered to one knee. The wind continued to pick up and the fires spread, stripping the paint off his torso. Before he could pull his 'Mech back to its feet, a barrage of long-range missiles struck him all over, threatening to keep him down.

"Go, Four, go!" he grunted, bringing his *Savage Coyote* about and running with a trail of sickly black smoke streaking into the wind behind him.

A 'Mech, obscured by the dust, fired its lasers at her as it steadily approached down the hillside. With her slug rounds loaded, she fired one last time at the attacker before making for the relative safety of the base.

The run back to Six-East was tense. Odraz constantly checked her sensors and three-sixty vision strip for anyone following them. The fire on Misaki's 'Mech had burned out, but the cracks in his cockpit were visible from hers, and she could hear the pain in his breathing over their open comm the entire way.

As they reached the base and powered down in the hangar, personnel scrambled to help Misaki from his cockpit. The base's paltry medical team tended to his burns while Odraz climbed from her cockpit, adrenaline spent, legs barely supporting her in the icy cold air of the 'Mech bay.

Technicians clamored to repair her machine as she struggled along the gantry to reach the command room. Misaki forced himself off the gurney to follow, the base's lone doctor struggling to follow and tend his wounds as they rode the crew elevator to the gantry.

The doors slid open and she did her best to steady herself, looking around wildly until she spotted Remont talking with the shift commander.

"Six-West, what happened?!" she said as he turned and held his hands out defensively.

"I am trying to ascertain that. We just got someone on comms."

Beside them, base crew shouted into mics over the static in their ears and the commotion of the command room. Nothing Odraz overheard sounded hopeful, but she tried to piece everything together in snippets.

The Hellions had equipped all their machines with jump jets and scaled the mountains to Six-West. They still didn't know why they had come, but Six-West was in ruins, with the civilians wounded, without power, and still counting their casualties. Its three warriors were dead, with only one kill each.

It was unclear what had been taken, but there had been a definite plan, with the facility included in the trial and infantry brought to ransack the larger structures. Finally, the all-terrain haulers used for moving minerals and personnel across the jagged, broken surface of the planet, the ones loaded with crew and equipment rotating off-world, had been destroyed. They had attempted to escape along the canyon floor at the base of the facility, but their speed was no match for the Hellion 'Mechs.

Odraz was in shock, backing up into Misaki and the doctor, gasping for air. Tears welled in her eyes as she turned away and pressed her hands into her face before trying to unfasten her oppressively tight and hot coolant vest. She gasped for air as her head swam, losing focus on the room around her.

She could see her sister's face, determined, eyes narrowed, glancing across to her through the thick underbrush as they darted toward their prey. Signaling to her to run as they heard more coming. Fixating on her as the sun went down and they became increasingly alone. Remorseless, as she pinned her from above, moments before blacking out, leaving her sister the inevitable victor. It would be years before she ever saw her again, and now she was gone for good.

Remont watched her quietly, looking lost. From across the room, Urima watched it all play out, looking displeased.

"Great Father, what do I do?" Odraz whispered, voice shaking.

"We need a way out of this, Odraz," Misaki said flatly as he was being patched up.

"Perimeter?!" she called out with a cracking voice, trying to assert some kind of order to the room.

"Clear, no sighting!" the tech called back.

"What did they have at Six-West that was so important?" she asked, looking between Remont and Urima.

Remont cocked an eyebrow dismissively. "Quartz...ProtoMechs, not that Hellions would want them. There is nothing worth attacking the base over."

"Not...exactly," Urima interrupted, causing all eyes to turn to her. Odraz said nothing, but her eyes demanded an explanation. "We have some testbed designs being worked on there."

"...BattleMech designs?" Odraz asked.

They all balked at Urima before Misaki cleared his throat.

"Maybe we should..." he said, thumbing toward the separate office behind them.

Odraz, Remont, Urima, and Misaki filed into the room, shutting the door behind them.

"Why did I not know?" Remont asked, visibly upset.

"It was being handled internally," Urima said, on the defensive.

"Wait," Odraz said, holding her hands up. "Internally...within the scientist caste..."

Urima shifted uncomfortably. "It was determined that warrior involvement was not required at this juncture," she said cautiously.

"You gotta be joking," Misaki croaked as he checked his bandages.

"How can you possibly—this wanton *chalcas*—" Remont sputtered angrily.

"Hold on, Remont—"

"Yes, listen to MechWarrior *Odraz*," Urima said, her gaze boring into her. "She knows a great deal about the sacred order the castes must follow."

The room went quiet as looks were exchanged. Urima's eyes were on Odraz like a rabid dog's. What had she noticed? A secretly acquired retinal scan, or fingerprint, something she'd said?

Odraz's pulse raced as her right hand instinctively drifted to the knife on her belt. Could she do it here, in front of everyone, before she exposed their secret? Had she told anyone else? Killing a *chalcas* scientist might be enough of an excuse—

"By order of Khan Silas Kufahl," Urima said to widening eyes, "the scientist caste may undertake whatever means necessary to preserve the Way of the Clans...including the development of new hardware without the involvement of the warrior or technician castes."

Remont shook his head at her words, while Odraz narrowed her eyes and stopped moving for her blade.

"There is simply no time to waste with warriors and their trials when there is critical work to be done," Urima continued.

Remont sat on the desk behind him, eyes on the floor, processing this new development. Misaki winced and sucked air through his teeth as he shifted uncomfortably.

A knock sounded on the door, which Odraz bade to enter. The tech told them Londerholm II was raised and awaiting response before disappearing behind the closing door.

"Odraz..." Remont said softly. She looked at his tired eyes, and he looked back into hers, hurt but not defeated.

"We have one small passenger VTOL," Odraz said. "That should carry the three of us to Six-West easily. Are there any weapons there we can use?"

Urima smiled.

It would be six days before reinforcements could reach them from Londerholm II. More Hellions could come at any time. At Six-West, every member of the base had been watching the distance for approaching hostiles while retrieving the dead, patching structural damage, and clearing the tarmac.

Waiting by the access ramp to the underbelly of the base were Odraz and Remont. Across the field they could see the smoldering wreckage of the haulers; great, black, wheeled caterpillars, twisted and split open, while emergency crews toiled sadly around them.

Odraz stood there in the cold wind, numb on the outside, her knees threatening to give. Inside, she was screaming. There was still so much she had to say to her sister. Her partner and friend all through life, her stronger half, pulled away by her ambitions and dreams. For months, she'd wanted to talk to her again, to try to fix things, even just ask about the baby, but they could never risk being seen together.

And now they never would be.

Remont sat on a crate, his sight locked on the emergency crews as dust stuck to his wet cheeks. "My son..." he choked out. "I had a son..."

"Remont, I'm so sorry..." she said, placing a hand on his shoulder. His fingers met hers as her vision began to blur from the tears forming in her eyes. "It should have been me."

"It *is* you," came a voice from behind.

Odraz turned her head to see Urima walking with conviction from the vehicle bay in the mountain wall. She clenched her jaw and used her free hand to wipe her eyes, locking them onto the older woman.

"Officially, of course. But it seems your deception cost your sister her life. You have my sympathy," the scientist said in an almost sincere tone.

"And now?" Odraz asked, with hesitation.

"And now," Urima said, gesturing back down the ramp, "we go on."

The small vehicle bay opened up as the back wall separated to reveal a rudimentary, hidden BattleMech hangar. New OmniMechs emerged, in configurations never seen before. Inside, there was a spare for Odraz in the form of an ungainly machine with spindly arms, crouching on squat, reverse-jointed legs.

In her gray warrior's jumpsuit, Odraz took a few steps toward the OmniMechs with equal measures of awe and revulsion. Remont hardly seemed to notice.

Odraz sighed. "So this is what they came looking for. What everyone died for."

"*Cephalus, Septicemia, Osteon*," Urima said, pointing at the machines in turn. "They were still being worked on at the time of the attack. Bad timing...but we did get some useful data, it seems, from our ProtoMechs."

"Bad timing..." Odraz tasted the words in her mouth.

"Tactically speaking, of course. The loss of life is terrible. But, with the vector they took on approach, and good visibility for the moment, we think we can track them back to their point of origin and declare a trial of our own." She turned to look Odraz in the eye, expectantly.

Odraz glared back at her. "You want *me* to do this?"

"I think you understand what we are trying to achieve—the importance of the task our Khan has charged us with."

"And what about the caste system?"

"What is the role of the warrior caste?" Urima prodded, a glint in her eye.

Remont looked up from the ground. "Is this a trick, or a bad joke?" He returned his gaze to the wreckage. "It is the place of warriors to protect all other castes. To lead."

"But?" Urima continued.

"But what?!" he snapped back.

"But they haven't," Odraz said, almost to herself.

The old scientist nodded, but Remont looked appalled. "Wait..."

"We have been asking for reinforcements for months, and never got them. Command knew we were vulnerable," she said, holding back tears. "Clan space has been falling into chaos, there are reports of famine and disease in every other system!" She was starting to get worked up now. "There has to be a change."

"How can we go down this road any farther..." Remont muttered. "One warrior... We were trying to start a...a family, but..."

"We have to. If we want to fix anything, we have to," Odraz said, looking back at Urima.

"The Khan wills it. And our survival as a Clan may depend on some... reinterpretation. You can help us, Odraz. As a warrior," Urima urged before starting to walk away, "or you can cling to the old rules. And the consequences for breaking them."

Urima disappeared into the hangar to attend to her duties.

Resolve setting in, Odraz sought Remont's eyes, and when they met, she nodded and made to leave.

"There's nothing we can do here," she said, wiping her eyes again for good measure. "We can grieve later. They need us."

"Do not trust her," he said from behind.

"As long as she keeps our secret, I remain a warrior. I can help turn things around."

"This is going to kill us all."

"I am dead already...but as long as I have this name—" She rubbed her thumb over the name etched into her neurohelmet. "—I will do something with it."

She fastened her helmet and vest, heading down the ramp, eyes locked on her new 'Mech, those same eyes her sister had looked on her with all those months ago in their clandestine first meeting, no longer simply hard and determined, but filled with something greater: a purpose.

MechWarrior Odraz climbed into the cockpit of her new *Septicemia* OmniMech and led the six other scientist combatants into the dark, sprawling mountains to the north. The winds were still calm, but that would soon change as the long winter ended, and the planet orbited back toward its sun. Soon it would be dawn, and with it, a chance to make things right, and to make dreams come alive.

CHAOS CAMPAIGN SCENARIO: ROCKING GIBRALTAR

TOM STANLEY

The Gibraltar system was seized by the Marian Hegemony in 3147. Since then, their attempts to convert the populace into accepting their rule proved difficult. The warrior-monks of the Brotherhood of the Rock—along with others—harassed and resisted Hegemony rule. The constant attrition, fighting, and low morale made occupying the system too costly. Consequently, the Free Worlds League liberated the system in mid-3151.

This scenario can be played as a stand-alone game or incorporated into a longer campaign using the *Chaos Campaign* rules (available as a free download from *https://store.catalystgamelabs.com/products/battletech-chaos-campaign-succession-wars*).

For flexibility of play, this track contains rules for *Total Warfare* (*TW*), with *Alpha Strike: Commander's Edition* (*AS*, or *AS:CE*) rules noted in parentheses, allowing the battle to be played with either rule set.

> Captain (ret.) Conán Diether scanned the news on his printout. He was supposed to be enjoying his retirement, contemplating his newfound civilian life after Operation Hammerfall. Yet here he sat, waging guerrilla war, making life difficult for the Secunda Cohors.
>
> He looked up at the scout, codenamed Sparrow, still standing at attention. She was one of many volunteers who'd pledged to help the Brotherhood of the Rock any way she could, and she knew how to agitate a riot in the cities. He tapped the paper printout on the table. "So you're sure the 'Mechs are moving this way?"

Sparrow nodded. "It's a solid plan. Have them think they found a rebel stash here to disrupt and use that time to have some real fun in the city." Her near feral smile and glint in her eye made Conán shiver briefly, glad to see she was on his side.

"All right then, go on. You invited them to the ambush all polite-like, we'll hold down the heavy metal here until it is too late for them to spoil your fun."

Miles Gregarius *Arturo Igors clicked his mic on to address the cohort. "We're approaching the rebel base, if the rumors are true. The plan is simple: go in, break their spirits, break their backs, then we can parade the spoils of war and defeated rebels to the cities. We'll teach these beasts proper manners yet."*

The cheers erupting from the rest of the Hegemony MechWarriors filled his ears as he led the advance toward their target.

SITUATION

MIDDLEMARCH
GIBRALTAR
FREE WORLDS LEAGUE
2 NOVEMBER 3150

Secunda Cohors, of III Legio, has sent units that are harassed by a group of resistance cells managed by the Brotherhood of the Rock, warrior monks whose self-appointed task is to protect Gibraltar from outside threats. They've sabotaged supplies, incited riots in the cities, and overall made life hell for the Marian forces in the system. One tactic features leaking false intel to the Marians, distracting them away from the cities for other objectives to be met. Members of the Brotherhood serving as the decoy give every measure of their life for each second they can steal from the legionnaires. The Legio's *Prefect*, Mohamed Kilgore, has planned to strike Gibraltar hard and fast, then control the cities with parades and threats.

GAME SETUP

Recommended Terrain: Foothills #2 (*MapPack: Grasslands*), Grassland #2 (*A Game of Armored Combat*)

Attacker arranges two mapsheets with their short edges touching, creating the battlefield. Defender chooses one of the two short edges at the battlefield's ends as their home edge; the opposite short edge is Attacker's home edge. Attacker's home edge points north; Defender's, south.

On the battlefield, Defender places four Level-2 buildings (*TW*: three with CF 40, Medium, and one with CF 60, Heavy. *AS*: three with CF 6, Medium, and one with CF 8, Heavy) representing the "rebel base." The buildings must be placed in pairs of two, with each building in a pair between 4 to 7 hexes away from each other and the two pairs of buildings no closer than 3 hexes to each other.

If playing with miniature terrain instead of mapsheets, Attacker places no more than 4 hills on each side of the playing surface (to give LOS breaks) and places up to 5 Woods or trees. (Rules for converting between hex maps and miniature terrain are on page 68 of *AS:CE*.)

Attacker

Recommended Forces: Secunda Cohors, III Legio, Marian Hegemony
Attacker has two heavy 'Mechs and three medium 'Mechs. Roll on the Marian Hegemony table (see p. 128, *Empire Alone*). Attacker picks one 'Mech for *Miles Gregarius* Arturo Igors to pilot. His Skills are Piloting 2, Gunnery 3 (*AS*: Skill 3), and he has the Blood Stalker SPA (see p. 93, *AS:CE* or p. 73, *Campaign Operations*) but will lose the benefits if any of his allies attack his target as per the rules in *Empire Alone* on page 122. All other pilots are Veteran quality in Pilot and Gunnery Skills (*AS*: Skill 3).

Defender

Recommended Forces: Brotherhood of the Rock, Free Worlds League
The Defender consists of two heavy 'Mechs and a lance of heavy vehicles. Roll on the Free Worlds League tables (see pp. 124 and 130, *Empire Alone*). Defender picks one 'Mech for Conán Diether to pilot; his Skills are Piloting 4, Gunnery 3 (*AS*: Skill 3). The remaining 'Mech's pilot has Skills of Piloting 3, Gunnery 3 (*AS*: Skill 3). The vehicles' crews have Skills of Piloting 4, Gunnery 4 (*AS*: Skill 4).

WARCHEST
Track Cost: 250

Optional Bonuses

+100. Fanatical Brotherhood (Attacker Only): Defender forces improve their Skills by 1.

+200. Faulty Preparation: All of a player's ammunition bays contain half its normal rounds. Roll 2D6 for each weapon not requiring ammunition; on a 9 or higher, the weapon is considered nonfunctional until a time determined by the GM. (*AS*: Roll 2D6 for each unit; on 10+, it begins play with a Weapon Critical Hit. Units with ART-, AC, BOMB, LRM, or SRM add +2 to the roll.)

OBJECTIVES

Commander Killed: Kill the opposing Commander. **[+50]**
Break the Base! (Attacker Only): Destroy all four buildings. **[+150]**
All Toys Broken: Destroy or cripple all units on the opposite team. **[+200]**

Keep Them Entertained (Defender Only): Keep active enemy units on the field after turn 10. If all Attacker 'Mechs are crippled/Destroyed, add this bonus to All Toys Broken. **[+150]**

SPECIAL RULES

"The Citizens are Revolting!" (Attacker)

Attackers at Turn 10 will get transmissions about riots breaking out in the city they were supposed to subdue. Each turn afterward, roll 2D6; on a result of 9+, the Secunda decide to cut their losses and retreat through the north part of the map. If Arturo is killed or crippled, add 1D6 to the roll.

Forced Withdrawal

Attacker can only withdraw if their commander is dead, or they fulfill the above special rule. They are determined to destroy the buildings and break the rebels here.

Defender can only withdraw when more than half the starting CF of all buildings is destroyed. The buildings aren't vital to their resistance cell, but it must look like they are.

The rules for forced withdrawal are on page 258 of *Total Warfare* and pages 126 to 127 of *Alpha Strike: Commander's Edition*.

AFTERMATH

The Brotherhood's hit-and-fade tactics infuriated the less cohesive Secunda while they were on the planet.

Captain (ret.) Diether limped his *Rifleman* off the battlefield while the false base burned. He'd lost supplies in the diversion but not any personnel; a small setback, but well worth it when news of the riots reached *Miles Gregarius* Igors, causing the Marian to double-time his 'Mech back to his post, damaged and bloodied.

His *Prefect* stripped him of his 'Mech and confined him to desk duty due to his "stupidity and greed." A month later, he took command of a Bulldog tank for a patrol to earn his *Prefect*'s good graces again. Monks ambushed the Bulldog and left his body outside of it as a message to other Hegemony troops.

The scout only known as Sparrow vanished into the cheering Gibraltar public when the Marians lifted off-world. Her last gifts to Conán Diether were an envelope containing a crumpled patch of the Tamarind Regulars and a note detailing how she couldn't get over her losses in Operation Hammerfall until now, thanks to the Brotherhood.

THE PONY EXPRESS
RIDES AGAIN

MIKE MILLER

On 7 August 3132, four out of five hyperpulse generators (HPGs) across human space were disabled, often with irrecoverably burned-out cores. Houses, Clans, and other private individuals attempted to slap together assorted JumpShip command circuits to deliver emergency communications to systems lacking a working HPG. In theory, such circuits can relay messages to destinations many jumps distant in merely hours once per JumpShip charging cycle. However, using a nation's merchant stellaris for communications alone was inefficient.

The more ship-efficient communications protocol used during the late Terran Alliance and Age of War was to relay electronic messages between civilian JumpShips recharging at jump points. With well-known shipping schedules and the vast fleets of civilian ships of the era, it was possible to relay news, mail, and media content faster than individual JumpShips if not competitively with a command circuit. Challenges for planning transmissions included but were not limited to the following:

Short routes. Few JumpShips traveled farther than a handful of jumps (often just one) to maximize revenue.

JumpShip Shortages. A common issue since the Succession Wars, there were times when message-carrying JumpShips might find themselves with no ships to share data.

Deviations from schedule due to hardware, customers, bureaucracy, and numerous other issues that have afflicted shipping for millennia.

Part of the solution was distributing copies of messages to multiple ships at a jump point in the assumption one set of messages would eventually get to the destination. Jump point statites ("communication buoys") at low-traffic systems lacking recharge stations buffered messages. The algorithms for message sharing at jump points were quite elaborate, including random hash IDs to avoid duplicates, expiration tags, and delivery tokens to avoid endless accumulation of data. Overall, this implemented a point-to-point protocol. If human space had been homogeneously developed, then the point-to-point protocol meant news could cross the Inner Sphere in less than a year.

Given some planets were more developed than others and JumpShip traffic focused on those worlds, communication hubs developed that sped distribution. For example, physical traffic from New Avalon to Terra takes about four months due to the thirteen jumps involved, while during the Age of War, data relayed between ships might get there in less than four weeks. Ships leaving Terra redistributed news to other House capitals on similar timelines. From House capitals, regional capitals, and major trade worlds, messages flowed to even the most distant and least-visited planets within six months. Most systems of any value would hear of news once it reached such hubs within two months. Hence "pony express" couriers could deliver news to most worlds of the Inner Sphere in about six to twelve months, though it was extremely expensive to send it any faster, as dedicated courier chains were required.

The process was highly profitable, too. The required commgear on JumpShips did not impact cargo capacity, but even a month's worth of messages, media content, and government communiqués from one planet added a handsome supplement to freight and passenger revenues. Coordinating delivery of these messages to customers was performed by specialized mail companies. (Prior publications have confused the role of DropShips in Age of War interstellar communications. Electronic messaging was delivered directly between planets and JumpShips. The "veritable galaxy" of courier DropShips carried physical mail, whether it was a message too vital to entrust to photons or just mom's homemade cookies for a distant child.)

Prior to the Succession Wars, JumpShips were common enough that dedicated courier ships were economical on important routes. As the Hegemony disengaged from the Age of War's conflicts and sought diplomatic rapprochement with the Houses, it extended courier chains to House capitals by 2500. These hundred-odd couriers formed command circuits to and from Terra, allowing one-way messages to be delivered in hours and two-week round-trip communications between House leaders and Terra. It also cut cross-Sphere communications markedly. The typical twelve- to sixteen-week one-way message delivery from Tharkad to New Avalon plummeted to two weeks.

This process did depend on powerful commgear, which fell out of service in the face of HPG competition. While modern JumpShips retain commgear able to punch signals across the astronomical units from jump point to planet, their bandwidth is limited. Modern ships only

needed to contact traffic control and collect some crew mail, a "low data" system in modern terms. There was no longer as much need for the "high data" systems of pre-HPG JumpShips to carry multiple weeks' worth of news, entertainment, and messages to neighboring systems. (HPGs, speedy as they were, had bandwidth bottlenecks of their own imposed during ComStar's anti-technological reign. During the Succession Wars, many holovid shows were delivered by physical media on DropShips.)

When the Blackout struck, the Republic of the Sphere's population relocation programs had produced large numbers of JumpShips, even if the total quantity remained far below that of the Star League. But there was the matter of getting high-capacity communications equipment on JumpShips. In an ideal universe, reapplication of Age of War protocols would lead to resumption of reliable interstellar communications, perhaps twelve months from Circinus to Filtvelt, given the smaller quantity of JumpShips in service compared to the 26th century.

However, the Inner Sphere never runs according to ideal principles. In the mid-3130s, it wasn't clear that retrofitting JumpShips was worthwhile, since it was thought the HPGs would be fixed soon. Most ship owners didn't want to burn money when interstellar trade was in freefall and the new commgear might prove unnecessary, though some (like the Solar Express group) leaped at the opportunity. Then, just as everyone was settling on "low data" exchange protocols that would pass encrypted, read-only text messages using existing JumpShip commgear and using Terra as a hub, Terra walled itself and some favorite neighbors into the Fortress Republic in 3135.

A consortium of media firms and worlds like Solaris VII and Nanking took the opportunity to push their plans for "high data" exchange protocols. This would create data packages of holovid-rich planetary news, entertainment shows, personal messages, and government communiqués using new, high-bandwidth gear on JumpShips. However, no one could agree on billing or communication standards. With two-way interstellar communications running on time scales of months, high data protocol standardization proceeded slowly. Often, it didn't progress at all, but stalled or even went backward as competitors sued each other, and interstellar lawsuits during the Blackout were not speedy affairs.

Then, of course, there have been the wars. While there is no all-encompassing conflict like the various Succession Wars, there have been numerous border conflicts, civil wars, and conquests of ailing neighbors. Conflicts also make standardization challenging.

Another issue stems from the decentralized nature of these networks: lack of security. Despite all the efforts to secure messages transported in JumpShip communication caches as encrypted, read-only data, different systems have assorted security loopholes. Everyone from the Combine's Internal Security Force (ISF) to criminals has reasons to interfere with interstellar communications. At any time, up to a quarter of participating JumpShips may have security-compromised commgear.

(The Lyran Intelligence Corps [LIC] and ISF both spent much of the 3140s crippling Clan planetary communication nets, thanks to JumpShip vulnerabilities. Notoriously, LIC managed to distribute broadcasts of a convincingly simulated Jade Falcon Khan Malvina Hazen caught in "microphone gaffe" moments, confusing civilians and warriors alike. In these widely viewed clips, the simulated Hazen discussed her support for Warden politics and "only using the Mongol Doctrine to get idiotic Crusader genes exterminated from Clan Jade Falcon.")

The Falcons' reaction of restricting interstellar communications content has been mirrored across the Inner Sphere. (Their execution of several thousand communication workers was not duplicated.) As of 3151, major would-be media hubs like Solaris VII and Nanking are struggling to introduce "high data" standards and prove their many infotainment products are safe for other planets to receive.

Ideally, well-coordinated communications with the current number of JumpShips in the Inner Sphere could put national capitals only a couple of months apart for important diplomatic messages. Front-line troops should be within two months' reach of their capitals, less on command circuits.

What's really happened is most star systems can only deliver a directed message to a neighbor about once every week or two at best. Guaranteeing messages get delivered two, three, or more jumps away by a certain date based on commercial traffic is almost impossible. Transmission speed for most networks has averaged about eleven days per jump, worse than hiring a dedicated courier ship. The only significant nation to arrange a coherent JumpShip communication circuit is the Rasalhague Dominion, which has established circuits between Rasalhague and the provincial capitals.

LOCUST ALONE

BENJAMIN JOSEPH

THE SCRAP SANDS
EASTERN DESERT
MAHRAH III
EDGE OF THE LYRAN COMMONWEALTH
6 JUNE 3135

I flee across the sands as dust clouds gather on the horizon. They're coming for me.

The *Locust* -5M settles into a desperate rhythm beneath me. The thud of the 'Mech's feet against the sand matches the rapid beat of my heart in my chest. I force myself to focus on the desert below, and away from the clouds behind me.

The sands out here are treacherous, but I can ride them. I can do this. I can feel the places where they run soft and deep. I can sense the spots where a sure footing can be found. It takes skill to run this fast through the desert, to keep a sure footing at this speed, but I was always good at that. Let the other MechWarriors tell tall stories about their marksmanship. Lois Khanna has always been about speed.

Yet still, the dust clouds behind grow closer.

Beneath me, I can hear the actuators protesting at the pace. The *Locust* sounds older than it is, and Lord, I know how that feels. Behind me, I can feel the old connection cable rattle against my neurohelmet as we run. A loose connection like that needs a professional's eye. Instead, I have to make do with two clumsy hands and a roll of repair tape. We have been alone for such a long time.

Yet I am not eager for company.

The *Locust* clears the top of the next dune, and finally, there it is. A wall of rock rises from the sands, glowing red in the sun. A long dark crack splits it, top to bottom, a narrow canyon barely two 'Mechs wide. It'll cut my speed, but whoever's behind me, they're gaining on me anyway. Once upon a time, I could've outrun any 'Mech, any vehicle on this planet. But I am tired. So very tired. At least in the canyon I might lose them, hide out.

I'm coming in fast—*too* fast. I can imagine the frowns of my academy tutors, their eyebrows raised as they point out the rubble and debris scattered across the base of the cliffside. Any one of them could trip or cripple a small 'Mech at this speed. I ignore them, as I always did. They never understood what I could do.

Instinctively, I time the *Locust*'s steps between the loose rocks, jinking and dodging past boulders and scree. They pass by in a blur. Once upon a time I would have reveled in this, running the gauntlet, threading the needle. Now, I just feel my bones ache.

Behind me, I hear the low growl of primitive vehicles—and the heavy pounding footsteps of something larger. Something with legs. There's at least one other 'Mech out there, eating up the sand with the steady, confident pace of a well-maintained predator.

I've almost made the entrance, almost reached the shadow of the towering rock formations, when I hear the first shot. A burst of hypervelocity rounds smashes into a boulder as I race past, and I know I'm in trouble. They have ammunition.

This planet had been abandoned, forgotten for decades before our scout force landed. Solid slug rounds are rarer than water out here in the desert. If my pursuers have enough to waste on me, then I have a fairly good idea who's out there—and it's not good news.

My *Locust* jinks left and right as I run, keeping the movements erratic, throwing them off. They may have ammunition, but I'm betting they still can't aim worth a damn. Especially not now.

Shots ricochet from the rocks around me, but then I'm inside—engulfed by the shadows of the canyon. I turn down the first passage I see, but before I vanish around the corner, I catch a glimpse of my pursuers. A gang of small, armored trucks, armed figures clinging to the sides—and there, behind them, a few taller, unmistakably humanoid shapes. Great.

In the shadow of the ravine, I'm finally forced to slow down, and the heat levels on the *Locust* subside a bit. I check my weapons out of habit, but the Mk VI cannon hasn't worked for months, and I can't remember the last time I even tried the smaller lasers. No way to know if they'll work until I'm forced to find out. I really hope I don't have to find out.

The ravine twists and turns, narrowing and expanding around me. I don't know this area, this canyon specifically, but I've spent years on Mahrah. I can follow the signs. I chase the slope of the ground, following it upward, seeking an exit. There's no hiding in here now—

not after they saw me enter. But if I can find an exit first, I might just get another head start. After that, I don't know. That's a problem for later. I just keep moving. I always keep moving.

There. I can see the sand gathering at the end of this route. The ground is sloping upward, the sand is getting thicker, piling up in small dunes that mark the start of the desert proper. There must be an opening up here. I pick up the pace, squinting my eyes against the inevitable glare of the sun as I burst out.

Then a shape steps into the passageway as I charge forward. Huge, heavy, and gleaming in the sunshine.

No.

At full speed, I can't stop, I can't slow, I can't dodge. The enemy 'Mech blocks the entire opening, and it's big, far bigger than me. As I charge forward, the pilot steps their machine forward, bracing themselves, then smashes their 'Mech's shoulder against my smaller *Locust*.

Ferroglass shatters, and I feel the sharp pain as shards rain down on my bare skin. My world tumbles around me, the *Locust* spinning out of control. Off balance, the 'Mech smashes against the side of the ravine, sending my stomach into my mouth.

Then the world steadies, and slows, and I stop breathing.

The other 'Mech, my attacker, squats atop my fallen ride. I look up into my death. It's a *Hunchback* model, and the giant, rusted muzzle of its heavy autocannon is centimeters from my cracked cockpit. The bigger 'Mech looks almost as worse for wear as my *Locust*. There are missing armor panels all over, some patched with rusted steel, others left to hang loosely from their mounts. Rust is everywhere, and something else. Something brown-red and thicker than mud. The smell creeps into my cockpit through the cracks and holes. It smells like death.

The stained muzzle of the cannon fills my sight. The recoil from firing it looks as if it would blow the *Hunchback* in two—but I'd be in many more parts than that before then.

It would be a quick death, though.

Then I hear them. The *tap-tap* of their feet against the *Locust*'s skin as they pull themselves up. The screeching sounds of their victory chants. The riders and raiders from the armored trucks. One of them presses his face against my cockpit, making me jerk back in my seat. He's wearing a mask, like they all do, and little else besides. His skin is streaked with dried blood and daubs of bright yellow mud. The smell of death is stronger now.

They have tools they jam into the cracks and holes of my canopy. I try to fight them off, but I'm weak, and my head hurts. There's blood on the seat.

Then they reach in for me, and it all goes black.

"Hello, Lois." His voice pulls me from the darkness.

The voice is soft and low, like the hum of a laser cannon warming up. The speaker is tall and thin like a spider, and he hangs back in the shadows. The room is sparsely lit, flickering lights from control consoles and the odd intact overhead light giving the place the look of a haunted house. I can only see his limbs, long and awkward, as he leans back against a console, arms folded, his face lost to the shadows. He's wearing what was once a military jumpsuit, folded to the waist and tied down. Above, his torso seems bare, although it rattles with fetishes and talismans as he shakes his unseen head.

"Always running, Lois. All this time, you never came back to us."

I try to ignore him. My head hurts, but at least the room isn't spinning. It's hard to see much in the shadows, but I feel like I recognize this place. If I know where I am, maybe I can think up a plan. I'm tied to the chair I'm sitting in, but it's only rope. Crude rope, coarse against my wrists. Surely, I can deal with rope.

"You should have stayed with me, Lois. We're all that's left now..."

"Screw you, Stevens." The words escape my lips before I can help myself.

The spider in the shadows is very still. Then, slowly, with a clatter of his necklaces and amulets, he unfolds himself and steps forward, bending his face down into the light.

"You have misplaced your anger, my girl."

He looks awful. Stevens was always lean, but this is something else. Almost alien. His skin is pulled taut against his skull. There's no fat on him. His eyes are painted, rimmed by the same mud I saw on his followers. His mouth is darker though, red. I can't bring myself to look too closely. The dried blood traces strange symbols and runes across his bare head. His eyes are the worst. They're dark, the pupils almost lost in the black, and they seem fixed on something past me, beyond me, something I don't think I would see even if I was able to turn around. He sends shivers down my spine, and I react the way I always react to things that scare me.

"What kind of screwed up game is this, Stevens? You're what, some kind of chieftain now? You're *Lyran military*, for god's sake! The galaxy is falling apart out there! We should be trying to get home, trying to help, and you're hiding away playing dress up and tea parties with cannibals?"

He just listens without moving or reacting. Not a muscle twitches on that freakishly painted face. Then he sighs, a gentle exhalation like an engine releasing pressure. He stands again, his head shaking. Lost to the shadows, his voice comes down at me as if from the heavens.

"You don't understand. You *still* don't understand." He smashes his fist against a console. It's a sudden burst of violence, gone as quickly as it came. His body twitches for a moment before he continues, his voice low and soft once more. "No, you've just forgotten. Forgotten how they looked in Command, when the Blackout came. How scared they were. How pathetically helpless. The great Lyran Commonwealth, reduced to its knees, sending scouts like us out to scrabble in the dirt for scraps of tech that might let them cling to 'civilization.'

"This planet, though... These people, they've been forgotten since the Third Succession War. No communications, no supplies, reduced to scraps and superstition for a hundred years. And yet they took down our DropShip and Baumann's *Griffin* before we'd even set up a base camp. They were showing us the way, even then. We just couldn't see it at the time.

"You cannot cling to civilization in the darkness, Lois. You must embrace the chaos, and let it harden you. Adapt, or die."

"If you can't beat them, join them," I recite in a sing-song voice.

He shoots me a glare full of venom.

"*Learn* from them, soldier. These people fight like we never could because they fight for life, for food, for water. We grew fat and lazy in the Inner Sphere. We think ourselves warriors, but we are nothing without our machines. These people—they are *warriors*. Natural killers. Cut off from the corruptions of the Inner Sphere, they thrive again."

I can't help laughing. "Thrive? Have you even seen what's going on out there?"

He smiles. "The weak die, and the strongest rise. It's the way of life. Together this planet grows stronger, day by day." He sighs. "I won't let them take us back, not now."

There's something in the way he says it that stops me in my tracks. I can feel my brows furrowing, the wheels turning, my brain stiff with thirst.

"What are you talking about? Who would take us back? The JumpShip got called back home as soon as they dropped us, and who knows if they even made it? It's chaos out there. No one is coming to take us back. Not so long as we sit here and let them forget us!"

He just stares at me. After a moment I begin to look around, and now I know where I am. I know. I'm here, in the heart of the old HPG relay we'd been sent to find years ago. It's still a mess, half the equipment burned out, just as we found it when we landed. No, not quite the same. Among the rows of silent machinery and vacant screens, at the back, where the basic short-range radio equipment is buried, a few lights are blinking.

My eyes widen.

"They came back for us. There's a ship in system trying to contact us."

To my horror, he continues to smile, like a proud tutor watching his favorite student. He shifts to a console and touches one of the few blinking buttons. A crackling image forms on the monitor across from me, a blue outline of a strong jawed man in a pristine uniform.

"This is Captain Trejo of the JumpShip *Nero*. Recon Lance Delta, do you copy? Is anyone alive down there?"

My blood is cold. "Tell them. Damn it, contact them, Stevens! They can help! They can save us. They can bring food and supplies. Maybe we can actually fix the relay. They can get us off this hellhole…"

"No." He says it so softly, yet it falls with the weight of a boulder in the sand. "You still don't see it, do you? You grasp their help so quickly; you deny your own strength. We do not need their food, their supplies…their weakness. They will only make us fat and weak again. I understand now. All these years alone on this planet. I will not let us return to that pathetic life of dependency."

"You're insane." I finally say it. The word that's been bubbling on my tongue since the start. "You're crazy. We will all die on this damn rock!"

He crouches before me, the light gleaming from his bald head. "You are stronger than you know, Lois. We all are. You just have to see it."

Stevens makes a sound with his mouth, a click or a call, and a shadow detaches itself from the darkness. It appears so silently and smoothly it feels like the night itself is coming for me. But it is just a man. One of the idiots that follows Stevens, wearing the same mask and adorned with blood. He is naked from the waist up, and his body is lean and strong.

"Show her," Stevens says, without taking his eyes from me. "Take her and show her our strength. Let her decide how strong she is."

His minion approaches, and hauls me upright, my hands still bound. He clicks and whistles as he does so, his face cocked at an angle. As he leads me into the darkness, I hear Steven's voice, so soft and confident, behind me.

"In the end, you're one of us, Lois. You know that. A survivor."

They strap me to the outside of my *Locust*. They've pulled away what remained of the shattered cockpit canopy, leaving just the framework struts. There, above the pilot's seat, they tie me down, spreadeagled and stretched out in the hot sun.

I fight. Of course I fight. I twist and turn; I bare my teeth and bite anything that comes close. But there are so many of them, and my shoulder is a throbbing mass of pain from the crash. I struggle and curse at them, but it doesn't change a thing.

They have dragged or driven my *Locust* into the courtyard outside the old HPG station, a small semicircle of walls, topped with rusted turrets. Only one in three still seem to work, the rest droop sadly, barrels to the sand. Around the edges of the courtyard, surrounding my 'Mech, they have gathered what they must imagine is a terrifying force. There are armored trucks, a single hovercraft, a handful of converted and armored IndustrialMechs. All of them coated with the same yellow mud, and the same dried blood. Fetishes and talismans of outstretched hands, and vast, all-seeing eyes dangle from every surface.

In the center of this strange audience, they drag me on top of my *Locust*, and tie me down as the sun begins to burn my bare skin. For a moment, I dare to think this is the end. That this is the worst torture their twisted minds can imagine.

Then I feel the fusion reactor warming up.

The *Locust* stands, slowly, unsteadily, as if the pilot is still unsure of the controls. It takes one step forward, then another, and the gathered creatures on the ground raise a huge, ragged cheer.

I scream curses back at them.

One more step, then another.

Then, we are running.

The ride is furious, and it jerks me from side to side so hard that I feel as if my skeleton will break loose from my skin. There is heat from above, and heat from below. The sun burns above me, slowly cooking my skin, dazzling my eyes, while below me, I feel the building heat of the damaged fusion reactor, the miniature sun below. My skin blisters on both sides, and I roar out my pain to the desert.

All that answers me is laughter.

I can hear the laughter of the pilot, the 'Mech thief below me, but there is more. I see shapes materialize beside the *Locust* as we run. The trucks, the IndustrialMechs from the courtyard. They are following too. Masked figures hang from every surface, whooping and calling out their strange cries as I scream my rage at the uncaring sky. This is not a joyride, though. There is a purpose to this journey.

The *Locust* bounds over the top of a dune and dips its head. Then I see. I see why I am here. Below us, in the valley of the dune, is a small group of homesteads. Gathered behind a low wall, topped with tiny figures who frantically gesture at the raiding party emerging from the desert alongside the *Locust*. The 'Mech stays like that, head dipped, as the others stream past, as they fall upon the encampment. Forcing me to watch.

I begin to struggle harder. They've used ropes again, just primitive ones of twisted flax. One of my hands is held tight, but the other one has been lashed to a broken armor strut. I can move it, just a little bit, and the metal beneath is rough-edged and sharp with rust. I thrash harder, forcing the rope against the edge, again and again, as the smoke begins to gather below.

The WorkMechs hit the wall first, tearing into it with their claw-like limbs and industrial cutters. The small-caliber weapons of the defenders ricochet uselessly off the heavy steel plates bolted to their frame. Around the perimeter, the armored trucks and the hovercraft circle, taking potshots at the figures on the walls, forcing their heads down, as the walls start to crumble.

I struggle harder, faster. The rope seems to be fraying. I can feel it move; I can feel it give. I scream as I force my aching stiff muscles to move again and again.

Then I am free.

For a moment I don't realize it. My brain cuts out and my body just acts without me thinking. I swing my arm over, frantically pawing at the knots on my other hand. Suddenly, I hear shouts of alarm from below. Without warning, the 'Mech lurches sharply to the side, sending me flying.

I scream as I come down hard, my still-connected arm wrenching in its socket. I'm dangling down the side of the cockpit, my life held by the same rope I was just desperately trying to loosen. I can see the pilot from here, my old neurohelmet ill-fitting on his shaved skull as he glares back at me. He swings the control stick the other way, sending me spinning once more. The *Locust* shakes like a dog with fleas and I am praying for the ropes to hold. There's no grip to get on the pitted armor plates of the cockpit struts. My arm screams in protest, and I wonder what will break first—the rope or my flesh. My free hand flails wildly in the air as I'm thrown once more—and it comes down on something flexible and soft.

I pull. Hard.

I hear a scream from below, and the cockpit lurches again. He's flipped me over, my free hand dangling down through the broken ferroglass. Into the back of the cockpit. Where the old fraying connector cable runs to the loose socket at the base of my helmet.

I yank the cable, again, and he roars in pain. The feedback must be awful. I can see him scrabbling now, trying to pull my helmet from his head, but he's clumsy, hurt and unused to the strap.

With my bound hand, I grab the ropes tied to my aching arm. My other hand grips the cable, and I pull. I strain every muscle I have, increasing the tension, pulling his head back into the seat.

It shouldn't be possible. Not even if I was twice the woman I am. But I was never a good repair tech, it's been so long since anyone looked at that joint. So long.

With a spark of power, the cable tears free from the back of the helmet, and I hear the scream as the feedback rips through his mind. Beneath me, the *Locust* goes still.

There's blood in my mouth, every muscle aches, but I can't rest. I pull desperately at my remaining bonds. The rope comes free after a moment, and I swing down into the cockpit. Drool drifts from the lips of the hijacker, sprawled on my seat. I tip him down onto the sand below and check the cable. A few rounds of repair tape on the broken connection, and it looks like it might work again. For a little longer. Maybe.

I spin the *Locust* around. Behind me, the compound is burning, and my heart aches. But I can't help them. There's only one thing I can do now.

I run.

I flee across the sands as the dust clouds gather behind me. They're coming for me, but they won't catch me. Not this time. I'm pushing both of us hard, every muscle creaking, every fiber straining, the connector rattling loose at the back of my helmet. Whatever happens, we're running now for the final time.

The wind whips through the open cockpit around me. It feels like freedom. I'm lost in the rhythm, acting on instinct, every step, every movement timed to the beat of the blood in my veins. This is what I live for. Speed. I can feel the adrenaline sparking through my body, burying the pain of my injuries. It feels good to not be running away. I have a destination.

The low, squat shape of the HPG base rises up before me. It wasn't hard to find. I've spent years in the desert, I can navigate by the sun, by the sands. I could find my way back here blindfolded.

I slow down as I come up on the courtyard. I can't say why, but I trust my instincts. I step into the opening of the walled semicircle, and there he is.

The *Hunchback* is standing in the center, facing me. Its crude, blocky arms are spread as wide as they can go, and I know who the pilot is even before he speaks. His voice broadcasts from the larger 'Mech and echoes from the walls around me.

"Don't you see how strong you've become, Lois?"

I shut him out. I'm here for one thing only. I keep my eyes on the *Hunchback*, on the giant autocannon attached to its shoulder. The other 'Mech is over twice my weight, even battered as it is, and the autocannon is a big part of that bulk. I have to assume it's loaded, and one hit would tear my *Locust* in half.

A *Locust* shouldn't fight a *Hunchback*. Not alone. I may not have been the best combat pilot in the academy, but I remember that much. If a *Locust* did have to deal with a beast like this, you stay at long range, move fast, rely on speed to save you, circle around, pick your target apart from the rear. That's the strategy. That's the play. I know it. He knows it.

But his minions are bearing down on me from behind, and the thing I want, the reason I'm still here, lies behind him. The only way out is through.

I thrust the control sticks forward, and charge.

It takes him by surprise. There's a precious few seconds before he reacts, and I'm already at almost full speed, running straight at him. He tries to back away, to bring the big autocannon to bear. It fires, with a roar that almost deafens me, but the burst goes wide over my shoulder.

The recoil throws him off balance, he stumbles backward, searching for a footing. His machine is old, older than mine even, and the gyros in *Hunchback*s were never that good to start with. I'm close enough now that I can see him, his skinny, wiry frame grappling with the controls inside his cockpit. I see his eyes wide and gleaming in the sun. He *knows*.

I'm a terrible shot. Everyone who's fought alongside me will tell you. I barely scraped by in the academy, but damn if I don't know how to go fast. And running at a hundred klicks an hour, a 20-ton 'Mech is a weapon all on its own.

I've learned from last time. This time I'm the one springing the surprises, taking him off balance. Just before I reach him, I let the *Locust*'s feet push off, thrusting forward and upward, throwing the *Locust* off the ground, into the air, just a little, enough that I hit the *Hunchback* not in the chest, but higher up. My cockpit smashes against his, and I feel the breaking of glass again.

I feel the *Hunchback* wobble, arms flailing for balance, but it's over. It's gone. Like a tall building it topples, falling backward in slow motion, my *Locust* on top. I see Steven's face as we fall together, and for the life of me, I swear that monster is smiling.

Then we crash into the building behind, and everything goes black once more.

When I wake up, the world is burning. Everything is agony. I'm staring upward at the sky, half broken by a ragged edge of steel-reinforced concrete that seems to have been smashed apart by some vengeful god. Then I remember where I am.

I pull myself from the cockpit of the *Locust*, slowly. Painfully. A cockpit with no glass has its advantages, I find. The *Locust* is lying on its back. One leg is twisted the wrong way, almost sheared clean off by the impact.

The *Hunchback* lies there, silent, and shattered. Its cockpit has ceased to exist, rammed back into the body of the 'Mech by my *Locust*. There is no movement from within. No cry, no sound except the flickering of fires in the wreckage surrounding us.

We crashed backward through the wall of the complex. Several stories lie above us, half collapsed. The outer complex is ruined. But the part I need is deeper inside. There's still a chance.

I limp inside as the sound of the approaching mob begins to ring in my ears.

I remember the way to the control room. Not from when I was tied up, but from the times before. Years ago, when the uniform I wear wasn't stained or torn. When my bones didn't ache. When I called Stevens not by his name, but his rank: leutnant.

When the world was brighter, when the future was clearer.

God, I'm tired. I'm so tired.

My left arm hangs loose, the shoulder a ball of pain. My ankle screams in protest at every step. My leg has been sliced deep in the crash too, and I can feel my life running out of my body in a thick flow that leaves a trail behind me as I walk. The monsters behind me are close, and I cannot outrun them now. But I have one last thing to do before I die.

I find the one console in the shattered control room that still has lights on, and lean on it, breathing hard. I can barely stand up. I find the button I'm looking for, and the sudden illumination of the screen makes me squint.

For a second, I can't find the words, my mouth doesn't work. I'm so tired...

"JumpShip *Nero*. Come in, JumpShip *Nero*. This is Lois Khanna of the Third Lyran Regulars. We're here. We're still here."

BATTLETECH ERAS

The *BattleTech* universe is a living, vibrant entity that grows each year as more sourcebooks and fiction are published. A dynamic universe, its setting and characters evolve over time within a highly detailed continuity framework, bringing everything to life in a way a static game universe cannot match.

To help quickly and easily convey the timeline of the universe—and to allow a player to easily "plug in" a given novel or sourcebook—we've divided *BattleTech* into eight major eras.

STAR LEAGUE
(Present–2780)

Ian Cameron, ruler of the Terran Hegemony, concludes decades of tireless effort with the creation of the Star League, a political and military alliance between all Great Houses and the Hegemony. Star League armed forces immediately launch the Reunification War, forcing the Periphery realms to join. For the next two centuries, humanity experiences a golden age across the thousand light-years of human-occupied space known as the Inner Sphere. It also sees the creation of the most powerful military in human history.

(This era also covers the centuries before the founding of the Star League in 2571, most notably the Age of War.)

SUCCESSION WARS
(2781–3049)

Every last member of First Lord Richard Cameron's family is killed during a coup launched by Stefan Amaris. Following the thirteen-year war to unseat him, the rulers of each of the five Great Houses disband the Star League. General Aleksandr Kerensky departs with eighty percent of the Star League Defense Force beyond known space and the Inner Sphere collapses into centuries of warfare known as the Succession Wars that will eventually result in a massive loss of technology across most worlds.

CLAN INVASION
(3050–3061)

A mysterious invading force strikes the coreward region of the Inner Sphere. The invaders, called the Clans, are descendants of Kerensky's SLDF troops, forged into a society dedicated to becoming the greatest fighting force in history. With vastly superior technology and warriors, the Clans conquer world after world. Eventually this outside threat will forge a new Star League, something hundreds of years of warfare failed to accomplish. In addition, the Clans will act as a catalyst for a technological renaissance.

CIVIL WAR
(3062–3067)

The Clan threat is eventually lessened with the complete destruction of a Clan. With that massive external threat apparently neutralized, internal conflicts explode around the Inner Sphere. House Liao conquers its former Commonality, the St. Ives Compact; a rebellion of military units belonging to House Kurita sparks a war with their powerful border enemy, Clan Ghost Bear; the fabulously powerful Federated Commonwealth of House Steiner and House Davion collapses into five long years of bitter civil war.

JIHAD
(3067–3080)
Following the Federated Commonwealth Civil War, the leaders of the Great Houses meet and disband the new Star League, declaring it a sham. The pseudo-religious Word of Blake—a splinter group of ComStar, the protectors and controllers of interstellar communication—launch the Jihad: an interstellar war that pits every faction against each other and even against themselves, as weapons of mass destruction are used for the first time in centuries while new and frightening technologies are also unleashed.

DARK AGE
(3081-3150)
Under the guidance of Devlin Stone, the Republic of the Sphere is born at the heart of the Inner Sphere following the Jihad. One of the more extensive periods of peace begins to break out as the 32nd century dawns. The factions, to one degree or another, embrace disarmament, and the massive armies of the Succession Wars begin to fade. However, in 3132 eighty percent of interstellar communications collapses, throwing the universe into chaos. Wars erupt almost immediately, and the factions begin rebuilding their armies.

ILCLAN
(3151-present)
The once-invulnerable Republic of the Sphere lies in ruins, torn apart by the Great Houses and the Clans as they wage war against each other on a scale not seen in nearly a century. Mercenaries flourish once more, selling their might to the highest bidder. As Fortress Republic collapses, the Clans race toward Terra to claim their long-denied birthright and create a supreme authority that will fulfill the dream of Aleksandr Kerensky and rule the Inner Sphere by any means necessary: The ilClan.

CLAN HOMEWORLDS
(2786-present)
In 2784, General Aleksandr Kerensky launched Operation Exodus, and led most of the Star League Defense Force out of the Inner Sphere in a search for a new world, far away from the strife of the Great Houses. After more than two years and thousands of light years, they arrived at the Pentagon Worlds. Over the next two-and-a-half centuries, internal dissent and civil war led to the creation of a brutal new society—the Clans. And in 3049, they returned to the Inner Sphere with one goal—the complete conquest of the Great Houses.

SUBMISSION GUIDELINES

Shrapnel is the market for official short fiction set in the *BattleTech* universe.

WHAT WE WANT

We are looking for stories of **3,000–5,000 words** that are character-oriented, meaning the characters, rather than the technology, provide the main focus of the action. Stories can be set in any established *BattleTech* era, and although we prefer stories where BattleMechs are featured, this is by no means a mandatory element.

WHAT WE DON'T WANT

The following items are generally grounds for immediate disqualification:

- Stories not set in the *BattleTech* universe. There are other markets for these stories.

- Stories centering solely on romance, supernatural, fantasy, or horror elements. If your story isn't primarily military sci-fi, then it's probably not for us.

- Stories containing gratuitous sex, gore, or profanity. Keep it PG-13, and you should be fine.

- Stories under 3,000 words or over 5,000 words. We don't publish flash fiction, and although we do publish works longer than 5,000 words, these are reserved for established *BattleTech* authors.

- Vanity stories, which include personal units, author-as-character inserts, or tabletop game sessions retold in narrative form.

- Publicly available *BattleTech* fan-fiction. If your story has been posted in a forum or other public venue, then we will not accept it.

MANUSCRIPT FORMAT

- .rtf, .doc, .docx formats ONLY
- 12-point Times New Roman, Cambria, or Palatino fonts ONLY
- 1" (2.54 cm) margins all around
- Double-spaced lines
- DO NOT put an extra space between each paragraph
- Filename: "Submission Title by Jane Q. Writer"

PAYMENT & RIGHTS

We pay $0.06 per word after publication. By submitting to *Shrapnel*, you acknowledge that your work is set in an owned universe and that you retain no rights to any of the characters, settings, or "ideas" detailed in your story. We purchase **all rights** to every published story; those rights are automatically transferred to The Topps Company, Inc.

SUBMISSIONS PORTAL

To send us a submission, visit our submissions portal here:
https://pulsepublishingsubmissions.moksha.io/publication/shrapnel-the-battletech-magazine-fiction

Printed in Great Britain
by Amazon

42141144R00136